IDRIS
KEEPER OF THE LIGHT

Anita Nair

4th
An Imprint of HarperCollins Publishers

First published in India in hardback in 2014 by Fourth Estate
An imprint of HarperCollins *Publishers*
HarperCollins *Publishers* India, Cyber City, Building 10-A, Gurugram,
Haryana – 122002, India
www.harpercollins.co.in

First published in paperback in 2018

1 2 3 4 5 6 7 8 9 10

P-ISBN: 978-93-5277-614-6
E-ISBN: 978-93-5029-782-7

Typeset in 10.5/14 NewBskvll BT
by Jojy Philip, New Delhi 110 015

Printed and bound at
Repro India Ltd.

HarperCollins *Publishers*, Macken House, 39/40 Mayor Street Upper,
Dublin 1, D01 C9W8, Ireland

IDRIS

KEEPER OF THE LIGHT

Anita Nair is the bestselling and critically acclaimed author of the novels *The Better Man*, *Ladies Coupé*, *Mistress*, *Lessons in Forgetting* and *Alphabet Soup for Lovers*. She has also authored a crime series featuring Inspector Gowda.

Anita Nair's other books include a collection of poems titled *Malabar Mind*, a collection of essays titled *Goodnight & God Bless* and six books for children. Anita Nair has also written two plays and the screenplay for the movie adaptation of her novel *Lessons in Forgetting*, which was part of the Indian Panorama at IFFI 2012 and won the National Film Award in 2013. Among other awards, she was also given the Central Sahitya Akademi award. Her books have been translated into over thirty languages around the world.

She is also the founder of the creative writing and mentorship programme Anita's Attic.

Praise for *Idris*

'Nair's prose unfolds like an Ang Lee film, as a vast geographic panorama sweeps in front of the reader's eye, frame by exquisite frame. The individual sentences are zen-like in their balance and poise, more beautiful for the absence of extra words. Nair brilliantly captures the music of many tongues as she traverses the different terrains.' – *Outlook India*

'Meticulously researched and quite, quite unforgettable – Anita Nair brings alive the 17th century. It's not just about the language and the story, but also as much about the landscape, which she describes to the fullest, which add an element of mystery. Fascinatingly imagined, this is a riveting tale which celebrates details.' – *Verve* [Pick of the Month]

'The novel is a breath-taking adventure, a passionate love story and a voyage of discovery with the tall, dark, mysterious traveller, Idris, as the still centre of the story.' – *The Hindu*

'Packed with riveting adventure, exploits, mystery, intrigue, sensualism, and passion, and full of fascinating insights into the 17th century, the book keeps you riveted and hungry for more as the historical tale moves from land to sea and back to land. The amount of research that Anita has done and the seamless way she has integrated the historical traditions of the Malabaris with the character of Idris, the eternal traveller, seeking the measure of earth and man, goes on to show the calibre of this author.' – *The New Indian Express*

'This beautifully crafted novel chronicles Idris's travels ... Anita Nair does a marvellous job of bringing such rich and various settings and cultures from another age, to vivid life. With the help of intensive research and a forceful imagination, she draws readers to share life aboard the ships, feel the rocking waves and fear thunderous monsoon storms ... A remarkable narrative.' – *Sunday Herald*

'[A] new historical to sink your teeth into.' – *The Week*

For my parents Soumini & Bhaskaran,
without whom no realm of imagination would be possible

But now your heart is set: you want to have
the tale of all my trials – and I must add
more tears to those I have already shed.
What should I tell you first? What should be last?
I've had so many griefs at heaven's hands.
Let me begin by telling you my name,
So that you, too, may know it

The Odyssey of Homer

(A verse translation by Allen Mandelbaum)

PROLOGUE

AD 1625

(AH 1034)

For a fleeting moment, the howling paused. The boy shifted within his cage of bones. He unfurled his tiny fist and looked at the pebble that had brought him there. A pigeon's egg, black as his Fatima Naaya and smooth as her cheek. He held it against his lips and whimpered, 'Aabo.'

In that ephemeral stillness when the howling had paused, he felt he was home again; in Fatima Naaya's arms as she held him tight and pressed his face into the crook of her shoulder and sang softly: abaayo amiino, jijineey rabtaaye, aabe majoogto...

The boy whimpered and shifted again. When the howling resumed, he shuddered, squeezed his eyes shut and willed his ears to stop hearing. For when the wind funnelled through the jagged sides of the high mountain pass, even Allah sitting on his throne in heaven must wince, the boy thought.

'The boy needs to be wrapped up better,' Ali the camel handler had said at dawn. They were about to start on the march that would take them further on the silk route. They had spent several restful days amidst the lush grazing grounds of Xaidullah, but it was time to get onto the caravan road in Karakash Valley.

The boy had gone to sleep the night before with his father pointing out the stars and planets to him. 'That is Al-Zahra, the lamp of the evening sky,' Aabo had said, pointing to a slender thread of brilliant light on the horizon. He had snuggled deeper into his father's side. A little later, his father had roused him from his sleep. Aabo's voice was quivering in excitement. 'Look, inan, look how the crescent moon is flanked by Al-Zahra and Al-Mushtarie, the biggest planet in the heavens! What a wondrous sight it is, the brightest and biggest of celestial bodies together with the crescent moon! It is a sign from heaven to remind ourselves that Allah will prevail for peace upon earth.'

The boy didn't understand the wonder in his father's words but he had fallen asleep with the image of the moon and the planets. In the hour before dawn, as he sat rubbing sleep out of his eyes, he heard Ali mumble at the reddish planet in the sky, 'I do not like it. Al-Mareekh is a sign of evil and bloodshed.'

But Aabo had smiled calmly at Ali and said, 'That is old wives' talk. It doesn't befit a man like you. We will not change our plans. Besides, in the Surat An Nur, it is said 'God is the light of the heavens and the earth. Allah will watch over us.'

But soon the landscape had begun to change and both men and beasts had begun to tread warily, not knowing if each step was leading them to heaven or hell. Ali had darted meaningful looks at his master but Samataar Guleed wasn't worried and so neither was the boy.

The pass was like a saddle between the mountains and about 130 feet wide. Even though it was springtime, there was not a scrap of grass and the wind rushed at them, shrieking and with icy talons. A strange silence clamped their mouths as the caravan went past bones of animals strewn here and there.

The boy was grateful now for the thick woollen robe he wore over everything else: the breeches, shirt and woollen jellabiyad.

Intaadan falin ka fiirso, Aabo said all the time. Should he have looked before he leapt into the burrow beneath the cage of bones? If only he could let go of the pebble he clung to, he could stick his fingers into his ears. But he dared not. The pebble was his talisman and this was not just a crying wind, it was the devil's own. Outside his cage of bones, the shaitan roamed, seeking a victim to devour.

He had seen it. How the shaitan had lifted even Madoowbe, his father's favourite mule, with its giant packs, and sent it hurling against the mountain wall with a horrible, flat, slamming sound. He had heard the other mules bray and scream as the shaitan wind tossed them into nothingness. He had watched the double-humped camels try and resist the velocity of the wind and fail.

From within this skeleton of a camel he had crawled into while chasing after his black pebble, he had seen the entire caravan – seventy-seven animals and thirty men – disappear into a gorge. The shaitan wind with its long, bottomless throat had sucked all of them in. With the ease of Aabo sucking on a marrow bone.

'There is a technique to this, or you will choke,' Aabo had said, tapping the marrow bone on the edge of his plate to dislodge a tube of dark flesh. 'Eat this now. When you are older, you can do it on your own.'

The wind, like his father, knew the technique, the boy thought. To suck and suck and not choke. 'It will do you good to keep in mind that the shaitan is only the other face of Allah,' his father had told him once. 'All that Allah can do, the shaitan can just as well. The shaitan cannot create life, only Allah can. That is the difference. Which is what you must remember when the shaitan stares you in the face. Think of all that I have taught you. If you cannot, try to remember the names of all the suras. That much you can do, can't you?'

The wind rattled the bleached camel bones. Tiny bits of shale cut at his exposed face. The boy pulled himself into a smaller, tighter ball. Aabo would be there somewhere, he knew. If he waited here, Aabo would find him. Nothing could touch his Aabo. He was the tallest man in their village; the strongest and most devout of Allah's followers. Allah would take Aabo within the folds of his jellabiyad and keep him safe from the wind.

Say the suras; speak it, son, Aabo whispered above the howling wind.

Al-Fatiha, the boy chanted. The opening. Then came Al-Baquara, the cow. What was next? Was it Aal-e-Imran or was it Ar-Raad, the thunder? Would the shaitan wind bring in his friend, Raad the thunder? The boy shivered. The names of the suras seemed to dance before his eyes. Nahl, the bee. Hijr, the rocky tract. The boy swallowed. His throat ached with dryness.

Then they came to him, the names, other names. All forty-six words that Ali had taught him. 'You little dhoocil,' Ali had shouted when he had bitten his hand the first day Ali joined the caravan. Ali had yelped and reached out to cuff the boy when someone called out, 'No, Ali, no, he's the master's son!'

Ali turned his yelp into a loud guffaw. 'So this is the little caravan master! If this is the son, I wonder what his father is like.'

The boy had looked up, surprised by the sound of such free-flowing mirth. He had wiped the taste of Ali's skin from his lips with the back of his hand and asked, 'What is a dhoocil?'

'You don't even know that,' Ali smirked, 'but you behave like one. A rutting buub in fact.'

'What is a buub?' the boy had demanded.

Ali peered at him. 'You know, it is very hard for me to decide if I should call you a dhoocil or a buub. No, I think I'll call you a dhoocil. Do you like that name? You know what we Somalis say: A man without a nickname is a goat without horns.'

'You still haven't told me what a dhoocil is,' the boy persisted.

Ali opened his little skin pouch in which he kept his jaad leaves. 'See this,' he said, pulling out a black shiny pebble. 'This is yours if you will recite for me a poem I teach you. I will repeat it to you three times today; once each time after the three namaz left for this day. Tomorrow, after the Fajr namaz, if you can recite the poem to me, then this pebble that I brought back from Medina is yours.'

The boy watched Ali brew his tea with dried jaad. He took the pebble and clenched his fingers around it. He would have it, he swore to himself. 'Tell me,' he said.

Ali smiled, holding his hand out for the pebble. 'Not now. Come to me after the Asr, then after the Maghrib and Isha namaz, and I'll tell you the poem then.'

'What's this, Ali? The boy is only four years old. His father will be furious,' Hamid the cook whispered.

'He will learn the ninety-nine names of Allah in time, but who will teach him this except Ali, the Sheikh among camel trainers?' Ali laughed. 'Aqoon la'aani wan iftiin la'aan.'

To be without knowledge is to be without light. Hamid shook his head and walked away. He wanted no part of it. And what was the little master going to do with Ali's brand of knowledge?

The boy thought of the black pebble. It was both his Fatima Naaya and the window to the world he was yet to see. When he held it against his cheek, it brought back the satiny skin of his favourite aunt, his surrogate mother. When he pressed it against his closed eyelids, he could see the distant lands the men often talked about. A pattern formed in his mind. The poem grew. Now clenching the pebble in his fist, the boy spoke again, the only thing he could remember. A poem of forty-six words. A poem woven from words for a camel that Ali, Sheikh among camel trainers, had sung to him: Aaran. Abeer. Afkuxuuble. Awr. Awradhale. Baarfuran. Baarqab. Baatir. Baloolley. Buub. His mind paused there.

Ali called him buub. Young, unbroken male camel. It was Ali's term of endearment. Where was Ali now? Would Allah have found Ali a place in his jellabiyad too? Ali is as vulgar as his camels, Aabo said, but Ali is a good man. Would Allah recognize that? Stop dawdling, buub, go on, Ali's voice rang in his head...

Caddaysimo. Caggabbaruur. Cashatab. Cayuun. Daandheer. Duq. That's what Ali called Hamid. Duq. Old female camel. Fussing all the time. The boy remembered how he had giggled the first time he heard Ali call Hamid a duq. He couldn't laugh now. How could he? The shaitan would hear him and carry him off like it had everyone else. Go on, he told himself. Sing, boy, sing...

Dhaan. Dhoocil. Farruud. Garruud. Geel. Gool. Guubis. Gulaal. Guran. Gurgurshaa. Hal. Hayin. Irmaan. Kareeb. Koron. Labakurusle. That was the name for the two-humped camel. Aabo had bought twenty-four of those for the caravan. They understand this terrain best, he had said. And with the labakurusle had come Ali. Leading the flock, swaying ever so gently as he sat between the two humps of Sanaam, the tallest of the camels. The other handlers walked alongside their charges.

Spring was only setting in and the labakurusle still wore their shaggy fur coats. The boy had been frightened at these beasts that looked nothing like the camels he knew. He had seen Ali's face, which looked like cooked meat – a reddish grey and lined. And then Ali had tried to pick him up. That was when he had sunk his teeth into the beast master's palm. Had he ever said sorry to Ali, the boy wondered. When they were together again, he would tell him that he had bitten him only in fright. And Ali would smile and call him luqmalliigle. Young camel who means no harm. But one day you will be a mandhoorey, the best camel of the herd, Ali would say.

Nirig. Rati. Qaalin. Qaan. Qawaar. Qoorqab. Qurbac. Rakuub. Ramad. Sidig. Tulud. Xagjir. The song ended. The boy felt his eyes grow heavy. But he must not sleep. What if they thought he was dead and went away?

In a caravan, there is no place for mistakes, or for energy to be expended on the correction of mistakes, the boy had heard his father tell his men. Aabo had worn his stern face as he spoke. The boy hadn't understood what he meant. Would chasing a pebble into a cage of bones be termed a mistake by Aabo, he asked himself and felt salt burn the back of his eyes.

How long did he remain in that little lair, protected from the shaitan wind by earth and bones? How many places did his mind drift to? How many arms did he nestle in? How many voices spoke in his head? The boy wandered between sleep and dream, quiet and noise, hope and utter desperation till finally a voice rang through: Idris.

The silence. The boy knew then that the shaitan wind had died itself out. Again that cry: Idris. Inan.

Who would call him boy except Aabo?

The boy roused himself. His legs and arms had gone to sleep. His throat was parched and when he tried to open his mouth and call out, 'I am here', no sound emerged except a mewl.

The boy dug into the earth with his elbows and tried to push aside the cage of bones. It moved. Knowing that his life depended on it, he flung all of his being into moving the mighty skeleton. He felt a side of the ribcage rise. Quickly he wedged himself into the gap and began to crawl out.

Inch by inch at first, and then afraid that the bearer of the voice would go away, giving him up for dead, Idris the boy, son of Samataar Guleed, pushed again with all his strength. The skeleton rose, and in that brief moment before it fell back into place, propelled by its own weight, the boy wriggled out.

Behind him, as the gigantic camel ribcage fell back onto the ground it had rested on for over a score of years, a bleached bone splintered off the vertebrae and flew through the still cold of the early afternoon and pierced the boy's right eye.

He screamed.

The boy tossed. His body burnt. Why had they put him on a bed of coals? He wanted to rise and run. But he wouldn't move. Then, slowly, through the heat and anguish, he felt a cool hand stroke his brow. A voice spoke to him in his head. Was it a voice he knew? Or was it the voice of Allah, the Most Gracious, the Most Merciful?

'There is a wind that blows over the desert. It starts as spring dies. A hot, dry wind laden with suffering. The wind blows for three or four days without respite. And so it goes on intermittently for a period of fifty days. That's why we call it khamsin. You are too young to remember, but when you were a baby, we were caught in the middle of a khamsin and even you retreated into silence. In the desert, when the khamsin blows, the sand ripples will make your heart cry in delight. But how can you see the beauty of the khamsin when to open your eyes to it is to be hurt? For the khamsin is the wind of the sand. When the khamsin blows, it sneaks its way into everything. The folds of your clothes, into your food and bed; it comes to live in your scalp and the gaps between your toes. It sears your skin and seizes your thoughts. It rattles within your head and whines in your ear. You learn to count then, son. You learn to count to fifty. For when you have crossed each day off this relentless wind, you come to fifty and to its end. So you must now. This is what you must do now. This was the first khamsin of your young life. There will be more khamsins, but if you survive this first one, you will survive everything else that comes. Start counting in your head now.'

Idris counted. He had been taught to count till a hundred. Half of that was fifty. If he got to fifty, he would be able to rise and run again. One, two… he began. The pain in his head made him retch. He felt the little strength in him ebb. He felt himself slide into a blackness. Black as Fatima Naaya's skin.

Black as his Kabaah pebble. Sometime later, he felt his senses swim into place. He began again. One, two, three, four, five… Each day he managed to count just a little more, each day the pain in his head diminished, each day he got a little closer to fifty. And then, on the day he reached fifty, he managed to lift the weight that pressed down upon his eyes and opened them. Through his left eye, he saw his world again. Through his right eye, nothing. He shut his eyes and opened them again. He saw Aabo with his left eye, and with his right, only a blackness. 'Aabo,' he whimpered. 'Aabo.'

He saw Aabo loom over him, gaunt and hollow-cheeked. Behind him was a shadow. Ali, the camel handler. 'The little master is with us.' His voice shook as he fell to his knees and raised his arms to the heavens.

'Praise be to Allah, you are with us again,' Aabo whispered. For the first time in his life, Idris saw his Aabo cry. Tears welled up in his eyes. Idris felt the salt of his father's tears in his mouth, the wetness of it on his skin. A mild sting in his left eye. Only in his right eye, he felt nothing.

'Aabo,' he said. 'My eye…'

'Hush, hush,' Aabo said, taking him in his arms. 'Don't talk now. You must build your strength first.'

Idris sank into the comfort of his father's arms. No matter what, Aabo would know what to do. He felt his father's fingers pop a raisin into his mouth. His teeth sank into its flesh. Sweetness flooded his mouth. He felt Aabo rock him gently. He heard Aabo whisper: 'Sleep, my son, sleep.'

PART 1

January–April AD 1659

(Rabi Al-Thaany AH 1069–Rajab AH 1069)

I

No one saw him at first. He stood amidst a clump of trees, hidden by the shadows and the hue of his skin: black.

They called him names behind his back. Once, a mother and two sons had teased him as he walked past them. Kaka, Kaka, the boys had cawed derisively, flapping their arms like wings. The woman had laughed and hastily covered her mouth to muffle her laughter. 'I know it's cruel, but I don't think I've ever seen anyone so black!'

The boys still wet their beds remembering how they had been sat upon and pummelled to the last breath of their life. Of the mud trickled into their bruised, gasping mouths. The woman still had nightmares about the boy who had almost gouged her children's eyes out with his fingers.

He was unlike all the other boys of his age in the neighbourhood. He didn't speak much. He seldom asked for anything or started quarrels. Mostly he was content to merge with the shadows. Only when his pride was hurt would he emerge, and then it required two grown men to hold him down, tame his fierceness with a vice-like grip and soothing words.

As the boy stood shivering amidst the trees, feeling the fingers of mist swirl around him, he felt again the unfairness of it all.

In the month of Magharam, the seasons cusp. Half the month is cold, with a vicious bite in every breeze. Dawn is sheathed in mist and dusk is early and abrupt. The stars shine brighter than ever and the night skies are enough to make every man believe in the power of the unknown. The wind winnows through the paddy fields, making the heads of burgeoning paddy shiver in anticipation. Fruit trees unfurl tiny blossoms. And then slowly the month moves into summer. Longer days, warmer hours, beads of sweat. The sun ascends the skies as its brightest star. The boy liked to capture the passage of each changing month in his mind, to dwell on detail and hue, but as he stood now, surrounded by the silence and weighed down by the hammering in his heart, he didn't notice how the night had begun to change into day. All he knew was that soon it would be the hour.

He had watched the men as they walked through the fields, finding their way in the dark with an instinct honed at the kalari. His cousin Kesavan talked about it every now and then. It's there in you. All you need to do is find that harmony when the body becomes all eyes.

Where could they be going? They would make their first attempt to ambush the Zamorin's bodyguards at daybreak, but there was still time for that. What would they do between now and then? The boy had heard the whispers that floated through the corridors of the kalari his cousin trained at. He had heard mutterings at the weekly fair among traders and amidst pilgrims at the temple. Aswathi Thirunaal, the new Zamorin, wasn't to be dismissed as an ineffectual sovereign. There was talk that he would soon march forth into the kingdom of Kochi and establish his might over the Raja there. The Kochi Raja was supported by several vassal kings as well as the Portuguese. But the new Zamorin feared no one, least of all the white-faced parangis with their guns and cannons. He was aggressive and ambitious, and would allow no one to take advantage of him. He would be prepared at all times, the Chaver had realized.

All of Thirunavaya town was prettied up to celebrate the Mamangam that took place once every twelve years on the banks of the Nila river. Everyone knew that the Mamangam festival was held so that the Zamorin could proclaim his might and all his allies and vassals could make a public display of their allegiance to him. But people also came from all over to see the sights, and to buy and sell goods that traders from different parts of the world brought there.

Only the Chaver had no time for such frivolities. When honour was at stake, what man of good lineage would squander energy on appeasing his appetites and acquiring gewgaws? Honour was all. That was what the Chaver lived by. An honour that could be retrieved only by the death of the Zamorin.

Every fibre of his being ached to be part of the group of Chavers. To wield the sword as its blade sliced through the Zamorin's bodyguards of thirty thousand and more. To let the urmi slash through the air, the snake-like, moving metal blade whipping away opposition and heads. The boy was only nine years old, but he had already mapped his destiny. He too would be one of the Chavers when the time arrived.

The boy closed his eyes and held his breath. His cousin had taught him how to gauge each thing around him even with his eyes shut. The coarseness of the bark, the patina of the leaves. The cool mist, the biting breeze. The powdery earth beneath his feet. The birds in the trees. The insects in the grass. A twig falling. The celestial bodies moving. Time speeding.

Suddenly a hand descended on his shoulder and pinned him to the ground. The boy struggled, not daring to make a sound. He did not want to be the reason why the Chaver Pada's attempt was foiled. He did not want to be an object of derision in the ballads the Pulluvas would sing as they wandered through hills and plains.

'Bhagwati,' the boy called to his guardian deity, the goddess of the Thirumandhamkunnu temple, 'help me.' He wriggled, trying to turn his head and bite the hand that had him in its grip.

'Ssh...' a voice whispered from high above. The grip slackened a bit, allowing the boy to turn his head. He saw a man blacker than his black with a head bald as an egg and shaped like one. On this face was a strange glistening eye alongside a real eye. Was it an apparition of the devil? Something cold clutched at him. His mouth opened to let the scream emerge when a palm clapped over it, shutting the sound out.

'What are you doing, dhoocil? Do you want to give yourself away?' a voice said. A deep, sonorous voice as if from the bottom of a well, fashioning words he knew but had never heard before.

The boy allowed his body to unclench. The man loosened his clutch. From his great height, he leaned forward to look at the boy.

'Who are you?' the boy asked. 'And what is a dhoocil?'

The man smiled. A fleeting, wistful ghost of a smile.

'A dhoocil is an untamed camel. But what would you know of camels? Do you even know what it is?'

The boy shook his head. He knew a camel was a strange-looking animal, but he had never seen one. He had heard Itukka Menavan, his grandmother's consort, refer to one of their relatives as a camel. But he didn't think Itukka Menavan had seen one either. He didn't think even the Gurukkal at his cousin's kalari had.

'Does it bite? Does it have horns?' the boy asked, staring at the man's glittering eye. 'And this eye... can you see with it?'

'So many questions.' The man sighed. 'Some camels bite. No, camels don't have horns and no, I can't see with this eye, but I can see better because of it.'

The man squatted on the ground. The boy looked at the

length of the leg the man stretched out even as he curled the other under him.

'Who are you hiding from?' the man asked softly.

'No one,' the boy hedged.

'Then why hide?'

The boy was silent for a few moments. Then, rousing himself, he demanded, 'Who are you?'

The man's eye widened. 'Who am I? I wish I knew, my boy, I wish I knew. But to suit your purpose now, my name is Idris. Idris Maymoon Samataar Guleed. Previously of Dikhil. Now an eternal traveller seeking the measure of earth and man.'

From the chiaroscuro pattern beneath the trees, the boy saw something unpeel itself. He stiffened.

'Hush,' the man said. 'That's Maccanto. Here, eeye, come here.'

'It's a dog. Why do you call it eeye?' the boy asked, watching the dog place its snout on the man's knee. He had never seen a dog like this. A black and white dog that merged with light and shadow. A dog with a small, long, narrow head with a long, tapering muzzle and an elegant neck descending into a well-muscled body, and long legs. But it was the eyes the boy noticed. Set within black patches on a white face, the deep brown eyes gazed at the boy as if it could read every thought that coursed through his head.

'It's the Somali word for dog,' Idris murmured.

'Somali? What's that?' The boy frowned.

'It's the language I speak among others.' The man smiled. 'It is the language of the land I was born in.'

The boy stared at the man who was bent at his waist, whispering in the dog's triangular ears that lay flat and close to the head. The dog looked at the boy, then moved towards him.

The boy groped on the ground for a stone.

'Don't be hasty, boy. Maccanto will not hurt you. But if he thinks you are going to hurt me, he will remove your arm with one bite of that beautiful mouth.'

The boy dropped the stone. The dog trotted towards him and licked his face. The pink tongue wiping clear all fear and anxiety. The boy put his arm around the dog.

'You are from one of the Chaver families?' the man asked softly.

'How do you know?' The boy's eyes flashed. As if sensing the change in him, the dog growled. A small growl that said, 'Watch it, boy. That's my master you are talking to.'

'Maccanto,' the man admonished. The dog licked the boy's face again. And the boy tightened his hold on the dog, feeling a surge of love for it.

'I can see it, boy. I can see how every fibre of your being is filled with indignation at being left behind. But you are a child. And children ought not to be burdened with the demands of honour. They were right to leave you behind. So which one of the houses are you from?'

'I am Vattoli Kandavar Menavan,' the boy announced with pride. 'The son of Kuttimalu, and the nephew of Vattoli Chandu Nair.'

The man looked at the boy. He saw the coral pendant the boy wore at his throat. I should have known. How did I not see it?

II

Ten years ago, Idris had been part of a trading group on their way to the Vaniamkulam chanda. 'It's the biggest cattle fair in the world,' the Yemeni, Umar, had told him. 'I know you prefer camels, but this is a sight worth seeing. Go with us. You never know what a walk in that direction will bring your way.'

The Yemeni and he had travelled together along the Malabar Coast from Bhatkal in a sambuq headed towards Kozhikode. Idris and he had sat on the deck of the wooden vessel till the Yemeni broke the silence. 'Brother, where are you from?'

Idris had pondered for a bit on how to phrase his reply. Where should he begin? And in the end, he had arrived upon what he was to use for the rest of his life. 'I am Idris Maymoon Samataar Guleed. Previously of Dikhil. Now an eternal traveller seeking the measure of earth and man.'

The Yemeni's eyes widened. 'Idris Maymoon. The glorious interpreter. Is that a real name or one you found for yourself?' He guffawed. 'Whatever the truth, I like it, brother Idris. You say nothing and you say everything.'

It was an acquaintance forged on that bit of ambiguity that had tickled the Yemeni's fancy, and would be no more. Idris preferred it that way. He knew the folly of having friends. Friendship was a responsibility; it demanded making an effort to nurture relations and never asking why. It meant expectations and subsequent disappointments. A lone traveller needed no friends; what he needed to cultivate were acquaintances. Someone to pass the time of the day with. Someone who would find him a bed for the night and a meal, if he were to ask for one. Someone who would see him leave with a little more than a sigh and no regret. Idris and the Yemeni would presume no more of each other.

They watched the waves of the Arabian Sea and shared a meal of dates that the Yemeni brought out. 'Amru bin al, one of the Prophet's Sahabas and the Arab conqueror of Egypt wrote: The sea is a boundless expanse. Trust it little. Fear it much. Man at sea is but a worm on a bit of wood, now engulfed, now scared to death,' the Yemeni said. 'Tell me, brother, what does the sea do to you?'

Idris shrugged. 'I'd rather be on a real camel than a ship pretending to be a camel.'

The Yemeni smiled. 'So why are you on this ship then?'

'I needed to move on,' Idris said quietly. 'And be away from the scrutiny of a certain man. The sea seemed the best place for that.'

'You are a fugitive?' The Yemeni was curious.

'No. I have committed no crime yet. But if I stayed on, I would have. I would have had no option.'

The Yemeni looked into the distance. The sambuq was their home for now. As long as they shared this space, they were brothers. The African had a proud tilt to his head. There was nothing sly or secretive about him. But he had few words, and even those didn't reveal much.

'What will you do when you get to Kozhikode? Do you have a plan?'

'No.' Idris shook his head. 'I haven't thought that far.'

The Yemeni smiled in relief. How could you not trust such a man?

'It is time we ate,' he said, gathering his things around him.

Idris nodded gravely. Breaking bread with a stranger was the ultimate sign of acceptance. He liked the Yemeni too.

On the deck of the sambuq was a small area reserved for cooking. The Yemeni was a seasoned sea traveller. He had laid in supplies which Idris hadn't had the time to. He had boarded the ship with one thought alone. To flee. In fact, he had chosen to come to Bhatkal, a lesser port, than go to Hinnaur where he feared he would be recognized.

Idris watched as the Yemeni lit a small fire. 'This may be nothing like you have eaten before, brother,' the Yemeni said as he carefully brought out a pot in which crushed wheat lay soaking. From one of the other travellers, the Yemeni had procured half a chicken, plucked and skinned. Idris watched as he simmered the meat and harees. From a little container, he poured a trickle of clarified butter into the pot.

When the water was almost absorbed, the Yemeni took the pot off his makeshift stove and used a pestle to pound the mixture. Then he brought out a serving dish and poured the harees into it. He gestured to Idris to join him.

The Yemeni then brought out a box. Salt. He poured the coarse grain into the mortar and pounded it before sprinkling it over the food in the serving bowl. Idris still didn't speak. To say anything would be to undervalue the Yemeni's offer of brotherhood and peace.

'Will you join me, brother?' the Yemeni asked softly. Will you go against me, African, is what he implies, Idris thought. Why do they all fear me so? Is it my height? Or is it my dead eye gleaming?

'I will,' Idris said, and squatted on his haunches. He watched the Yemeni stir in more clarified butter into the dish.

The harees tasted strange yet familiar, and it filled him with a sense of comfort. 'Sometimes we leave out the meat and add cinnamon and honey to it,' the Yemeni said, using his fingers to fork the harees into his mouth. The dish soon emptied as the men ate their way through it.

The Yemeni put the pot with the bones and bits of chicken back on the embers. 'That will be our next meal and our last hot meal till we reach Kozhikode,' he said as he measured out two cups of water carefully.

Idris looked heavenward. Allah had been kind to him again. Without the Yemeni, he would have starved.

Idris and the Yemeni walked to a quieter part of the deck, where they stood looking at the waves.

Night had fallen, but the warmth of the day still clung to the air. The ship had dropped anchor and the sound of waves slapping against its sides filled the darkness.

'That is the Al-Mushtarie,' Idris said, pointing to the planet rising in the sky resplendent with stars.

'What?' the Yemeni asked, looking in the direction of the African's finger.

'It is a planet and not really a star,' Idris explained.

'You are a stargazer. Tell me, do the stars really hold our destiny? The Hindus believe that the stars determine the passage of our lives.' The Yemeni's voice was low and there was a strange wistfulness in his eyes and the curve of his mouth.

Idris continued to look at the sky in silence. Then he spoke. 'There is a story that when the mother of Imaam Shafi was expecting him, she saw a dream of how the Al-Mushtarie descended on Egypt. The interpreters of dreams said a son would be born to her whose knowledge of the Deen would exceed all that was known and the people of Egypt would benefit from his teachings.'

A meteor shower flashed. 'Did you see that?' The Yemeni's voice rose in excitement. 'It was like a cascade of pearls...'

Idris smiled at the poetic excess of the otherwise matter-of-fact Yemeni. Stars and the night sky did that to even the most staid of men; they turned them into soft-edged dreamers.

'I am a trader,' the Yemeni said. 'I buy goods from one place and sell in another. But do you know what I really want to do?' He drew out a pouch tucked into the folds of his jellabiyad and opened it on the palm of his hand. Pearls trickled out. One of them propelled another into the air and sent it flying. The pearl rose into the night, an arc of glistening beauty that almost went over the side of the ship, but Idris reached out and snared it in his palm.

The Yemeni smiled. 'She was only seeking to return to where she came from, but you saved her. And now she's yours.'

Idris leaned forward to thrust it back into the Yemeni's heap of pearls. 'Don't be silly. I can't take this.'

'Why not? Wise men say, if you save a life, you become responsible for it.'

'I didn't save a life, brother.' Idris laughed.

'You saved her from ignominy. She's beautiful. She should adorn a woman's throat or a pasha's crown. If she had fallen into the sea, she would have rested on the ocean floor, forever forgotten. Keep her. If nothing else, in a moment of trouble, you can sell her to pay for your way forward,' he paused and looked slyly at Idris, then continued, 'as you seek the measure of earth and man.'

Idris accepted the gift. It would have been ungracious to protest any more. He wrapped it in a piece of cloth and placed it in the little skin pouch along with the black pebble. Pebble and pearl. One had changed his life. What would the other bring his way, he wondered.

When they docked at Kozhikode and the Yemeni announced his plans to go to the Vaniamkulam chanda, Idris allowed himself to be persuaded.

How had he got separated from the Yemeni's group? He had walked on while the others rested. He wasn't afraid of losing his way or being confronted by the natives. Mostly he overwhelmed people into an awed silence with his height, the colour of his skin and his gold-enamelled eye. Besides, he could speak their tongue.

He hadn't told the Yemeni that he spoke some of the local dialect. He had joined the Keladi ruler Shivappa Naik's court at Bidannur as a young man and been part of it for some years when the ruler decided that Idris should accompany his men to Bekal to rebuild the fortress there. Idris had learnt to speak Malayalam then as he helped with the groundwork. But he had been summoned back to the court before they had actually begun work and then had to flee when he realized that the palace intrigues would force him to take sides.

He had thought the Yemeni's group would catch up with him, but at a fork in the path, he had taken the left instead of the right. It was when night descended suddenly that he realized he was well and truly lost. No home would offer him a bed for the night. There wasn't a mosque nearby to seek shelter in. He tried to merge with the shadows when he saw a wall in front of him. Idris leapt over the wall and found himself near the bathing pond of a large house. The pond had a little enclosure with a thatched roof. He would spend the night there, he decided, and at the crack of dawn, retrace his path to the Yemeni.

No one from the house would venture out at night. The Hindus saw djinns everywhere. In trees and caves, in stones and water. And the night held greater terror for them than anything else. For they believed that was when the djinns stalked their prey. He would be safe here. Even if they did spot him, they would think he was a djinn, he thought wryly.

It was a hot summer night. Fireflies drew love songs in the air and only a gibbous moon watched. A hot summer night when a young woman walked into the pond house and gave Idris the fright of his life. If she screamed and he was discovered, there would be no reprieve. The laws of the land were harsh, bordering on barbaric. How many counts of crime would be heaped on his head? Intent to burgle, intent to rape, trespass, violation of caste codes… He shuddered and held himself still. Perhaps she would go away without noticing him. And she would have, if his eye hadn't given him away.

Was it the madness of a summer night? Or was it the yearning born of being celibate for many months? Or was it that thing poets sang about – that thing called passion – that abrupt cessation of sense and a rapacious need to hold someone close? Or was it merely the magic of the moment?

III

The month of Medam was always unbearable. Kuttimalu thought it was almost as if she were impaled on the horns of a giant goat, unable to move, unable to think, unable to even breathe.

'What else do you expect? This is summer, girl.' Nani Amma, her mother, snorted.

'The equinox is just over and do you know what they say?' Itukka Menavan said and spouted a long verse in Sanskrit.

A retort sat at the tip of her tongue like a tamarind seed waiting to be spat out: Yes, tell us what the meaning of that shloka is, and why I wish I could spend all day neck-deep in water. But Kuttimalu didn't speak, for she was certain he didn't know what it meant. Besides, she knew her mother wouldn't like it. It had been almost a decade since Itukka Menavan became Nani Amma's consort but she still treated him as if he were a newly acquired pet, to be indulged and pandered to.

Itukka Menavan fancied himself as an astrologer and a scholar. He spent long hours studying the palm-leaf texts he procured from here and there. He had discovered that an effective way of silencing his listeners was to fling complex Sanskrit verses at them.

Kuttimalu wasn't overwhelmed by Itukka Menavan's rhetoric. The old fool didn't know that she had studied Sanskrit and arithmetic as a child. Many years ago, a brahmin had stayed in their madom for a few years. He had nowhere to go, he said. 'I do not need much, just some rice and milk and vegetables to feed me, and a roof over my head. In return, I shall teach the children of the house Sanskrit and arithmetic. And music, if they can sing.'

Koman Nair, her uncle, had waved his hand imperiously.

He wasn't a local regent, but he was wealthy enough to have the airs of one. 'We do not expect our guests to pay for the hospitality we extend to them.'

Kuttimalu, six years old and wide-eyed, had hidden behind a wooden pillar and eavesdropped on the men's conversation. *Please, oh gods, let Ammavan not send him away. Please let him agree to his request. I so want to learn all that the old brahmin says he can teach.*

The brahmin shrugged. 'It isn't payment. It's merely taking forth education. Music, arithmetic, Sanskrit, what real use do Nair children have for these? It's at best a leisurely pursuit; what is it you say – nerampoku – a time pass!'

Koman Nair had frowned. 'You don't have to.'

'I don't have to. I want to,' the man said gently.

'In which case, so be it!' Koman Nair said. He rather liked the conceit of having a brahmin residing in his madom. And the man appeared to be a scholar. Koman Nair would make sure that everyone in the ten deshams around him knew of this.

Kuttimalu had muffled her cry of delight. Ammavan didn't approve of girls making noise. You don't laugh; you smile. You don't speak in your natural voice; you whisper. You don't meet a man's gaze; you peer at a point beneath his chin. Ammavan had many such edicts. And now it remained to be seen if her uncle would allow her to be one of the students.

Kunju, the caretaker, had led the boys to the madom. The girls had giggled at the sight of the boys, who were being forced to abandon their games and attend classes instead. Kuttimalu had tagged along and slipped in when Kunju went back to bullying the servants.

The old brahmin had smiled at the girl in the room and then pretended he hadn't noticed her. No mention had been made of a girl student. The brahmin didn't think education was to be decided by gender; it was the mind that he sought to fill.

When Kuttimalu was discovered, everyone expected

Ammavan to erupt. Nani Amma had boxed her ears and hissed, 'Why do you do things to annoy my brother? Why can't you be like other girls? Why do you always have to be different?'

But Ammavan smiled and said, 'Nani, leave the girl alone.' He had turned to her and touched her cheek in a rare gesture of tenderness. 'Very well. You may continue to fill your head with this and that for some more time.'

When Kuttimalu turned eleven, the old brahmin left. He was going back to his village, he said. 'My horoscope said I would commit a caste offence and would be excommunicated for life. So I chose to leave my home during that period. For what is a man without his caste?'

Koman Nair nodded gravely. He had wondered at the length of the brahmin's stay. Usually they left in a day or two, some stayed a week, but none had stayed this long. 'Yes, what is a man without his caste?' he agreed.

'The madom will seem empty without you, the children will miss you,' he said. He had taken to meeting his brahmin guest most evenings. There was so much he didn't know that this man seemed to have a complete understanding of.

The old brahmin smiled. 'I will miss the children too,' he said quietly.

Why don't they just come out and say that they will miss each other, Kuttimalu thought from her habitual hiding place. After the brahmin left, Kuttimalu tried to keep at her arithmetic and grammar, but her learning grew rusty with time. Only the music remained. Notes she took and sang again and again till they were more her own and not what she had been taught.

Tired of Itukka Menavan's pronouncements, Kuttimalu rose from where she sat. The heat was stifling, even the floor felt warm to the touch. She walked listlessly within the airless, poky inner rooms of the naalukeutu, then stopped suddenly. She knew what she was going to do.

It was dark and no woman in her right mind would step out at this hour. But Kuttimalu could find her way alongside the vadakkera, the northern wing of the house, through the kitchen, and take the path that would lead her to the bathing pond. She knew nobody else would be there. She would take off her mundu and allow the waters to wash over her breasts and slide between her legs. She would let her hair float in the waters and no one would reprove or castigate her.

Humming under her breath, she threw the cloth that served as a towel on a little clothesline slung up alongside one wall of the pond house. She unclasped the knot of the cloth she wore around her waist and dropped it alongside the towel. The breeze, cooled by the waters of the pond, caused her skin to erupt in goose pimples. She shivered. Then she stepped into the water with a gasp and a sigh.

She kicked off the edge of the pond lazily. The water was cool and in the skies above, the stars gazed down upon her, as did the moon. She felt a gaze follow her. But there wasn't anyone there. Was some wandering god watching her cavort? She smiled, a slow, languorous smile of desire. If you are, then come take me, I am all yours, my celestial lover, teach me to fly as you do.

She shook her head and dived beneath the water's surface. Her sambandhakaran hadn't been to see her for almost a fortnight now. Would he come back or stay away for good, she wondered. She didn't particularly care either way.

He had spotted her when she had gone to worship at Thirumandhamkunnu temple and decided he wanted her. Just like that. As though she were one of those countless cattle bought and sold at the Vaniamkulam chanda every week. A brief ceremony had followed. A lamp lit. A cloth exchanged. In the privacy of their room, he had seized her, his new bride, as he would a cow he had just acquired. Patting her buttocks, cupping her breasts, pinching her cheeks, slapping her playfully on her thigh with a laugh, and then he had lowered himself onto her saying almost sotto voce, 'You are quite something…'

He was a brute of a man who thought the marital bed was an arena for him to practise his battle moves. He arrived. He thrust himself into her. He left. And not once was a tender word spoken. Or even that most banal of queries uttered: How are you?

But he was a powerful man from a well-known tharavad and in his veins coursed warrior blood. Such men cannot allow gentleness to root in them. They are dedicated to a cause, her brother Chandu said, when she complained to him. So Kuttimalu had learnt to still her protests and give her body to him and ask no more. One day, perhaps, there would be somebody else.

It's a strange life we lead, she told herself as she floated on her back. Our husbands are not really husbands; they are merely sambandhakarans – consorts with whom we share some nights and the call of the flesh; they fill our wombs but seldom our hearts; they come and go while we wait; when one leaves, another takes his place. For a piece of cloth he will buy the tenure to my body and if my soul craves for more, I will tell myself as my mother did and hers before that: Still your tongue and desires, girl, we Nair women keep our names and homes, isn't that enough? Shouldn't that do? Your destiny is not hitched to that of a man's. Any man's. Learn to accept what you receive and no more. The Nair woman's heart should never ache with expectation. Leave that to others in whom the warrior spirit has no place.

All very well to proclaim, but what do you do when you get lonely? What do you do when your man leaves and you dare not ask, when will you visit me next? This eternal waiting, that's what made you shrivel within.

Kuttimalu's gaze settled on the firefly again. It seemed to have stayed in the spot where she had seen it first. That's odd, she thought and on a whim, she swam back to the edge of the pond and climbed up the steps. The firefly rested in one corner, high up, close to the rafters. There was a little platform that ran alongside the wall where the women kept their oils, gram powder, sandal paste and loofahs. If she stood on it, she would be able to reach the firefly.

Kuttimalu pulled herself up on to the platform from the edge of the pond and walked to the firefly. As her fingers reached through the darkness, she touched skin. Warm skin. Fine silk. She gasped. Her mouth opened in a scream, but before she could make a sound, a pair of arms clasped her to a chest that was taut with muscle. Her mouth tasted the salt of sweat. Her nostrils flooded with the scent of the unknown. She heard a whisper, 'Please don't, thampurati. I mean no harm.'

She stopped struggling. His grip loosened and his arms fell to his side. But she stood there pressed against him. Skin against skin. All of her ached to touch and feel this man whose eye was a firefly, whose skin was silk and whose voice rumbled through the night, thunder with the sibilant fall of rain. He had called her thampurati. Mistress of the house. But he enunciated the syllables as one not familiar with the intonation. He knew the language, she realized, but he was not from here. He had hidden in the pond house rather than come to the main house. Which meant he was either a fugitive or someone who would not be allowed entry into their precincts. He knew the rules. And so did she.

Her fingers crawled up his chest and examined his face. She tilted her neck back and looked up at him. 'How tall are you?'

Beneath her fingers, she felt his mouth stretch into a smile. 'Not who are you?'

She laughed. Madness. What madness was this? She had called for a celestial lover. She had yearned for one. And here he was, in flesh and blood. She let her fingers slide back onto his chest.

'Does it matter who you are?' she asked.

'Not really,' he whispered. They stood still, her naked body pressed against his as if it was the most natural thing.

It felt right. It felt good. As though she had been waiting for it all through those brutal couplings with her sambandhakaran. The hardness of this body, the gentleness of tone, the softness of touch.

'I thought you were a firefly. Your glittering eye...'

'Fireflies are strange creature, thampurati. Do you know that a male flies through the night and those little pinpricks of light are what he uses to announce his intent? The female firefly sits on a branch and waits. If she likes the poetry of his light, she sends him a poem of her own, inviting him closer. He will then go to sit next to her. They will let their antennae touch. If she likes his smell, she will let him mate with her. Who would have thought the firefly has such complexities of passion?' His voice rambled on as if to buy time.

She laughed against his chest. 'I like your smell.'

He didn't know what to do, or what to say. What could he say? He knew it was dangerous, but he didn't want to stop the onslaught on his senses.

'It doesn't matter to me who you are or where you've come from. I know you are not of this world. How can you be? I do not know any men who are as tall as a palm tree and have a firefly for an eye. I do not know any men who merge with the night and whose skin has the sheen of silk. You cannot be of this world. I don't want you to be,' she murmured, her mouth tracing little arcs on his chest. 'Will you teach me to fly? For I am certain you must know how to.'

Something in him snapped. That iron control that had held him motionless in the dark corner, not wanting to betray his presence by a movement, a breath. That severity of thought that had made him curb the rush of blood as her body pressed against his. It was as though the feel of her mouth had caused his nerve ends to explode.

'I am not of this world,' he murmured and with one swift move, he raised her from her perch on the platform and brought her face close to his. Their breath mingled. 'But I make you this promise. That I will teach you to fly. All the way to heaven and beyond. Will you go with me, thampurati?'

'I will fly with you. Go with you wherever you choose to go,' she said against his lips.

He kissed her.

So this was what a kiss was like? Her sambandhakaran had no such use for his lips or hers. His mouth opened to feed his appetite, spew venom or betel juice. But this man, oh this god, his mouth was a master that knew exactly what to do. The quiet unfurling of the mouth, the softness of the lips, tongues coiling around each other, his, hers. The touch and go, the pressure, there was no knowing where it began, where it ended, this devouring of each other, this steady stoking of subterranean fires.

He raised his face for air. She clung to him. 'Are you going to stop with this?' the greedy little child in her demanded of him.

He laughed and bent to kiss the base of her throat where a coral pendant rested. Then he pushed her down onto the platform and blew gently into the well of her navel. Her back arched in response, inviting him to explore and discover.

What pleasure gates had she opened for him? What reservoirs of tenderness did she draw from him? What was this winged chariot they rode through the clouds?

Would there be another like him, she anguished as his mouth, his fingers, his maleness sought her in countless ways, each movement twisting that gut of pain in her.

They clung to each other, unwilling to let go. Her thighs drew him closer, deeper into her. His fingers trailed over her scalp. Such need, such a deep need to memorize every aspect of each other. Every bump, mole and hair follicle.

His mouth swooped down on the gentle slope of her belly. The smoothness, oh the unbearable smoothness of it. He pressed his eyes, the living and the dead eye, against the flesh. How could it be that even his eye that was no eye could harvest such joy?

No, my love, you cannot go without my leaving my mark on you. His teeth parted and nipped. She flinched, then smiled. She stroked the bruise with the tip of one finger and traced the curve of the mouth that had hurt her.

Already a certain wryness had entered her smile. A bruise would be her only keepsake of this madness. Of this glorious passion. A bruise that would fade, leaving behind a fleeting thought: did it really happen? Or did I imagine it all?

Kuttimalu walked away, not daring to turn back. What if she turned and was greeted with silence? It had to be lust after all, she told herself, or how would he have let her go? Not once did he say, 'Go with me…' If he had, she would have. One look was all she needed. One hint of intent, and she would have gone to him.

He stood there, watching her walk into the night and out of his life. It had to be lust after all, he told himself, or how could she have left? She didn't turn back once. One look was all he needed. He would have asked her to go with him, no matter what.

A deep sadness cloaked him. She hadn't even asked him his name.

'Thampurati,' he whispered to the night and all the assembled spirits there, 'I am Idris. Idris Maymoon Samataar Guleed. Previously of Dikhil. Now an eternal traveller seeking the measure of earth and man.'

He waited for her to seek him out. Perhaps, at the crack of dawn, she would make her way to the pond house to see him one last time, hold him one last time. But there was no sign of her. A slash of orange striated the eastern horizon and bird calls heralded the arrival of day. It would be dangerous for him to wait any longer. As he walked towards the wall, he was struck by a thought. He went back to the pond house and took from his skin pouch the pearl the Yemeni had given him. He knotted it at the end of the cloth she had left behind. Perhaps she would remember him occasionally, if not every day.

IV

So this is my son, Idris thought, looking at the boy who sat still as a rock. Only his fingers moved as they fondled Maccanto's forehead.

He had given her more than a pearl, it seemed. A rush of feeling for the boy overcame him. Idris had never allowed himself to probe his thoughts after that night. To do so would have been to twist the knot that had come to live in him.

He hadn't come back to the Malabar Coast since that time, and had instead found new places to travel to. But he had heard of the Mamangam ten years ago and had decided he would attend the next one. A few months ago, he had arrived in Kozhikode and attached himself there to a group heading to Thirunavaya. Only kismet had made him seek this copse of trees, he thought, as his eye gleaned the features of the face before him.

'Is it an uncle or a cousin who is part of the Chaver Pada?' Idris asked. 'Or your father?'

The boy looked at him and smirked. 'Father! I never had one. He was my mother's consort but when her belly swelled with me, he stopped coming. He died soon after. She has a new sambandhakaran now. A fair, soft worm who doesn't know one end of a spear from the other.'

Idris looked away, trying to hide his smile; a faint flush of hope.

'It's my oldest cousin. You should see him. He's tall. Not as tall as you are, but he's strong. His thighs are like stone and his biceps stand out like this.' Kandavar clenched his right bicep and drew a curve in the air above it with his left hand. 'And he's so agile. You should see him in the kalari. He leaps in the air and kicks his opponent down with a mere nudge of his big toe. It's the pressure and the speed, you see, all he does is plant his big toe right in the centre of the other man's forehead and the man falls back like a log.... And he's clever. And kind. Everyone loves him.'

'So does this paragon whom you are trailing have a name?'

The boy stiffened. 'I will not have you mock him.'

Idris grimaced. 'You dhoocil... let up. I wasn't mocking him. But if he's all that you claim he is, why set out to assassinate the Zamorin? Everyone knows that so many times, over so many years, the Chaver have only met with failure. He knows he's going to his death.'

The boy stood up. 'You are a trader. That is obvious. What do you know of honour? Or its claim on the warrior blood that runs in me and my cousins. We do not fear death.'

Idris reached out and took the boy's hand in his. 'You are right. I know nothing of the blood that runs in your veins or what it demands of you. But you are a child. You cannot take on your shoulders the burden of battles.' Seeing the boy's eyes seethe with indignation, he added, 'Yet. Listen to me, it will be your turn but not yet. There is still so much you need to learn and know. So much to see and understand.'

The boy's head dropped, accepting the truth of the pronouncement. 'That's what my mother tells me too. She says I need to curb my impatience.'

The dog leaned forward and licked the boy's face. He put his arms around it and hugged it as if he would never let go.

'Maccanto likes you,' Idris said.

'I like him too. Very much,' the boy said, his face buried in the dog's fur.

Idris smiled and stood up. 'In which case, he is yours…'

The boy stared at him. 'But he's your dog!'

'Now he is yours.'

'What if he pines for you…'

Idris adjusted the turban he had wound around his head. 'He won't if I tell him.'

He felt the boy's eyes take in the clothes he wore, suddenly conscious of how he must look. Many years ago, Idris's father had given up wearing macawis, replacing the sarong with the white full-length tunic, the jellabiyad, with pockets in its sleeves. Idris had worn one till the time he became part of the Naik's court. There he had given up his jellabiyad for the clothes the Mohammedan traders in India wore. A long tunic and loose trousers, a cloth turban wound around the head. It made him less conspicuous and hinted at who he was and what he did. But the boy had probably never seen anyone in anything other than the cloth that people here wore around the waist, be it man or woman.

'Wait,' the boy said slowly. 'Do you have to leave? Can't you stay? I am certain my uncle will be happy to meet someone like you. I can see you every day then. And Maccanto too!'

Idris leaned against the trunk of a tree. He smiled at the boy. 'That's a plan. But no promises as to how long I can stay.'

The boy didn't speak. Instead, he looked at the man's face, trying to fathom the expression in his living eye, and asked, 'What should I call you?'

The living eye blinked. The dead eye stared. Half a thought here. Half a thought there. The cold unseeing eye spoke up: *No one would know. So why not, Idris*?

'Call me Aabo,' Idris said softly.

'What's that?' the boy asked.

'Aabo. It's what a boy like you would call a man like me in my part of the world.'

'Aabo,' the boy said, savouring each syllable. 'I like it. Aabo, Aabo, Aabo.'

Idris felt a strange sense of exhilaration rush through his being. *So this is my son and he calls me father*. Was this how his own father had felt each time Idris had called him Aabo?

A roar rent the air. From the distance came sounds of a baying crowd and of a manic people intent on seeing blood drawn. Through the copse of trees, through the early hours of dawn, the sound carried to the boy and the man. The dog growled; from a lazy pet, it became the guardian beast with ears cocked and a mouth full of teeth ready to sink into anyone who threatened his master and his charge.

The boy and the man looked at each other. 'Come,' Idris said. 'We have to go. But first, wear this around you. The mob has no mind. Any stranger would be suspect but in my cloak, you would be considered my son. And they won't hurt a trader even if he's a foreigner.'

The boy draped the garment around him. It felt strange to be wreathed by cloth, and one that had sleeves he had to put his arms into. 'I could be your son. I am almost as black as you are,' the boy said, holding his arms aloft and feeling the cloth move with him,

'Yes, you could be, inan,' Idris said. He had never called anyone son before. He had never had a son until now.

The boy smiled, gathering the folds of the cloak around him. 'There is no one in my tharavad who is as black as I am. I don't care. Neither does my mother. She says all human beings can only be black or white. Have you seen a green man or a blue woman, she told a woman who said something to her about the colour of my skin...'

The three of them – man, boy and dog – walked towards the clearing and the source of the kerfuffle.

The clearing led to a lower terrace. Three or four terraces led off that one. Trees hid the Thirunavaya temple. On the highest terrace was an elevated ridge of hard laterite rock. And on it, at least twelve feet high, was the manittara. When the Zamorin stood on the platform, almost thirty feet higher than the riverbank, everyone would know that he, and he alone, was the master of all he purveyed. Anyone who thought otherwise would bear the brunt of his wrath.

The Chaver Pada had decided to attack the Zamorin before he reached the manittara. They had wanted to catch him unawares when he went to bathe in the river at the bathing pavilion built specially for his use. The leader of the Chaver Pada had decided to take a risk, knowing that only some of the Zamorin's bodyguards would be with him.

Traditionally, the Chaver attacked the Zamorin only when he stood on the manittara. It was a matter of custom. But are we here to enact a ritual or claim our honour? Rama Panicker had demanded. And the rest of the group had agreed. But somewhere, something went wrong. An informant, a careless tongue, or was it just bad luck that the Zamorin woke up with a fever. And so neither the Zamorin nor his coterie were present when the Chaver walked into a wall of bodyguards assembled there to prevent any such ambushes. Swords flashed. Blood spouted. Limbs were severed. Men died.

In the early hours of the day, the boy saw the plight of the Chaver. Of men who knew that death was certain and yet went headlong into battle.

An elephant was brought. A young male elephant to whom

everything was a game, a coconut or a severed head. The bodies were dragged all the way to the lowest terrace. The crowds jeered. Somewhere a voice murmured, 'I know this is how it is done, but these are warriors, men of honour.'

'Shut up, you fool. They are traitors and traitors deserve nothing better!' someone else snarled.

'Hear, hear,' the crowds booed down the lone voice of dissent.

The voices clamoured in the boy's head. The smell of blood and sweat, and the overwhelming smell of crushed mailanji leaves, as the crowds pressed against the hedge that grew on either side of the road. A tangy, spicy fragrance that would forever remind him of the road that was the destiny of every Chaver. The road to the end of the terrace.

For here was the manikinaru. A deep well cut into the laterite. It was here they brought the bodies of the Chaver. No rituals, no sacred chants, no touch of the holy fire to ease their passage to the other world. Just a cursory toss into a well of debris. Beneath each layer lay the remains of those who came before them. No one knew how many lay there. An ankle in an eye socket, a femur nudging a skull, a metatarsal hooked into a clavicle. For centuries now, men had sought to avenge their honour. For centuries, men had gone forth knowing that they would not return. But when you are a man, a man of honour, you think not of pain or death; you fear your own cowardice more.

The elephant kicked one body into the well. The crowds bayed for more. Fourteen such Chaver, one after the other. Then the elephant reached for a head, coiling its trunk around the hair and flung it into the well as if it were a coconut. As the head flew through the air and fell into the well, Kandavar felt a chill settle in him. It was his cousin. In the open eyes was the incredulity and wonder of having been taken by surprise. His cousin hadn't even realized he was dying as his head was severed. How could his life have been taken just like that? The boy clutched the older man's arm in fear, in shock. 'Aabo,' he cried.

'Enough,' Idris said. 'You have seen enough.'

Taking the boy's hand firmly in his, Idris wove his way through the crowds that now thronged around the well to peer down at the heap of bodies that lay within. Later in the day, someone would throw pails of quicklime over the bodies. And water. So that not a whiff of traitor stench would ride up the nostrils of anyone present. Even if one of the Chavers had a heartbeat left in him, the scalding would extinguish it.

Buried beneath a mound of flesh and bones, honour crumpled and torn asunder, what man could escape his melting flesh? What man would wish to? Twenty days later, the manikinaru would be covered with a layer of soil. And over the next twelve years, the wind and rain, sunlight and dew would chew their way through the bodies of the Chaver. Until it was time for another Mamangam, another mass grave.

'Shouldn't you go home?' Idris asked. 'Won't they be looking for you?'

The boy didn't speak. Instead, he continued to walk back towards the copse of trees. He walked till they were deep within, camouflaged by the trees and shadows. The boy sat beneath a tree. The dog went to sit by him. Idris looked at the two of them. He opened a pouch and from it took a handful of raisins, almonds and apricots.

'Here, eat this,' he said.

The boy looked at the offering. It looked like seeds and goat shit. 'What is it?'

'Fruit from distant lands. Eat it. You will feel better.'

The boy looked away. He didn't think he would ever know hunger again. Or thirst. 'Aabo,' he said, laying his palm against his chest, 'it hurts here.'

The man swooped down on his son and took him in his arms. Had anyone ever held the boy so, he wondered. He doubted it. 'Hush, hush,' he said, rocking the boy gently. 'One day soon, the soreness will become less. One day soon, it will go away. One day soon... you must trust me. I know. Your Aabo knows.'

Idris sang to his son the words that Fatima Naaya had erased his fears and sorrows with: Aabaaya amino, jijineey rabraaye, aabe majoogo, haoyo majoogto.

With every refrain of the lullaby, he fed his son a raisin, an almond and an apricot. He would let the boy sleep for a few hours or for as long as it took for the lacerations in his soul to heal. The boy had seen what no child should have. So had he, in his time, but he had his Aabo who, fortress-like, had gathered him in his arms and safeguarded him. My son has no one, Idris thought. I am his Aabo, but how can I make my claim? How can I be there for him?

The dog rose and came to lie beside Idris. 'What shall we do, Maccanto?' Idris asked the dog. 'Shall we go with him and let ourselves be known, or shall we disappear into the night like we have many times before?'

The dog licked his foot.

'I take it that's a yes. So we shall go with him and Allah will have his way. Neither you nor I nor anyone who walks this earth will be able to change that, Maccanto.'

Half asleep, the boy heard a soft murmur in a strange language. He thought of the many times he had climbed the jackfruit tree by the bathing pond to lie on one of its broad branches. All around him, from within the foliage, he would hear bird sounds. What they said to each other made no sense, but something about the chattering comforted him. Aabo's language was like that. He lay nestled against the older man's chest, reluctant to be parted from the protective warmth. No man had ever held him this close before. He kept his eyes shut and heard Aabo's heartbeat.

Idris felt the boy stir. But when he continued to lie against his chest, he smiled. Our blood calls to each other, he thought. That settled it. All doubts fled. This was Allah's doing. Why else had Idris, who had come to trade at the Mamangam, wandered into this copse of trees? It was kismet that he and his son should meet. Allah, the most merciful, knew that his son needed his father now more than at any other time. Allah, the most benevolent, had arranged it so. Who was he to fight Allah and kismet?

Idris stared at his son's face. He hugged the boy and kissed his brow.

The boy opened his eyes and spoke. 'Aabo, we must go.'

Idris nodded. 'Yes, we must.'

The boy sat up. 'You must meet my mother. She will like you, I know. And you, her.'

Idris looked away. Idris, who feared neither man nor beast, demons or death, felt his mouth go dry. Would she recognize him? Would she seek to distance herself, and worse, his son from him? She may not want her past to intrude into her present.

But Idris, previously of Dikhil, seeking the measure of earth and man, had never learnt to take a step backwards, and so with his son, he walked ahead.

V

In the evening light, Baapa Gurukkal saw three figures cross the clearing and walk down the hill towards his kalari. All around the kalari, the trees grew thick and almost impenetrable. From his vantage point, Baapa Gurukkal wondered who they were and what had brought them this way.

At the padipura, they hesitated. Baapa Gurukkal could now

see them clearly. A young boy of about nine years of age, a tall man who was a foreigner, and an unusual-looking dog with long legs and a pointed snout. Who were they and why were they at his gatehouse?

'Are we allowed entry, Gurukkal?' the boy called out.

'What about the dog?' The man had a strange accent. Baapa's ears perked.

'You can bring the dog in. I don't mind dogs. But dogs are haraam in my religion and so I am not allowed to handle them,' Baapa said carefully.

'Aabo, you are a Muslim too. But you have Maccanto!' the boy whispered.

'Whoever is kind to the creatures of god is kind to himself,' Idris murmured. 'So the Quran says, but it is the decision of our host, to touch them or not.'

Baapa Gurukkal said, 'Salaam walaikum.'

The man smiled. 'And peace be upon you as well, brother. Wa' alaykum salaam.'

As the boy watched with his hand on the dog's head, restraining its impulse to leap or lick, the two men embraced.

'How did you find your way here?' Baapa Gurukkal asked.

'The boy had heard your name spoken by his cousin who attended Ithappa Gurukkal's kalari. Besides, it is unusual for a Muslim to run a kalari, so it wasn't hard to find you.'

Baapa was silent. Ithappa and he were on opposing sides. But there was a mutual respect and admiration. An understanding that while they may owe their allegiance to different flags, their professions bound them in a brotherhood that recognized only what they brought to their chosen path of payatu.

'We didn't know where else to go,' the man added quietly.

Baapa Gurukkal nodded.

'This is Kandavar of Vattoli house,' the man said.

'And you? Who might you be?' Baapa asked softly.

'I am Idris. Idris Maymoon Samataar Guleed. Previously of

Dikhil. Now an eternal traveller seeking the measure of earth and man.'

Baapa smiled, a slow smile imbued with understanding of what was being stated and what was hidden. 'That is a practised answer. So tell me, what brings you here?'

Idris allowed the mask to slip. 'Once I lost something in these parts. Perhaps my quest is to seek it. Retrace my path in the hope that I may find it again.'

Baapa nodded. His eyes darted briefly to the boy, who stood fondling the dog's ears.

'Sometimes what we discover may not be what we set out to find. Are you prepared for that? Would you know what to do with your discovery then?'

Idris tried to read the expression in the man's eyes. Was it so obvious, he wondered. But he couldn't give himself away, much as he desired to call out to the world: I have a son. I have a son!

'A traveller has to keep an open mind. A traveller travels, not knowing what comes next. A traveller is one who erases the word expectation from his lexicon,' Idris said.

'For a foreigner, you use the language well.' Baapa didn't smile, nor did he bother to hide the wryness in his tone.

'When you learn a language, you take a step without feet,' Idris murmured. 'And a traveller has to travel with both his mind and feet, brother.'

Baapa raised an eyebrow. In time this tall man might reveal to him what he was really doing here. Until then he would have to be content with his intrepid statements and revelations of veiled truth. 'Come, you must be tired. And the boy.'

'We will leave tomorrow morning. But I shall return again and would like to stay awhile with you.'

Baapa nodded. 'You are welcome to stay for as long as you choose.'

'I would like to pay you. So if you will…' Idris took his money pouch.

'God owns the land, the water and the air. What are you going to pay me for?' Baapa held up his hand. 'A roof that already exists and a handful of rice that would otherwise end in a rat's belly. Tell me stories instead. Let that be your payment.'

The two men smiled at each other. More than anyone else, Idris knew the true value of stories. Of how they could feed a hungry man and heal the ailing. Of how they opened doors and offered solace for the weary. For Baapa, Idris would bring forth the stories he knew, and some he would make up as he went along.

'The boy has gone to sleep,' Baapa said.

Idris turned to where the boy lay curled up on the verandah of a small building where the farming implements were stored. His head rested against the dog, his arm curled around it.

'It has been a long day for him, but he is sturdy. Not easily fazed,' Idris said as he walked towards his son.

Bending down, he scooped the boy up in his arms. The dog stood and shook itself.

'Lead the way, brother,' Idris said.

Baapa Gurukkal woke up suddenly. His wife Bilkis's arm lay heavily across his middle. He looked at her with tenderness and a certain weariness. Bilkis was his third wife and she clung to him even when she was asleep, almost as if she was frightened that she too would go like the others had. His first wife had died in childbirth, leaving behind a stillborn child. His second wife was bitten by a cobra. Baapa hadn't wanted a wife thereafter. But someone had an astrologer read his horoscope and there was nothing in there to indicate further bereavement. Then it was suggested they ask the question of the planets. What had gone wrong the first two times?

A battery of astrologers went to work. There was a particular system for doing so. A mirror, a gold coin, a bowl of milk and yoghurt, fruits, palm-leaf manuscripts and a white cloth were placed alongside brass lamps filled with ghee into which wicks were inserted. Next the omens were read: the time when the query was stated; the rhythm of breath; the image that flashed through the mind of the astrologers gathered there. They turned to gauge Baapa's posture and body language. They deliberated on the first alphabet of the first word spoken by him in their presence and the expression in his eyes and they looked at everything surrounding them at that point. And then the language of events was deciphered so that the heavenly games of planets could be fathomed. A celestial pointer provided the answer: the trees.

All around the kalari was a forest of trees that seemed to almost press the house down. Baapa's first wife had wanted to build a wooden cradle for her unborn baby. She had chosen a fine rosewood tree and had it chopped. But she didn't live to rock the child in its rosewood cradle. Neither had the baby survived. Baapa's second wife had hated the sound of two jackfruit trees brushing against each other. She had looked at the trees that loomed over the house and had ordered for them to be cut. So we have some air and light in the house, she said. The next day, a cobra bit her when she went to the betel-leaf vine to pluck a few leaves.

'The trees are not to be touched, ever. When it is time for them to leave this world, they will wither and die. Then you can chop them down. Until then, not even a branch is to be lopped off. The goddess who once lived here considers the trees to be her children. Will any mother let her child be harmed and watch without retaliating?' one of the astrologers had asked.

Baapa tossed and turned in the bed. Sometimes he thought the burden of his inheritance was becoming increasingly hard to bear. He looked at his young wife again and thought of the visitors asleep in the guest house attached to the padipura. What would Idris have done in his situation? he wondered.

Suddenly it became a matter of supreme importance for him to know.

There was enough moonlight for Baapa to trace his path to the guest house, but he took a torch nevertheless, waving it so that sparks flew off its lit end. A cold breeze blew and the call of a nightjar echoed. Baapa shivered. The door to their room was open. He hesitated. Some indefinable need had pushed him out of his bed and brought him here, but what if Idris was asleep? He could hardly rouse him and ply him with his unformed thoughts.

'What brings you here, brother?' Idris's voice rumbled through the night.

Baapa was startled. Then, gathering his wits, he murmured, 'So you couldn't sleep either…'

Idris straightened. He had been reclining against the wall. He had taken his outer clothes off and sat bare-bodied, allowing the night air to caress his skin.

'I haven't slept since I was four,' he said.

'Since you were four years old?' Baapa's voice was incredulous.

'I was trapped in a cage of bones. For eighteen hours I crouched in there with my eyes pressed shut, hearing only the howling wind. I survived, but each time I close my eyes, yes, even my dead eye, the wind howls. I will never sleep again, until perhaps that last sleep.' One more lesson learnt as a traveller: never lie if you can tell the truth, no matter how improbable it may sound. You won't have to work yourself into knots corroborating your story later. Besides, he knew instinctively that Baapa would trust him, with no questions asked, if he spoke the truth.

'Is that why you took to wandering the earth?' Baapa moved to sit beside Idris.

'Put that way, perhaps. To have a home of one's own would necessitate a routine and regular hours. How can I, when I can't sleep? To lie awake night after night while my wife and children sleep and dream. This way, every night I have a new sky to gaze up at. This way, each night I dream with my eyes open.' Idris smiled. 'Do you think I am being fanciful?'

Baapa looked at the man before him. The muscles of his chest, the tightness of his belly. The foreigner may form words differently and he may sound like a poet, but his body was hard and had endured much.

'Not really,' he said slowly.

'We are traders. My father and his father before that. We traded in skins for perfumes and spices. My father wanted more. So he sought silk and we had to go across mountains – the silk route – have you heard of it?'

Baapa nodded. His home had been a haven to many a traveller and trader from distant lands.

'But when my father died, I sold our caravan and disbanded the men and set out on my own. I traded sights and stories, and to aid my passage I negotiated deals, became a courier of sorts, and sometimes served in the courts of small kings who liked having me as a part of their entourage.' Idris's tone made Baapa flinch.

Baapa didn't know what to say. He had come here wanting to exorcize his doubts, still the demons, but here was one whose demons were greater, more vicious. Idris smiled in the darkness. 'Brother,' he said, as if he had just caught the vagrant thought in its flight path, 'I travel because I don't know what else to do.'

'Like I wouldn't know what else to do but this.' Baapa's arm swept the expanse of his heritage, his home, his life. It was a gesture full of resentment. Baapa dropped his arm abruptly. Where had that come from? He had never felt as he did now. Confined by the demands of who he was.

'Tell me.' Idris spoke gently. Baapa was the older man. But it seemed Baapa needed the ministering, the guiding light of the Zohaal, to lead him back to hope.

VI

Cheraman Perumal heard of the brahmin warriors from Tulunaad. As a king he knew their prowess with weapons would help him extend his territory. Such was the sovereign Cheraman Perumal's reach and power that the twelve Tulunaad brahmin warriors accepted his invitation readily. Besides, it wasn't as if Tulunaad or Valluvanaad were very different from each other. The trees that grew there grew here. The birds that sang there sang here. They ate almost the same foods and everywhere the sky was the same. A brilliant blue when the sun shone and a mass of grey when the rains came. And during the night, the stars that prevailed upon their destinies were the same. Why would they hesitate to move to a new land then?

The brahmin warriors were accomplished masters of all eighteen concepts of warfare. But it was the padinettam adavu or the eighteenth concept, which involved flinging sand in the enemy's eye with a quick movement of the shield and feet, that made them virtually invincible. When a man has such knowledge, what place is there for fear in his life?

So they moved to the new land and founded a version of their garadi there. In time, they too took to calling their martial arts school by the local name for it – kalari. Or perhaps it was their garadi that came to be called kalari. It didn't matter what it was called, for everyone knew that within these gymnasiums warriors were born. They had another role too. As the king's men, they fought battles for him and made him more powerful than ever.

When Cheraman Perumal left for Mecca, their new lord was the Zamorin. Nothing else changed. The Tulu brahmin warriors continued to fight the Zamorin's battles and as the years passed, their sons succeeded them.

Who knows which year it happened? Who knows if the sun was blazing that day or hiding behind rain clouds? Who knows if a breeze blew that day, lifting leaves off the ground and making the paddy kernels shiver in their husks? Who knows? But that day the twelve brahmin warriors, descendants of the original twelve Gurukkal, were returning home amidst victory calls.

Each call proclaimed their prowess and strength; of how they had led the battle against the Vetath king and won it for the Zamorin. Flags and pennants were waved; voices grew hoarse with pronouncements of victory. Only one low-caste fellow, an untouchable, appeared to be unmoved.

He ought not to have been there in the first place, but flush with triumph, they had been willing to overlook the fact that a Nayadi stood in the distance, beating coconut husks with a stick. But when he continued to stand there, they were irked. He wasn't in their path, nevertheless they expected total obeisance from him. That he would fall on his face so that his lowly, untouchable visage wouldn't blight their horizon, pollute the air they breathed, taint the perfection of their victory. But the Nayadi, with a total disregard for who they were or what they had accomplished, continued to beat the husk methodically with a swinging, threshing motion.

The twelve Gurukkal paused. They stared at him with narrowed eyes. The creature needed to be driven off the face of the earth. But for now they would just chase him off the periphery of their vision. In fact, they wouldn't even bother dipping into their arsenal of combat techniques. A handful of gravel would do. One of the Gurukkal reached down and grabbed a handful of gravel. He knew exactly how to raise his arm and spread his fist at an angle that would make each bit of gravel a stinging bite. He knew it would make the Nayadi scream for mercy and run!

The gravel rained. But the Nayadi, with a turn of his body, a fleck of his wrist, twirled his stick so it dissipated the gravel shower. And as the twelve Gurukkal watched, he continued threshing the coconut husk.

How could they let this go? All twelve of them grabbed handfuls of gravel and began pelting the Nayadi. But once again, it seemed all that the Nayadi did was execute a little leap this way, a little leap that way, the cocking of an elbow, a turn of the neck, a sway of the hip, a slash of the stick, and he remained untouched by their fierceness and wrath. In fact, some of the gravel bounced back and fell around them.

The brahmins slumped to the ground while the Nayadi continued to beat the fibre out of the coconut husk.

'How did you do that?' one of them called out, unable to help himself.

'There are more skills than you may know of. There are more concepts to warfare than you are masters in,' the Nayadi said. 'That's all there is to it.'

The Gurukkal looked at each other.

'We have to learn it from him,' Deva, the man who had called out first, said.

'Are you insane?' the oldest of them snapped at him. 'He's an untouchable. Accept him as a master? Do you even realize what you are saying?'

'Let's leave this place before anyone discovers what happened. We'll find a way to get even with the creature. He won't be awake all day. We'll have his throat slit in his sleep,' one of them suggested.

But Deva wouldn't let go. 'We may have won the battle, but we lost the war, don't you see? Killing him by stealth is not what honourable men do.'

'Are you getting all noble here?' someone murmured fiercely.

'No, all I am saying is, he has something that we don't.

And if we are serious about what we do, we should acquire that knowledge,' he said.

The men burst into laughter and walked on, all except Deva Gurukkal.

He stood there watching the others leave and the Nayadi thrash the husk. It seemed to him that he was at a crossroads. Good sense demanded that he follow the others; his innate love for his vocation whispered that if he did so, he would be filled with regret for as long as he lived, for having let this opportunity go.

On their own, his fingers slid into the waist band of his mundu and brought out a pouch of coins. From another pouch, two betel leaves and a sliver of areca nut. With these, he walked towards the Nayadi. He placed his offerings on the ground and waited.

'Unless you make the request, how can I respond?' The elderly Nayadi smiled.

'Master, will you accept me as your student and teach me all you know?' Deva Gurukkal said.

The Nayadi nodded.

'The nineteenth concept. And marma chikilsa,' Baapa Gurukkal said. 'That was the heritage.'

Idris frowned. 'Marma chikilsa?'

'Yes, it is the science of how to hurt or heal by pressure on the sixty-four vital spots. The Nayadi taught Deva Gurukkal that as well. He taught him all he knew, but Deva Gurukkal had no place to take his new-found knowledge to.'

Deva Gurukkal was not allowed to even enter the gatehouse. 'When you made the choice to become the Nayadi's disciple, you chose to shut the door in your own face,' the oldest of the Gurukkal said.

'We performed the funeral rites in your name. We do not know who you are,' another one called out.

Deva Gurukkal let his eyes sweep over the house that had been his home once. He felt as if the finger of Shani, the death finger of Saturn, had been used to penetrate all the sixty-four vital points in his body. Who was he now? What was his name? What was his caste? Where did he belong?

From somewhere, the wind whispered in the Nayadi's voice. 'You forget that every hurt can be healed. You forget that maruthattu exists. An antidote for every wound inflicted. That revival is possible. All you need to do is look beyond the obvious and make use of what is available. Think, Deva. Think, son.'

Crouched on the ground, a fallen warrior, a beaten man, Deva now rose and stood tall. In Ponnani, he would go to the temple of Islam and there he would become a new man. If Cheraman Perumal could, so could he. He was, after all, the direct descendant of the men brought by Cheraman to maintain his suzerainty. Soon Deva, now a Muslim, chose a bride from a Muslim family and founded his own kalari.

'My grandfather moved away, bringing with him our family secrets, and set up this kalari. If you go to Changampully in Thirunavaya, you will see that he chose to replicate the original house of the Tulunaad brahmins here. I am the sole descendant of the line that branched away. I have no choice but to be me. Do you see now, Idris? Do you?'

The dawn was approaching. Birds called. Light streaked the skies. From the house came the sounds of life waking up: someone drew water from the well; hens squawked as they were let out from their coop; a cow lowed. The boy stirred in his sleep. The dog stretched itself.

'Is there something else you wished to do?' Idris asked gently.

Baapa Gurukkal rose. He was nimble as a goat despite his bulk.

'I don't know. I could never get myself to think beyond what was expected of me. I was destined to be Baapa Gurukkal and I became that. Everyone thinks it is a blessing to have the skills I possess. I am not so sure. There is very little that separates a blessing from a curse. Talent is such. When you know you have it, you see it as a blessing from Allah, but when others expect you to fulfil their desires with that talent, you are burdened by that expectation. You become the cursed one. Bound to eternal slavery by that talent, that cursed talent!'

Idris looked away. Later in the day, Baapa Gurukkal might regret this moment of soul baring. Later in the day, he would be stricken by awkwardness. It was best not to meet his eye, so he wouldn't remember what he saw in Idris's eye. Pity for a man shackled by his heritage. Envy for a man rooted to his talent. It was best that Baapa Gurukkal be allowed to forget his momentary weakness.

Idris cleared his throat and murmured, 'I have to wake the boy. We must leave soon.'

Baapa Gurukkal nodded. 'There is food in the main house,' he said as he left. 'Let me fetch it here for you. Though you know you are welcome to come into my home, it may be best for the boy to not do so. It would be considered a caste offence by his people.'

Idris watched the dawn unfurl around him. What would this day be like, he wondered.

VII

Kuttimalu stirred in her sleep. She turned on her side and felt the warmth of skin against hers. She opened her eyes and stared at the man asleep next to her. She ought to rise and start on her day. But he was here. Why hadn't he left as he usually did? Stealing out of the house in that hour before dawn, rousing his attendant so that he may ignite the torch and lead the way back to his home.

She touched his cheek with her forefinger. He was not a bad man. In fact, she truly liked him. There was nothing brutish or selfish about him. When he took her in his arms, it was with gentleness, and he made love to her carefully, as if she were a bud, bruised easily. But he was a brahmin and the caste laws so rigid that he could consort with her but not eat at her home.

All he allowed her was the preparation of his betel leaves. His eyes would gather each detail as she snapped the stalk of the leaf and laid it on her palm; as she removed the veins of the leaf, scoring it with a fingernail. He would watch her as she placed the leaf on her palm and daubed it with a mark of lime and laid slivers of areca nut on it. She would fold the betel leaf into a little parcel and he would be waiting. When he opened his mouth, she would sometimes tease him by taking the betel leaf pouch as far as his mouth and then moving it away. Last night, he had grabbed her fingers and nibbled at them in jest.

Later, he had wanted that she sing. Then he had made love to her as if it was the last time. And now, as he lay at her side, she felt a stab of fear. Was he leaving too? Was that what this was all about?

He opened his eyes and caught her gaze. He smiled, then took a deep breath.

'What is it? What is wrong?' she asked, trying to read his expression.

Neelakantan Namboodiri rubbed his eyes and sat up. There was a mist outside. A dense mist. He had to reach home as quickly as possible, but he was reluctant to leave Kuttimalu and this isle of calm. It was going to be an arduous day.

He touched her lips and traced the lines with the tip of his forefinger. 'What would I do without you?' he said.

She smiled and clasped his fingers.

'Something is troubling you,' she said, sitting up.

'I have to officiate at an ordeal,' he said in a low voice.

She stiffened. He felt her body tense and turned to her. 'I hate what we do in the name of law. I hate the inhumanity. And yet...'

'And yet?'

'And yet, how else are we to maintain order in our society?' Neelakantan rose and went to the window.

It had begun as a straightforward enquiry the day before. Most often, the accused confessed and after the punishment had been meted out, everyone left. Not this time. The accused was a barber, his crime: stealing a gold chain. The barber had gone as usual to tend to the men of a tharavad. He wasn't a stranger; in fact, he had been their barber for the past fifteen years. 'We trusted him,' the head of the family said. 'We have known him for so long, and he is a good barber.'

Neelakantan sat with the other men as part of the court of enquiry. 'Bring the accused to the kottil!' He spoke as chief officer at the enquiry. He hoped the accused would confess without them having to take it to the next step.

The accused had been thrown into a hole in the ground. Eight days of food hurled down into his face twice a day. Eight days of eating and sleeping in his own filth. Hour after hour of not knowing if it was day or night. Every breath inhaled was of his shit and piss and the fear that there was no escaping this, one way or the other.

The barber was brought to the kottil in chains. His hair was matted and he had a small beard. He smelt. The rank odour of the unwashed and something else – hopelessness. His eyes were glazed and his feet dragged with every step.

'What say you?' Neelakantan asked. Any moment now, the barber would burst into tears and reveal where the gold chain was hidden, he thought.

'I am innocent,' the barber said instead, raising his eyes. 'I have been their barber for the last fifteen years. Why would I steal anything from them now?'

No one had expected this. Didn't the barber know what would come next if he failed to confess to his crime?

The head of the household rose in agitation. 'So you are accusing me of lying?'

The barber didn't speak.

Neelakantan frowned. 'This is a court of enquiry and not your home. We will not tolerate such lack of decorum.'

The man subsided, murmuring under his breath. Of course he knew this was not his house and that he should rein in his temper. But did that mean he had to listen to a thief accuse him of perjury?

Neelakantan looked at the accused. 'There were witnesses,' he said.

'There always will be when it comes to the rich and powerful,' the barber said, every syllable dressed in bitterness.

'Do you hear that? Such arrogance,' someone in the crowd hissed.

'It is the righteous indignation of the innocent,' someone else said from the corner of his mouth.

Neelakantan swivelled his head to glare at the whisperers.

'You were seen picking up the waist chain from the ground,' he said.

'I was seen bending down to the ground. Do you know what I was doing? I saw a pebble with a pointed end. I thought it might pierce someone's foot. There are four toddlers in that house. So I picked it up. That was what I did. Tell me sirs, why isn't anyone questioning the witnesses about the missing waist chain?' the barber asked. The court of enquiry was a farce. He might as well die speaking his mind.

Neelakantan narrowed his eyes. The barber had a point, but how could the court of enquiry admit to that? 'So you will not confess to the crime?'

The man shook his head. 'I am poor. I am ignorant. But I am not a thief. I have my pride. I do not want to better myself on what doesn't belong to me.'

Neelakantan and the other officers exchanged glances. 'In which case, your innocence will be proven tomorrow by the fire ordeal,' he said.

The accused turned pale. His lips trembled. He fell to his knees and stayed there, beseeching them with his silence.

Neelakantan had been unable to bear the sight. To see a man so broken, so defeated – this case disturbed him in a way he hadn't expected it to. He needed consolation. And so he had sought his Kuttimalu.

'I must be on my way,' he said, gathering the abandoned pieces of cloth. One to tie around his waist and one to drape around his shoulder. He paused at the doorway to look at her again. Kuttimalu was dressed only in her jewellery. Her unbound hair hung to her waist and in the little light in the room, she looked like a goddess, he thought. With the body of a woman and not a girl's. She had a son; a boy of nine years who glowered at him when they crossed paths, but you wouldn't know to look at her.

She smiled, basking in the warmth of his gaze.

Neelakantan stepped out into the verandah and the attendant sprung to his feet, waving the torch this way and that to fire up the embers.

Neelakantan frowned as the torch failed to light.

'Ebhiya, you idiot, you let the torch go off... can't you be trusted with even this?'

The man didn't speak. He banged the lit end of the coconut fronds harder on the ground and then waved it furiously in the air. The torch blazed to life and he walked ahead, leading the way. Neelakanṭan followed. He turned for a last look. He couldn't see her, but he knew she was there, watching till he entered the padipura and disappeared from her line of vision.

VIII

They left Baapa Gurukkal's kalari a little after sunrise. 'Vattoli tharavad is only ten nazhikas away,' Baapa said. 'What is the hurry?'

'Nazhika?' Idris asked, puzzling over the word.

'A nazhika is twenty-four minutes.' Baapa smiled.

'The boy's mother must be worried. He sneaked out of their home without telling her. I must make sure he reaches home before they start a manhunt for him.'

Baapa nodded. 'Go then. But you know you are welcome to return anytime you want. Khuda hafiz.'

'Khuda hafiz,' Idris said.

A thin mist wrapped the countryside, but the sun was already piercing through the veil of cool.

'Are you tired?' Idris asked the boy.

'No, Aabo.' Kandavar smiled. He had made a little green ball by plaiting the leaves of coconut fronds around each other and rolling it deftly. He threw the ball ahead for Maccanto to fetch. 'Go, go, Maccanto, fetch the ball,' he called, laughing.

Maccanto raced after the ball, barking, wagging his tail furiously.

It was Idris who first saw the assembled crowd.

The trial ground had been swept clean of leaves and twigs. A woman had sprinkled a mixture of water and cow dung on the ground. It was part of the ordeal – the ritual cleansing. Only then would the gods make an appearance.

Idris stood with the crowd. Kandavar and the dog waited under a tree some distance away. Idris wouldn't allow them to go any closer. 'No,' he said. 'This is not for a boy to witness.'

Kandavar's jaw set at a mutinous angle. 'It is for this boy to see.'

Idris felt a swell of pride. But he hid it and said, 'What about Maccanto then? What if someone did something to him? There are only laws for humans in this land; none to prevent a dog from being tormented!'

Maccanto, as if to press the point, licked the boy's hand. Kandavar tugged at its ears gently. 'All right, I'll stay back then,' he relented.

'Away from the sight of the crowd,' Idris had called out as he walked forward. One or two of them had darted curious glances at the tall, black stranger. But the thought of grabbing a place in the front to witness the trial took priority over the presence of a stranger.

'What is he accused of?' Idris heard a man whisper.

'Theft. A gold waist chain apparently,' someone whispered back.

Idris heard the collective drawing in of breath.

'Have they found the chain?'

'No, they think he probably hid it. There are witnesses who saw him take it from the ground where it had fallen!'

Idris felt chilled to the bone. Murder, killing a cow, theft – these were all capital offences in this land, he had heard.

A brahmin stepped onto the trial ground, a wet cloth

wrapped around his waist. He murmured incantations as he walked around the trial spot.

'Yes, yes, call all the deities as witness to this,' a voice laced with bitterness mumbled. 'Only they will be able to save the barber.'

Idris watched as the brahmin asked two attendants to place a copper pan on the fire.

'Even the pan must be of a particular size. Four fingers deep with a diameter of sixteen fingers. When it comes to ordeals, they are as exacting as their caste laws,' a voice said in Arabic. Idris turned to see two foreign traders. From their clothes and complexion, he knew them to be Kutchis. Idris moved closer to them. He would stand out less if he was with them. The crowd would dismiss them as a group of curious foreigners and think no more of it.

The attendant brought a copper vessel brimming with sesame oil and poured it into the pan. Soon the oil was bubbling.

There was a small commotion as the accused was brought to the trial ground. 'Have you come to witness this farce?' he called out, his voice weary but defiant.

The crowd fell silent. Idris looked away. What was he doing here, witnessing a man being tormented? And yet.

The court of enquiry stood apart, their faces grave and their brows furrowed. They waited for Neelakantan to ask the dreaded words of the accuser. The head of the household was present, his face showing nothing of what was on his mind. 'The barber has not confessed to the crime. Do you require him to take this ordeal or do we let him go?'

The man's expression hardened. 'Let the gods decide if he is guilty.'

Neelakantan sighed. He truly hoped the barber was guilty. The alternative was too terrible to even dwell upon.

The barber was taken to the bathing pond near the temple and asked to cleanse himself. 'Wash your mouth well,' the guard called out. 'When you swear your innocence to the gods, your mouth must be clean.'

Still in his chains, the barber waded into the pond and stood neck-deep in water. As the water cleansed him of the filth and horror of the past few days, he held his breath and went below the surface. One of the guards tugged at the end of the chain he held. He didn't want the barber trying to drown himself before the ordeal. Such things had happened in the past. A few seconds later, the barber emerged and walked back to the edge of the pond.

The guards led him into the temple. A lone lamp was lit within the sanctum sanctorum. They removed his chains. 'Don't even think of escaping,' one of them said as they shoved him in.

Idris watched from a distance. What words of prayer would the condemned man say? He shivered.

A guard held the barber by the arm as another took a palm leaf with the accusation written on it and wrapped it around the waist of the accused. A bronze kindi was brought and its water spout held over the barber's hand. As the water gushed out of the vessel over the barber's fingers and palm, the guard said loudly so that all who stood there may know that this was a matter between one man and the gods, 'Say your prayers so that the gods bless you and cleanse your hand for what comes next.'

The barber darted a look of contempt at the guard. 'Get on with it,' he muttered under his breath. 'Why make such a brouhaha of it? Who are you trying to convince?'

The guard didn't reply. This was only customary behaviour in an accused. Some wept for mercy. Some went silent in shock. And some others became aggressive.

The brahmin washed a ring of iron in water and cast it into the oil.

The crowd hissed at the sight of the ring disappearing into the bubbling oil.

The court of enquiry now walked up to the accused. The crowd fell silent. Idris thought he had never known such a silence. Even the birds in the trees and the cicadas in the bushes paused. The greatest terror, Idris realized then, was not felt under a starless night sky but in broad daylight. Under a clear blue sky, as the sun shines, fear is deadlier.

'Hold your right hand out,' a guard said.

Two scribes approached the barber. They took the man's right hand in theirs and examined it. 'No sign of injury or disease,' one said while the other took his stylus and wrote the words on a palm leaf. 'It is hereby noted that he has a mole on the first joint of the index finger.'

The oil bubbled.

'What are they waiting for now?' one of the traders whispered.

'Watch!'

A peepul leaf was thrown into the pan. It turned crisp with the heat of the boiling oil.

'Speak the truth,' Neelakantan said again. 'Speak it three times so the gods may hear you, and also all those assembled here. And your conscience.'

The barber looked in the direction of the temple and said aloud, 'I did not commit this theft of which I am accused. Nor do I know who did it.'

He said the words again. The third time, his voice shook.

The brahmin stepped forward and whispered an incantation over the oil.

'Now retrieve the ring,' Neelakantan ordered in a hollow voice.

When the barber plunged his fingers into the oil, everyone there closed their eyes. The barber hollered in pain as the bubbling oil scalded his palm. Idris watched, his living eye unable to shut out the sight. Was there a smell of cooking flesh? Or did he imagine it?

Still screaming, the barber held up the ring. His face had turned deathly pale and his hand was a deep red. The barber tossed the ring to the ground unable to bear the pain and shook his injured palm in the air as he jumped from one foot to the other, babbling incoherently. Two guards held down the shrieking barber while the scribes stepped forward again. One of them took the barber's palm in his as carefully as he could, pretending not to be moved by the colour of the cooked flesh, the swelling and the blisters that had popped on the skin. They examined his hand even as obscenities tripped out of the barber's mouth. A white cloth was brought and the hand was wrapped in it quickly and deftly. One of the scribes placed a seal on the binding.

The scribe announced, 'In three days, we will return to this very spot and the seal will be broken in front of the court of enquiry. The gods will decide what the verdict is. All of you who have witnessed this – it is incumbent upon you to return and witness the verdict. The gods demand it and so do the laws of this land.'

The Kutchi traders looked at each other in dismay. 'Three days. We don't have that kind of time. Perhaps we can speak to the court of enquiry and explain.'

The crowds watched the accused being led away. Idris saw the complainant wipe his brow with a cloth.

Idris went with the traders. Over their heads Neelakantan saw the looming figure of a black man. His one eye glittered white and the other gold. Who was this stranger?

'We can make no exceptions,' Neelakantan said. 'It is the law.'

Idris dropped his gaze as the man peered at him. He was used to the curious glances people threw his way. Everywhere he went, people stared, but this was something else. Idris turned and walked back towards the clump of trees where the boy and the dog waited.

Neelakantan sat back in the palanquin and closed his eyes.

The morning had drained him of all strength. He hated these inhuman laws. He hated the thought that he had to be part of this cruelty. Most of all, he hated himself for not having been able to say no when called upon to head the court of enquiry. He opened his eyes and gazed into the distance. The tall black man with the curious-looking eye was walking towards a copse of trees. He saw a white dog emerge and behind the dog, a boy. His eyes narrowed. He had seen the boy before.

A fist clenched at the pit of his stomach. Kuttimalu's son. Kandavar. His mother called him Unni.

Neelakantan saw the boy and man together and he felt as if someone had clubbed him. There was a strange resemblance between the two. But how? His Kuttimalu... would she? No, he told himself firmly. Kuttimalu was feisty but she couldn't have been as rash as that. Besides, where would she have met him?

His fatigue was making him imagine the improbable, he decided.

IX

Idris held all emotion and thought in rein. He would not load this moment with any significance. To do so would be suicidal. He was just seeing his son home. And then he would leave. That was all, he told himself with every step.

The boy led the way as they drew closer to the house. The dog ran at his side and Idris walked a few paces behind. They stepped into a gigantic stretch of paddy fields. A distant hill edged one end of it, but there were bright squares of ripening paddy all around. Idris could see that they had already started harvesting from one end. He muttered a prayer of thanks under his breath. In all the commotion of the harvest, he wouldn't be as conspicuous.

The padipura here was both house and gate, tall and imposing. It was two storeys high and had a thatched roof. Idris had heard that only the Zamorin's palace and the temples were allowed tiled roofs. All houses, be it a Nair tharavad or a Namboodiri illam or a Muslim home, had to have a thatched roof. That was the rule.

Two planks stretched across a deep stream of water from the bank of the paddy fields to a narrow piece of land on which the padipura gates – twin wooden doors – lay wide open. But a burly man with a stout pole sat on one of the curved outer seats.

Kandavar ran across the plank. Maccanto trotted after him, unwilling to let the boy go out of sight. The burly man stood up. 'You ran away again, did you? Two men have wasted a whole day looking for you. Where did you go? Your mother has been weeping all day.'

Kandavar hung his head.

'And what is that with you?'

'This is Maccanto, my new dog. Don't you know a dog when you see one?' Kandavar said, patting the dog's head.

'Don't get too cocky. I was asking about that man there, on the edge of the paddy field.' The burly man frowned at the sight of the stranger, who seemed as tall as a palm tree and just as stately.

Kandavar stiffened. He could hear voices, including the deep gravelly voice of his uncle Chandu Nair. The boy shivered.

Chandu Nair stood across the threshold and peered at the tableaux before him. His nephew and a dog at the gatehouse door. And on the other side of the bridge stood a tall black man with a gold eye, draped in strange looking garments.

'Summon him in,' Chandu Nair said to the gatekeeper.

'But, thampuran, he is not from here,' the gatekeeper said, not hiding his surprise.

'Neither were you, Manickam, when I found you.' Chandu Nair's voice rang clear. 'Or have you forgotten?'

Manickam's face fell. He hadn't forgotten. Manickam had come from Madurai with a head of cattle ten years ago. At the Vaniamkulam chanda, his master had sold the cattle for a tidy profit. Humped cattle were not so common in these parts; in fact, you could buy an elephant more easily. The Kavalapara Nair had bought them all.

No one knew what actually happened, but the following day, Manickam's master was found dead. Snake bite was the verdict. He had been poisoned by a group of jealous traders, someone said. Some others said he had gambled all his earnings away and killed himself. Manickam had been left destitute. A boy of twelve with nothing to call his own except a piece of cloth around his waist and a tiny silver pendant strung on a thread round his neck.

Chandu Nair, on his way home, had seen the weeping boy. He had heard the rumours too, and on a whim, he took the boy in.

'No, thampuran, I haven't. The doors of the Vattoli tharavad offer shelter to all those who need it.'

Manickam put his hand to his mouth and called out, 'Traveller, you are welcome to rest at Vattoli tharavad's gatehouse.'

The boy's face lit up. He ran across the bridge, calling out, 'Aabo, Aabo, my uncle wants you to come in.'

Idris hesitated. Then the need to be with his son for a little while longer, the desire to catch a glimpse of her again, overrode caution and he stepped on to the wooden planks.

At the gatehouse, Manickam waited to usher the stranger in. 'Who is he?' he asked softly.

'He is Idris Maymoon Samataar Guleed,' Kandavar recited.

'Previously of Dikhil. Now an eternal traveller seeking the measure of earth and man.'

Manickam scratched his head. What was the boy saying? He peered at the stranger again.

'Come,' he said, injecting a note of deference into his voice.

Idris looked around him. In most homes the padipura was only a gatehouse, but here it was a little house on its own. Beyond the wooden gates was a short corridor flanked by ledges on either side. At the end of the corridor were two rooms to the left and right. One room had a wooden staircase which led to another one above. Idris climbed the staircase and found himself in a big airy room with six narrow openings cut into the walls. In times of trouble, archers would use the openings to shoot arrows at intruders. For now it offered a splendid view of the fields and the hills. There was a ledge alongside a wall and on it, a pile of rolled-up palm-leaf mats. It was a palace compared to some of the places he had been in.

'Traveller, you may rest here. The thampuran will see you in a while,' Manickam said.

'I have to go now. My mother is waiting for me,' the boy said from the doorway.

The dog stood at the foot of the stairs. Idris saw the confusion in its eyes. 'Take Maccanto with you,' he said. 'Let him get used to your home.'

There were matching openings in the wall overlooking the house. He went to stand by one. He saw his son and their dog walk down a broad, smooth path of hard baked clay. On either side of the path were raised banks of mud two fingers high. Soon they disappeared behind the giant old jackfruit trees with their dark, glossy leaves.

Idris sat on the ledge. He waited.

Some time passed. Idris didn't move. He would wait till they sent for him or someone came to see him.

The evening was turning into dusk when Manickam came to the door. 'The thampuran would like to see you. Make sure you stop at least ten feet away from the steps leading to the house. The caste laws here are very strict. And no one will mistake you for a Nair.' Manickam covered his mouth as a grin escaped him.

Idris's eye twinkled. 'That they won't.'

Idris bent low as he went through the doorway. He would have to remember each time, or he would slam his face on the lintel. He paused at the inner doorway of the gatehouse and gazed at what lay before him.

A magical world hemmed in on either side of the gatehouse by a massive bank of earth, on top of which was an interlaced fence of dry, prickly bamboo thorn. Within were trees. Idris expelled a breath at the sight of the trees. So many kinds. Some familiar, like the coconut and areca nut, mango and jack, teak and rosewood, tamarind and red silk cotton, and some he had never seen anywhere in his travels. Winding their way up several trees were pepper vines laden with spikes. A few of the spikes had fruits turning red at the base. The air smelt moist and green. Occasionally, the breeze brought a whiff of fragrance from a flowering tree. The rows of trees stretched as far as the eye could see. How much land did this tharavad own? He saw three elephants tethered to trees. A majestic tusker and two cow elephants. The mahouts gazed at him curiously as he walked past them.

Closer to the house, edging the front yard, were betel vines.

Manickam walked up the pathway towards the house. Idris followed, trying to look unmoved by everything he saw.

The gateman paused on entering the front yard. 'We'll walk twenty feet in and stop there. That is the custom.'

Idris said nothing, but halted on the flat, hard ground that seemed to have been made smooth with a mixture of cow dung and charcoal dust.

Chandu Nair stood on the verandah of the house, watching the tall black stranger take in his surroundings.

'Do you like what you see?' he asked curiously.

'It could be jannah,' Idris said softly.

'And that is?'

'Heaven in Arabic.'

'Obviously you are not from here, traveller. But you speak Malayalam.'

Idris nodded. He had learnt the nod as he had the language. 'I was attached to the court of the Keladi ruler Shivappa Naik in Bidannur. When he decided to renovate the Bekal fort, I was sent there, and so I learnt to speak Malayalam.'

'You are no longer attached to the court?'

'No,' Idris said firmly, to suggest he was unwilling to disclose the whys and wherefores.

Chandu Nair took the hint and opened his brass chellapetti. Within were several betel leaves and nuts.

'Where did you find the boy?' he asked, taking out a leaf and deveining it with a small knife.

'Near the market at Thirunavaya,' Idris said. 'I think he was lost. He seemed distraught.'

'Rubbish!' Chandu Nair snorted. 'All of nine and he thinks he is a Chaver already. This family has lost many sons, Mamangam after Mamangam. I have forbidden this pointless exercise in honour.'

Idris did not speak. A hen and her chicks scratched in the dust. A calf ran across the yard with its rope tagging behind it, scattering the hen and its chickens. The hen squawked loudly to gather its children. Where was the boy and Maccanto? The house seemed to have swallowed them whole.

'You are a trader, I presume.' Chandu Nair spoke through a mouth full of betel leaf and nut. His lips and tongue were stained red. 'What do you trade in?'

'I am more of a middleman. I merely facilitate trade,' Idris said.

'So what brings you here? But first tell me, where are you from?'

'From across the sea. Dikhil. It is a small place bordered by Somalia and Abyssinia,' Idris said, wiping his brow. He saw incomprehension in Chandu Nair's eyes. He may as well have told him he was from the moon, Idris thought ruefully.

'So why are you here in our land?' Chandu Nair persisted.

'I go where there is a call for my services,' Idris said. How long would the interrogation last? And what was it that the man really wanted to know?

'So if I were to ask you to be our guest for a little longer, would you be able to accept our invitation?' Chandu Nair asked quietly.

Idris felt his heart pound. 'I could, but why?'

'The boy seems very taken by you. Perhaps you could show him how to think of other things, rather than grooming himself for certain death twelve years from now.' Chandu Nair sighed.

Idris nodded. 'Guest or employee?' he asked slyly. 'I made a vow many years ago to work for no man. Or woman.'

Chandu Nair stood up. 'Guest then!'

'To come and go as I please. You will give me total freedom to train the boy's mind and perhaps even take him with me on short trips,' Idris said quickly.

'Of course. The gatehouse will be your home then.' Chandu Nair prepared to leave.

'Who is this Kesettan the boy refers to?'

'Kesavan, my older brother's son. Why?' Chandu Nair's voice rose. 'My older brother died many years ago.'

Idris cleared his throat. Should he announce the death or let the family discover it on its own?

Manickam walked in just then, leading a man. 'Thampuran, this man has come to see you from Angadipuram.'

Chandu Nair's eyes widened. A strange expression contorted his features.

'Thampuran,' the man said. 'Kesavan thampuran attained his heavenly abode last morning. He was one of the Chavers this year.'

'What?' Chandu Nair's voice rose in distress. He slumped against a wooden pillar. 'He was only twenty-one years old.'

Idris folded his arms and stood silently.

Chandu Nair turned to Idris. 'You see, don't you? You see what you need to do. In twelve years my nephew too will be twenty-one.'

Idris nodded and turned to leave.

From a room upstairs, he saw a movement. A flash of a hand as someone moved away from his line of vision.

Kuttimalu covered her mouth with her hand. So this was the man who had brought her son back. Kandavar had been strangely reticent about him, giving nothing away. What divine mischief was this? Her fingers slid over the gentle curve of her abdomen. The bruise his teeth had left had faded a few days later. But there were times when she still felt it throbbing under her skin. As if to remind her that it hadn't been a dream after all. That she couldn't delude herself into thinking that Kandavar wasn't his.

From the corner of her eye, she saw Kandavar watching her.

'What is it, Amma?' he asked cautiously. 'You look like you've seen a ghost!'

'That man, down there, talking to your uncle,' she said cautiously.

'That's Aabo.'

'Who?'

'Idris Maymoon Samataar Guleed. He asked me to call him Aabo. He is the one who found me and brought me home,' the boy said, going to the window. He could see Idris walking back to the padipura.

'He is not from here, is he?' Kuttimalu asked, joining her son at the window.

'No. From some place called Dikhil, across the seas. He is blacker than I am. And he has a gold eye.'

'I know,' she said, stroking her son's arm while her gaze remained fixed on the back of the man.

'How?' Kandavar tilted his chin at her. He was only nine, but he was almost as tall as her.

'I caught a glimpse of him,' she said.

'I am hungry, Amma,' he said.

Kuttimalu dropped a kiss on top of his head. 'It's not even twilight and the lamp hasn't been lit. How can you be hungry? You had an enormous lunch.'

'I don't know, but I am hungry, Amma.'

'If the rice is ready, you can eat,' she said smiling, turning to leave. The boy watched as she stood at the kitchen door hurling instructions.

'I am so hungry that I could eat an elephant,' he said again.

She smiled at him. 'Wait a bit, Unni.'

She called him Unni as did everyone else in the family. For the servants he was Unni Thampuran. Little master.

'The rice is still cooking. And you had better not let your new friend come in. Ammavan will be furious.'

'Who? Aabo?'

'No, your dog,' she said, thinking of her brother Chandu Nair's expression if he were to see a dog inside the house.

'Maccanto?'

'What a peculiar name!'

'It means honey in Aabo's language. And you don't have to worry about Maccanto. He understands. He won't come in unless I tell him to,' the boy said. He had already planned how, in the night, he was going to smuggle the dog into the room he slept in. 'Amma, will you make some koova tomorrow?' Kandavar asked, seeking to change the subject.

'Did you hear that, Kunji?' Kuttimalu called out. 'Do you have any of that koova powder left?'

Kunji, the kitchen maid, crinkled her forehead. 'I think there is some left, thampurati. If Unni Thampuran wants it, I'll make it for him.'

'No, you make it, Amma. Your koova tastes the best!' He tugged at her arm. 'Aabo gave me some dried fruits to eat. They were like nothing I've eaten before. One was a drop of sweetness; the other had a smokey, chewy taste and the third was crunchy. It was harder than a groundnut and tasted better. Everything about Aabo is strange, isn't it, Amma?'

Kuttimalu nodded gently. That brief glimpse of him – she didn't know what she felt.

When Kuttimalu discovered she was pregnant, she had thought of killing herself. The child would betray her, she had thought. And if discovered, the caste laws would demand that she be sold into slavery. Or her family would murder her to avoid the dishonour and scandal. But she couldn't do it. There will be a way. There is always a way, she told herself.

When Kandavar arrived, an old crone in the tharavad cackled, 'Who would have thought that your grandfather would be born as your son? The boy's a perfect replica of your grandfather from head to toe.'

Kuttimalu had lain there with her baby suckling at her breast and gazed with gratitude at the old woman for camouflaging the truth. For once she was glad that her mother had died a few months ago. Nani Amma was the only one who could have refuted the old woman's claim.

And so Kuttimalu's secret stayed a secret. The boy was named Kandavar after the man who had impregnated her grandmother with his dark-as-night skin and long limbs.

Then Neelakantan Namboodiri entered her life and her days and nights entered a plane of content. There were no high notes, but there were no low notes either. She smiled, hardly laughed, and never cried. Should anyone expect more of life? she asked herself sternly if ever a pang of regret clutched at her. Perhaps, in another life, she would know a different set of emotions.

'You are not listening to me, Amma,' Kandavar said, tugging at her arm again.

Kuttimalu looked down at her son's face and smiled. 'I was thinking...'

'About what?'

'About the time you were born.'

'Did I cry?'

Kunji, stirring a pot on the stove, snorted. 'No, you popped out cracking a joke! What's wrong with you? All babies cry when they are born – or they are dead!'

Kandavar flushed.

Kuttimalu saw her son's face cloud and hastened to change his mood. She stroked his arm. 'The rice must be ready. Wash your hands.'

At the north-eastern corner of the room was a well with two wooden shutters that were latched at night. During the day, they stayed wide open. The first thing Kunji did on waking up was to open them with a bang, and the last thing before going to bed was to shut them, again with a bang.

Kandavar stepped down into the sunken area by the well. The pulley was made of wooden slats in which were three small wooden balls, so each time the rope was lowered or raised over the runner to fetch water, it made a series of loud tumbling sounds. The music of the well, Kunji called it. Kree ka da ka da...

He splashed water on his face, arms and legs and went to the room adjacent to the kitchen. He sat on the ground, crossing his legs. Kuttimalu smiled at him and began ladling conjee into a flat-rimmed bronze bowl. She added a dollop of ghee and pushed the duck-shaped wooden salt box towards him. He opened the salt mariga and took a pinch of salt. Kunji brought a leaf of the jackfruit tree folded into a cone and pinned with a sliver of the coconut-leaf spine. Kandavar dipped his leaf spoon into the bowl and spooned the gruel and rice into his mouth. Kuttimalu watched, amused at the speed with which he ate.

'Some more?' she asked, ladling more conjee into his bowl.

'It's my kinnam, right?' he said, peering at its edge.

'It's yours,' Kuttimalu said with a laugh.

'How do you know that?' he demanded.

'Like you know. I look for the same dent as you do to make sure it's yours.' She paused.

'Unni, this kinnam existed before you, and will continue to exist after my time and yours. It isn't good to be attached to our possessions. If it goes missing one day, you will grieve. And grief is to be saved for greater sorrows.'

She paused, then said gently, 'There is something I must tell you. Kesavan...'

The leaf spoon slid out of his fingers.

'I saw, Amma, I saw him and the other Chavers thrown into the manikinaru like they were a pile of rubbish.' He buried his face in his hands and wept with loud heaving sobs as he remembered the horror of seeing his cousin's severed head. Then he raised his head and said through his tears, 'I would have jumped in and brought him home. But Aabo dragged me away from there. If it wasn't for him, I wouldn't be here.'

Kuttimalu closed her eyes, unable to bear the irony of it.

X

'You must be very special,' Manickam said, as he set down the bowls of rice and vegetable curry a little past twilight.

Idris looked at the food in dismay. Not a sliver of meat or fish. How was he to eat this? And how would the boy have any strength if he ate only this cattle fodder?

Manickam frowned at Idris's hesitation to dive into the food. 'What? You don't like this?'

Idris didn't respond. He held up the jackfruit leaf and looked at it curiously. 'Am I to eat this?'

Manickam slapped his palm on his forehead. 'Aiyyo, where have you come from? Here, watch me.'

Manickam fashioned a spoon out of the leaf and said, 'If you are going to eat your rice as conjee, you will need this. Or you can use your fingers. I didn't know what you preferred. So I brought both.'

'No meat, no fish, this is too insipid!' Idris mumbled.

'They are strict vegetarians in there.'

'But they keep chickens.'

Manickam shrugged. 'Someone told thampuran that the dogs need to be fed more than rice to make them fierce. So the chickens were introduced.'

'Good! Maccanto would have rebelled and attacked the chickens otherwise,' Idris said, stirring the rice with the leaf spoon, wondering how he was going to eat it.

Manickam rose and left the room. He came back with a covered dish containing two boiled eggs. 'This satisfy you?' he asked with a grin.

Idris grinned back. 'Is that yours?'

Manickam nodded.

'But how?'

'Two of the hens have taken to laying their eggs in a little burrow behind the gatehouse. When my taste buds tire of their veggies, I boil an egg or two, sprinkle some pepper and salt on it, and that makes the meal palatable.'

Idris and Manickam sat across from each other and ate quickly.

When the meal was over, the two men sat gazing at the fields. 'What did you mean by saying I must be special?' Idris asked suddenly.

Manickam's mouth twisted into a wry smile. 'Do you know why I was appointed the gatekeeper and set up here at the boundary of their home?'

'You are a sturdy young man.' Idris smiled. 'No one will mess with you.'

'That I am. But also because I am not one of them. After all these years, I am only allowed to go as far as the end of the path and am not even allowed to step into the front yard. They believe my presence will pollute them. And here you are, a stranger, a foreigner, and they let you step into the front yard.'

'Oh, that!' Idris wiped his face, his shaven head. He hadn't felt heat like this in a long time. Humid heat that seemed to turn even his bones into water.

'I am a foreigner and that makes me hard to categorize. So I get to go to places where you natives wouldn't be allowed entry. I get to do things that you may be penalized for.'

'Ah, now I know why you travel. So no one can contain you within their laws or customs.' Manickam shook his head in amazement. Why hadn't he thought of that? He sighed. It was impossible for him to even consider it. Only someone like this Idris could get away with it.

Whereas it was his destiny to remain as gatekeeper to Vattoli tharavad; pilferer of eggs and bodyguard to the thampuran. This cursed land and its laws! He wished he could leave. But where would he go?

Someone called from across the field. Manickam stood up and said, 'You should step aside. We mustn't be seen by them.'

He hastened to open the gates. A man holding a torch aloft led the way and another man followed. Even in the hazy light of the torch, Idris recognized the face.

It was the man who had been leading the court of enquiry. Idris frowned. What was he doing here? Then it dawned on him. This must be her new consort. Kandavar had spoken of a fair, soft worm: this must be the worm.

Idris moved out of sight to stand by the ladder. The dark room, he hoped, would swallow him whole. It was best if the worm didn't see him. He needn't have bothered though, he mused, when Manickam had shut the gates again. The fair, soft worm had been impervious to anything and anyone.

But then, such is the nature of worms everywhere, he told himself. Lacking a spine, they do not seek out triumphs of courage but can be dangerous in a quiet, sly fashion, burrowing into your heart and home and robbing them of everything that you thought was yours.

XI

'I didn't expect you tonight,' Kuttimalu said.

Neelakantan leaned against the headboard of the bed. He had gifted her this bed. The thought of being with her on a bed she had lain on with another man repelled him.

He had first spotted her at the Aryan Kavu. She was with a group of women, worshipping at the temple. He watched how, while the other women stood with eyes shut and heads bent towards their clasped fingers, mouthing prayers, she alone was more interested in what was around her than in front of her. He saw her eyes darting this way and that, a dimple scoring her cheek at the sight of a monkey perched on top of a pillar.

She wasn't a girl. He didn't want a coy creature who would weep if he kept away for a few days. Her body curved and dipped pleasingly enough, and Neelakantan had been enchanted by that dimple in her cheek.

He had his official caretaker make enquiries. She hadn't had a sambandhakaran for some years now, he was told. She had a son. Yes, the family was willing, if he was interested. Chandu Nair, her brother, had heard a great deal about him and wasn't averse to the liaison. And so, Neelakantan came one evening and in the presence of her family and with only a bronze lamp officiating as light and divinity, he offered her a cloth and his troth for as long as either of them desired it.

'What are you thinking?' Kuttimalu asked. There were deep furrows of thought on his forehead. Something was troubling him, she knew. If only he would say it.

Neelakantan wiped the frown off his face with a smile.

'It's the ordeal that I had to officiate at this morning. I have to go back there again three days hence,' he said slowly, stroking her hair.

I could be a cat or a dove, Kuttimalu thought as his fingers continued to run through her hair again and again. Something to hold and caress, and no more. It was this, the need to break the self-absorption, that prompted her to ask, 'And what do you think will be the result of the ordeal?'

His fingers paused. He stiffened at the thought of what lay ahead. 'The scribes have noted the state of the barber's palm when he pulled the ring out of boiling oil. Then they bound his hand and placed a seal on it. Three days from now, we will all gather and the seal will be broken. If his hand has healed, he will be set free. Else…'

Kuttimalu shivered. Why had she even raised the subject?

'Will it heal?' she asked, thinking of the accused man.

Neelakantan shrugged. 'Miracles have happened…' His voice was hard as he continued, 'We do not live in an easy land, Kuttimalu. Our laws are stringent and will not tolerate any deviation.'

Kuttimalu met his gaze. Why was he telling her this, she wondered.

'By the way,' he said, thrusting the chellapetti towards her. 'I think I saw your son today. What was he doing so far from home?'

Kuttimalu clenched her face to still the turbulence within her. Had he seen her son's father? She opened the betel-nut box. 'What do I say?' She sighed. 'He decided he wanted to see the Mamangam festivities and ran away with some boys from the kalari his cousins go to.'

'He wasn't with any of the boys when I spotted him. There was a tall, black foreigner with him.'

Kuttimalu began to smear lime on a betel leaf to hide her trembling fingers. 'Yes, I was just getting around to telling you that. He got separated from the others and the foreign trader – for that's who he is – found him and brought him back.'

She paused and added, 'My eldest brother's son Kesavan was one of the Chavers. He…' She stopped, unable to continue as her eyes filled up. Her brother's wife had a new consort but Kesavan was still her nephew and her heart went out to his mother. How could any mother bear the death of her child?

Neelakantan rose from the bed and went towards the window. The skies were lit up with a million stars but one star glowed above all the others. Mrygyavydha. The deer hunter. Rudra of the skies. It was a star that often comforted him when chaos ruled his thoughts. A constant that anchored him, helped him to believe in what he considered was good and right. Tonight, though, the star prodded him to ask the question that had loomed in his mind all day.

'Is he here?'

'Who? Kandavar?'

'Your son's father.'

Kuttimalu joined him at the window. She followed his gaze and saw that it was fixed on the Mrygyavydha. The brightest star in the sky. She could see that he was willing himself not to turn and look at her. What was he afraid of seeing in her eyes?

Many years ago, when her son was born and the old crone had proclaimed him to be the exact replica of a man she had never seen, she had allowed herself to be part of the conspiracy. The old woman, Ittiamma, had watched her suckle the baby and murmured, 'You have a silly habit of wanting to speak the truth all the time. Sometimes the truth doesn't do anyone good. Neither the teller nor the listener. Or the innocents who are involved. Look at your son. Untouched by life or what came before… so innocent… so helpless, Kuttimalu. Do right by him. That is all you need to remember.'

Kuttimalu hadn't responded. But she understood the purport of Ittiamma's words.

'Unni Raman Nair died while I was still carrying my son. He was bitten by a snake. I thought it was common knowledge,' she said, prevaricating. She unclenched his grip on the wooden bar of the window and turned him towards her.

'He was a brute of a man. It is with you I have discovered what content is,' she said, laying her cheek against his chest. It was the truth.

He wrapped his arms around her. The turmoil in his heart quietened.

In the night skies, the stars gleamed. Witness to many truths and renderings of truth.

He lay on his side on the woven bamboo mat. Maccanto lay at his foot. The boy let his big toe slide along the length of the dog. Maccanto turned his head and licked the boy's foot. Kandavar felt a fierce surge of love.

His mother and everyone else would be horrified if they saw him now. Kandavar had waited for the household to fall asleep. He was a lone child and his mother had no sisters. But it didn't really matter. His second cousins tied by blood were his playmates and companions. Sometimes Kandavar wondered about the call of blood between cousins. Would his bond with his cousins be absolute, as between two brothers or a brother and sister? If they had to choose, would they choose him or their siblings? But now, Kandavar had Maccanto.

He had gone to bed with the other children in the thekni, the room opening to the central courtyard. Like the others, he had unrolled his bamboo mat with its thin cotton pillow and chorused the night prayer seven times: Hanumane, Hanumane, pedi swapnam kaattaruthe…

He had looked at his cousins as they sat on their beds, hands clasped, eyes closed, beseeching the monkey god. How could the monkey god help keep nightmares away? Our dreams are our own, as are our nightmares. How could any god, even someone as powerful as Hanuman, determine the shape of their nights? But Kandavar knew enough to not question the custom of the house. He parroted the words as he was expected to.

He had to wait for at least two nazhikas before it was safe for him to creep out of the thekni and walk along the corridor, past all the rooms where various people slept. He emerged into the poomukham, the large front room that jutted out from the main building and with all three sides open. He could see the padipura in the distance. A hazy silhouette in the night that shifted as the moon went behind the clouds.

Bedroll tucked under his arm, Kandavar crept towards the veranda that ran around the house to the north-western corner where the granary was. Only grain slept in the pathayam. Paddy seeds that lay on their side, nestled against each other, trapped in a gigantic wooden chamber and dreaming of when it would be time to be taken and put to rest in the earth they had sprung from. He had heard Aabo say that he never ever slept. Was that how the paddy seeds felt as they waited?

Kandavar felt a wet snout nuzzle his knee. Maccanto had arrived to find him. He hugged the dog, murmuring, 'You knew I would come, didn't you?'

He squatted on the floor, unrolled the mat and placed the pillow at one end. He lay down and felt Maccanto flop beside him, a little sigh of relief – was it contentment? That was precisely how he felt too.

A cool breeze blew. Kandavar shivered and hugged the dog. The night sky was ablaze with stars. They were the souls of the Chaver, he thought. Men who had died for honour and turned into stars for everyone to see every night. That was their reward – eternal fame. He was certain that his cousin Kesettan too had turned into a star.

One star burnt brighter than all the others. It must be the soul of the first Chaver who set forth to wrest the rights of the Mamangam from the Zamorin.

In the morning he would ask Aabo for the name of the star.

Fingers of mist wafted in through the slits in the wall. Idris shivered. He pulled his robes around him and turned on his side. Slivers of the night sky. A star here, a star there. Idris thought of how the stars cut a swathe of light through the dense blackness of the night. The constellation of Al-Jabbar was resplendent and he traced its zones as a matter of routine. Al-

Nilam. The string of pearls that drew energy from the vastness of space. Then came the girdle, Al-Nitaq, and the Mintaka, the area that balanced justice and truth. All the raw energy in the upper echelons, when it distilled down into the lower regions, became divine reason. He had stared at the heavens, seeking familiar stars: Rijl Jouzah al-Yusra, the foot of the mighty giant Al-Jabbar. Saif, the giant's sword.

Idris brought out his pouch of hashish and filled his small pipe. He would need it tonight to quell this strange restlessness. He searched the skies for a star. Wherever he was, it was that celestial light that rooted him to the earth and drew a map around his feet. Ash-Shira: the leader. The brightest star in the sky. Without the Ash-Shira, Idris and countless travellers like him would be lost. A Greek sailor had told him it was called Al-Jabbar's dog. Idris had liked that. Here was a star that would be with him through all his travels. It was the star Idris had chosen as his familiar from the moment it had been pointed out to him by an Arab he had met on his travels. The Arab had an astrolabe, which he had shown Idris how to use. In the course of that celestial navigation, his eyes had wandered back again and again to this one star. All these years, he had clung to the Ash-Shira in the skies and the image of a woman bathed in shadows and moonlight. The darkest night would never deter his step when he had this to light his path, still his fears and walk with him.

The Serer people of Sine and Saloum called it Yoonir. To them, it was the symbol of the universe. The rain priests drew on its path to predict rain. The Dogon of Manden Kurufu thought the ancestral spirits Nommo lived around this star. The yellow people called it celestial wolf. These people of Malayalam – what was their name for it?

What was their name for a man who lay staring at the stars while his son slept in a house where the father was not allowed to enter? What was the term for a man whose one eye never blinked or shed a tear, even though it saw that in that house where his son slept was also the woman whom he had loved once and who now lay beside another man?

What was their name for a man who didn't know how to explain to himself his presence here? Or what he was to do next? Would he gather his son and woman into his arms? Or flee the place, like he had always fled the past?

XII

In the early hours of the day, Idris left. He could no longer bear to be there. It was all too much and too sudden. He thought he would go back to Baapa Gurukkal and stay there till he could collect his thoughts and find the balance that suddenly seemed to have escaped him. He left a few of his things behind so they would know he intended to return.

As he walked towards Baapa Gurukkal's kalari, he saw the ordeal ground. There was nothing to indicate the horror of the previous morning, except for the clearing where the stones used for the fire sat, dusty black witnesses of a warped justice system. How could anyone give credence to such a barbaric ritual and deem it to be ordained by god? Somewhere in him, the futility and helplessness he had felt through the night churned and twisted. Life needn't always be beyond his control.

Baapa Gurukkal asked no questions. Idris was grateful for that. Instead, he listened carefully as Idris described the tree he was looking for. 'It is a single-stemmed tree with a crown of leaves on top. The wood is very soft and there is a cluster of fruit at the base of the leaves. It has big green fruit that turn yellow when ripe and there are many black seeds within the yellow-orange flesh when you slice it open.'

Baapa Gurukkal led him towards a clump of trees to the rear of his house. 'Are you talking of this tree?'

Idris smiled at the sight of the babbay tree laden with ripe fruit. 'Yes,' he said. 'This is it!'

'We call it omakaya in Malayalam. The parangis call it mamao.' Baapa Gurukkal smiled. 'But that's besides the point. Why do you need this tree?'

'It's not the tree I need as much as the fruit,' Idris mumbled, reaching for the ripest of them.

'Wait,' Baapa Gurukkal said. 'There are riper ones inside the house. My wife had them plucked this morning. But what do you need them for? To eat?'

Idris shrugged. 'What else?'

Baapa Gurukkal grunted but didn't probe any further.

The two men walked back to the house. Idris wondered what the other man would say if he were to tell him what he intended to do.

As though he had read his mind, Baapa Gurukkal asked again, 'Tell me... what did you want the fruit for?'

Idris took a deep breath. He gestured for the other man to seat himself and then narrated to him the ordeal he had witnessed the previous morning.

'But I still don't understand. What do you want omakaya for?' Baapa Gurukkal said. The house was silent. Even the chickens had stopped clucking and scratching the earth. The question hung in the air like a fruit, ripe and about to explode.

'In the land I come from, we use the babbay for more than just eating,' Idris said. 'It is best I don't tell you what I plan to do. I shall, in time, but for now...'

Late in the night, Idris went back to the ordeal ground. The guards had long since gone to sleep. The fire they had lit had burnt itself out. Only the barber was awake. He was lying beneath a tree. Idris lowered himself to the ground. The barber turned towards him, startled at the sight of the apparition. His hand was on fire, throbbing with pain, and it seemed death had come to take him away.

The apparition put a finger to its lips. Then it took the barber's bound hand in its own and began applying a golden yellow ointment to it. The barber felt the fire cool, something close to relief trickled down the cloth to his burnt flesh. 'Keep adding this to the cloth every time you can, when no one is watching,' Idris murmured, handing him the ointment in a coconut shell.

The barber nodded, too overwhelmed to speak. He watched as the apparition slid into the night and became one with it. Was it a yaksha or a gandharva? he wondered as hope suffused him. The gods had heard his plea of innocence and had sent a celestial messenger to heal him.

On the third day, Baapa Gurukkal went with Idris to the ordeal ground where the court of enquiry had gathered. All the others present on the day of the ordeal had to stand witness to what would happen next.

The barber's face was serene and untroubled when he was brought forward. A collective gasp of surprise filled the ordeal ground. Why wasn't he trembling with pain, whispering with terror, weeping for mercy? Could any man be so unmoved by pain and fear?

His bound hand was held aloft. Everyone could see the bandage was stained yellow with oozing pus. The seal was broken and the bandage was unwound. Again there followed a gasp of bafflement. For the barber's hand seemed to have healed. He was innocent.

The barber fell to his knees and raised his arms in supplication. 'The gods have spoken. They have declared me innocent.'

'But how? What is the explanation?' It was a rhetorical question by one of the men on the court of enquiry, but the barber chose to answer it.

'The spirit of the tree I lay under came to me. The spirit took my hand and stroked it. A golden glow wrapped my scalded hand and I knew my innocence had been recognized.'

'I suppose you are the spirit and the golden glow was the pulp of the fruit,' Baapa Gurukkal murmured.

Idris smiled. 'It is a traditional medicine for burns, especially for children, in the land I come from. I added to it some aloe I found in your garden. It worked well enough.'

Over the heads of the crowd, Idris felt a pair of eyes descend on him. He turned his head slightly. Neelakantan Namboodiri was gazing at him with a strange expression.

Idris held his gaze, and slowly he tilted his chin and lowered it in that customary gesture of silent acknowledgement.

XIII

Idris waited for two weeks for a glimpse of Kuttimalu. For some overture or signal to suggest that she knew he had returned. But there was nothing. Each night, he searched the skies for a glimpse of the Ash-Shira. There was no sign of it either. Idris was beginning to despair.

It seemed to him that she didn't step out of the tharavad at all. He saw an elderly woman sweep the yard and sprinkle a mixture of cow dung and water on the ground. He saw another old woman pluck betel leaves from a creeper. He had heard that Nair women were not bidden to stay indoors. In fact, at temple festivals, they would be present wearing all their jewellery so that they may be seen and admired. Where was his son's mother? Manickam, who had the evening watch for the week, had a ready answer.

'Probably they have decided that she must not step out because you, a foreigner, are present here.'

'What would I do?'

'You have to understand, it is not about you as much as about what goes on here. In the month of Karkitakam, when the rain falls like a sheet all morning and night, the untouchables – the parayan and pulayan – will hover by these tharavads. If they spot a Nair woman, they hurl a stone or a twig at her. And if, heaven forbid, the stick or stone touches her, she will be excommunicated and will have to make a home with those untouchables. So which young woman, unless she is desperate or foolish, will step away from the shadow of the tharavad? It may not be Karkitakam but the fact is you are not one of them and what if you accidentally crossed her path?'

Idris nodded without speaking. What desperation had brought Kuttimalu to the pond at night, all those years ago?

The next morning though, Kandavar and Maccanto arrived with a story to tell. 'My mother says there is a demon in the pala tree by the pond. It is drawn to the fragrance of the tree.'

'Do you believe in demons?' Idris smiled at the boy.

'I don't know. If I see one, I may know what to believe. That's what I told Amma.'

'So what did she say?'

'She said she had seen one many years ago. And that if one goes there on the second night, in the darker phase of the moon, one may see it,' Kandavar said.

Idris felt his heart hammer. There was a message there somewhere. Or, was he reading too much into an innocent statement? His instinct told him otherwise. It was the second night, in the darker phase of the moon. The night would cloak all.

'Will you go with me? We'll take Maccanto. He will be able to sense the demon if it's there and we can run before it grabs us and drinks our blood,' the boy said.

Idris tugged at the little knot of hair on the boy's crown.

'Hmmm... maybe I should go first and let you know if it exists. Demons are frightened of foreigners, I am told.'

Kandavar nodded. He was relieved not to go demon spotting, but he had been afraid Aabo would think he was a coward if he said so.

All day Idris waited. At night, he went up the stairs as usual. Manickam was a slob. He slept through his watch most nights, his giant snores reverberating through the padipura. Idris waited for the song of snores to begin.

He stepped out of the gatehouse when it was safe and walked along the ridged boundary of the paddy fields, towards the eastern wall. The pond and the bathing house were in that direction. A million cicadas filled the night with their singing. To Idris, they sounded like knives being sharpened. What was he doing, he thought as he inched his way into the night.

The branches of a mango tree spread over the fence. But it was too high for him to clamber onto. On his side of the fence was a tamarind tree. Idris remembered climbing it and dropping to the ground on the other side of the fence. He was thirty-eight years old now. Hardly the age to be clambering up trees and jumping over fences. But he did it again.

Idris fell to the ground with a soft thud. The bed of leaves at the foot of the tree muffled the sound. He gasped for air, drawing in lungfuls to regulate his breath. The hammering of his heart seemed to rise above the din of the cicadas. Idris leaned against the tree and steadied himself. It was pitch dark.

He looked around, uncertain. There were so many trees here. Which one was the pala?

The breeze brought a wash of scent. Idris drew in the fragrance greedily.

He stumbled in the dark as he walked towards the pala tree. Its tiny flowers filled the air with its perfume. A scented trail.

'You mustn't come any closer,' she said.

Idris sucked in his breath in shock at hearing her voice again.

'Please stay there. I can see you from where I am.'

Idris paused. There was no moonlight, so how could she see him? He stood near the tree, waiting for her to show herself, speak his name, reveal what this rendezvous was all about.

'Is he what you thought he would be?' she asked. Idris remembered her first words to him: How tall are you? Not, who are you?

Here it was again, that strange directness. No leading up to the moment; no sieving of thoughts.

'Who?' Idris asked softly, prevaricating.

'Your son.'

'Do I have a son? No one told me.' Idris allowed his anger to surface.

'How can you not know he is your son? Besides, how could I have sent word to you about a son being born?'

He flinched. 'And whose fault is that? You didn't even ask me my name.'

'You didn't either.' Her voice came from behind a row of areca nut trees.

He thought he heard a tautness in her voice. Was she angry?

'Idris Maymoon Samataar Guleed. That is my name,' he offered abruptly.

'Yes, I know. And I have also heard the rest of it. Previously of Dikhil. Now an eternal traveller seeking the measure of earth and man,' she murmured with a dry laugh.

'I know your name is Kuttimalu. You have a new consort, Neelakantan Namboodiri.'

'What else did he tell you?' She sounded displeased.

'Is there more?'

'What did you expect?' she demanded. 'The one I was with died. I am a woman. I have both desires and fears. I cannot live on memories alone.'

'So why keep the pearl? Why wear it?' he asked, smiling in the direction where he thought she was. Would she touch the pearl at her throat? he wondered.

'It is a beautiful one.' She caressed the pearl with her forefinger.

'Would you like a couple for your ears?'

She snorted. 'Why are we discussing jewellery?'

'What would you like us to discuss?'

'Your son. My son,' she said in a forlorn voice. 'Only you can clear his head of all this Chaver nonsense.'

'Is that why you sent that coded message to me?'

'What else do we have to discuss?'

'Us, Kuttimalu. What about us?'

'There can be no "us", I want you to understand. When Kandavar was born and he emerged with skin like this night, an old woman came to my rescue. She dug up a memory and proclaimed that he was the image of a man my grandmother had for a husband once; the man who was supposed to be my mother's father.

'If she hadn't, my own brothers may have thought nothing of killing me. The alternative is worse; I could have been sold as a slave to the foreigners who come over the sea; I would have ended up as a whore and have no one to blame for it but myself. Is that what you want for me?' she hissed.

He moved through the darkness swiftly. Long years of shepherding the night had taught him to see in the dark. He gathered her in his arms before she could protest or flee.

'I will take you away from here. Do you hear me?' he whispered fiercely against her hair.

'What are you doing?' She tried to shake him off. 'What is wrong with you?'

But he wouldn't let go. He looked at her, holding her at arm's length. She wasn't a girl anymore. That much was certain. But somewhere in her still lived that impetuous creature who had clung to him and cried, 'Teach me what it is to fly.'

The pearl at her throat glistened. Her skin was like silk from China and she smelt of sandal and camphor and something else – excitement riding on fear and arousal.

'I will be there for you,' he said again. 'We will leave together, you and I and our son.' He pulled her close to him.

She stopped struggling. 'Once I may have gone with you, but now there is too much at stake. They will hunt us down and slaughter us. And then they will turn us into a cautionary tale. Don't trust a foreigner. Don't take him home. Don't let the women of your house anywhere near one. Don't let the children of such a cursed union survive. I cannot bear the thought of losing my child. Can you? For one night we were just us. Now there is Kandavar. Now there is only him.'

His hold on her loosened. She stepped away. 'Neelakantan Namboodiri already sees what he shouldn't. He asked me about my son's father. I lied. But I do not know if he believed me. It isn't safe for you to be here. It isn't safe for any of us. My consort isn't a bad man. He is slow to anger. But that makes him more dangerous. His wrath would be a hundred times worse to confront than that of a hot-headed man.'

Idris listened. She could protest all she wanted, but one day she would seek him out. He knew this for certain. Idris, who sought the measure of men everywhere, knew the workings of a woman's heart too, its precise beat and meter.

PART 2

May–October AD 1659

(Sha'baan AH 1069–Muharram AH 1070)

XIV

Since then, how long ago was it, almost four months now, Idris had not seen Kuttimalu even once. He had kept away as much as possible. He had made short trips to see Baapa Gurukkal and once to Kodungallur to pray at the big Jumah mosque after the holy month of Ramadan which he had spent at Baapa Gurukkal's kalari and, thereafter, as far as even Kochi. He had been away for more than two months when he returned to Vattoli tharavad.

'I cannot live on charity,' he explained to Chandu Nair. 'In Kozhikode and Kochi, I can still broker deals that will be enough to keep me in funds for a while.'

Chandu Nair had nodded in admiration. 'We are good to fight but for all else, we need others.'

'That's good enough. Our prophet is reported to have said: Archery is power, archery is power, archery is power. He didn't say: trade is power.' Idris smiled.

'But one day, trade will be power. Do you see what the Portuguese and the Dutch, the English and all those who came in as traders are doing? How they have divided amongst themselves this land and all its riches? Trade is power, my friend. It is the clink of coins that makes things happen and not the twang of the archer's bow.' Chandu Nair's voice fell. 'I will never be able to fathom the making of money. It is beyond me.'

The summer was at its fiercest and the heat had everyone in its stranglehold. Wells had dried up and the fields were a parched brown while the skies were a brilliant blue, with not a hint of a cloud. Chandu Nair fanned himself slowly. 'But I am glad you have returned, Idris.'

Idris nodded. How could he have not returned? The boy was here. Kandavar had come running to the padipura, eyes alight with delight, his face radiant, Maccanto matching his stride, his feathery tail wagging furiously. That was enough for a man to retrace his steps.

'Aren't you hot in that thing you wear?' Chandu Nair asked suddenly. 'Even this thin mundu we wear feels like too much. I can't imagine how you wear that…'

'Jellabiyad.' Idris had taken to wearing the jellabiyad once again. In the heat, it was easier than the tunic and trousers. Often, he wondered if he too should opt for the mundu like the men here. But he feared that if he did, he would feel a displacement that would shake his core. When a man doesn't have a land to claim as his own, when the words that roll off his tongue are another's, when the scents and stars are unfamiliar, he must cling to what he can – accoutrements and memories – to remind himself of who he is and where he came from. 'You get used to it,' he said.

That night, Chandu Nair broached again the subject of Kandavar's tutelage. 'My sister and I fear that if he goes to the kalari our family has gone to traditionally, his head will be stuffed with nonsense like honour and pride in death.'

'And you don't believe in it?' Idris asked, curious to hear such a non-Nair like pronouncement.

'There is neither honour nor pride in fighting for a cause that is history. A feud that stretches so far back, no one remembers what it was about. And how does it matter now? But no, we continue to fill the heads of our young men with this nonsense. If you ask anyone a year from now if they remember the names of the Chaver who died five months ago, all they will come up with are wild guesses. No one will remember them or grieve for them. No one, except the families of the young men, will feel the loss…'

Idris cleared his throat. 'My religion talks of jihad. The Prophet has said: "If ever there is a man who does not fight in a battle or help a fighter to get ready for a struggle, or cooperate in the effort, or at least do the best service to the family of a fighter in his absence, divine wrath will come upon him in this world itself, before the Day of Resurrection."'

'I know something of your religion, Idris. I know the call for arms in a jihad. But do you believe in it?'

The cicadas were louder than ever before. The summer heat drew out their song with a greater ardency. Once again in their music, Idris heard the brandishing of knives. What did he believe in? He hadn't ever asked himself this.

'And anyway, this isn't jihad. Or, is it?' Chandu Nair asked in the silence.

Idris dropped to his haunches, stumped by a thought. No matter what he believed in, everything changed when it came to one's own blood. Would he want his son to be a jihadi?

'It is of no consequence what I think, thampuran. I will speak to Baapa Gurukkal. I will keep my eyes and ears open. We will find a kalari that will teach Kandavar to respect life rather than death.'

A few weeks later, when the monsoon winds had brought sheets of rain and the land was a sea of puddles, Idris returned bringing news of a kalari. 'It is highly recommended by Baapa Gurukkal,' he told Chandu Nair. 'We will have to wait for the monsoon to end though. The students of the kalari are having their Karkitaka chikilsa. The treatment regime cannot be interrupted.'

Chandu Nair nodded. He knew the importance of the health regime everyone underwent in the wet month of Karkitakam. Medicated oil massages, herbal concoctions and a controlled diet to cleanse the system of the residual evil of a year's excesses.

It was Kandavar who was riddled with doubt. It was not the kalari his uncles had gone to. Would he be at a disadvantage by not going to the one that made the Chaver what they were? But Aabo seemed convinced about Ravunni Gurukkal and so it seemed was his uncle. Only his mother wept. 'He is too young to go away,' she cried, holding on to him.

'No, he isn't,' Chandu Nair said, frowning. 'He is already past the age when boys begin their training. And when the kalari closes periodically, he will be home.

'Besides,' he added, looking at his sister's swelling belly, 'it will be time for your baby to arrive and you will not miss him.'

Kuttimalu looked away without speaking. You do not make up for the absence of one child with the presence of another, she wanted to tell him. But she knew it was an argument that would go nowhere.

Kuttimalu swept her palm along the curve of her belly. She draped a thin mundu over her upper body these days to ensure that the pregnancy wasn't apparent. The evil eye was a strange thing. It needn't always emanate from the barren and desperate. Sometimes, all it took for the evil eye to wreak its havoc was a passing thought: Ah, so she is pregnant! How nice it must be for her to have a baby. She looks well, and the baby will emerge with glowing cheeks and flailing limbs. That was all it took. A passing thought that would twist the cord and strangle the child.

Kuttimalu hoped it would be a girl and she would look every bit like Neelakantan Namboodiri, right down to the cleft in his chin.

She realized that he hadn't been entirely convinced about

Kandavar's paternity. She had seen a thoughtful expression on his face when his eyes fell on her son. Perhaps, for the next few months, it was best for her son to live away from home and take with him the tall black man with the gold eye.

The Gurukkal was a stout man with a massive chest and a grave face. The skin of his face stretched like the sheath of a drum, tight and clear.

Kandavar felt the Gurukkal's gaze on him. Almost as if bidden by that penetrating look, he raised his eyes to meet the Gurukkal's. Kandavar felt as if the Gurukkal could read his every thought, his oldest memory, and felt a strange elation course through him. The Gurukkal knew and would understand what it was to be governed by the call of his blood.

'This is my nephew,' Chandu Nair spoke up. 'We should have started him at the kalari two years ago, but it didn't happen. But he must begin his tutelage at a kalari at least now.'

The Gurukkal's gaze moved to the older man's and then further, to the padipura, where a tall black man and a dog waited. He nodded.

'But you are from one of the Chaver tharavads. Shouldn't he be sent to one of the four kalaris that you go to?' the Gurukkal asked, his eyes darting to the boy again.

Chandu Nair's eyes narrowed. He wasn't used to having his decisions questioned. 'The Chaver has to be called by the Thirumandhamkunnu Bhagwati. The goddess decides who will be a Chaver. Not the kalari.'

'And you never were called?'

Chandu Nair met the Gurukkal's eyes steadily. 'No.' His reply was brief.

'Who suggested that you send your nephew here?' the Gurukkal asked with a small smile.

'Idris Maymoon. The man at the padipura,' Chandu Nair

said, wondering if he had made a mistake by coming to this kalari and its rather capricious Gurukkal.

'But I don't know him.'

'Neither does he know you,' Chandu Nair snapped, his impatience bursting through. In the normal course, he would have summoned the Gurukkal to his tharavad, but this was a small kalari and he had been curious to see for himself what it was like. Besides, Idris had sung paeans about its Gurukkal.

The Gurukkal raised his hand and summoned a student. 'There is a man at the padipura. Call him in. Tell him I wish to speak to him.'

Chandu Nair sighed. The day had begun well, but now it seemed to have lost its way. Should he have just sent the boy to one of the four kalaris? There would have been none of this interrogation, this... He watched in amazement as the Gurukkal bid Idris to seat himself. Chandu Nair looked nervously around. 'Our caste laws...' he began, seeing Idris hesitate.

'In my kalari, I determine the caste laws... besides, he is a foreigner. Anyone can see that. How can a foreigner be anything but a foreigner? What answer can he give me if I ask him about his caste?' the Gurukkal said firmly.

'Baapa Gurukkal told me about you,' Idris rumbled in a low voice.

The Gurukkal's expression didn't flicker. 'So you speak Malayalam well enough,' he said. 'And what did Baapa Gurukkal say?'

'That you would teach my boy here to fight, not with just his body, but his mind too.'

'Your boy?'

'I found him when he was lost; perhaps even saved his life. And I have been taught that once you save a life, you are responsible for it.' Idris opened his palms in a gesture of exegesis.

'He has been part of our household for some months now. But why are we discussing Idris instead of my nephew? The boy will be ten soon,' Chandu Nair interrupted waspishly. 'He is already two years late, but his mother was unwilling to let him go too far from home. Fortunately, our man here stepped in and remedied the situation.'

'My name is Idris Maymoon Samataar Guleed,' Idris said quietly. 'It is time for the boy to begin,' he continued. 'Why? Do you doubt it?'

The Gurukkal ran his finger along the wooden plank he sat on and looked at the skies as if searching for a portent.

'No, I don't.'

Kandavar's neck ached from swivelling it this way and that as he looked first at his uncle, then the Gurukkal, and now Aabo. A pink tongue licked the tips of his fingers. A snout pushed into his palm. The boy glanced down at Maccanto.

'The dog will accompany the boy,' the Gurukkal said abruptly.

'If you don't like the thought—' Chandu Nair began.

'The dog can stay; what about you, Idris Maymoon Samataar Guleed? Will you too stay?'

Idris nodded. He had decided it was time to resume his travels. But the thought of leaving the boy caused his resolve to weaken. Once the boy was gone, there would be no reason for him to stay back at the tharavad.

But here at the kalari, he could stay with the boy. And Vattoli tharavad was only half a day's journey away. Kuttimalu may pretend that he didn't exist, but he knew how aware she was of him. Even if they both tried to sidestep it, there was something unresolved between them that stood like a wild elephant in a room, eating up space and catching the light on its massive gleaming tusks. A potential malevolent force that someday would run amok without warning and destroy everything that came in its way.

XV

The river ran alongside. In that stretch, even the sluggish Nila became turbulent, bouncing over the rounded rocks with the youthfulness of a stream, curling and curving and never for once hinting at the treacherous currents that would suck in even an able-bodied swimmer and smash him against the jagged rocks that lay hidden in the depths, ripping his skin open and gouging out chunks of flesh as if he were no more than a palm fruit fallen into the waters.

A row of steps hewn out of laterite stone led to the river. Idris sat on one, watching a kingfisher that perched on a low hanging branch. Suddenly, it flew towards the river, dived and rose with a small fish in its beak. Idris smiled at the valiance of the little blue and brown aerial warrior. Focus, focus, that is the key, Ravunni Gurukkal told his students. When you have that, all else will follow.

The kalari was on a higher ground from the river, facing east as it was supposed to. It had been created by excavating the ground one kol deep. A kol was a unit of measurement that was about two-and-a-half feet, Idris had been told with some amusement. The earth that had been dug out, Ravunni Gurukkal explained, had been used to build the surrounding walls by about another kol from the ground. It was from these walls that the bamboo poles for the roof rose into the air.

Idris entered the kalari through an opening set in the centre of the eastern side of the kalari. This, too, had to be a precise width: one kol. A set of steps led down into the sunken floor of the kalari. It was cool and airy inside, and the walls of earth muffled all sound. He looked up and saw, high above, the steeply sloped roof of the kalari made of plaited coconut palm leaves and supported on a frame of wooden slats and bamboo poles.

'There is a science to that as well.' Ravunni Gurukkal spoke from the entrance of the kalari. 'It should equal the width. And the kalari should be located in the south-west or north-west corner of the land. It is the only way we can avoid the mrytoyogam. You see, every piece of ground has a certain predilection to cause accidents or death.'

Idris swallowed. The sailors were guided by the stars. The farmers sought the stars for planning crops. But what science was this that used heights and depths, direction and wind to stave off destiny? He touched the rock-hard walls and felt a strange excitement course through him as he thought of everything Kandavar would learn here.

The Gurukkal descended into the kalari. Idris wondered at the man's gesture of touching the floor and then raising his right hand to touch his forehead and chest.

The Gurukkal caught Idris looking at him. 'With this I ask the forgiveness of the earth mother for trampling on her.'

Ravunni Gurukkal saw Idris's eyebrows rise a fraction. 'Right, if you think that's too far-fetched, let's assume that with such a ritual entry, every student who enters the kalari learns to put behind him all distractions and clear his mind of all that the world outside entails.'

Idris nodded. He looked around him, knowing he might never see this again.

'I can let you in here only because the deities haven't been installed yet,' the Gurukkal said, walking to the south-west corner. 'I will have to shape seven tiers of earth here and on this, what we call the puttara, a deity will be lodged on each level.

'The seven steps of the puttara are the seven presiding deities of the kalari. Only a warrior who knows what each of these seven represent, and absorbs the governing power of that deity into his spirit, will succeed in the battlefield.

'First is Vignesha, at the base of the puttara, who gives you the power to overcome obstacles.

'On the second step is Bhumi, who teaches the patience of the earth.

'On the third step is Vishnu, who grants the power to decimate. Vishnu has the chakra as his weapon and as it whirls it destroys all enemies.

'On the fourth step is Vadukisca or lightning. The weapon by itself has no power. It is only the action with the weapon that bestows the power associated with speed and quickness.

'On the fifth step are the power and blessings of the guru.

'And on the sixth is Kali in her raudra aspect. Here is the repository of fury.

'Finally, on the seventh is Vagastapuruso, who blesses the warrior with a fierce animal growl that will terrify an opponent.

'There are other deities too, who live in this space.

'In the north-western corner will be Andhiviran, in the north-eastern corner Bhadrakali, and in the west, three times seven Gurukkanmar, the past gurus, all of whom have to be worshipped. It is only if all of them make their home here that the kalari will prosper and my students prosper.'

The Gurukkal watched Idris as he continued to speak. 'This season, I am taking in only eighteen boys,' he said. 'Too many would mean I do not have enough time for each of them. Of these, I wonder how many will return the next season.'

Idris chewed on his lip thoughtfully. If one decided to become a warrior, the kalari would nurture that calling by paying attention to every aspect of war craft. Each student's individual prowess with a weapon would be identified and he would be taught until he had mastered that weapon. Kandavar may have come to a kalari where life was respected, but it wouldn't make him any less of a warrior, Idris thought with a sinking heart.

The Gurukkal walked down the path, towards the river. Idris walked with him. The sounds of splashing and shrieks of delight rent the air. The fragrance of the waxen white frangipani flower with its yellow heart hung heavy and low. A butterfly with blue-black wings flitted past them. 'This is beautiful,' Idris said, almost whispering.

'Weapons are not. It takes away a man's natural softness and teaches him to be hard and controlled. Weapons can make a boy forget what it is to be human. So I need them to be constantly reminded that weapons only constitute one part of their lives. For the rest, it is the man who must prevail,' the Gurukkal murmured.

Neither men spoke as they watched the boys play in the river.

Kandavar was settling in quite nicely, his habitual restlessness curbed by all the tasks the Gurukkal had set out for him.

Suddenly, Kandavar's gaze locked with Idris's and they smiled at each other. The Gurukkal watched the brief interplay. 'The boy's life is linked to yours,' he said.

Idris turned his head. 'That is a strange assumption to make. My life cannot be linked to anyone else's.'

'Oh yes, I forgot.' The Gurukkal snapped a twig between his thumb and forefinger, the crack resounding in the silence. 'The eternal traveller.'

Idris didn't respond. Then, after a long moment, he said, 'He is special. He is destiny's child. I was meant to be in his life, or why would Allah have caused our paths to cross?'

The Gurukkal rose to his feet. 'You are a curious man, Idris Maymoon Samataar Guleed. I wonder what lies behind those walls you have built around yourself.'

Idris smiled. 'There is nothing but flesh and blood. I am like you, Gurukkal. A man.'

The Gurukkal didn't refute it. But his expression indicated that he knew otherwise.

'We start lessons in two days. I am waiting for the auspicious day.'

Idris nodded.

He would stay for as long as they let him. Kismet had taken him to the Mamangam, which had been aborted the day after he met the boy. The Zamorin hadn't recovered from the fever in time to reign over the festivities and the celebration had been concluded in a desultory fashion. If the boy had come to Thirunavaya a day later, their paths might never have crossed. Allah the most merciful had wanted them to meet and know each other.

But he also knew that one day he would wake up feeling a giant fist curl around his chest, squeezing air out of his very breath, till he felt suffocated and cramped, and ached to escape it all. Then it would be time for him to go away on yet another voyage.

Idris was in a pensive mood. The Gurukkal's observation had unnerved him. He couldn't allow himself to be tied to anybody or anything. But the boy had coiled silken ropes around his legs and knotted them around his heart.

Was this love?

Idris had often reflected on the nature of love. He had known how to measure and fathom what his Aabo had stoked in him; he had understood his feelings of tenderness for Fatima, his foster mother; Kuttimalu had been a fire in his blood and would still be if she would let him. But, for the boy, it was beyond all of this. Was it love that he felt for his son? But love brought hurt. Love left in its wake regret, and Idris wanted none of that.

Idris pinched the bridge of his nose between his fingers. His next voyage, he decided, would be to the kingdom of Odisha. He had heard of giraffes taken to that kingdom by the sea. If a giraffe could survive there, so would he.

XVI

'You are very tall. What does your mother feed you?' the boy asked.

Kandavar looked up from the two ladybugs he was trying to race against each other. He shrugged. 'Elephant dung mixed with a powder made of heron's beak and dissolved in butter made from tiger's milk.'

'Are you serious? No, you can't be,' the boy said when he saw Kandavar's face spliced by a grin. He came closer. 'My name is Rairu. What is yours?'

Maccanto watched the exchange, tongue hanging out, his head turning this way and that to look at the two boys.

'Kandavar. And this is Maccanto,' he said, pulling at the dog's ears gently.

'Will he bite?' Rairu asked, stepping forward.

'Not unless I tell him to. Or if he thinks you are going to hurt me,' Kandavar said proudly. 'Come sit at my side and he will get used to you.'

Rairu edged along the riverbank and sat down near Kandavar. The boys smiled at each other. Soon Kandavar and Rairu had chosen a ladybug each and were urging their beetles along with a small twig. The race ended when the beetles managed to escape.

'We look like night and day,' Kandavar said, placing his forearm alongside Rairu's.

'I'd rather be as tall as you are,' Rairu said, throwing a pebble into the water. 'You will always be able to see above everyone else. What use is this fair skin?'

'What do you think will happen in the kalari tomorrow?' Kandavar asked suddenly.

Rairu shrugged. 'He is not like other Gurukkals, I am told. He has his own way of doing things.'

'That's what Aabo said.'

'Who's he?'

Kandavar shrugged. 'I don't know. He is from some distant land. You have to travel by ship to reach there. For many days… Imagine that!'

Rairu narrowed his eyes and looked at the western horizon. 'The sea is that way. Do you think if we followed the river, we'll come to the sea?'

'And what will you do when you reach the sea?' Idris asked in amusement.

The boys turned, startled. Maccanto pranced around Idris, his tail wagging furiously.

Rairu watched Maccanto's tail in fascination. 'Near my home, there are these tall grass fields by the river. The dog's tail looks like the grass waving in the wind.'

'He is a poet,' Idris murmured.

Rairu frowned. 'No, I am a warrior. That is what I will be.'

'You can be both poet and warrior,' Idris bent down to tell the bristling boy.

Kandavar felt a twinge of jealousy. He didn't like Aabo lavishing attention on someone else.

'Aabo,' he said, trying to snap the unseen threads that bound his Aabo to his new friend.

Idris turned his head and Kandavar felt his golden eye bore through skin and flesh and unearth his secret fears. Idris pulled Kandavar towards him. 'Look at Kandavar here,' he said to Rairu. 'Whether it is a ball of plaited leaf or a wooden doll, all you have to do is show him once and he'll replicate it. He is an artist and he will be a warrior too. You don't have to be one or the other.'

Kandavar smiled.

Idris sat on the riverbank with the boys on either side of him. It was mid-morning but the rains had washed the heat out. Every bit of the land was a glistening green. It wasn't just the desert sand or the snow-covered mountains that hurt the eye, Idris thought. Sometimes the lushness of green did too.

'Aabo,' Rairu said, taking up Kandavar's name for him. 'What is the sea like?'

Idris smiled. It seemed he had acquired yet another son. Should he correct the boy, he wondered. Perhaps teach him to call him Abti for uncle. After all, Aabo was not a term to be used so incautiously. 'You can call me Abti,' he said gently.

'Why?' The boys frowned.

'Because I say so. You must always find a name that is your very own for the people who matter to you.'

Kandavar shook his head. Sometimes Aabo said the strangest things. But Rairu seemed to like the idea. 'So only I may call you Abti,' he said, 'not Kandavar.'

Idris nodded. The boy was indeed a poet, drawn to the unusual and the fanciful. He would see colours where others saw a monotone. He would hear chanting in the bee's drone.

'Abti,' the boy said, savouring the word as if it were a daub of honey on his tongue. 'What is the sea like?'

'It's enormous. Lie on your back and look at the sky. That is how the sea is. Vast and endless. You have no sense of where it begins and where it ends. And like you don't know how high the sky is, you will never know how deep the ocean is… it falls deeper and deeper, a bottomless abyss.'

The boys gazed at the sky, trying to see the ocean in it.

'What is the colour of the sea?' It was Kandavar who broke the reverie.

Idris lay back with the boys. He scratched his chin and tried to remember. 'Sometimes it is like the blue of the kingfisher's wing. Sometimes it is green, like the waters of the pond in your home. Sometimes it is a deep black like the mashi so you think you can dip a quill in its inky depths and write. Sometimes it shimmers like the dragonfly's wing.'

'Abti, you are a poet too.' Rairu laughed.

'He is that, and an eternal traveller.' Kandavar giggled.

Idris sat up and glared at the boys. In one swift motion, he scooped Kandavar under his arm and began tickling him. The boy wriggled, giggling. 'No, no,' he shrieked.

'Yes, yes,' Idris said, tickling him harder. 'Are you making fun of me?'

He let go of Kandavar suddenly and grabbed Rairu, who had been laughing at Kandavar's plight, and began tickling him. When Rairu too had been reduced to a writhing, giggling mass, Idris flopped on the grass.

The boys flopped alongside, snickering. 'You are mad, Aabo,' Kandavar said.

'It must be his gold eye.' Rairu giggled. 'It makes him see and do things no one else can.'

Idris closed his eyes. The poet may be right after all. It was the gold eye that made him who he was.

'Abti, the sea... you were telling us about the sea,' Rairu spoke up.

'The sea has waves. Small waves that rush to the shore and throw themselves at it in a heap of froth. And then a big wave comes, rolling and surging, and sweeps you off your feet. The sea roars, like a slumbering animal. It has a smell: salty, fresh, and something else.' He paused. The fragrance of a woman, he thought. That was the smell of the sea. Which is why sailors sailed the sea. It was that fragrance that kept them riding the waves.

'Aabo, you sound like you wish you were on the sea... do you miss it?' Kandavar tried to hide his tremulousness, but Idris heard it. An unspoken fear: *will you go away*?

'I like the sea. But I like the land too,' he said.

He turned and saw Kandavar's face clear. And on Rairu's face was something else, a desire to know the ocean, hear its boom and taste its salty spray. The poet, he thought, will one day seek the sea.

'Maybe one day I will take you boys to see the sea,' he said, rising to his feet. The boys jumped up.

From the kalari, the Gurukkal's eyes followed them as they walked along the river's edge and climbed up the steps, onto the high ground.

XVII

Kandavar glanced at Rairu's face. His eyes were closed and his hands folded in prayer. The Gurukkal had said it was easy, but Kandavar had blanched at the list. How many did he have to pray to? All the gurus who dwelt in the kalari, and also the twenty-one masters; the eight sages, the eight forms of Brahma, Vishnu, Siva, the forty-three crores of gods… he couldn't even remember the rest.

The Gurukkal had smiled at Kandavar's expression of horror. 'Did you think it was easy to be a good abhiyaṣi? A practitioner of payatu has to know more than how to wield weapons. He has to have physical strength and mental stamina. Susruta, the great physician, has said: Growth of the body, radiance, harmonious proportions of the limbs, a kindled fire, energy, firmness, lightness, purity, the power to endure fatigue, weariness, thirst, heat and cold, and even perfect health – this is what is wrought by physical exercise. Along with it, you need to exercise your brain as well.'

Kandavar tried to hide a yawn. Why were they being told all

this? All these names of dead people who seemed to have had nothing to do other than make these incomprehensible, boring statements. What he wanted was to start learning the adavu. The kicks and jumps and the weapon exercises. He wanted to fly through the air and knock an opponent down by pressing his index finger against the man's marmam. Kandavar had heard the older boys talk about such feats in the room they had been assigned to sleep in.

'Ravunni Gurukkal can cripple a man for a week by just striking his fist at a particular marmam. That's the thing about the vital points in our body. There won't be a single bruise or flesh wound when you aim for a vital point but the man will need intensive treatment to be on his feet again,' one of the older boys had said.

'But how?' Kandavar had asked in amazement.

'He knows how to. But he won't teach us any of that till he is certain we can handle such knowledge.' The older boy's response seemed oblique to the younger ones, but nobody dared ask him where these marmams were located in the body. He was known to have a vicious temper.

'Maybe it's because he is such a bully,' Rairu had murmured, 'that Gurukkal doesn't teach him any of that. If he thinks we can do it, maybe he will show us how to. He will.'

Kandavar had nodded. He decided he would give the Gurukkal no cause for worry.

'Your mind is wandering,' the Gurukkal said. 'What are you thinking about?'

Kandavar felt Rairu's gaze on him. For a brief moment, he thought about mouthing a lie, of saying something that would please Gurukkal. Only for a brief moment. Then he said, 'All of this... I don't understand... how will any of this make me a warrior?'

The Gurukkal sighed and turned to the class. 'Ah, the boy has doubts even before he has begun!'

Kandavar flushed.

'At least you had the courage to speak the truth. That is an auspicious beginning.' The Gurukkal waved his hand. The older boys moved back against the wall. Only Kandavar and Rairu were left standing on the floor. He gestured for them to step back a few feet.

As the boys watched, they saw the Gurukkal clench his jaw and take a deep breath. Slowly his body and limbs began to assume a position and they saw how he seemed to cease being a man and metamorphose into a rooster. Like a cock ready to leap into attack, all parts of his body – hands, legs, neck and fingers – turned into weapons for combat. He stood on one leg, stretched his body and neck so the muscles in his neck protruded with tension, fixed his gaze on them as if they were a predator, curved his palms and nails into hard pointed edges and shivered ever so slightly, manifesting rage and the desire to draw blood.

The boys trembled. Then, to their astonishment, the Gurukkal turned one by one into animals, some familiar, some they had only heard of. The serpent and the peacock, the elephant and the cat, the horse, the lion, the wild boar.

When the Gurukkal was done, the silence in the kalari hung heavy inside each boy. How would they ever learn any of this? And this was just the first of many lessons.

'Payattu,' the Gurukkal spoke slowly, 'is more than just the body turning supple and executing leaps and jumps. Your mind must match the body and take you to the place you wish to be, and only then the body will follow. That's what differentiates you from the animal kingdom. The rest is all preparation and practice. Are you convinced now?' He fixed his gaze on Kandavar.

The boy nodded.

'Come here,' the Gurukkal said. 'We will start with the basic kaal-uyarthal. Anyone can raise a leg and kick. But what is necessary is to find a balance at the core of your body, for this will help you to move to the next stance even as you finish one... balance, that is the key. In leg exercises and life.'

The boys looked at each other. Kandavar almost rolled his eyes and then thought better of it.

'Here, look at me, and then Raman will help you,' the Gurukkal said, stretching his right leg out and kicking elegantly forward to a point above his head. 'Lock your knee and stretch your toes and, most importantly, look at a specific point on the opposite side of the kalari. This position is called the nerkaal. The straight leg.'

Kandavar took a deep breath and tried to emulate the Gurukkal. He tottered as he raised his leg in a kick and almost fell.

Blood rushed to his face. He righted himself and looked at the other boys. Were they tittering? No one was. All of them had been there before. Besides, the Gurukkal had a way of admonishing with a phrase or two that felt worse than hot oil falling on the skin. It ate into your skin and left you shivering in anguish.

'Try again. And again. And again. And eventually you will be able to do it,' the Gurukkal said, beckoning to Raman to demonstrate.

There were eight leg exercises of leaps and kicks, seated and standing, with indrawn and sweeping movements. Raman went through the rota of exercises with an effortless ease that made Kandavar feel inadequate. He had thought he would be able to accomplish the exercises effortlessly. But he couldn't even get an easy kick like the nerkaal right.

Rairu was far better.

Kandavar tried again. He tottered again. He slumped. Would they send him back? Had it ever happened that a student had been kicked out of the kalari on the day he began?

'Stop,' the Gurukkal said, after many minutes of watching Kandavar still battling with the nerkaal. He waved his hand to indicate Kandavar should wait by the wall.

Kandavar's heart dropped into the pit of his stomach.

The other boys pretended not to see what was going on. Kandavar's eyes brimmed. He blinked furiously so the tears wouldn't roll out and shame him further. When it was time to finish for the day and they began the ritual of paying their respects to the deities, the Gurukkal said, 'Join them and do as they do.'

Kandavar followed the boys as they circumambulated the interior of the kalari, one by one, beginning with the guardian deity in the south-west corner. Still facing the puttara, they stepped back on the left foot and with their right hand, they touched the floor, raised their fingers to their forehead and chest, then went up the steps.

'Kandavar, you will wait for me outside till I emerge,' the Gurukkal called out.

What now, he wondered, trying hard not to show the fear he felt.

What will the Gurukkal do in there, he asked one of the older boys.

They shrugged and walked away.

Kandavar went alongside the kalari. He was tall enough to peer over the wall that was the base for the poles on which the thatch rested.

Inside, he saw the Gurukkal pick up a weapon. It was a churavadi, the short stick. He crouched before the brass lamp facing the puttara. The Gurukkal seemed to have turned into a cat.

He was chanting, and then he struck the stick three times on the floor with his right hand.

Kandavar saw the Gurukkal rise and drag the stick along the floor as he moved backwards. When he reached the steps, he turned to his right, threw the stick high in the air and leapt up and out of the kalari before the stick fell to the ground.

Kandavar fled to the entrance and tried to pretend a calm he wasn't feeling. But his heart hammered in his chest with the frantic fervour of a woodpecker pecking away at a tree.

The Gurukkal looked at him and said, 'There is no need for stealth. All you need to do is ask me what you wish to know.'

Kandavar licked his dry lips. How had the Gurukkal known?

The Gurukkal strode forward, muttering, 'Follow me.'

Kandavar trotted after him, not sure where he was being led and for what.

The Gurukkal stopped abruptly. A line of ants was running up a tamarind tree. 'Watch these ants,' he said.

Kandavar looked at the ants scurrying up the tree. 'What do you see?' the Gurukkal asked.

'They have six legs each.'

'Good enough. Now look here and tell me what else you see...' he said, pointing to an ant which was rushing ahead, looking very purposeful.

'The ant is carrying a load that is bigger than it is,' Kandavar offered.

'Which do you think will reach faster?'

Kandavar shrugged. 'The ant on the tree...'

'Why do you think so?'

'It's simple. It doesn't have a load.'

'Well then, do you understand what I mean when I say that you are bringing into the kalari a burden. You think too much about what your knowledge will do for you. That is what cramps your legs and draws the strength away. Don't think too hard. Let the body find its rhythm. Later you can ponder on where this knowledge will take you. First pursue it. Enjoy it. Do you have any questions?'

Kandavar shook his head.

Then he looked at the Gurukkal and said, 'What were you doing in the kalari after we left?'

'Choovadumayakkal. Wiping all the steps and the impurities we brought into the kalari. So that when we return tomorrow, it will be fresh ground to start upon all over again.'

It had seemed so much more to Kandavar. A protracted secret ritual that enabled the Gurukkal to acquire skills that no one else could. But it made sense. He would forget everything that had gone wrong at the kalari and start afresh tomorrow.

XVIII

He had returned home after the thulavarsham. The north-eastern monsoons were accompanied by low, rumbling thunder and great flashes of lightning that lit up the land even at night. He had wanted his mother to see all that he had learnt in the months he had been away. She was huge with the child in her belly. She was tired all the time, she said. And no position, sitting, standing or lying down, was comfortable. 'I wish it was time for the baby to emerge,' she said, wearily rubbing her aching back.

He watched his mother step down to the courtyard and lean against the eastern wall. He wished Aabo were here too, so the two of them could see all that he had learnt.

'Your Aabo,' his mother said, as if reading his thoughts. 'Where did he go?'

'He didn't say. He said something about a kingdom called Odisha he would have to reach by the sea. He said the waves were huge and fell on the shore, roaring like a hundred tigers. He said, if you ever did ask, I was to tell you that he would be back. For everything that is precious to him is here.' Kandavar repeated from memory the quiet words Idris had spoken in his ears, the night when he had announced he was leaving.

'I have to go,' Idris had said, taking his hand in his giant palm. 'I have done nothing for many days now. A man cannot live doing nothing.'

The protest had died on Kandavar's lips even though he didn't understand.

A man cannot remain rooted in one spot, the Gurukkal had said one day. In the kalari, they taught you this. There was a time to be idle and there was a time to be on the move. But even when you were idle, you were simply collecting your energies, preparing your sinews and tendons for that time when you would need to draw upon every vestige of strength that lay dormant in yourself.

Idris had pulled Kandavar close and wound an arm around him. Kandavar had snuggled deeper into the embrace. It felt almost as good as snuggling up to his mother. Or Maccanto, he thought, breathing in the fragrance that emanated from Aabo. A hint of lime, a whiff of sandal, sun-washed cotton; the cloves and cinnamons Aabo liked to chew on. And there was something else. A faint tang like tamarind, a smokiness, a hint of heat, like dried coriander seed; it smelt familiar, like the ground mailanji leaves his mother used to paint her fingers vermilion. And it smelt strange. Perhaps that was Aabo's real fragrance. Familiar and strange.

'When will you be back?' he asked sleepily.

'Sooner than later.'

He had heard the smile in Aabo's voice.

'Good,' he had murmured. 'Don't go away for too long, Aabo. I'll miss you.'

'I'll miss you too. But you must work hard here at the kalari and when I return, you can show me how well you have used your time.'

In the morning, Aabo was gone. Kandavar thought, I didn't even hear him slip away. I will ask Aabo to teach me this when he returns. To move with the stealth of a shadow.

'Where did you disappear to?' His mother's voice dragged him out of the reverie he had slipped into. 'I thought you were going to give me a demonstration of all that you've learnt.'

Kandavar smiled sheepishly, and then stilled his face into a mask, turned to the south-west corner and made the salutation.

One by one, the awareness of his surroundings – his mother with fatigue etched into her face and every line of her body; a flock of hens squawking and scratching in the undergrowth beyond the yard, a woman servant foraging among the yam plants, the chopping of wood somewhere, the deep rolling note of the crow pheasants, the cheep-cheep of sparrows, the blue of the morning skies – all of it slipped away, and all he sensed were the deep runnels of breath as he tightened his core muscles, ready to take the stance. In time he had learnt that the only ritual there was to this business of being a warrior was practice. But practice with clarity. You had to hear right. You had to observe every detail right. For if you learnt it wrong, you would never unlearn it. At a crucial point, the wrong learning would prevail, overriding countless hours of practice. To combat this, he had to develop focus. Ekagratha, the Gurukkal called it. A single-point focus that would enable the power within to surge up.

It became their routine. Kandavar practised all that he had been taught while his mother watched.

'Why don't you go and play? This is your time away from the kalari… shouldn't you be playing a game, climbing a tree or something?' Kuttimalu asked one morning. She really didn't want to get up from where she sat, but the aunts wouldn't allow it. Exercise was key to a smooth pregnancy, leading up to a quick birthing. Time enough to rest after that, they said. And they encouraged Kandavar to keep his mother on her feet.

'I have no one to play with, and Aabo isn't here,' Kandavar mumbled, shredding a yam leaf into a long strip of green. Aabo had shown him how to do this as well. To curl the thumb so the edge of the nail sliced into the leaf, and to drag it along, almost to the edge, and then curve it so that a strip emerged. His younger boy cousins had been sent away to another kalari.

Kuttimalu tried to hoist herself up. Then, to Kandavar's horror, she shuddered and cried out. Her face was pale and there was sweat on her brow. 'Fetch the aunts,' she whispered.

Kandavar fled and in a matter of minutes, life changed.

The aunts took his mother away to an inner room. He followed at a discreet distance and maintained a vigil at the end of the corridor. He saw the midwife arrive. He heard his mother scream, the high notes raking the walls of his heart and making his teeth ache. At one point, he rose and walked to the front of the house, where his uncle was pacing the floor. It had been a long time since the house had heard the cries of a woman in labour.

'Will Amma die?' he asked his uncle, unable to contain his fear.

'Don't talk nonsense,' his uncle snapped. Then, softening at the anguish in the boy's eyes, he added, 'All women scream when they are about to have a baby. You should have heard her when you were born! Why don't you go climb a tree? It will take your mind away from this caterwauling!'

Kandavar smiled. He realized his uncle was trying to comfort him. But he wished Aabo was here. Only Aabo knew how to make him feel less afraid.

He went to the yard, looking for Maccanto, who came rushing.

He wound his arms around the dog's neck and buried his face in its side. 'Maccanto, I am so afraid. I wish Aabo were here.'

Maccanto turned his head and licked the boy's face.

Kandavar felt Maccanto's breath on his ear and cheek. A warm rush of air that soothed him more than anything his uncle had said. 'I have to go now, Maccanto,' he said. 'I cannot leave my mother alone. You understand, don't you?'

They wouldn't let him enter the corridor. 'This is not a place for children. Don't you have anything to do?' One of the aunts frowned.

'Chase a hen, or go for a walk with that dog or climb a tree,' Kunji offered, more gently.

He glowered at them, wondering why everyone wanted him to climb a tree. He sat cross-legged on the floor at the end of the corridor, arms folded and head held pertly. Try and budge me from here, he said without uttering a word.

All through that day, until dusk descended and the cawing of the crows stilled, he sat there, rising only to eat or pee. He could see the night descend through the window. A cool breeze blew in through the wooden bars. If only he could see his mother once.

Suddenly, there was a flurry of movement. Voices. Screams. Hustle and bustle. Unfamiliar sounds. And then a long-drawn-out wail…

Kandavar sat up, his heart hammering. The baby was here. In one fluid movement, he was on his feet and racing to the door. But before he had reached the other end of the corridor, one of the aunts grabbed him, snarling, 'Where do you think you are going?'

'My mother… the baby,' he stammered.

'Your mother is fine. And you have a baby sister. White as the moon.' She smiled, thinking of that little scrap of a girl who had been born. She looked robust enough to take the family line forward even if Kuttimalu didn't have any more children. Almost instantly, she wished that thought away. Gods in heaven, I didn't think that. The baby looks frail and wan. Will it survive? Only if you bless her, the old woman called out to all her favourite deities.

'I want to see her!' he said, trying to twist his arm out of her grip.

'Are you out of your mind?'

'It's my mother. And my sister. I have every right to see them,' he said, sticking his chin out.

'Your mother just had a baby. No one can go in there, or see her or the baby, for the next fifteen days,' she said, turning him around.

'But why?' he asked, unable to believe his ears.

'That's the way it is. When you are born, and when you die, there is a fifteen-day period of waiting. Until then, souls are in limbo and we shouldn't disturb their passage into this world or the next,' his uncle said from the head of the corridor.

There seemed to be a 'that's the way it is' for every question he asked in the course of the next fifteen days. No one could go into the room his mother and baby sister lay in. No one could touch the baby. The water heated for her bath would be infused with leaves of various trees and would have to be heated to a particular temperature. Neither cold nor hot water was permitted to be added to the bath water.

Kandavar hovered outside the door of the room and breathed in the hot, fetid smell of oils and ghee, blood and milk, damp and smoke, sandal and camphor, and waited for the moment when he would be permitted to enter.

On the eighth day, his mother demanded he be allowed in. Kandavar stood at the doorway, taking in the sight of his mother and his baby sister. His mother smiled at him. He smiled at her and then his eyes fell on the baby and a giant fist squeezed his heart. He ached with an immense love and tenderness for the little mite flailing her legs and hands in the air.

'Come closer and take a good look,' she said. 'You haven't ever seen a baby before, have you?'

There had been a dearth of girls in the last three generations of the tharavad. More boys had been born than girls. And of the girls, two had died at childbirth and one of snake bite. Only Kuttimalu's mother and her sister had survived. The sister hadn't conceived, though she'd had three consorts. Kuttimalu had two brothers and two sisters. The oldest brother had died; one of the sisters had died when she was three years old, of fever, and the other sister in childbirth. Kuttimalu was the last living fecund woman. And this girl child would be the one to keep the family line and tharavad alive.

Kandavar understood some of this. But beyond all that, he had a sibling now. Someone who would be there for him. Someone who would love him as he would love her. The next time his mother had a baby, his sister would be with him when they sat vigil at the end of the corridor. He would teach her everything he knew and show her all the wonderful things that had caught his eye. And he would share both Aabo and Maccanto with her. He stepped forward.

'You have to wait for a few days more to pick her up,' his mother said gently, moved by the expression in his eyes. 'But come and look at her,' she added.

He bent down and peered at the baby in the wooden cradle Neelakantan Namboodiri had sent across the day before. A wooden cradle that had been carried over by two men. Hewn from the finest of Nilambur teak.

Kandavar looked at the baby and felt a great horror descend on him. Something was wrong. 'Amma,' he cried. 'Vava is hurt...'

'What?' Kuttimalu said, propping herself on her elbow. 'What's wrong?'

'She doesn't have a chukkumani!' he said, clutching at his own penis protectively. 'A rat must have come and bitten it off!'

Kuttimalu burst into laughter as her son stared at the baby's genitalia in horror, imagining a rat running off with a baby penis.

'Girls don't have a chukkumani,' she said, giggling, using the childish idiom for a penis. A knob of dried ginger. Men should remember that, she thought, when they strut around thinking they are lords of the world. It takes a woman to turn that knob of dried ginger into a fair representation of manliness.

'So how do they pee?' he asked curiously.

'Oh, they manage all right,' Kuttimalu said wryly.

Kandavar peered at his sister. A small bead of pity rolled into his thoughts. The poor thing! She didn't have a chukkumani. She would never know the joy of playing with it when there was nothing else to do. Or aiming a stream of pee at a hopping frog or drawing alphabets in the sand with a jet of urine.

He sighed and touched her cheek gently, with the tip of his finger. He would make it up to her.

XIX

Kandavar sat up, wide awake. He had gone to sleep along with the other boys. The Gurukkal was very strict about time. The boys had to rise early, so it was imperative they went to bed early. 'You need to sleep for eight hours. That is when the mind rests and the body grows,' the Gurukkal had said, catching Rairu and him wandering one night. 'And what were you doing out so late?'

The boys had hung their heads. The Gurukkal sighed.

'I wanted to see how the full moon shone over the water,' Rairu said. 'Somebody said, when that happens, a beautiful woman rises from the water and all the fish in the river come to the surface as her attendants…'

'Someone told you that? Or did you imagine it yourself?' The Gurukkal's voice was tinged with exasperation. The boy was too dreamy for his own good. 'Anyway, enough of this chit-chat. Go to bed now, and I don't ever want to see the two of you out at this time of the night. I may not be so kind the next time.'

The boys had slunk away and each time Rairu came up with night-walking schemes after that, Kandavar talked him out of it. But tonight, it was Kandavar who had a plan.

He leaned across and pressed two fingers down at a point near Rairu's ear. He woke up instantly. It was the quickest and quietest way to wake someone, Aabo had told him.

'Rairu,' he said, 'Rairu, get up…'

'What?'

Kandavar pressed his palm down on the other boy's mouth. 'What's with you? Do you want to wake up everyone?'

'What is it?' Rairu sat up, rubbing his eyes. He peered out at the night sky and asked, 'What time is it?'

'I need to go home,' Kandavar said.

'What?' Rairu asked, his eyes wide as the bronze plates with rounded edges they ate from. 'Home? How can you go home?'

'I need to see my baby sister. I have this strange feeling. I have to go to her,' Kandavar said urgently.

'You are imagining things. Your mother is with her. So are the rest of your family. What is wrong with you, Kandavar?' Rairu said, lying down on the palm-leaf mat.

'No, I am not,' Kandavar hissed angrily. The hiss of an angry serpent. 'I don't imagine things. That's what you do. All the more reason why you should take me seriously.'

Rairu stifled a yawn and sat up again.

'Listen,' Kandavar said, 'something strange happened. I was asleep when I felt a warmth near me. I turned on my side and that's when I saw her. It was the Thirumandhamkunnu Bhagwati. The goddess sat at my side and bent over me to whisper in my ears. She said, "Are you going to sleep when your sister needs you there?" So how do you expect me to stay back?'

'And you call me a dreamer!' Rairu said wryly.

'This is not a dream. The goddess came to me to tell me that I was needed at the tharavad. I saw her. I heard her. How can I not obey her? I am going. I am telling you, so you can explain it to the Gurukkal.'

'Explain what?' Rairu demanded, petrified at the thought of voicing what seemed like a silly story even to his ears.

'Just tell him what I told you,' Kandavar said, rising to leave.

'It's the middle of the night. God knows what creatures will be out at this hour… jackals and leopards, wild boars and snakes.'

'You forget the yakshis and rakshasas,' Kandavar said with a smile.

'That too,' Rairu retorted with a shudder. Kandavar may laugh but everyone knew that yakshis and rakshasas stepped out when the moon had risen, their nostrils quivering for human blood, their fangs glistening, and they pounced on silly idiots who threw caution to the winds and stepped out into the night.

'Don't worry. Maccanto will warn me of any dangers. Besides, I am wearing this,' Kandavar said, fingering the talisman slung on a thread at his hip. 'I'll be fine. Enough of talking now… it's time for me to go.'

'When will you return?'

'You'll see me when you see me,' Kandavar said. 'Sooner than later.'

From his post on the verandah, Maccanto watched Kandavar emerge. The dog stared as his master strode softly into the darkness. He leapt up and rushed to him. Instinctively he knew he shouldn't make a noise. 'Good dog,' Kandavar whispered. 'We have to go home,' he said, stepping into the grounds. 'You will have to lead me home.'

Maccanto ran ahead. His home was somewhere else, but he knew what his master meant. And he knew how to get there.

Maccanto stopped at the steps that led to the river and sniffed the air. Then he turned around and whimpered. A tiny sound to indicate the chosen direction.

Light streaked the skies as the weary boy and dog trudged home. The doors of the padipura were closed. Kandavar sat down on the low wall, catching his breath. Maccanto collapsed at his feet, his pink tongue lolling from the side of his mouth.

They had run through the night, the boy and the dog, pausing for a few minutes after every two nazhika. If the Gurukkal discovered him gone, he would think nothing of sending a group of the older boys after him. And they would find him, he was certain about that.

So he had kept a steady pace. Aabo had taught him that if one was running a great distance, the trick was to find a speed that didn't exert you into early fatigue. 'Take a lesson from Maccanto,' Aabo had said. 'See how he paces himself.'

Maccanto had seemed to know the way. Kandavar had trusted the dog's sense of direction and let him take them home.

Kandavar heard the giant wooden wedge being drawn. The bronze locks were turned and the doors opened with a long-drawn-out creak. Manickam stepped out yawning, his arms stretched above his head. He stopped in his tracks, his eyes widening at the sight of the boy and the dog.

'What are you doing here?' he asked.

Kandavar shrugged and stood up.

'Are you on your own? How did you find your way home?'

Kandavar cocked an eyebrow at Maccanto.

Manickam shook his head. 'You are going to get into serious trouble over this...'

Kandavar didn't speak. He expected that he would be punished.

One of the women was sweeping the yard. The brisk movements of her broom on the hard earth made harsh, scratchy sounds. Little puffs of dust rose in the air.

'Is everyone well at home?' he asked abruptly.

'They were until last night. Have you run away from the kalari?' She giggled.

Kandavar didn't answer. Instead, he strode towards the house, unable to postpone the moment any longer. As long as his baby sister was all right, he didn't care what they did to him.

They were angry with him. No, anger was too mild a word, he thought. Furious was better. His uncle was furious with disapproval. His mother was furious at his recklessness. The aunts were furious because his mother and uncle were. Even the hens strutting through the yard seemed to cackle words of reproof at him. Only his baby sister seemed pleased to see him. She gurgled her pleasure and grabbed his finger with her fingers.

His mother stroked the baby's cheek as she spoke to him. But she made no effort to hide her exasperation. 'But Unni,' she asked, 'what did you think could happen to her? I am at her side all day and night. You know that till the fortieth day, they won't even let me step out of this room. You know what they say – till the fortieth day, a woman who's had a baby shouldn't even utter the word "nazhi". Even curling your tongue around a difficult syllable is considered strenuous. So, like a demon guarding a treasure, I am here with your sister, Unni.'

Kandavar didn't have an answer. But he had complete faith in the goddess's instruction that he must rush to be with his baby sister. The reason would reveal itself.

It happened later that evening. His uncle had wanted to send him back right away, but his mother had pleaded for him to be allowed to stay the night. 'Let him leave early in the morning. He is a child, after all. He needs to rest.'

Chandu Nair had twisted his mouth into a grimace and walked away.

'Stay out of his sight,' his mother had warned. 'He is very displeased with you.'

Kandavar had nodded. He had no intention of leaving the room until he was satisfied that his sister was safe.

The snake had found the perfect resting place. A long spout stuck out of the wall, a few feet up from the ground. The snake had climbed easily and crawled into the mouth of the spout. It was dark and dry but cool, and the snake felt safe from the countless dangers that walked the countryside. It had buried its head under its coils as it did customarily and waited for the day to end. There was no need to take any pointless risks. Especially because everyone thought he was a krait though he was only a wolf snake. A chena thalayan who just wanted to be left alone. He was a young snake, two-and-a-half kol long, and he felt the stirrings of lust occasionally. In the evening, the snake roused himself and decided to set out. He was hungry, and truth be told, he would have liked to copulate too. There were no female snakes nearby but he could hear the click-click of a lizard. It seemed to be coming from the other end of the hole. The snake uncoiled itself and decided to slither out of the spout and get the gecko before it disappeared.

Kandavar had finished his ablutions for the evening, said his prayers, and now he sat by the window, looking out at the sky. He wished Aabo were here. Had he made a mistake after all? When he went back tomorrow, there would be recriminations and punishments. But what he feared more was the jeering and mocking. He shuddered.

Then he heard a movement.

His eyes darted around the room. The baby was fast asleep. A stone lamp had been lit at dusk and the flame threw shadows on the walls, but there was nothing else. A gecko that was perched on the wall by the cradle unfurled its tongue towards an insect. But another gecko butted in and grabbed the insect. The first gecko veered towards the intruder in rage. Kandavar watched, amused by the two quarrelling geckos. And then, from the corner of his eye, he saw a movement again.

A snake emerged from the ovu, the drain into which women and children were encouraged to pee at night. A slender blue-grey snake with bands on it.

Kandavar's eyes widened in horror. He looked around him wildly, seeking a weapon to pulverize the threat that was crawling towards his baby sister. As he watched, unable to move, he saw the full snake emerge.

It was a vallikettan. A krait that could fell a grown man in hours and kill a baby in minutes. He remembered the Gurukkal saying, 'Deep inside, we are all animals. In fact, we have the same weapons that animals do. Teeth and nails. And brute strength. But mostly we let the animal in us hide. That is how it should be. But if you are ever stuck in a situation where you have no weapons at hand, call upon the animal in you. Let it emerge. Use your teeth and nails to draw blood. Don't think twice about it. Be the animal you want to be.'

Kandavar leapt across the room and grabbed the snake with the lightning movement of a cat. 'No, you won't,' he screamed and bit into the snake.

The snake flailed in terror but felt its life ebb away as the teeth sank deeper and deeper, severing it almost into two.

When Kuttimalu entered the room from her bath, she saw her son standing there with blood dripping from his mouth and an almost dead but still dancing snake at his feet.

'Unni!' she cried in horror.

'This is why the goddess sent me, Amma,' he said.

He buried the snake himself. The next morning, they would do a ritual to appease the snake gods and he would beg for forgiveness. But, for tonight, the snake was a deadly predator that he had been sent to deal with.

PART 3

NOVEMBER AD 1659–MARCH AD 1660

(SAFAR AH 1070–RAJAB AH 1070)

XX

It had been almost ordained that the two men meet. At the Mishkal Palli in Kuttichira near Kozhikode, Idris had felt Sala Pokkar's eyes linger on him. He watched the man walk away after the prayers with the gait peculiar to seamen and camel drivers. As if constantly seeking to find the centre of gravity by slightly bowing their knees outwards... This man could be the key to finding a vessel that would take him the distance he wanted to go.

'Salaam walaikum,' Idris offered by way of greeting.

The young man, sturdy, with skin like cedar and a shiny shaven head, stopped and murmured, 'Wa' alaykum salaam.'

Idris felt the young man size him up with more curiosity than fear. He took a deep breath and spoke in Arabic.

The man blinked. He shook his head. 'What is he saying?' he murmured under his breath in Malayalam. 'I should have gone to the madrasa and kept up with my Arabic studies as Vaapa advised me to.' He dredged his memory for all the Arabic words he knew, cleared his throat and came up with a phrase, 'I don't understand...'

Idris smiled and rumbled in Malayalam, 'Would you know of a ship sailing out in the next few days?'

Idris thought it was recompense for the frustration of those first few weeks spent, many years ago, attempting to get his tongue around the sounds of the language, when he saw the amazement on the young man's face. 'You... you speak Malayalam?'

Idris smiled. 'I have to, since you don't speak Arabic. But tell me, is there such a ship?'

Sala Pokkar frowned. 'There may be one, I am not certain. Where can I find you to let you know?'

'I will be here. The mullah – ah, what do you call him? The musaliyar here has offered me a bed in his home,' Idris said.

'The musaliyar? That is unusual. He doesn't even like strangers. What did you offer him?'

Idris smiled and shrugged. 'Nothing.'

Sala shook his head. 'I don't believe that! You must have offered him something he wants because I know he will not offer anyone bed or board for money.'

Idris smiled in amusement at the young man. 'Nothing, I assure you. I do have a talent for calligraphy and I promised to give him a few lessons.'

'Calligraphy?' The young man stared. 'What's that?'

Idris walked towards a mango tree in the mosque grounds. He dug deep into his jellabiyad and pulled out a scroll. A Chinese trader had sold him several sheets of a heavy, almost cream-coloured paper and on it Idris had chosen to work the calligram. A mystic merger of Muhammed and Dhul-al-Fiquar, the sword. A Bismillah with the Quranic Hudhud, the hoopoe. And beneath it, a few lines of the Nashki script.

'But what do you write with?'

From a pouch Idris drew out the reed pen and said, 'This is my instrument. I dip the qualam in the ink and let Allah lead my hand.'

'What does it say?' The young man's voice had dropped to a whisper.

Idris murmured, 'La-in basatta ilayya yadaka litaqtulanee ma ana bibasitin yadiya ilayka li-aqtulaka innee akhafu Allaha rabba alAAalameena – if thou dost stretch thy hand against me, to slay me, it is not for me to stretch my hand against thee to slay thee: for I do fear Allah, the cherisher of the worlds.'

The young man looked away. Idris realized that nothing of what he had said had made any sense to the young man. Bookish knowledge was evidently not his forte. 'What's your name?' he asked.

'Sala Pokkar,' he replied.

Idris took a twig and drew the name on the sand that covered the grounds. Sala Pokkar's eyes widened.

'That's your name in the Nashki script that calligraphers generally use.'

'So that's what it looks like?' Sala Pokkar said, his eyes unwilling to part from the markings on the sand.

'I could teach you. No man should live a stranger to his name,' Idris said.

'In which case, I'll need to go on the ship that you board, Ikka,' the young man said. Ikka. Older brother. Idris smiled. It seemed he had acquired a sibling now.

'Do you have any skills, Sala Pokkar?' Idris asked.

The young man smiled. 'I am a khalasi, Ikka. Have you heard about us? All I need is a davar, a wooden winch, a wooden handle we call kazha, and thick coir ropes to raise and lower the heaviest weights in the world. So I'll find a job anywhere I go. You don't have to worry that I will be a burden to you.'

Idris nodded. It was best everything was spoken up front before they set out together.

The next morning, Sala Pokkar was at the mosque with a beaming face and barely suppressed excitement. 'There is a ship. It is a small Arab vessel that will dock at Thekkepuram to take on supplies. But the Parangis who are the Zamorin's new best friends are bloodthirsty leeches. They levy an exorbitant fee for docking rights at Kozhikode, so most ships, including this one, set sail the very next day. They will take us, I am told. I'll work for my passage. You'll need to pay for yours. Is that all right?'

Idris nodded. He would work for his passage too, but not in the manner Sala called work. There would be stories to tell, deals to broker, calligrams to fashion, medicines to dispense, alternative worlds to lead them into… Idris smiled at the thought.

'So when is the ship expected?'

'Five to six weeks, I am told.' Sala Pokkar shrugged.

'Good, then we must be on it when it sets sail from here.'

'Ikka, don't you want to know where we are going?' Sala Pokkar's eyes widened.

'It really doesn't matter to a traveller. But anyway, where are we going?'

'Serendip! It is an island…'

Idris sat up at the name.

Many years ago, Ali the camel trainer had told him a fairy tale: Of a land called Serendippo, a lost camel, and of princes who made discoveries they had not sought. It was when Idris read Khusrau that he knew it to be the island that was called Tamarabarani. To the Portuguese, it was the Trapobana, to the Arabic Tenerism, and for the yellow people it was the Pa-out Chow or the isle of gems. So many names for a little island. He would seek his own Serendippo, Idris decided, and let it set the path for further travel.

'I have always wanted to go there,' he said.

'Really? They say it's just like here… Why travel to another place that's like home anyway?'

Idris peered at Sala carefully. He wasn't all brawn and wide-eyed innocence then. 'Let me tell you a story…' said Idris.

Once, many years ago, several hundred years ago, there existed in the country of Serendippo a great and powerful king by the name of Jaffer. He had three sons who were very dear to him. He was a good father and so was determined that their education should hone all their faculties.

He found the best possible tutors and the tutors were pleased with the progress of the three princes. But the king was still unsure, so he decided to test them. He called each one of them and offered him the kingdom. But the princes refused, saying they still had so much to learn about kingship.

The king was secretly pleased, but to ensure that his sons learned to survive on their own, he pretended to be very angry and exiled them.

The princes set out and soon they reached a foreign land like they had never seen before. At the port, there was much commotion. Apparently, a merchant had lost his wife and camel. The princes walked away from the port, towards the town. On their way, they found clues of a missing camel. They concluded that the camel was lame, blind in one eye, missing a tooth, carrying a pregnant woman, and bearing honey on one side and butter on the other. In the town, they found a hostel to spend the night and while there, they discussed their findings. Someone overheard them and went to the merchant's house, where he was bemoaning the loss of his wife and camel. The merchant was dumbfounded. 'They abducted my wife and stole my camel!' he shouted.

And so they were taken to the emperor of the land. The emperor was curious about the description they gave of the animal. 'How could you know so precisely a camel you have never seen?' he demanded.

The oldest prince said: 'We saw that grass had been eaten from the side of the road where it was less green, so the camel must be blind on the other side. There were bits of chewed grass on the road that were the size of a camel's tooth, so they must have fallen through the gap left by a missing tooth. The tracks showed the prints of only three feet, the fourth being dragged, indicating that the animal was lame. We knew that butter was carried on one side of the camel and honey on the other because ants had been attracted to melted butter on one side of the road and flies to spilt honey on the other.'

The second prince stepped forward. 'I guessed that the camel must be carrying a woman because I noticed that near the tracks where the animal had knelt, the imprint of a foot was visible. There was some urine nearby, so I wet my fingers and as a reaction to its odour I felt carnal longings stir within me, which convinced me that the imprint was of a woman's foot.'

'I guessed that the woman must be pregnant,' the third prince concluded, 'because I noticed that near the urine spot were handprints which showed that the woman, being pregnant, had helped herself up with her hands after urinating.'

At this moment, a traveller entered the court to say that he had found a camel with a pregnant woman on its back, wandering in the desert, and had brought them back.

'You want to go there because of a story that wasn't even set there.' Sala Pokkar guffawed. 'Simply because the princes were from Serendippo?'

'Better than going there for a tale of magical riches,' Idris retorted. No one ever laughed at him. Everyone was too intimidated or awed. It was a rather pleasant sensation, he thought, to be teased. 'I just want to see what it's like.'

'By the way, the island is also called Ceylon. It doesn't matter to me but I thought you should know. Besides, a ship is a ship. The sea is the sea. What will make it different is you,' Sala Pokkar said, rising and dusting his clothes.

'Here,' Idris said, pulling out three Vir-raya fanams. 'We'll need supplies. It's better you buy them. You'll get a better rate than I will.'

Sala Pokkar's fingers trembled as he took the gold coins.

This was unimagined riches. 'It's a lot of money,' he said. 'Do you know the value of this?'

Idris smiled. 'Do you?'

Sala Pokkar shook his head.

'The smallest coin is the copper kashu. I hope you are aware of that. We may not need one now, but you can buy a little monkey for four kashu. Sixteen kashu make one silver taram.' Idris held up a star-shaped silver coin. 'With one of these, you can buy enough rice for a whole day for a family of six. Twenty-eight of this make one fanam.' Idris smiled at Sala Pokkar's baffled expression, but continued, 'So yes, it is a lot of money, but we also have a long way to go. For all that we need, a fanam will suffice. For the rest, I want you to buy Calico cloth. Go to Chaliyam and find both the plain ones and the ones with a lotus design on it. Ask them to pack the bales carefully. Tell them to insert strips of thazhampoo after every tenth layer. It will keep the cloth fragrant, no matter how long we keep it bundled.'

'And you trust me? That I won't make off with these riches.' Sala Pokkar laid his palm against his chest.

'If you do, you will never sleep again,' Idris said. 'But that is not the point. Go, do as I ask you to. We have less than a month to prepare for the voyage.'

'And then?'

'And then, we will see.'

That night, Idris lay staring at the ceiling. All day, he had felt a peculiar sense of loss. As he lay waiting for dawn to arrive, he tried to examine every corner of his mind, trying to locate the source of the loss jostling within him. Suddenly he knew what it was. He closed his eyes, exasperated with himself. But his mind wandered back to the boy. How was he coping? He felt an odd sense of misgiving. Perhaps he should go back one last time to convince himself that he was doing right by leaving Kandavar and sailing away.

XXI

Idris cleared his throat. Chandu Nair stood up and walked to the edge of the verandah. He paced up and down a few times. Then he stopped mid-stride and stared unseeingly at Idris.

'The boy worries me. He needs to be taken in hand,' Chandu Nair said, shaking his head in helplessness.

'I heard about his latest escapade. But he is only a child,' Idris said.

'I thought he would shape up at the kalari and the Gurukkal, to be fair, is doing his best, but his impetuousness… what is one to do with it?'

'He is young. Time will teach him to be careful.'

Chandu Nair wiped his forehead with the edge of the cloth hung over his shoulder. 'I wish… but he already thinks the goddess speaks to him. That is how the Chaver set out on their suicide mission. They believe they have to heed the goddess when she asks them to. He is so young, but already so headstrong. And the Gurukkal tells me that he has the makings of a great warrior. A dreadful combination. The boy worries me.'

Something in Idris wanted to clamp his tongue but something else more fiery, the greed in him to have his son at his side, made him say, 'I am going away for a bit. A voyage. Let the boy go with me.'

Chandu Nair stared. 'Go with you? But where are you going?'

'I told you I am a trader. It's been a while since I was out in the world. So I have to relearn many things…'

'That's all very well. But where will you go?'

'I am not sure yet. Here and there. I may be gone a year. That's how long it should take,' Idris said. He didn't want to reveal to Chandu Nair that his travels would involve the sea. He had heard at the Naik's court that upper-caste Hindus considered it a grievous sin that might even cost them their caste. Which was why they depended on the Muslims and Christians to source for them whatever they needed from lands that could be reached only by sea. More fools they, he thought.

'You do know that it is forbidden by our religion to travel across the seas,' Chandu Nair took the palm-leaf fan and moved it languidly to break the stillness of the late morning.

'The ocean is where our gods dwell. It is their resting place, and to disturb them would be to incur their wrath. And who knows what monsters lurk in its depths?' Chandu Nair continued, pausing the lazy movement of his hand.

'I didn't see any monsters when I crossed the seas,' Idris said gently. He didn't want to offend the man, but he had never heard as much rubbish as he had in these past few months in Malabar.

'That may be so. Perhaps there are no monsters. But in the *Manusmriti*, it is said that the brahmin who crosses the sea will be denied a shraadha. We are not brahmins but the rules hold good for us as well. And without the appropriate rituals after death, how can one's soul find eternal peace? If one crosses the ocean, the offender is grouped with prisoners, sellers of soma – alcohol – a perjurer, one who eats food given by the son of an adulterer, and strangely enough, a bard and an oilman.'

Idris tried to hide his smile. These Hindus, he thought, would make a taboo of anything. It seemed to him that, in the final tally, the things that were not allowed far outranked what was allowed. 'I can understand a seller of alcohol and a liar. But why a poet and an oilman?' Idris asked.

'That's what the scripture says, but the truth, if you ask me, is this. How can one keep the caste laws when one is not on land?' Chandu Nair said, gesturing to the spread of land around them.

'I promise you the boy will not cross the seas,' Idris said. 'All we will do is trail the coast till Serendip. And the sea there, I have heard, is hardly a sea, more like a canal,' he murmured under his breath.

'Let me think about it,' Chandu Nair said. It seemed too big a decision to take without careful consideration.

Idris, knowing that he was dismissed for the moment, went back to the padipura.

Chandu Nair watched the tall black man disappear between the trees.

Could he trust his nephew to him?

That evening, Idris watched the rain fall. Through the curtain of rain, he saw the land swell in its greenness. How could he think of taking the boy away from here?

In the morning, Idris had his answer. Kandavar would go with him, Chandu Nair said. 'You see, if the boy stays away, he will fall behind in his mastery of the kalari adavu and when he sees that he will never be as good as the rest of his classmates, it may deter him from offering himself as a Chaver,' Chandu Nair said slowly, not meeting his eye.

Idris looked at the man's face with pity. He realized that Chandu Nair felt a great distaste for what he was doing, but was compelled to do it to safeguard his nephew from certain death.

'You promise that you will look after him,' Chandu Nair said abruptly.

'I will. As if he were my own son,' Idris said.

He heard a gasp from behind the kilivadil. Through the many closely spaced spindles and a decorative opening in the centre of the wood screen behind which women usually sat to listen in on an important discussion amongst men, Idris could see a shadowy form. The kilivadil was both barrier and veil, so the women could see without being seen.

'What about the boy's mother? Has she agreed?' Idris asked, knowing Kuttimalu could hear him.

'She will not question my decision.' Chandu Nair frowned.

Idris didn't speak. He would have to find a way to ask Kuttimalu what she thought. If she wasn't happy with Kandavar going away, he wouldn't take him, Idris decided.

Chandu Nair suddenly peered in the direction of the wall with the kilivadil. 'What is it?' he asked, walking towards it.

When Chandu Nair returned to Idris's line of vision, he looked pleased. 'My sister says she is happy that you will look after Kandavar as if he is of your own blood. We hold great esteem by such a kinship. The blood tie. When will you leave on this voyage?'

'Soon,' Idris said. He felt a flatness creep into him. There was nothing to keep him back. It occurred to him that Kuttimalu was eager to see him go, and with their son. A new baby from the new man had taken precedence over old ties. 'I will explain to the Gurukkal and bring Kandavar back here so he can take his leave. Once we leave, it will be many months, maybe even a year before we return…'

'A year?' Chandu Nair exclaimed. 'He is only a young boy!'

Idris shrugged. 'He will be more than a child when he returns. That is what going away from home does.'

XXII

Kandavar stared at the vision of the tall robed man standing at the helm of the boat as it approached the river bank. Aabo, he thought. Then he shook himself, thinking he was imagining it. But the boat drew closer. And Maccanto was racing to the shore, barking and wagging his tail in high excitement. It was Aabo.

Later that night, as Kandavar talked to Rairu about what had happened, it felt almost like a dream.

'Can you imagine?' he said, his excitement causing the

words to tumble out in a jumble of staccato sentences. 'Aabo has returned to take me with him on a voyage. And no one has any objections. Neither my mother, nor my uncle. Not even the Gurukkal.'

Idris walked in on the two boys and Rairu turned to him with an eager face.

'Abti, why can't I go with you and Kandavar?' Rairu demanded.

'Your family will never agree to it. They don't know me. Besides...'

'Besides what?' Rairu's eyes flashed.

'Nothing,' Idris said firmly. Besides, Rairu would stick out, making them conspicuous. And that was one of the secrets of travelling safe. To be able to blend in without calling attention to oneself. Kandavar in a jellabiyad or even a tunic and trousers would pass for his son. No one would question a father and son travelling together. In fact, Idris decided that he would grow out his hair instead of shaving his head every few days.

Idris shook his head. 'There is no way you can go with us. Instead, use your time well here at the kalari so that when Kandavar returns, you can help him make up for lost time.'

Rairu turned on his heel and walked away. He wouldn't speak to Kandavar either.

Kandavar tried to reason with him. 'But why are you angry with me?' he pleaded. 'It's not my fault.'

Rairu turned his face away and wouldn't utter a word.

'There is nothing you can do,' Idris said gently. 'He is angry and jealous. And you know what your uncle says – there is no cure for baldness or jealousy.'

Kandavar giggled, thinking of how his uncle would rub his bald-as-an-egg head ruefully as he mouthed the words.

'Let him be for now. He resents that you are going away. He will get over it in time. You just have to be patient.'

And so Kandavar had trudged after Aabo and Maccanto, away

from the kalari. But just as the boatmen steered the boat to the right and trees began to cover his line of vision, he saw a flash. A wave of a hand. Rairu. Kandavar smiled in relief, then waved his arm furiously in acknowledgement. Aabo had been right.

Kandavar tried to be as dignified as Aabo when it was time to leave home. No one would have known that the night before, he had lain at his baby sister's side, crying silent tears. Once the excitement had worn off, he grew frightened at the prospect of leaving home and his mother and going away to some distant land. He was terrified at the thought of what was expected of him. He would have traded places with Rairu, he told himself. But there was no going back. Everything had been decided, and when dawn broke, he would leave with Aabo for the seaside city of Kozhikode – the seat of the Zamorin.

Kandavar went into his mother's room and opened a wooden chest that held her jewellery box and other expensive possessions. The chest smelt of sandalwood and thazhampoo. Kandavar rummaged through it impatiently. Beneath a stack of mundu, he found what he was looking for. A red silk cloth bundle. He took it out carefully and opened the bundle to take out the katari which his favourite cousin had given him some months before he died at the Mamangam. He touched the blade of the push dagger. He forked his fingers through the horizontal handle set between the close-set vertical bars so the blade of the dagger sat over his knuckles, for a better grip. If he saw the Zamorin out on the street somewhere, he would know what to do. He would sink the blade into the Zamorin's belly and turn it so that the intestines would sever and then he would wait there as the Zamorin bled to death. Everyone would know that he, Vattoli Kandavar Menavan, had accomplished what countless Chaver before him had been unable to.

In the morning, Kandavar touched his uncle's feet and sought his blessing. He could hear his mother sobbing and the baby whimpering. He bit down on his lip so that his face wouldn't crumple at their distraught faces. And then he walked with Aabo towards the padipura. Maccanto followed them.

At the padipura, Kandavar stopped. 'You cannot come with us,' he said, bending to hug the dog. 'Manickam will look after you.'

The dog sat on its haunches and watched the boy and man leave.

Kandavar and Idris walked in silence for a while. Then Idris turned to the boy. 'You are very silent. Are you all right?'

The boy nodded.

'Are you scared?' Idris asked, noting the tightness around the boy's lips.

'Yes,' he said in a small voice.

'Good,' Idris murmured. 'Fear is good. It makes us careful. And it is important that we be careful on a journey.'

'Will there be monsters where we go?'Kandavar's lip shook tremulously.

Idris laughed and drew the boy towards him. 'The only monsters we need to fear are the ones in human form.'

'What?' Kandavar asked.

'Nothing. Don't think so hard. Just keep your eyes open, and your mind.' Idris smiled. 'Now there is something that I need to tell you, and it is to be a secret. Do you understand?'

And so Kandavar acquired a new name and identity. He would be Kandavar Bilal, son of Idris Maymoon Samataar Guleed, previously of Dikhil.

There had been little time thereafter for rumination. 'We have to get there as quickly as we can,' Idris said, hurrying Kandavar when the boy paused to rest. Some of the way was covered by boat but mostly they had to walk. On the fifth day, Idris and Kandavar entered Kozhikode.

Kandavar was silenced by the sights and sounds of the city. At the kalari, the older boys had talked of the wonders of Kozhikode. Raman, who was the self-appointed authority on all subjects under the sun, had said, 'You are certain to see strange sights. People from all parts of the world. People with three heads and people walking on their backs. As for animals, don't even get me started…'

Where were the people with yellow skins and three heads? Where were the monkeys that perched on top of coconut trees and drank toddy? Where were the crocodiles basking in the sun and talking parrots that you could converse with? All he saw were avenues of trees and houses set so close together that they seemed to lean into each other. There was a long road with shops on either side selling fruit and another that sold spices.

'Where are we, Aabo?' he asked in a small voice a little later.

Idris patted his head as they walked alongside a tank with steps leading into it from all four sides. 'Kuttichira. We'll meet Sala Pokkar here. He will be travelling with us. Remember, at no time should you mention who you really are. You mustn't see it as falsehoods but we have no option. You know the caste rules so it is best that we let everyone think you are my son. So your name is Kandavar Bilal and the rest is the truth. You were living until now with your mother's family and you went to a kalari, and you will name Baapa Gurukkal as your kalari master if questioned. That is the other thing to keep in mind: Don't volunteer any information until asked.'

Sala Pokkar was waiting under a tree outside the mosque. His face lit up when he saw Idris. 'I thought you were never coming back,' he said.

Idris smiled. 'Why would you think that?'

'It is almost six weeks since you went away. But who is this?' Sala Pokkar asked, lifting his chin in the direction of the boy.

'My son,' Idris said and pulled the boy towards him. 'Kandavar Bilal. You can call him Kandavar, though.'

'Bilal I know. It's in the book. But Kandavar, isn't that a kafir name?' Sala Pokkar asked. He didn't seem surprised that Idris had produced a son, he was more perturbed by the name.

Idris shrugged. 'It's just a name. Like you, he speaks no Arabic. He grew up here,' he added.

Sala Pokkar nodded. He had more pressing news to deliver. 'Ikka, the ship will set sail tomorrow. We need to hurry and load our things in it before sunset.'

Kandavar felt he was in the heart of a whirlpool as Idris and Sala Pokkar made preparations for the voyage. There wasn't even time to exclaim at the sight of the ocean or its vastness at his first glimpse of it at Beypore.

Kandavar rushed towards the water, drawn to the grey-green expanse. The sea was everything that Aabo had said it would be and more. For a moment, he wished Rairu were here. The wave swirled around his feet and retreated with an astonishing speed. When the next wave broke, he bent down and cupped a handful of water and drank deeply of it. The next moment, he spat it out, grimacing at the taste. 'It's salty!'

'But that's how nature wants it to be, inan.' Idris smiled at Kandavar's expression. 'Oceans are salty. Rivers are sweet. Lakes are brackish and the rain, it tastes of nothing.'

Sala Pokkar looked at Idris in admiration. He made even the most ordinary things sound profound. It was true. The rain tasted of nothing. He had never thought about it.

'We have to go,' Idris said abruptly. This was no time to stand on the sand and spout poetry. 'We take a small boat to where the ship is anchored, we load our supplies and ourselves and we sail at first light. We don't have much time.'

'Will he be able to handle what lies ahead? It's not what he is used to. He has never seen a ship before and knows nothing of what it means to sail the seas.' Sala Pokkar's eyes darted to the boy.

'He will cope,' Idris said. 'We have to go now.' He turned to the boy, who was running in and out of the waves.

Kandavar had his first glimpse of a ship from the raft. He stared at the floating house that Aabo called 'kappal'. How did it stay afloat on the waves? What about food and water? And where would he pee? Kandavar felt a wave of homesickness wash over him like the foam-crested waves of the ocean.

When Aabo had suggested that he go with him, it had seemed like a dream come true. But now, he wondered if he should have stayed home, where all was familiar and known.

'It's a sturdy little patamar,' Idris said, assessing the fat-bottomed vessel. 'It will help get us to Serendip quickly enough.'

Kandavar felt his eyes pop out of their sockets as they drew closer to the ship. It seemed there were many people on it. Two men were scrubbing the wooden floor while a few others bearing loads on their heads were descending into the belly of the ship through a hole in the floor. One man was counting drums of water and three others were mending what looked like a giant white cloth. All going about their chores without even a thought that they were on water and not land.

In the course of the week it took to reach Serendip, Kandavar found his sea legs. He discovered that the patamar was rigged with two masts with a triangular sail and a head sail. It had a bamboo deckhouse with a coconut palm-leaf thatch and there were twenty other people on the vessel. And that the stars determined the way they went.

'How do we know where we are headed?' Kandavar asked, eyeing the horizon once the ship set sail. The sea stretched as far as he could see and beyond. And the land had almost receded.

'The al-kamal,' Idris said, smiling at the worry in Kandavar's gaze.

'The what?' The boy's head jerked in surprise.

'Wait till it's night and I'll show you how the stars hold more than our destinies.' Idris smiled and leaned back against a coil of rope and closed his eyes to still all conversation. Sometimes it was the only way he could steer away from the claustrophobia that threatened to suffocate him when surrounded by people he knew and loved. Strangers were all right. They could be kept back and dealt with. But the people you loved thought it was the prerogative of love to intrude. To swamp your space.

The night swallowed the vessel and the sea. Idris could see the boy's face by the light of the lantern. Time for a lesson, he thought, and uncurled himself. 'Come with me,' he said, pulling the boy to his feet.

The al-kamal operator was standing on the deck, fiddling with his wooden board.

'What is he doing?' Kandavar whispered.

'Celestial navigation,' Idris murmured back. 'See that notch on the board. He will try and position the al-kamal so the North Star falls within it. That is the North Star,' he said, pointing out the star in the skies. 'In your country you call it Dhruva, in mine we call it Al-Kibblah. In Damascus, where I went many years ago, they call it Mismar, which means needle, and among sailors, it's called the Ship Star.'

They watched the operator hold the bottom of the board level with the horizon so the north star fell within the notch. There was a string attached to the centre of the board. The operator drew the string towards his face and knotted it at the point where it touched his nose.

'That is the celestial location, the point where we are. As long as the operator can level the board with the horizon and fit the star within that notch, he can gauge where we are based on how much he needs to loosen or tighten the string so that the knot touches his nose. That is why it's called the guiding line.'

The boy nodded. How much had he understood, Idris wondered.

'Why that particular star, Aabo?' the boy asked, his gaze fixed on the star on the horizon.

'Yes, why that star, Ikka?' Sala Pokkar spoke up. He had crept after them to see what had brought them to this side of the deck.

'The North Star doesn't change its position, unlike other stars. No matter where you see it from, it's constant. That's why the Al-Kibblah is used to fix the guiding line.'

Kandavar threw his head back and stared at the night sky. A million stars shone above him. He felt dwarfed by the immensity of the universe. And frightened too. There was so much to see, learn and understand. Where would he begin? Kandavar fixed his gaze on the North Star. He would call it Aabo, for wasn't Aabo his own personal guiding star? As long as he could see Aabo, he would know where he was. All the other stars might merely distract him, but the Aabo star would keep him safe.

Idris felt the boy draw closer to him and slip his fingers through his. He closed his eyes as a queer dread filled him.

XXIII

The vessel scudded along the Malabar Coast. A steady breeze blew – from midnight to midday the land breeze and from noon to middle of the night the sea breeze – taking the vessel along. In the quiet of the evening, Idris took to telling his stories of travel and the sights he had seen. One of the older Arabs on board was mesmerized. 'I thought I told the best stories,' he said, 'but yours are better.'

Idris smiled and raised the tip of his fingers to his forehead to acknowledge the compliment. In the lull that had fallen, the Arab said, 'I hear you are a stargazer. If this had been the end of the monsoon on the Malabar Coast, we would be sailing into the tail of the elephant. The constellation that the Portuguese call Rabo del Elephanto. Have you seen it in the sky, young man?'

Idris shook his head, mystified. The monsoon was called an elephant, he knew. The grey clouds coming and going with thunderous sounds and much stomping, storming and boisterousness, like a herd of elephants, but he hadn't heard of such a constellation. He wondered at the veracity of the other man's observation, but kept his counsel. He didn't want to be tossed out of the ship for having offended the old man, who was venerated on the vessel.

'Who reigns in Serendip?' Idris asked, wanting to change the subject.

The elderly Arab cleared his throat. 'First of all, the white skins call it Ceylon. No one calls it Serendip except us.'

'Yes, I know,' Idris said softly.

'I do not know what you know of the politics of this region. For one, the old order is falling apart. Once upon a time, the struggle for supremacy in the East was dominated by the Portuguese and the English, who were determined to capture the trade. But now a new power has joined the fight for trading territories – the Dutch. They have entered the pepper politics. Everyone knows that whoever has control over pepper in these parts will inherit the rest of the trade. The Dutch are beginning to dispossess the Portuguese in the new territories they had earmarked as their own. They took over the rein of power in Serendip by invitation. The Zamorin is in talks with them to negotiate an agreement that could help him in his battle against the Kochi Raja, I hear. As for King Raja Singha II of Kandy in Serendip, he has already invited the Dutch to help throw out the Portuguese from the island. So it is into a Dutch Galle that we will sail.'

Idris said nothing. He was a trader and a black man. It didn't matter to him in whose power Ceylon lay.

They skirted past Vizhinjam and set sail towards the Cape. Some distance away a lofty mountain seemed to loom into the skies. The captain of the ship had decided to drop anchor, not wanting to risk sailing the waters in the dark. When night fell, the side of the mountain glittered with countless stars.

'What are those stars, Aabo?' Kandavar asked, pointing towards the mountain.

'Yes, what are their names, Ikka?' Sala Pokkar echoed.

Idris shook his head. With every league they travelled, he knew less and less about the new territories or the skies they were entering. 'Those are not stars. And yet, they twinkle like them,' he said slowly.

'Ask your Arab,' Kandavar murmured, unwilling to prise his eyes away from the mountain of stars.

The old Arab cupped his chin in his palm and smiled when Idris went to him with his query. 'So, traveller, it is your turn to hear rather than speak. Those stars you see are not stars but the creation of little birds who flock to the mountainside to build their nests. The natives say that the birds place a piece of clay on top of their nests and in the night, they stick a firefly or two on the blob of clay so they light up the mountainside.'

'Birds don't need light like we do,' Idris said, unable to hide the wryness in his tone.

The old man narrowed his eyes. 'No, they don't. But they know that the lights will dazzle the giant bats that abound in these parts and dash them against the rocks. The bats often hurt or kill the young of the birds and what parent will let that happen to his child? So the birds seek ways and means to protect their babies from harm.'

Idris was silent. He turned his face to the south-east where the island of Ceylon lay. His gold eye glinted in the light from the lantern. The Arab smiled. 'Your gold eye could be a firefly,' he murmured.

'What was he saying, Aabo?' Kandavar asked Idris later that night.

Idris shrugged. 'I told you about the birds that use fireflies to light up their nests.'

'No, he said something else to you after that.'

Idris snapped, 'Nothing that is of any consequence to you. Go to sleep now. Tomorrow we will go around the Cape. And it may not be a pleasant experience!'

Kandavar felt his lip wobble at Aabo's brusqueness. Aabo on the ship was not the same man he was on land. Sometimes Kandavar thought he didn't recognize this cold taciturn stranger who stood before him. Kandavar opened out his mat and lay on it quietly. He felt Aabo's eyes on him and turned on his side. If Aabo didn't want to talk to him, he didn't want to talk to him either. A cold, jagged rock of misery grew in his gut. He curled into a ball, pulling his knees to his chest to soothe away the pain that threatened to dislodge his heart. A tear slipped out of the corner of his eye. His mother, if she had been here, would have scolded him for not stretching out. 'How will your body grow evenly if you sleep with your limbs curled and bent, Unni,' she would remonstrate and tug at his leg.

When Kandavar was seven years old, he had seen an elderly aunt laid out after her death. He had sat up frowning the next time his mother prodded him to stretch his legs, murmuring under her breath, 'Why do you curl up like a millipede?'

'Tell me, Amma,' he said, 'Ittimema was laid out with her arms at her side and legs straight. Does that mean she is still growing in her grave?'

His uncle who had been within earshot had smacked

him then. A tight hard slap on his calf for back chat and for questioning his mother. Kandavar wouldn't have minded a smack now, or even three, if it meant he would be off this cursed ship where nothing was like home.

Idris paced the deck. He stopped and stared at the horizon unseeingly. The old Arab's words had disturbed him in a strange way. Kuttimalu had thought his gold eye was a firefly. Going away would cure him of the foolish, reckless longing that still gripped his loins when he saw her, he had thought. But was he sailing into danger? If he was on his own, it didn't matter. He would know how to extricate himself. But the boy was with him. He had promised Kuttimalu that he would make sure no harm befell their son. His eyes fell on the boy curled up on his side, facing away from him. He knew Kandavar was not asleep from the stiffness of the boy's arched spine. His sharpness earlier had upset him, he realized. But words to soothe away the hurt wouldn't come to him now. In the morning perhaps, he thought, pacing the deck again. In the morning the world would right itself again.

He walked back to his habitual place on the deck. He leaned against the coil of rope with his legs stretched out. He thought of Kuttimalu in her home. Did she ever think of him? Merely thinking of her weighed him down. What was he to do when the woman he wanted didn't want to be wanted? It was as if she was afraid to allow him entry into her life. She would offer him her body again if he insisted. As she had on that night before they left.

He had walked to the bathing pond almost as if a hand had tugged him along. It was close to midnight and as he had lain in bed looking at the stars, a voice had whispered his name.

The wind brought it to his ears. He sat up, startled. Idris, the voice said. Who called him Idris these days?

He had risen from the bed and gone to the slits in the wall. The breeze rushed down from the hills in the distance, gathering momentum as it raced across the paddy fields. Idris, the voice said again. A whisper that walked across his soul.

He had descended the stairs as quietly as it was possible. Manickam slept like the dead on the nights Idris was there. 'You are awake anyway, so why should I?' he had said. Then with a sly glance, he added, 'The sesame seed is dried in the sun for its oil; why does the silly weevil have to bake itself too?'

Idris had reached across and pulled Manickam's stubby nose. 'Are you calling me a weevil, you rogue?'

Manickam giggled. 'Ayyo…' he said, putting on an expression of mock penitence. Idris clasped the man's shoulder and spoke softly. 'One day I may learn to sleep again, but for now, this is my destiny! To stay awake with the stars. The nights that I am here, I'll keep guard. But don't let them catch you asleep when I am gone. They go to sleep, placing their trust in you. You cannot fail them.'

As Idris stepped into the passage, he heard a sound. It was Maccanto, who, when Idris was home, slunk away to be with him. The dog whined. Idris tugged at its ears. 'Jabaq-la'aan,' he whispered. Did the dog remember the Somali words he had taught it? Would Maccanto know to be quiet when he heard them?

Maccanto nuzzled his legs. 'Come along,' he said. 'Imow Maccanto, imow.'

Idris walked down the path to the bathing pond, not knowing what led him there.

She was waiting at the water's edge, staring at the inky waters of the pond. He cleared his throat so she wouldn't be frightened. 'I knew you would come here tonight,' she said.

He swallowed. 'I hadn't intended to. But a voice called to me.'

She turned and, like a bud unfurling, rose and climbed the steps towards him.

'What am I going to do?' she asked.

'What?' he asked, surprised by the query, the stricken note in her voice.

'Do you know how it feels? To be with one man while all of you yearns to be with another?' she asked.

'What?' he asked again.

'Don't play the fool,' she whispered furiously. 'You know exactly what I am saying.'

'What do you want me to do, Kuttimalu?' There. He had said her name.

'Don't.'

'Don't what?' he asked.

'Don't say my name. When you speak my name, I become a person to you. I move away from the realm of dreams where you and I belong.'

Idris looked at her. 'But we have a son. He is scarcely a dream. He is of our flesh and blood; yours and mine. How do you dream that away, Kuttimalu?'

She closed her eyes and took a deep breath to stem the words that rose in her. 'Look at me,' she said, removing the thin mundu with which she had wrapped herself.

His throat constricted. She was still suckling her daughter and her breasts burgeoned with milk. Her waist had thickened and her belly curved more fully than it had once. But he saw none of that. Instead, he saw the yearning in her flesh. How it sought his with a mindless hunger. The hardened nubs, the sheen of sweat on her skin, her panting breath.

He took her in his arms. 'Why now?' he asked. 'You've just had a baby.'

'I tried. I want you to know that. I don't want you to think that I didn't work at resisting you. This is madness, I told myself. A futile madness I should extricate myself from,' she said against his chest.

Her words were little kisses of warm breath on his skin.

'And?' he asked, tilting her chin up with a finger.

'And I am here. When you leave tomorrow, I want to hold on to this one memory you will have given me.'

Idris tightened his hold on her. 'I don't have to go. You don't have to live on memories.'

She smiled and touched the corner of his lip. 'You are a poet. Which is why you can be fanciful. But in me is warrior blood, and we do not allow our imagination to control us. There is no us, Idris. There, I have said your name. There never will be an us. All we may have is this tangling of limbs and desires. This…'

He raised her towards him and took her lower lip between his. Protests died as he had known they would. Her body was both familiar and new. A thousand ways to love her anew, a thousand ways to keep them together. That would be his arsenal of weaponry. I am a poet and a warrior, he whispered against the pulse that beat at her throat. I may be fanciful, but I also fight for what is mine.

He felt her defences melt away. She was a thousand mouths and a million hands. 'Every woman you make love to after this will remind you of me,' she whispered angrily, biting on his shoulder. 'You have to suffer as I do.'

She wept then. Even as he made love to her, quietly at first and then with a fierceness that made her gasp, she wept. He fed at her breast, first one, then the other, stealing her newborn's milk drop by drop. He teased her lips open and drank deep. Honey and cream. He thrust into her again and again. He would be child and man; cat and comet. He would gnaw at her spirit till he had tamed that resilience in her that made her say go. He would force her mouth to form the word she had forbidden herself to speak: Stay. But all through, she wept. Even as her body arched with pleasure and she came against his mouth and fingers, his skin and penis, all she would do was weep. Tears were her prism. Refracting forbidden what-if's; the rainbows of togetherness; the knowledge that this would have to end.

They lay on their backs, staring at the stars, and he said, 'So you will not ask me to stay.'

'You must go. And because you take our son with you, I know that one day you will return,' she said in a voice washed of all feeling.

Idris took her palm in his and placed it on his chest. She would allow no gentle caresses, no tender display of affection. The two times they had been together, he had learnt this about her.

'In Samarkand, there is a flower. We call it warda. It is the palest of pink and the red of blood. It can be yellow like the mango or sometimes pure white. It has a fragrance that will curl your nostrils and enter your blood stream. It is a beautiful flower. So beautiful that you reach for it to feel the silken softness of its petals and to draw in its fragrance, and then it draws blood. The warda has thorns, you see. It will allow no one to get too close.'

There was nothing left to say. They lay there for some more time, each lost in the need to savour this time eked out, these stolen, precious moments.

She sat up after a while. She leaned forward and kissed his forehead gently. 'Be safe,' she said.

He watched her leave. The imprint of her lips on his skin beginning to fade even as she walked away.

Idris felt the waves carry the ship forward. The night was pitch-dark with not a star in sight. He would have to believe in the healing power of time.

With time all would cease to matter: a lost eye, a dead parent, the love of your life. A betrayal, the thwarting of ambition or a frozen heart, you just had to give it time, he told himself.

XXIV

The waves rose high and tossed the little vessel this way and that. With every rolling motion of the ship, Kandavar began to feel queasy. He felt himself break into a sweat. Hot air whistled through his ears and he felt a queer fatigue even as his stomach churned. He retched loudly. Vomit flew through the air and splashed on the deck. Kandavar sank to his haunches, retching till he was spent. Sala Pokkar threw a handful of sand over the vomit from a bag kept for that purpose. 'It's quite natural to feel seasick,' he murmured kindly, seeing the embarrassment on the boy's face. 'Why, I am feeling quite sick myself. This is a nasty sea…'

Idris helped Kandavar to his feet and led him to the middle of the deck. He wet a cloth and wiped his face clean. 'Are you all right, inan?' he asked gently.

Kandavar nodded and clung to Idris, who held him against his chest. 'You will be all right,' Idris said, stroking the boy's head. 'Every good sailor will be seasick first. But soon your body will learn to find its balance on the waves. See, you are already halfway there.'

Idris pushed a giant coil of rope into a quiet corner on the deck and bade Kandavar to sit leaning against it. He took the boy's wrist in his hand and pressed down on the median nerve. 'This will help reduce the nausea. More importantly, I want you to look towards the horizon,' he said. 'No matter how much the ship tosses, the horizon will not move. And your brain will adjust to the motion of the ship.'

Kandavar stared at the horizon, willing the nausea to subside. The Arabian Sea had seemed like a pond when compared to the Cape they were heading towards. Three seas met somewhere ahead, Aabo had said, and how can you expect them to not fight each other for space?

Idris and Sala Pokkar went back to the foredeck, towards the club-shaped bow of the vessel. 'At this point west becomes east,' Idris said. 'Latitude 8 degrees, 50 minutes North, Longitude 96 degrees East.'

'What?' Sala Pokkar frowned.

'Nothing,' Idris said.

The elderly Arab from the previous evening came to stand beside Idris. 'Your boy hasn't sailed much, I presume,' he said.

'This is his first time on the sea,' Idris replied.

'Then it is Allah the most merciful who has made sure that his rite of passage didn't happen during the time the monsoon winds wreaks their fury. We will fall north of Caliture soon, so that we do not get tossed in the currents that come from the Gulf of Mannar. Even experienced navigators will not dare risk the current in these waters.' The old man tottered back to his cabin.

From Cape Comorin to Galle, the distance was seventy leagues. It wasn't a great distance, but what made it treacherous were the rocks that waited under twenty fathoms of water. At about the point that the water became fifteen to eighteen fathoms deep, the sails were drawn in.

'So it is time to say Khuda Hafiz,' Idris said as he saw the old Arab approaching them again.

'Not yet.' The old Arab laughed. 'Do you see that rock?' He pointed to a rock on which was an iron cannon. Alongside was a stake that held a flag fluttering in the wind. 'We have to wait for the Dutch to send us a pilot vessel. A ship can break to bits on the rocks around here. This way we can drop anchor safely and they know that we will never find our way back without their assistance. Meanwhile, tell me again the story about the barber and the ordeal. I shall miss your stories, Idris Maymoon.'

Galle was fortified on three sides and the sea, with its deadly crop of rock, closed in the fourth side. But it didn't matter to Kandavar. It was enough they were on land that didn't heave every now and then. They found rooms to rent easily enough and Sala Pokkar and Kandavar enjoyed exploring the city and its outskirts, even going into the hills to the east of the city.

They stayed on for a few weeks during which Idris brokered a few deals that made him some money even if they didn't excite him very much. He wanted to find a ship that they could board in a few weeks. Meanwhile, he worked on learning some Dutch words.

The Tamizh that they spoke in Galle was like Malayalam spoken in a sing-song. Idris had some Portuguese too. And Arabic, Malayalam and the Somali language. They called him the Man with the Golden Eye and Many Tongues.

One morning, Kandavar brought back to their rooms two fluffy chicks. 'Where did these come from?' Idris demanded.

'The watermelon woman gave it to me,' Kandavar said, holding the chicks in his palms. 'She had twenty-four chicks and she said I could have two since I liked them so much.'

'Chicks grow up and become hens or cocks,' Sala Pokkar mumbled. 'That is, if a kite or a cat doesn't get them first.'

'I won't let that happen.' Kandavar spoke fiercely. 'I'll guard them with my life. You forget I am a warrior. We protect our charges with our lives if the need arises!'

'Warrior?' Sala Pokkar guffawed and then mimicked Kandavar in a mock baritone. 'We will protect our charges with our lives if the need arises. You don't know what you are saying.'

Idris interrupted the conversation before Kandavar blurted

out the truth in rage. 'Listen to me, inan, I suggest you give the chicks back.'

Sala Pokkar saw the look of dismay in the boy's eyes and said, 'Ikka, I was just teasing him. I'll look after the birds.'

Idris said quietly, 'We won't be here very long.'

Kandavar frowned. 'Where are we going?'

'I'll tell you in a day or two,' Idris said, heading towards the door. 'But make sure you return the chicks to the watermelon woman.'

Idris walked towards the port, deep in thought. It was time to move on and find the boy a new horizon. He spotted a few seamen he had made friends with. They would be useful in helping him decide their next destination.

'How about Tharangambadi?' someone said. One of the seamen, knowing Idris's interest in such things, told him, 'That means place of the sighing waves. But the foreigners can't get their tongue around it and call it Trangebar. I would suggest Thoothukudi.'

'There are pearl fisheries there!' another seaman said.

Idris thought of the Yemeni Umar and the pearl and decided that was where they would head next.

They set sail for Thoothukudi on a balmy March morning. Kandavar did everything Idris asked him to, but said little. He ignored any overtures of peace that Idris made and kept to himself.

Seagulls raked the skies with their calls. It was a small fishing boat, and two of the men had cast their nets. Idris went to sit by Kandavar. The boy continued to look ahead. 'Why are you angry with me, inan?' Idris asked.

Kandavar didn't reply for a while. Then he said, 'I heard you tell my uncle that you were taking me away to broaden my horizon. So, don't I get to choose what that horizon should be?'

'Is there someplace else you had in mind?" Idris asked, surprised.

'No, but you should have asked me. I am not a servant like Sala Pokkar.'

'I apologize. Next time we will decide together,' Idris said softly. Then in a firm voice he added, 'Sala Pokkar is not a servant. He chose to come with us and I don't pay him any wages. So make sure that you don't treat him like one.'

Just then the men hauled in their nets, and fish the colour of gold and vermilion, fish that were flat and wide, thin and narrow, leapt within the snarls. Kandavar grinned. 'Aabo,' he cried, forgetting to be angry. 'Have you seen anything like this?'

'So, have your son and you made up your differences?' Sala Pokkar said, looking at the boy jumping this way and that in excitement.

Idris shrugged and smiled.

'Was he angry with you because you asked him to give back the chicks or because we left Galle?' Sala Pokkar murmured.

'I think it is because I didn't discuss with him the decision to leave Galle,' Idris said.

'You are his father. Why would you discuss it with him?' Sala Pokkar's voice rose in surprise.

'I told you that we lived separately for many years. He is yet to discover what it is to have a father.' Idris opened his hands in a mute gesture of helplessness.

The waves rose and fell with a steady rhythm that made the passage easier than the previous one. After two days at sea, when they landed at Thoothukudi, it seemed little more than a big village without walls, ditches or gates. Sala Pokkar looked around him in dismay. 'There is nothing here,' he said, making a face and thinking of the stately city built of stone they had left behind, with its houses, large gardens and markets.

Idris had thought the same. Thoothukudi was flat and arid, and seemed an ugly prospect for anyone coming in from Galle. He tried to lift their sunken spirits by promising a quick exit. 'In the next few days, they will open the pearl fisheries and everything will change.'

Once Sala Pokkar had adjusted himself to the thought that they were not going to be here for long, he set out to find them proper lodgings. The rooms by the marketplace were filthy and noisy.

He found them a house to rent among several houses built of stone, overlooking the sea to the south of Thoothukudi, on the way to Punnaikayal. Sala Pokkar had insisted, though Idris had hesitated at the thought. Walls and homes were not part of his psyche. 'I am a traveller,' Idris murmured. 'This feels too much like putting down roots. And I can't be rooted, Sala Pokkar... you have to understand that.'

'What are you? A bean plant, to put down roots in a month? Ikka, I love the sea, but once in a while I need to feel the earth, hard and unyielding beneath me, so I can love the shifting sea even more,' Sala Pokkar said.

Idris had liked the poetry of Sala Pokkar's words rather than the veracity of his argument.

The beach stretched on either side for miles. There was hardly a soul anywhere as they walked to their new home. Two porters and a donkey followed, bearing the things they needed in their new home.

Kandavar stood by the door and watched the waves. 'We will hear the sea all day and night,' he said, suddenly happy at the prospect of the sea at walking distance. He loved the ocean, it was ships he hated.

That evening, Idris gazed at the skies, seeking a familiar star, a sign to tell him his decision to come to Thoothukudi hadn't been unwise. It was a clear sky and the stars were out in plenty. He could see Hadar, one of the brightest stars in the sky, and so he could trace the constellation of the Centaur. But his eye was still familiarizing itself with this new horizon. Then he saw them, old friends who reassured him that nothing had changed. Al-Zahra in the west, as always a lamp in the sky, and an almost equally brilliant Al-Mushtarie in the east. He felt less afraid of what the future may hold and threw back his head to take in the expanse of the night skies. Overhead, like a slumbering portent of evil, blazed the red Al-Mareekh. His heart beat faster. What was he to make of this strange combination of heavenly bodies? What were they telling him? What should he watch out for?

'I don't know about pearl fishing, but they make very good quicklime here apparently,' Sala Pokkar said a day later. He had gone out to buy provisions and had returned with as much food as gossip, and a fine coating of white dust.

He hadn't meant to go there, he explained, but he had found himself near the kilns. He had stood watching as women brought several baskets of shells and coral while two men stacked the fire openings of the kiln with firewood that was almost two-and-a-half handspans long. The shells were emptied into the vertical shaft of the kiln and the fire started using up the coconut husk and leaves.

'The fire will burn for two days and then it has to cool,' Sala Pokkar explained.

'So how did you get covered in lime?' Kandavar asked, drawing circles with the tip of his finger on Sala Pokkar's arm.

'I went closer for a better look.' Sala Pokkar grinned sheepishly.

Later, Idris set out to see the kilns for himself. One of them was being opened at the base to take out the cooked shells. Two men used shovels to draw them out and then water was sprinkled by two women on the pile of quicklime. The men mixed the water into the lime with wood paddles. Next, it was the women's turn to winnow the lime to remove any lumps before it was set aside. The sight of the men and women covered in a fine white dust, and their mechanical movements as they went about their job, filled Idris with a sense of dread. One of the men bent double as a coughing fit overtook him. 'It's the lime,' he explained to Idris when the spasm was over. 'It will kill us eventually. Look at us. All of us have a nagging cough, bloodshot eyes and sores on our hands and legs from the constant exposure to the lime.'

'If we don't have the lime to sell, hunger will kill us,' another man said. 'So shut up and get to work!'

What must it be to be stuck in a life where every day was like every other day, knowing you were condemned to never escape it? They would have to get away from here as quickly as possible, Idris told himself. If only the pearl fishing would begin.

XXV

One evening not long after Idris took a boat to one of the larger islands off Thoothukudi. It was a desolate place with nothing but shrubs, some tall buildings and the sound of waves. Idris stood there for a while, watching the sea as it rose and fell tirelessly. As he walked back to the boat, he saw a man, who, it was evident from his clothes, was not a native. He saw the man size him up as well. Then the man bowed and murmured, 'Salaam walaikum…'

Idris returned the greeting and walked on.

'May I join you in your boat back to the mainland?' the man called out. 'Mine will take a couple of more hours to arrive.'

During the course of the boat ride, Idris discovered the man was called Muzaffar, he was from Malacca and an assistant at the Dutch factory. The tall buildings were the Dutch storehouses. 'Come by to the factory one day. I have a house alongside,' Muzaffar said as they neared land.

'How do I find the factory?' Idris asked, thinking he had spotted no building big enough to be a Dutch establishment.

'It is the church near the sea.'

'A church?' Idris said, unable to hide his shock.

'It's like this,' Muzaffar explained to Idris, who couldn't still understand how the Dutch could desecrate a place of worship, especially one that was of their own god. 'After the Dutch ousted the Portuguese in 1658, they sought permission to build a fort, but the Naik of this region wouldn't allow it. So they looked around and saw three capacious churches. They were Roman Catholic churches and the Dutch do not accept the power of Rome, so they converted one into their factory. It's still early days for the Dutch in the region, they will learn from their mistakes soon enough.' Muzaffar's face was grim as he spoke.

Two days later, it was with relief that Idris heard from him that a trial would be held at the pearl fishery.

They were seated in Muzaffar's house by the converted church. 'Don't get your hopes up too much,' Muzaffar cautioned. 'Sometimes sand just swamps the paar – that's what they call the oyster beds; sometimes the oysters don't reach their full maturity. Then they decide not to allow pearl fishing.'

Eleven boats set course for the paar, which was about a mile from the shore. Twenty-two paravars, the name by which the pearl fishers were called, dived into the water at the paar. Everyone gathered at the shore held their breath. The previous year had been a hard one. The rains had failed and a great drought had caused paddy fields to shrivel and die. Cows, oxen and buffaloes foraged the countryside, seeking a tiny shred of green. Their bones stuck out with every passing day. Rice had become so expensive that the poor could no longer afford it. The bellies of their children grew larger while their limbs resembled bony twigs. They sold what they could for rice and then they gave up and waited for death to relieve them of this dreadful hunger that didn't spare anyone. Everywhere one turned, there were clamouring mouths and needy hands. For the people of Thoothukudi, the pearls promised a respite.

Seven, eight, nine, ten fathoms deep… how far did the divers go? Idris waited for the surface to break and the divers to emerge. Suddenly three glistening heads surfaced, a big grin splicing each face, heads holding aloft a few oysters. The three divers swam towards the boat and dived into the water again.

'I wonder if the oysters are edible,' Sala Pokkar said.

Kandavar turned to him in horror. 'Eat that! It would be like eating a snail. Do you know who eats snails back home?'

'Sssh,' Idris said. 'The two of you are like seagulls fighting over a fish that the cat walks away with eventually. All noise and no gain!'

A thousand oysters had to be brought ashore before the headman would decide and then there was one more hurdle. The thousand oysters had to contain at least one rupee worth of pearls or the fishing would be stayed for that year. Idris watched the headman and some elderly paravars prise apart the oysters in an earthenware plate. They used the dried spine of a coconut leaf to tease the flesh. One of the oysters eventually threw up a pearl. The headman held it between his thumb and finger and studied it carefully. Would he throw the pearl back into the waves? That meant there would be no pearl fishing that year. Or, would he take it to the temple on the bay and lay the pearl as an offering to the sea goddess? All the paravars had been converted to Christianity by the Portuguese but when it came to the ocean and pearls, no one was going to risk offending the sea goddess.

The drummers and pipers waited, as unsure as everyone else. If it was the temple, they would lead the way with fanfare and music. The shore had been saved for the season and it would be time to celebrate.

Holding the pearl in his cupped palms, the headman turned towards the bay. The first note was struck on the drum. The crowds cheered and an excited whispering began.

The rest of the oysters were opened and it was discovered that the pearls, despite the drought of the previous year, were plentiful. In fact, the thousand oysters had yielded two rupees worth of pearls. Smiles lit up faces at the thought of the plenty that would soon be theirs. It was then announced that three days hence, the season would officially commence.

By evening, the boats had begun to come in. It was four years since pearl fishing had been allowed and the news had spread rapidly. Families came in their boats and set up tents on the beach. Cooking fires were lit. Traders came in with wares and set up temporary shops. People, conversation and palpable excitement filled the shore that had till then been shrouded in a desolate silence.

On the first day of the season, they woke up to the sound of drumming and muskets being fired at dawn. The three of them had a hasty breakfast and rushed to the shore. It was the first pearl-fishing season after the Dutch had captured the territory.

'I hear the Dutch commissioner is coming from Colombo,' Muzaffar had said.

They could see two Dutch sloops in the water. A procession of drummers and pipe players led the way, followed by a few soldiers bearing muskets. Next came a palanquin bearing a white man looking most uncomfortable in his tight-fitting clothes. Behind them were several servants. A couple of dogs ran alongside, barking at the noise and the strangers while a servant tried to shoo them away. Kandavar giggled at the absurdity of the scene and Idris murmured, 'Sssh... that must be the Dutch commissioner trying to make an impression! We can't be seen laughing at him.'

The procession halted and the man stepped out of the palanquin. His face was red from the heat. He mopped it with a white cloth. A Dutch flag was hoisted on a bamboo pole sunk into the sand. He spoke a few words which made no sense to anyone there. Then the interpreter stepped forward and translated: The company is happy that this year it will be possible to fish for pearls.

'Why should the company be happy?' Sala Pokkar asked. Idris glared at him.

The interpreter proceeded to explain the terms: Every toni and catamaran, boat and raft would have to be registered and a toll would be levied. All commodities, be it food or clothing, would be taxed on arrival into the camp.

The first day's takings were to be kept aside for the Naik.

It didn't matter what the religion of the boatman, the capanotti is, but taxes will be levied on the basis of diving stones. The Christians would pay the least, the Hindus a little more and the Muslims would pay the most. The Dutch would in turn offer them protection.

He stepped back. Then the soldiers stepped forward in a line and fired their muskets and the white man waved a piece of red cloth. Out at sea, the Dutch sloops led the way to the right and left, marking the territory of the fishery. Next, all the boats followed and when they were within the pearl-fishing zone, half the number of divers in each toni leapt into the water. Pearl fishing had begun.

Every morning, the boats set out to the paar before sunrise. Only the poor and desperate took their pearls to sell every day. Everyone else who could wait let the oysters keep till the end of the season, by which time the oysters would rot and open on their own. The pearls here were not as white or bright as the ones found at Ormus on the Persian coast. Besides, buying the pearls in the open market wouldn't fetch Idris the profit he was hoping to make. He thought of what Muzaffar had suggested. That he hire a few boats and paravars for himself. It was a gamble, he knew, but all trade was a game of chances and all he could hope for was that inexplicable streak of luck that came to those who propitiated chance.

Idris didn't think he could afford a toni. Instead, he looked for the cheapest option and found rafts that were little more than five or six bamboos held together and each would hold just two divers apart from the two who paddled the catamaran into the seas. So on the third day of the season Idris decided to go on the raft and Kandavar had demanded to go as well.

'I suppose I should stay back on the shore, to see you get a decent burial if you died at sea,' Sala Pokkar said.

'If we die at sea, the fish will eat us. There will be no bodies left to bury,' Kandavar tossed over his shoulder as he stripped down to his loincloth and clambered onto the catamaran that was bobbing on the waves.

Sala Pokkar crossed his arms and said, 'Has it occurred to either of you that I may be a good diver?'

'Are you?' Idris asked, surprised.

'You forget I am a khalasi. We don't just know how to lift weights. We also launch gigantic urus into the sea. A uru is sometimes twice as big as the ship we boarded at Beypore. And we do the repairs when required. I wouldn't be a good khalasi if I couldn't dive,' Sala Pokkar said, wading into the waves. 'I am coming too.'

Idris hesitated at the thought of taking his clothes off. In the end, he removed his tunic and trousers. He wore breeches beneath his trousers, and those he kept on. The paravars looked at him as he cut through the waves. Some of them had heard the missionaries preach. First, the Jesuits who had landed at Mannapad and then the Dutch missionaries. They had heard of the man, Moses, who walked through the sea. Idris could have been that man, they thought, only if he wasn't this black. According to the white men, Jesus and all his brethren were white men too.

'How far do you have to go?' Sala Pokkar called out.

Idris thought a while and said, 'From where you are, look at the horizon. We have to go five to six times that distance into the sea. We won't find anything much if we stay close to the shore.'

The boatsmen were strong paddlers and a good land wind blew steadily, helping the catamarans reach the oyster banks. When they got to the paar, the divers began preparing themselves. Idris watched as a rope was tied under their arms in a simple but tight knot and one end was left on the catamaran. Next, a rock as big as a man's head, with a hole in the middle, through which a knotted rope was passed, was fastened to the big toe of the diver and the end of that rope, too, was left on the boat. This was the diving stone the interpreter had referred to, he realized. Finally, a net shaped like a sack but with its mouth open by means of a hoop was given to the diver and its end left with the boatsmen, who now held all three ropes.

The divers leapt into the waves. 'The weight of the stone will take the diver to the bottom quickly,' one of the boatsmen said.

One of the ropes grew slack. 'He is at the oyster bed,' the boatsmen said, pulling at the rope until the stone emerged. 'He will use his big toe to nudge the oysters off the floor and as they rise, scoop them into his net.'

The first rope twitched. The diver was beginning to run out of breath. Idris saw the boatsmen pull at the ropes until the diver and his haul of oysters were hoisted up.

The diver sat in the catamaran, gasping while the oysters were emptied out. A few minutes later, he was ready to return again.

Kandavar wondered about the ocean bed. What would it be like? He gazed at Idris, then looked around him and quietly nudged a rope around his ankle, knotting it tightly before leaping into the water. The divers had made it look so easy, but as the ocean swallowed him, he felt the salt sting his eyes and soon his chest was ready to explode.

Idris stared at the empty space where Kandavar had been. Unbidden he thought of the red Al-Mareekh that blazed overhead every night. Of the camel trainer Ali, all those years ago, cautioning his father about it being an evil omen. Of the shaitan wind that had annihilated the caravan and robbed him of his eye. And now it seemed it would swallow his son whole. 'Sala Pokkar,' he shouted in panic. 'Sala Pokkar, Kandavar is gone. He…' He gestured towards the water, unable to speak even as he grabbed a rope and knotted it around his middle. 'I am going in after him.'

'I am coming too,' Sala Pokkar called back, grabbing a rope as well.

The ocean floor seemed a long way down and Idris swam around knowing he couldn't stay underwater very long. When he was almost out of breath, he tugged at the rope as he had been told to, and the boatsmen hauled him up. Sala Pokkar took a little longer to tug for help. But in those few extra moments, he had managed to reach the bottom and find Kandavar, who had slammed his head against a rock while trying to prise an oyster off the bed.

Idris felt his mouth go dry and his hands turn clammy as they helped Sala Pokkar hoist the bleeding, unconscious boy onto the boat. 'Inan, inan, Kandavar,' he called, shaking the boy's shoulder while Sala Pokkar crouched beside them, gulping in lungfuls of air loudly.

'Don't worry,' one of the boatsmen said as he saw Kandavar stir. 'He will be fine. He is a brave boy to want to see the ocean bed and without a diving stone.'

'He could be a very dead boy,' Sala Pokkar said, shaking his head, when he had recovered his breath. 'What was the idiot thinking of?'

'I owe you a debt for as long as I live,' Idris said, taking Sala Pokkar's hands in his. 'His foolishness could have cost you your life.'

Kandavar sat up slowly. He opened his palm and held out an oyster triumphantly. 'I found one; Aabo, I found one,' he cried in glee, oblivious to the bleeding gash on his forehead or the perturbed look on the men's faces.

Idris bit on his lip to stem the words of reproof that threatened to tumble out, called in his last shred of patience, smiled and reached across to pat his son's arm. 'I knew you would do it!' he said.

For the first time, Idris sensed the difference in the blood that coursed through them. A trader knew when to cut his losses and leave. A warrior persisted, seeking triumph to the last breath. He may have taken the boy out of the kalari, but the warrior blood in him would show itself again and again.

'I hope my oyster has a pearl,' Kandavar said, examining it.

'Hmm… we will soon know,' Idris said, determined to slip a pearl into the flesh if there wasn't one already in it. He couldn't bear to see disappointment in the boy's eyes. For the next few hours, there was nothing for them to do but wait as the divers continued to leap into the waves. When the wind picked up a little after noon, they headed back to shore.

Every evening, when the boats returned, Idris would be at the shore. The wives of the boatsmen and divers were employed to shuck the oysters. At the end of the fifth day, Idris looked at his harvest from the sea and bit his lip. The pearls found here were seldom used to make jewellery. The pearl dust was what fetched money. Pearl dust the foreigners sold in their lands to apothecaries. So, once he had paid the expenses for hiring three boats and six divers, the boatsmen and their wives and the obligatory toll the Dutch levied for protection, he hadn't made any profit. Idris walked back home, deep in thought. An overwhelming stench of rotting fish and something else – the decrepitude of hope as debts mounted – filled the air. Seagulls circled overhead constantly and crows strutted about, trying to grab an oyster to peck open.

'We may have to move on,' he declared that night.

'Are we rich then?' Kandavar's eyes gleamed at the heap of pearls Idris held in his hand.

'Scarcely,' Idris said, looking at the takings of the day. 'These pearls will be weighed not in chegos but by the ounce for pearl dust.

'What if we find more pearls like mine?' Kandavar asked, holding up his pearl, which was for his sister, he had said.

'You were just fortunate,' Idris said, hiding his smile.

That night the currents changed direction, something shifted on the ocean bed, sand swirled and settled. By dawn the oyster beds were completely covered by layers of sand. The paravars rose from the sea with pinched faces and empty nets. It was as if the paar had never existed. The season hadn't lasted even a week.

A silence fell on the shore. The flag came down. Someone said it was the curse of the Virgin Mary on the Dutch for desecrating her church, and the paravars for not resisting it. The boats began to leave. Muzaffar was asked to remove all accounts of the season from the ledgers and place them under another head. The Dutch commissioner saw the premature end of the season as a personal failure. A streak of ill luck that was best erased from memory.

PART 4

April–August AD 1660

(Sha'baan AH 1070–Thu Al-Hijjah AH 1070)

XXVI

It was a long, low island. The waves broke on its outer shore while between the inner shore and the mainland lay a gentle lagoon. Into this sheltered lagoon called Paliacatta Lake they sailed on a hot day towards the end of April. It had been a slow journey up the coast with several stops. Negapatnam, Caracal, Trangebar, until the vessel sailed into Paliacatta. The smell of salt and fish rushed up their nostrils. Sala Pokkar took a deep breath and smiled. It was a smell that had somehow eluded them at their other ports of call. The Dutch had obtained a settlement here in 1609 and the assistant at Thoothukudi had suggested Paliacatta to Idris. 'For the Dutch are traders at heart and will find a scheme of some sort to utilize you for.'

In Paliacatta, the Dutch took to him with the same ease as they had in Galle. They enjoyed the sight of the tall black man with a gold eye striding through the streets of Paliacatta with his son while his stocky cedar-coloured attendant hung on his heels. They opened doors and secrets, giving him their time and an opportunity to profit.

Precious stones. Textiles. Trading opportunities abounded in Paliacatta. And there was a new commodity: slaves. The drought had resulted in widespread famine. The poor, who were already in debt, had nothing left to sell but their homes. And themselves. An agent came to meet Idris with a proposal.

He would offer Idris a Tamizh slave for two guilders of Dutch money. Idris, he said, could in turn sell the slave for four guilders, to the Dutch who would pack the human cargo off to the East Indies. Two guilders of profit for nothing but knowing whom to talk to; the stroke of kismet on his forehead that allowed him to be at the right place at the right time. But Idris drew a line at slaves. There were other commodities to trade in, he told himself, even though the prospect of easy riches was tempting. Especially as he had to recoup the losses incurred at Thoothukudi.

They had rented a small house in the village to the south called Diramamy.

Sala Pokkar had found them the upper rooms of a Muslim merchant's home. It overlooked the sea and a strong breeze blew in every afternoon, dispelling the heat and humidity. At night, darkness enveloped the waves and Idris would often sit on the verandah, staring into the horizon, without speaking a word for hours.

When the holy month of Ramadan began, Idris and Sala Pokkar fasted and prayed and the house came in useful then, allowing them to wait within while the summer heat raged outside. Kandavar was unable to understand the need for such a rigorous fast. 'You mean you can't even swallow your own spit?' His eyes widened at the thought.

'It's just for a few days, inan. It's good to be able to put the body and mind through such a cleansing,' Idris spoke softly.

'Why can't I do it then?' Kandavar demanded.

'Because you are a child and children do not have to take on adult responsibilities,' Idris said in a firm voice. 'But there is something you can do. During this time, I would like to teach you the Arabic script. Someday, if you and I need to communicate in a language your brethren don't understand, we shall have one.'

'I still don't get it.' Sala Pokkar scratched his head in bemusement. They had been in Paliacatta for almost six weeks now. 'The Dutch are not known to be like this. They are ruthless and cruel. They are hard traders. That's what the wharf gossip is, but you… they seem to like you, Ikka.'

'Everybody likes a man who belongs nowhere. He is a transient. He will never be a threat to them or their beliefs.' Idris smiled, opening his pouch of hashish.

Sala Pokkar sighed and leaned back against the wall.

Idris rubbed the hashish on his palm and pinched it into tiny bits. He mixed it with tobacco, then took out his tiny smoking pipe. Sala Pokkar watched him stuff the bowl of the pipe. Then Idris lit the oil lamp. He held a reed to the flame and used it to light the pipe. Sala Pokkar wondered what it must feel like to draw deeply of the black stuff Ikka liked to smoke every now and then, inhaling the smoke deeply and holding it in the bowl of his mouth. What did that swirl of smoke do when it filled his insides? What was the black stuff?

'What is this?' he had asked, the first time he saw Idris draw out hashish from his pouch.

'Hashish,' Idris had murmured.

Sala Pokkar had gasped in shock. He had heard of what it could do to smokers. Turning them into beings with dead souls or manic creatures or blabbering idiots.

Idris had touched Sala Pokkar's arm. 'I have a rule I made for myself. I don't let anything take control of me. Be it emotions or people or hashish… so don't let your mind go where it just went.'

'Are we going to stay here for some more time? We would need to tell the merchant, if so,' Sala Pokkar said. Idris, he had discovered, was more amenable to normal behaviour when the hashish rode in his blood.

'No,' Idris said. 'We will leave when the month is up. That was our original plan. We'll stick to it.'

'Where to, Ikka?' Sala Pokkar asked.

'When I left Kozhikode, I had wanted to see the kingdom of Odisha. So perhaps there,' Idris said, averting his eyes from the group of men and women huddled in the grounds of the merchant's home, waiting to be taken aboard the next ship to the East Indies.

'But how?'

'The Dutch have a ship, *Hercules*, that they built five years ago. It's a trading ship and it's heading that way.'

'But why would they offer us passage?' Sala Pokkar scratched his head. 'They don't like us. They think we are little better than animals.'

Idris nodded. 'But to them I am a giraffe and you a zebra. We are not animals they see every day.

'It's a big ship and apart from cargo, it's used to transport soldiers from Colombo and Negombo in Ceylon to Thoothukudi. But they have a problem on their hands: the large number of Portuguese prisoners. So they've decided to send them to Bengal,' Idris said grimly, lighting his pipe again and taking a deep drag. 'The ship will call at Paliacatta. It will be loaded with money minted here and precious cargo. A dangerous combination to have on any ship. So they will need someone who will listen to the whispers and keep them informed. They need me. Along with the Portuguese prisoners, money and valuable cargo, Sala Pokkar, you, Kandavar and I will sail on this ship.'

Idris took another deep drag of his pipe. As the hashish loosened the last knot in his being, he was struck by a thought. 'Where is the boy?' Idris asked curiously.

'He is playing with the boys in the street,' Sala Pokkar said. 'Showing off his leaps and kalari techniques.' Then, as if unable to help himself, Sala Pokkar asked, 'Was he in a kalari? He couldn't have just picked it up like that?'

Idris nodded. 'I found one that would have him.'

'And his Umma?'

'She has a new husband.'

'Oh...' Sala Pokkar's gaze dropped.

'It's allowed, you know.' Idris smiled at Sala Pokkar's discomfiture.

'Yes, I know talaq is allowed. But I don't have to like it.'

Idris nodded. He didn't like this bending of the truth either. Moulding it so that he wasn't really speaking a lie, and yet he knew he was.

When Sala Pokkar left the room, Idris pulled out his journal and began writing. His journal was once a friend; a place to unburden the random flutterings of a soul when it grew butterfly wings.

But in the past months, he had neglected the writing of his journal. Of what he thought and how he felt, he had maintained a silence. History had no place for a father's love for a son, or a man's yearning for a woman. History may be determined by these but in its recording, it dwelt on the effect and the making of the effect rather than nebulous reasons. So Idris, amateur historian, would only track his travels, not the pauses.

'What is it you write about?' Sala Pokkar asked curiously, walking back into the room and crouching alongside Idris.

Sala Pokkar had in the past few months learnt to write his name and form a few calligrams. But he wasn't interested in anything beyond that.

'Notes on our journey. The whys and hows.'

Sala Pokkar frowned. Why would Ikka waste his time writing about what had already taken place? He watched as Idris wiped his reed pen and put it away.

Idris rose from where he was seated. Sala Pokkar sighed and rose too. He didn't particularly want to step out now, but if Ikka was going out, he would as well. Not that Ikka expected it of him, but Sala Pokkar felt obliged to do so.

'No,' Idris said. 'Stay here. I would suggest that the two of you have your meal. Don't wait for me.'

Sala Pokkar stared. He opened his mouth to ask where Ikka was headed, then shut it abruptly. Idris had a strange look on his face that said: Don't ask me anything!

Idris slipped out into the street and walked briskly away from the line of houses, towards the harbour. Between the village and Fort Gelria, where almost two hundred soldiers were garrisoned, was a large, empty ground. Some evenings, Idris liked to take a walk in that direction. But that night, he headed towards the bancksael, the Dutch name for the customs house. Ahead of him, the mestizo peeled himself away from the walls of the customs house where he waited most evenings. The men who came to the customs house for goods clearance often stepped out with a need to celebrate. And Goncalo knew how to help them.

Idris looked at the man, who probably was the child of a Portuguese soldier and a native woman, and said softly, 'I am here.'

Goncalo nodded. 'The truth is, I didn't expect you.'

Idris shrugged. He had considered speaking Tamizh, but thought it prudent to not let anyone know he spoke the language. The Portuguese he spoke was adequate for him to get by. But it was beyond him to enter into a long, complex conversation. He understood the language better than he spoke it.

Goncalo didn't need words to fathom a man's mind. He could read shrugs and looks, a flick of the hand, a tic of the mouth. He could see when a man was hungry for a woman.

And this tall black moor was.

XXVII

Her name was Margarida. She was the daughter of a mestizo and an Armenian Muslim woman who had converted to Christianity. If her mother hadn't chosen to convert, she may have been a Muslim merchant's favourite third wife, if not his first. But the mother died and the father was stabbed to death and Margarida, age six years and eleven months, was left alone but for her Tamizh nanny, who took her to the village on the north side of the fort. A village of Christian fishermen where the woman still had a small hovel that was hers. For the next six years, the nanny did her best. The girl ate when there was food; starved when there was none. Goncalo, who brokered everything from slaves to cattle to rice to the Paliacatta cotton to girls, often called in on them to suggest that the nanny give the girl into his custody. 'You will never starve again,' he said.

Nanny, who had at first spat in his face, succumbed in the famine years. Nothing was important when hunger gnawed your insides as you slept. Nanny told herself that the girl and she wouldn't starve. Honour is for those who can afford it; the rest of us have to do what we can to eat.

She eyed her Margarida as if she were a fowl. 'But she is still young and scrawny. Who would want her?'

Goncalo chewed on his lip thoughtfully. 'How old is she?'

'Almost thirteen. Still a child... if you know what I mean,' Nanny muttered, tying a knot at the end of the cloth she wound around her. A knot for every sin she was committing, she told herself. So I can keep tabs on my pile of sins and keep a check on it.

'That doesn't matter. There are some who like children.

Demand them, in fact! The younger the better,' Goncalo said with a sheepish smile.

'No,' Nanny said. That was one knot she wouldn't allow.

So Goncalo had to wait till Margarida turned into a woman. He paid the old woman some money. 'Think of it as an advance against future payments,' he said. 'Feed her well. Men like a bit of meat on their women.'

With every morsel that Nanny fed the girl, her fingers twisted the end of her cloth. Would this feeding of Margarida be considered a sin? It felt a little like fattening an animal for slaughter. But what was the option? The girl was an outcaste and no one would have her. Neither the mestizos nor the Muslims. She would end up as a common whore. Goncalo would make sure that she wouldn't be merely an orifice to assuage a need. And Nanny would make sure that she put something away so that one day, Margarida and she could leave this cursed town and make a new life where no one would know them.

After her first period, Nanny showed Margarida how to drape the Paliacatta celai around herself till it covered her lower half three times, and to bring the rest of the cloth at her waist and above to cover her breasts. 'Now take the cloth over your shoulder and bring it across your back and tuck the end at the waist.'

When Goncalo had his first glimpse of the girl in a Paliacatta celai, his mouth watered at her luscious beauty. His fingers itched to caress the mother-of-pearl skin. But she was too valuable for the likes of him. Maybe after her maidenhead had been sold a few times over, he told himself. For now he would announce the arrival of Margarida, the virgin mestizo. 'A blouse would add to her charm,' he told Nanny.

'Only whores wear blouses,' Nanny mumbled.

'And she is one now,' Goncalo said quietly. 'Even if she does not go with the local heathens, it will do you good to remember she is one.'

Margarida was petrified the first few times. The men were large, white and drunk. They stared at her in her Paliacatta celai and the blouse that Goncalo insisted she wear.

And they raped her systematically, almost as if that was the only way they knew how to fornicate. Biting her lips and parting her legs with a ruthless hand, thrusting into her again and again till they flooded her with a grunt and a heave.

Margarida wept the first few times. The men seemed to like her confusion and tears and that she lay like a helpless turtle squirming on her back and left a few coins as a little extra for the virgin whore. Then Goncalo decided it was time to advance her career to the next level. He took her into his arms and made love to her with a gentleness that made her respond. 'Yes, my darling, that's the way,' he murmured against her ear. 'Men like a woman to respond; not lie there like a plane of wood with a hole in it. You, my darling, could be a great seductress if you allow yourself to be one.'

Idris looked at the young girl sitting on a mattress. How old was she, he wondered. He turned to Goncalo. 'You said she was a woman. But I see a child before me.'

Goncalo smirked. 'She is fifteen. Hardly a child!'

Idris looked around the hovel that held nothing beyond a mattress and a lantern. Despite the strong sea breeze that came in through the window, the room was warm and humid.

'Show him you are a woman,' Goncalo murmured in Tamizh. 'I need him to feel grateful to me. Show him some of the tricks I taught you... I want you to turn him into a blabbering slave at your feet, my darling, and you will have twice the usual amount.'

Margarida studied the tall black man. Her eyes lingered on his gold eye. What would he be like, she wondered, narrowing her eyes. How was she to pleasure him?

She stood up and went towards him. Goncalo left, snickering.

Idris felt removed from his body as she wrapped her arms around him.

'Come,' he said, gathering her in his arms. He carried her easily back to the mattress in the corner of the room and laid her down. Then he swiftly pulled his tunic over his head.

Her eyes widened at the sight of his body. He looked bony and thin, but beneath that sack-like garment, he was quite muscular and had no body hair. She felt a sudden desire to stroke his skin.

She knelt on the mattress and raised her arms, inviting him to take his fill.

Idris sank into the mattress and pulled her to him. She was tiny. 'What are you waiting for?' she asked, raining little kisses on his face.

He didn't speak. Instead, he cradled her face between his palms and kissed her deeply.

She tasted of palm sugar. He felt a wave of remembrance suffuse him. Kuttimalu's mouth had been a well of wild honey.

Margarida always knew when a man's attention began to wander. She knew that when men held her, they were in truth holding someone else. Her face was supplanted by another woman's. She knew how to bring them back to her.

She purred from the bottom of her throat and rubbed herself against him, catlike. He shuddered. His mind might play games of its own, but his body needed a woman. A living, breathing creature who would match his caresses with her own, and gather him into her folds and crevices as if she would never let him go.

Idris held her by her tiny waist and inched her down on him slowly. Her body received him with a largesse he hadn't thought possible and in that dimly lit room, her little cat face pouted in concentration, her long, brown hair dishevelled, the pupils in her grey-green eyes dilated, he felt as if he had found his oasis. For the moment. He smiled at her, her naked body gleaming with perspiration. She leaned over him, nudging her small breasts towards his lips. A drop of sweat rolled off her brow and into his mouth. He tasted salt.

Memories dislodged themselves from that hidden chamber he strove to keep locked. His first love. She had been his first woman too. How could it be that all he could remember of her was a cornucopia of tastes and smells and not her face, or her voice? He thought of the fragrance of oranges at the nape of her neck and how the sweat between her breasts had tasted. She must have been the same age as this girl Margarida. Only darker, tauter, and a little wild cat in bed who liked sitting atop him and raking his chest with her nails and biting on his shoulder, hissing loudly her pleasure until he could bear it no longer. He would tumble her onto her back and enter her, thrusting into her hard and swift till she purred under him. Then she died. And like his eye, he thought no more of it. For you do not celebrate death by ruminating over it.

Margarida licked his nipples and whispered, 'Stop thinking of whoever it is you are thinking. Am I not enough?'

This one was more difficult than all the others, she decided. He kept drifting away. Where did his mind wander to? Sometimes, if the men were not pleased, if they couldn't find the release they sought between her legs, they refused to pay. And then Goncalo would lose his temper. He had his ways of punishing her. Never on her face or her arms, but on the insides of her thighs, so every movement for a week afterwards was hell.

She moved her body, clamping her thighs together. His body moved in rhythm with hers. His eye became glassy. Curious this, she thought. His gold eye gleams less when he is aroused. But he still was not all there, she decided.

With a little grunt, she hoisted herself off him and crouched at his side. Idris watched her, wondering what was on her mind. She looked at him from the corner of her eye and with a knowing smile, she went to work on him with her fingers and mouth.

In Damascus, there had been a woman in whose home he had sought refuge. The widow of Madinat al-Yasmin, with a chin like a pebble, round, smooth and hard, and a rapacious mouth that never tired of seeking and pleasuring him. Little flicks of the tongue, a deep cavernous mouth. She had smelt of jasmine, like her city, and had known how to trail the tips of her pendulous breasts along the line of his body till he could hold himself back no longer. The widow had sent him away the day before she remarried. He was a sword maker. 'The Damascus blade can cut a hair falling across the blade. You really don't want to check out how true the blade's reputation is. Do you?' she had said, trying the girdle of her robe. 'So, my dear Idris, it is time for you to find another haven.' She showed not the tiniest flicker of regret or remorse.

Idris had felt wounded, but he couldn't help admire her. Women, he realized then, could seek and draw pleasure with a single-mindedness usually attributed to men. Women too could love and leave. And so this Margarida, this child whore too, would make love without knowing what love really meant. A curious sense of sadness threatened to swamp him. He sat up and pulled her into his lap so they were locked in an embrace, her arms clasped around his neck, her legs around his hips, her breast in his mouth, his manhood deep within her. He thrust into her, banishing thought and memory, till all he knew was the sensation of release and escape from who he was.

She lay curled on her side, her knees pulled towards her belly. She looked exhausted, he thought. How old was she, he wondered again.

He sat down by her side and peered down at her. 'You look so young. Do you know what you are doing?' he asked in Tamizh.

Her eyes widened. 'You speak our language?'

He nodded.

She flushed. He must have understood what Goncalo said.

'Why did you pretend you didn't?'

'I didn't.' Idris shrugged. 'Your Goncalo assumed I didn't. Does it matter?'

She shook her head.

He was the first Moor that Goncalo had brought her way. Otherwise it was all the durais – Dutch soldiers and sailors – or sometimes mestizos. But none of the locals were allowed to come to her. 'You are not just anybody. Look at yourself in the mirror. You could be one of the Durai women.'

A breeze raised itself from the sea and wafted into the room. A tendril of her hair lifted in the breeze. The lamplight threw shadows on the wall.

'What if I decide to take you away from here?' he said abruptly.

She smiled.

'I wouldn't go,' she said, without a trace of emotion in her voice. 'This is my home. This is where I belong.'

Idris stared at her. How easily she said it. Even this child had a sense of belonging. And he, who knew so much and had been friend to kings and poets, had broken bread with conquerors and pontiffs, didn't belong anywhere.

'Isn't there anything else you can do?' he asked.

She shrugged. 'It's not a bad life… mostly. And when my nanny has put away enough, we will leave this city and go to another place. That is the plan.'

Idris nodded. For her sake, he hoped Margarida would have a semblance of a life. For his sake, he hoped he would never see her again.

XXVIII

It wasn't the usual practice, but Idris was given a berth in a tiny cabin in the mid-ship section of the *Hercules*. The crew quarters and kitchen were located there, and it would be home until the vessel pulled in at Petapolee.

Kandavar stood silently as the men spoke. He had made some friends in Paliacatta. Sons of weavers and traders. At first he had held himself back, afraid of the caste rules. But Aabo had seen the longing in his eyes and understood. Child that he was, he had turned to Aabo to make it right. And Aabo had. 'None of the rules of home apply here,' he had said softly.

'Just make sure you don't give away who you really are. If anyone asks, you are my son.'

Kandavar had nodded and run out into the street, grinning from ear to ear.

But one morning, Aabo had called him to his side and said, 'You remember, don't you, that our time in Thoothukudi didn't work out for me as I had expected. I made some losses, but I was able to recover my capital here. We need to go further up this coast so I can make some profit.'

Kandavar had nodded. After Galle, Aabo had explained to him each time where they were headed and why. So they were here on a ship again. Where would it take them?

It was Sala Pokkar who sought an answer from Idris.

'Ikka, do we go with them as far as they go? Or do we get off midway?' he asked, his eyes taking in the cooking pots, the grinder and the storage jars.

'We will see,' Idris said, his eye following Sala Pokkar's darting gaze.

'That's a martaban,' he told Sala Pokkar, touching an earthenware pot. 'It came from Myanmar.

'This,' he said, caressing the side of another, a glossy, dark-brown, almost conical jar with a high neck and a flared, rolled lip at its mouth, 'came from Siam. See these four handles on the shoulder of the jar. That's what they use to cover the mouth of the jar with cloth and tie it down. Such ingenuity, Sala Pokkar... so much to learn of a race from the jars they make.'

Sala Pokkar squatted on his haunches, overwhelmed.

'What happened?' Idris asked.

'I had never sailed beyond Kollam and when we came to Galle, I thought I had become a world traveller. How silly of me. These pots have seen more of the world than I have. I feel so inadequate, Ikka. I feel less than the cockroach on this ship that probably has seen more than I ever will.'

The sounds of the ship being loaded filled the wharf. Idris looked at the downcast face of the young man with tenderness. He pulled him up onto his feet. 'There will be occasions for you to feel sorry for yourself. Don't waste that emotion on a few pots and a dozen scurrying cockroaches. Go now to the bow where I have offered them your service to help with the ship's maintenance.'

Sala Pokkar bit his lip. 'What will I need to do there?'

Idris shrugged. 'Coil the ropes. Oil the pulleys. Who knows? I have said that you were one of the Beypore khalasis and trust me, that helped us find passage on the *Hercules* as much as my skill with languages. So you'd better show them what you can do with a pulley and a rope.'

'I need more than a pulley and a rope.' Sala smiled. 'I need my davar, a simple wooden winch, I told you about it once before. And I need the long wooden handle we call kazha. Only when I have those can I be a khalasi.'

Idris frowned. 'Oh,' he said, nonplussed.

Sala Pokkar guffawed. 'It's good to see you look so perplexed,

Ikka. It's a rare sight and for once I know something you don't. That feels good, Ikka. Really good!'

'Get away, you scamp.' Idris smiled. 'I am going to meet the ship's surgeon and offer myself as his assistant if he will have me.'

'What about me, Aabo?' Kandavar asked. 'What shall I do?'

Idris sighed. 'For now, nothing. But once Sala Pokkar and I have been assigned our places in the vessel, you can be with one of us.'

'But I can't not do anything.' Kandavar eyed the mast thoughtfully. Would he be allowed to climb it?

Idris wondered how he was going to contain the boy on the ship. He would be bored soon enough.

'Look at me,' Idris said firmly. 'See that coil of rope. Sit on that and focus on the horizon till you get used to the ship's rolling motion.'

'I am used to all that by now,' Kandavar said, his eye still on the mast.

'In which case, think of it as a lesson. Sometimes a warrior has to train himself to not move. That is the secret of being a good warrior. To gauge when to be still and when to pounce!'

The boy frowned. How could he sit on a coil of rope and stare at the horizon? Then he remembered the Gurukkal saying the same. The kalari master had insisted the boys learn how to sit still. Watch the animals. The rat, the snake, the cat, even the dog... all those who have to fend for themselves know the value of keeping still.

And so, on a balmy June day, when the skies and the sea were a brilliant blue, the 140-foot-long, three-masted *Hercules* set sail. Idris stood on the deck, watching the shore retreat. White-edged waves splashed against the sides of the 540-tonner merchant ship with her crew of fifty-nine, a hold full of prisoners and cargo. Idris, Kandavar and Sala Pokkar were paying passengers. But that didn't allow them any special privileges, he knew.

He felt Kandavar draw closer to him. The boy's warmth seeped into him. Would his life have been different if he had become a father earlier? Something changed when you became a parent. You thought of yourself in terms of your child. Something held you back from being who you wanted to be. This was why he had chosen to flee at first. He had to get away or he would suffocate, he had thought. But leaving was one thing and forgetting another. Every now and then, he had thought of his son. What was he doing? How was he coping? And so he had chosen to go back.

A seagull screamed and rose in the air. Idris's eye followed it as it circled the waters. A few fishing boats were out. A toni led the way for the *Hercules* into the open seas. He felt again that sloop of fear. He had never travelled the eastern seas.

That evening, after sunset, the sky was resplendent. The summer milky way was just about rising. Al-Zahra, Al-Mushtarie and Al-Mareekh were visible in a line. Kandavar pointed to the opposite side of the sky.

'What is that star, Aabo?

It was Zohaal.

'So what does it represent, Ikka?' Sala Pokkar asked, peering into the sky.

Idris leaned forward. 'Look carefully,' he said. 'The planet Zohaal has rings around it. It is said that when you dream of the Zohaal, you are destined to meet a person who lives in the wilderness and frolics with the deer and peacock, parrots, or any beautiful-looking animal.' He didn't dare tell him that it could also mean punishment, poverty, business losses or adversities.

Idris stared at the skies, trying to read meanings and portents in the heavenly bodies. Soon the waxing crescent moon rose and Idris felt his fear quell. The moon was noor, the divine light of Allah, and it seemed to him that Allah the most benevolent had glimpsed the turmoil in his heart and sent him a sign to say all would be well.

He saw the ship's captain and the surgeon stroll towards the bow. The captain had a telescope. He had heard of these miraculous instruments that allowed you to read the stars as if they were at arms' reach. He didn't understand these Europeans. Their minds worked in a way that he still hadn't been able to grasp. Have they ever, he wondered, lain under a starlit sky and sought to ask what lay beyond? That the stars existed to more than navigate unknown seas. They had such vast reserves of knowledge, but it seemed their souls were still not developed. Greed and the need to own; power and possessions – that's what drove them.

The ship's surgeon didn't need an assistant. But he needed a scapegoat, should his chest of contraband be discovered; and if he managed to make the voyage undetected, he needed a henchman who would trade his goods to the natives and bring him back the earnings. The tall, black man who stood before him, his real eye as unwavering and fixed in its gaze as his gold eye, seemed ideal. The Opperkoopman at Paliacatta had said as much. 'He is not one of them.' The senior merchant had waved his arm to indicate the house servants, the dark-skinned, wiry Indians. 'And he is not one of us either. He owes no one any loyalties. He will be a good man to have on your side.'

The ship's surgeon had peered into his snifter of brandy. The Opperkoopman lived in a house in Paliacatta that was built in the Dutch style with its distinctive, steeply sloping roof and curving eaves. Three rows of trees protected the house from the sounds of the street.

It was pleasant sitting out at night in the side porch. The constant boom of the waves seemed far away and the ship's surgeon could almost believe he was back home in Delft. They had dined on roast duck instead of goose, with turmeric root.

The duck had been stringy and tough but the ship's surgeon and the senior merchant had chewed resolutely. Somewhere in its fibre was a taste of home, as there would be in the brood pap, though the cook seemed to have added a touch of cardamom to the bread pudding.

Idris waited for the ship's surgeon to make up his mind. The frown lifted off the surgeon's brow and he nodded. 'The Opperkoopman seemed to think very highly of you, but have you done this kind of work before?' he said.

'I haven't.' Idris spoke in Portuguese as the ship's surgeon had. Soon, Idris decided, he would master the Dutch language too. The ship's surgeon was from a land far away called Delft, the Opperkoopman had said. 'Keep an eye on him for me,' he had told Idris. 'He is wilier than a pirate, but he has his uses. Ask to be his assistant and you will be able to snoop around without him getting suspicious.'

Idris cleared his throat and formed the sentence in his head. The problem with speaking as many languages as he did was that at times he found a Somali word popping up where he needed a Yemeni one. Or a Malayalam word instead of the Portuguese. 'I haven't,' he said again. 'But I am willing to learn.'

The ship's surgeon appraised him thoughtfully. 'And you are big enough to hold them down if I need to cauterize a boil. Or amputate a limb. The screaming is just as loud for the one as the other and they struggle just as hard.'

Idris's face was passive. Neither horror nor shock twisted his features. The ship's surgeon grunted in satisfaction.

'You can start by acquainting yourself with my instruments,' he said, opening a wooden chest laid out with what looked like a hundred surgical instruments, apart from the pestles and mortars, basins, needles, thread, cups and strainers. 'One day soon we'll need to get to work and I want you to make sure every scalpel and blade is shiny clean and sharp. They are to be used on living people and I may not be the world's nicest man, but I am not a butcher!'

The hours rolled into days and the days rolled into one another as the waves did. Ceaselessly, it seemed to Idris.

If light determined the transition from day to night, it was food alone that seemed to suggest that the day had hours and the week days. In the morning, there was bread and a porridge made of grouts, sometimes wheat, sometimes barley and, once a week, oats. For lunch there would be fish with peas or beans on Monday, Tuesday, Wednesday. Thursday and Saturday there would be a pound of beef for Idris and Sala Pokkar while the others had pork. On Sunday their ration was lamb's meat and beans while the rest of the ship had ham.

Kandavar disliked the food. He learned to eat meat, but fish was still hard work. With meat, he could chew and chew till it tasted of nothing, but fish smelt. Aabo insisted that he eat what was provided. 'You will need to preserve your strength. I will find a way soon but until then, imagine this to be your favourite dish and swallow it.'

Kandavar didn't know what he was going to do. How was he going to survive this voyage if he couldn't eat? On the Arab ship to Galle, the food had been cooked by Sala Pokkar, who knew how to cook the food he was used to eating at home. Aabo and Sala Pokkar had eaten their meat and fish, but he had resisted eating it till they reached Galle, where Sala Pokkar had dared him to try lamb and Kandavar had. Thankfully, he had got past his initial horror of eating meat, he told himself as he toyed with his food, or he would have starved on this ship.

He thought longingly of home. Of how Amma piled his kinnam with steaming rice and drizzled ghee over it, and then added a ladleful of parippu. The lentils and turmeric blending with ghee and rice and salt. His mouth watered. And his eyes, at the thought that home was a memory now.

Idris knew that the Dutch ship provided far superior victuals than the others. Apart from the three meals, there were dried apples and prunes and a supply of butter. But Kandavar worried him. The boy hardly ate anything.

At the end of the week, he realized something had to be done. Sala Pokkar and he and the few Tamizh men on board created a kitchen of their own. The rations were the same but Sala Pokkar added spice to their food. And Kandavar ate this food with a relish that made him smile.

More than anyone realized, Idris needed the comfort of food to propel him into the next day. On a full stomach, he could pace the deck till dawn broke.

'You have trouble sleeping,' the ship's surgeon said to him one day.

Idris shrugged.

'I could give you something to help you sleep. You need to sleep. The human body needs it to regenerate itself.' The ship's surgeon frowned at the strange black man who seemed to need nothing. That was dangerous in any creature. Such self-sufficiency turned a man into someone who couldn't be tempted or bought, corrupted or convinced. All he needed was himself.

Idris smiled. 'I will ask you if I need help.'

Sala Pokkar looked up from a bundle of rope he was coiling into neat rolls. 'What did he want?' he asked.

Idris shrugged. 'He was concerned that I wasn't sleeping.'

'It's not just him; I am too. What do you do all night, Ikka? How long can you gaze at the sky?'

Idris smiled. 'Trust me. Once you know the sky, you cannot stop looking. It holds all the secrets.'

'What secrets? I don't understand,' the young man said.

Idris smiled at the bewilderment in Sala Pokkar's eyes. 'What do you think of before you go to sleep?'

Sala Pokkar smiled. 'I think of my Umma and my brothers and sisters. I see Umma counting the eggs and my baby sister holding a fluffy chick. I think of going home laden with gifts. I think of how their faces will light up with a smile that won't ever go away.'

Idris squatted beside the boy. 'So, you go on a journey. That's what mine does too. My mind goes on its own travels every night.'

A little kitten came mewing up to the deck.

'Where did this come from?' Idris said, lifting the kitten by the scruff of its neck and peering at it.

Sala Pokkar looked at Idris anxiously. 'One of the cats had a litter and he attached himself to Kandavar.'

'And you!' Idris added with a laugh. 'Does he have a name?'

Sala Pokkar shook his head. 'Not yet.'

'Musa... you can call him that! That was the name of the Prophet's cat.'

Sala Pokkar took the kitten from Idris and nuzzled it. 'You don't mind?'

'Why should I? Whoever is kind to the creatures of god is kind to himself! That's what the Prophet said, my boy. Besides, I love all animals. I even had a dog.'

'But Ikka, isn't that haraam?'

Idris smiled. 'That is an interpretation. Do you know the story of the people of the cave? A dog went with some believers who were forced by their people to worship others besides Allah, and they took refuge in a cave. The cave was filled with a strange air that put them to sleep for a long time. Meanwhile, the dog kept watch at the entrance the entire time. Three hundred plus nine years, to quote the Quran! So, you see, the dog is a symbol of loyalty.'

Idris rose and walked to the edge of the deck. The sea stretched into the horizon, a blue-grey sheet of nothingness. In the days to come, Kandavar and Sala Pokkar would get extraordinarily attached to the kitten. He had seen it happen. And then there would be trouble. He had witnessed that as well.

Idris took a deep breath. Just then a shoal of silvery fish leapt above the waves. A gleam of silver. Love was like that. A leaping of the heart, above the mundane and banal. But oh, so fleeting!

XXIX

The wind rose in the afternoon. A crosswind that tossed the ship with such violence that even the seasoned seamen began to feel queasy. The pilot of the ship had long, worried discussions with the captain. They didn't want to be blown off course. Thunder clapped overhead and lightning ripped the sky. Kandavar felt a strange exhilaration shoot through him as he stood on the deck, watching the pyrotechnics. Soon it began to rain. Sheets of rain that made it impossible to determine where they were.

'I have never seen such a storm,' Kandavar called out in excitement, above the noise of the storm, to Idris.

'Neither have I,' Idris shouted back, looking worriedly at the fury of the storm. The Dutch looked after their ships very well. During the hot months, they made sure that water was thrown on the exposed parts of the ship morning and evening; to not do so would result in the timbers opening and taking in water when laden. They kept their pumps well oiled to crank if the ship filled with water during a storm. But this wasn't just any storm. It seemed like the apocalypse from the Sura Al-Qamar: *Then we opened the gates of the heaven with rain pouring down. And caused the earth to burst with springs, and the waters met for a matter already predestined. Indeed, we sent upon them a screaming wind on a day of continuous misfortune, extracting the people as if they were trunks of palm trees uprooted.*

'What are you saying, Aabo?' Kandavar asked, seeing Idris's lips move.

'Nothing,' he replied, shaking his head.

Sala Pokkar slid across the deck towards Idris, his face troubled. 'Ikka,' he called, 'we are doomed. We will all die at sea in this wretched storm.'

Idris held his arm. 'Calm down,' he said. 'We will survive the storm.'

'No, we won't.' Sala Pokkar's voice was shrill with fright. 'The pumps are not able to throw out the water with the speed with which it is filling up and the ship is loaded to maximum capacity. We will sink!'

Just then a thunderbolt struck the ship, almost setting the foremast on fire. But the rain doused it out. 'Take Kandavar away from here before another thunderbolt strikes,' Idris said, and rushed towards the captain's cabin.

'Later, later,' the man shooed Idris away.

'You have to listen to me,' Idris said, his voice thundering above the storm. 'We have to bale the water out before the lower deck is flooded.'

'Do you think I don't know that?' The captain frowned. 'But it's easier said than done.'

'No, there is a way,' Idris said urgently.

There were four bales of cowhide in the cargo hold. Among the Portuguese prisoners were three saddlers. They were summoned to stitch four of the hides into a large bucket. While the saddlers stitched the buckets and the carpenters made four holes in the deck, Sala Pokkar fastened a thick cable from the mainmast to the foremast and attached to it twenty pulleys for the twenty buckets. Then everyone went to work. Each bucket was filled and hoisted to the upper deck through the hole and the bucket emptied into the sea. In less than two hours, the excess water was baled out of the vessel. The rain began to abate and the pumps were set to work again.

For two days the storm raged, tossing the ship this way and that. The sailors had their work cut out for them and no one had any time for anything but the business of keeping the ship afloat. On the third day, the clouds lifted and the wind settled and everyone went back to what they were expected to do. The prisoners were sent back to their hold but the captain decided to add to their rations as a token of thanks for all that they had done. There was an air of relief on the ship. They had survived one of the worst storms ever. Only one man remained ill at ease: Andre, the half-caste sailor. He sat on a keg, staring at the middle distance. The storm had quietened, but the sky was the colour of ash and the sea still choppy.

Andre didn't know whether he loved or hated the sea. When he was on land, he yearned to be at sea. But when he was on the sea, he felt stifled and trapped. Liquor helped then. He didn't care what he drank. The local liquor of the natives or sometimes, what had been stolen or smuggled out from a ship and sold. Or, the arrack. It burnt away the sense of not knowing that gnawed at him all the time: was he white or native? Did he love the sea or hate it?

But with fifty-nine men on board and eighty-six Portuguese prisoners, the skipper wasn't going to allow a drop on board. Not that he denied himself. The captain had his brandy and superior victuals. As did the sailing master, the quartermaster, the first mate, the ship's surgeon, the book keeper and a few others. But the sailors couldn't have the comfort of a drop till the ship dropped anchor somewhere on this godforsaken coast. The captain wanted them to suck on a lemon instead. 'Good for your teeth and that turtle gait of yours,' the ship's surgeon had said, brandishing a copy of *The Surgeon's Mate* by someone called John Woodall in his face. 'Read this if you don't believe me. You, I hear, read English!'

Andre had said nothing then. But now, the yearning for a drink overwhelmed every other thought and feeling. He looked at the waters thoughtfully. If he jumped into the sea, would he be able to swim ashore?

Two of the men walked towards him. They were part of his bakken. Bowl brothers. All half-castes like him. They were not allowed on this part of the deck, in front of the mast, except at a certain time of the day. Andre sighed and turned away from them. He was in no mood to make conversation. What he felt was a nameless rage, a constant whining in his ears. The ship's surgeon had told him it was the sound of the timbers creaking and groaning, and it was only natural he should hear it below in the crew quarters and cargo hold, where he was most of the time. But Andre wasn't convinced. He knew one drop of liquor would still the sounds in his head.

That was when the kitten came sniffing at his feet, mewing at him and weaving between his legs as if it owned the bloody ship and him.

Musa the kitten had lost his fear of humans in less than ten days. The day Sala Pokkar had picked him up and scratched under his chin with the extended nail that he grew on his little finger, Musa the kitten forgot to be wary around humans. It seemed to him that everyone loved him. The tall black man sometimes held him to his chest and murmured in his deep voice soft sounds that warmed his little cat heart. The white man who often stood on the deck, staring at the horizon, brought him tidbits. Lumps of salty yellow cheese, bits of fish and once, a rag ball that Musa had chased and pounced on as if it were a mouse. Another white man who blew smoke from a strange-looking contraption often held him by the scruff of his neck and stared at his eyes. Everyone loved Musa. Everyone.

The two men paused and watched to see what Andre would do next. Andre saw them looking at him. What did they think he would do? Baby-talk this scrap of mangy fur? He grabbed the kitten by the scuff of its neck and flung it at the face of the ever-sneering Jacob.

'Oye,' Jacob jeered as he stepped back and caught the kitten neatly. He brought the kitten close to his face and stared at its unblinking yellow eyes.

Jacob didn't yearn for liquor. But he was bored and this seemed a good enough game. Catch the kitten.

'Here,' he called out to his companion and flung the kitten high in the air.

The kitten screamed as it flailed its limbs.

Rudi pressed his cheroot between his lips and raced across the deck to grab the flying ball of fur. He managed to reach the kitten in time but lost his cheroot.

'Bloody shit-pot,' he snarled and flung the kitten back at Andre. 'Keep your fur ball...'

Andre raised his arm and caught it. He looked at the kitten as if it were responsible for his plight and thought he would like to dash its head on a rock. But rocks existed on land. On a bloody ship, there was nothing. Even the nearest barrel was across the deck. He raised the kitten and aimed at it with his booted foot. He hoped it would hit a rock on the seabed.

The kitten flew over the deck.

Andre thought he heard a distant plop. It didn't make him feel better, but at least the mewing scrap was out of his face.

A shrieking something flew across the line of his vision and slammed against a bale of canvas. It lay where it fell, stunned or perhaps dead. Idris felt his heart in his mouth as he rushed towards the kitten.

Sala Pokkar ran towards Idris, his face twisted in anguish and horror. 'Ikka, the half-caste sailors... there was nothing I could do.'

He stopped abruptly when he saw Idris crouched by the

canvas, holding the kitten to his bosom and murmuring to it softly, 'Wake up, Musa, wake up. You are safe now. No one will hurt you.'

'Is he dead?' Kandavar asked, trying to hold back his tears.

'Not yet...' Idris said, stroking the kitten.

'I saw them, but I was too scared to approach them,' Sala Pokkar said, crouching at Idris's side. 'They flung him around as if he were a ball... and then that half-caste with a missing ear kicked him without even a change in his expression.'

'Will my Musa survive, Aabo?' Kandavar's voice broke. 'I will kill them, each one of them, with my katari. I swear I will, Aabo.'

Idris prodded the kitten's mouth open. Its gums were pale. Its heart beat rapidly and its breathing was loud. Idris stroked the kitten gently.

'Calm down, Kandavar,' he said softly. 'Don't agitate him further. Animals understand. Here, take him and stroke him.' He handed the kitten to the boy.

Kandavar cradled the kitten and baby-talked it as he stroked it between its ears. 'Wake up, Musa,' he whispered. 'Wake up.'

Idris patted the boy's back. 'We'll nurse him back... he will survive!'

The kitten mewed piteously and tried to move. One of its legs hung limply. It was broken. Sala Pokkar's eyes prickled. It was so tiny. How could men be such beasts? 'They have to be punished,' he said. Idris rubbed his brow. This was getting complicated.

Musa survived. Idris even found a way to splint the broken leg. He had the ship's carpenter fashion a box to keep the kitten in and restrain its movement. He strung a small cord around the kitten's neck so it wouldn't run away. Idris did what he could for Musa but he couldn't change Kandavar or Sala Pokkar's mind. They were determined to make the sailors pay.

'Not all of them, but that half-caste with the missing ear. He started it,' Kandavar said.

'I'll do it my own way. We'll get him one way or another,' Sala Pokkar added grimly.

A week later, Idris was on the bow of the ship. He was allowed access to most parts of the ship, except the captain's cabin. He didn't particularly want to see the captain's cabin, but the captain summoned him to the bow of all places, once a week, for a report on the Portuguese prisoners.

He could see Sala Pokkar work the block and tackle as a sail was hoisted. Some of the other sailors were there as well. The ship's mate had realized that Sala Pokkar understood the block and tackle better than the others did and had vested him with more responsibility than he would have otherwise. When the sailors grumbled, he snarled, 'He makes it twice as easy. And I don't have to worry about accidents with him around.'

They were hauling down one of the bigger sails and Sala Pokkar had set a two-line fall from the guiding sheaves to the sail. A stiff wind blew.

Idris watched absently as Sala Pokkar darted this way and that. From the corner of his eye, he saw Andre arrive where he had no business to be. He saw Sala Pokkar gaze at the man.

No, Idris thought. No, don't, he mouthed.

But Sala Pokkar was not going to let a chance slip by. It only needed a particular movement of the hand for the cable to slip out of the groove of the guiding sheave and for the system to come undone.

Andre didn't even feel the gigantic sail descend on him. The impact stunned him, which was a mercy, Idris thought, as he saw the iron pulley crush the man's leg, its vicious hook splicing open the flesh.

They blamed the wind as Sala Pokkar knew they would.

They blamed Andre for being in the wrong place. They blamed destiny for Andre losing his leg below the knee: Idris had to help the surgeon amputate when the wound wouldn't heal and gangrene set in. A leg for a leg, Sala Pokkar said when Idris glowered at him.

'I could have done worse,' Sala said. 'But I am not an unfair man.'

XXX

The *Hercules* sailed the coast at less than forty miles a day. The storm had pushed the vessel off its course. And it was almost eight days later than the estimated date of arrival when they arrived at the port of Petapolee.

The ship's surgeon stood beside Idris. His eyes narrowed as they approached the mouth of the river. 'We will drop anchor here. The half-caste Andre will have to be taken ashore. But we won't stop here for long.'

Idris nodded. 'This is a Dutch settlement. So what is the problem?'

The surgeon's mouth twisted. 'The English came here thinking they could replicate Paliacatta. But this place is humid and hot, and the mangroves are breeding grounds for everything that can kill a white man. Lily-livered white men like the English. The Dutch, we are a hardy lot. We survive. Nevertheless, I don't want disease on board. We have a long voyage ahead of us. And the captain will want to move on too, for the anchorage duty is greater for a ship like ours. Nine pagodas a day.'

Musa limped onto the deck and rubbed himself against Idris. Then he slithered between the surgeon's legs, holding his tail erect, purring and mewing. 'He is better, I see.' The ship's surgeon smiled.

'Thanks to you,' Idris said softly. The ship's surgeon had helped Idris set the kitten's leg rather reluctantly. 'Wring its neck and throw it over the deck. Better to put it out of its misery right away,' he had said at first, irritated at the thought of having to play doctor to a cat.

'I can't. My son loves it too much. And if he takes ill with grief, I will leave at the next port we call at,' Idris had said, laying the kitten on the wooden pallet. His eye met the doctor's gaze steadily. You need me more than I need you; the message was clear enough.

The ship's surgeon had grimaced, then said, 'Very well. I hope this works.'

Don't remind a man how reluctant he was to help you. He will remember that himself. Instead, thank him for what he did, and he will find a way to help you even before you ask him to. A sufi had murmured these words in his ears. Where had it been? Samarkand, or in the port of Jeddah, or Aden? Idris shrugged. He should remember to write his journal more regularly, he thought.

'You are lost in your thoughts again.' The ship's surgeon peered at Idris. 'Where do you go?'

'A distant port and a wandering seer,' Idris replied with a straight face.

The ship's surgeon frowned. Was he being sarcastic? But there was in Idris's seeing eye a faraway look. So perhaps...

The ship's surgeon was puzzled by Idris. Who was he when he was home? For that matter, where was home for him? He seemed to belong everywhere and nowhere. He felt something akin to pity for the tall African. When his own time here was over, he would sail home to Delft. To the prickly skyline of the Oude and Nieuwe Kerk and the many small spires of monasteries and chapels.

He could see it in his mind: the high walls of the city with its massive gates and watch towers; canals and markets – the Nieuwstrat, where freshwater fish was sold, and the Vleeschal at Voldensgracht, where they bought juicy sides of beef and pork, grains and fruits, the plenty that blessed each market bucket. The breweries and the tile painters and the stone bridges across the canals.

The salt of the breeze was unlike anywhere else. The ship's surgeon had tasted the salt of the sea in so many waters, but the Delft Sea was his own. It was unique, like the powdery crustiness of the bread brought by the baker's boy to their home every day. More than anything else, it was this the ship's surgeon missed. The salt of the Delft breeze and how the crust of the bread lent itself to chewing. And the crumbly moistness of the Reypaenar cheese in his mouth.

In the heat of the night, when even the finest cotton clung to his skin, he would close his eyes and imagine his wife and him strolling the wide streets with trees on either side, and of stepping into the fine town house with its whitewashed walls and cool stone floors.

His mind had wandered through its rooms, lingering at the cellar where she kept barrels and vats, and her pickled onions, turnips, cabbages and carrots in glass jars on shelves. He thought of the fireplace, almost unable to imagine a fire in the clammy mugginess of his cabin. It was the prettiest part of the house, with a line of Delft porcelain tiles on the chimney piece near which a small rug housed his favourite armchair and its pair. On the wall was a small painting that his friend Jan Vermeer had gifted him. A simple enough scene of a maid pouring milk from a pitcher into a pail. He had reached for a glass of water and gulped it down thirstily, wishing it were a glass of cold milk. Home was that piece of life and knowing that it was waiting for him. But this man, what did he have? Not even a plate to call his own.

What had the African told him when they had met in Paliacatta? 'In the land where I come from, we say, where I make my living, there is my home.'

'Petapolee is a port you can make a fortune from if you know how,' the ship's surgeon said suddenly, hoping Idris would understand the purport of his words.

Idris shook himself out of his reverie. 'What do you mean?'

'Well, someone has to go with the mestizo Andre into the port. It may as well be you. You will have all of this day and tomorrow, till the evening, when the boats come back to the ship to load supplies and some cargo. Ask for Karnam Krishnappa. He is a village accountant who owes me a favour or two. Tell him I sent you.' The surgeon smiled. The Karnam was a wily old man, but Idris would know how to handle him.

'What about customs duties, tolls and taxes?' Idris asked. 'I can't afford any of that.'

'We, that is the Dutch, pay a lump sum – 3000 pagodas or some such amount – every year for the clearance of goods, so as far as Masulipatnam, you can benefit from the Dutch umbrella,' he said. 'Why do you think I am asking you to go ashore here?'

Kandavar wanted to go ashore. So did Sala Pokkar. Idris stared at their expectant faces in dismay. He hadn't expected this. He had heard of Ibn Batutah, the Moor who travelled everywhere with an entourage of wives, concubines and almost a caravan of baggage. Idris had laughed at the mere notion of it. Now it made sense why Ibn Batutah had written mostly about courts and princes and less about real people. Unless you were on your own, how could you mingle with people? Now it seemed he was turning into a scaled-down version of Ibn Batutah himself. One son, one associate and one cat, all waiting to go ashore with him.

'That won't be possible,' he said to them firmly. 'I have to accompany the mestizo Andre to the shore. He is angry that he has lost his leg. He is furious that he has no place on the ship anymore. I don't want him near either of you or Musa. He is dangerous.'

'Oh,' Sala Pokkar said.

'But,' Kandavar began.

Idris held up his hand. 'No buts and whys. You must do as I ask. At the next port, we will have all the time to go ashore and explore. Be patient until then. In my village, we would say, you don't go searching for bones in a lion's den.'

XXXI

The ship's pilot had set a course from the east to the north as they entered the mouth of the river, and at a distance of a league and a half, he pointed out an isle covered in coconut trees to Idris to the north of the river. 'Once we have spotted this, I know that at a league's distance there is good anchorage at six fathoms deep,' he said. 'This is the safest harbour on this coast but because of this sand bar, only small boats can go further into the river.'

Idris looked at what appeared to be a tray, bobbing towards the *Hercules*. It had hardly any timber except a narrow reaper to hold together the board and thin planks sewn together with coir and calked with dammar, a sea resin. Ten men sat in it, rowing briskly, using their paddles to steer them towards the vessel. So this was the masoola. He sighed, hoping it would hold till the mestizo and he had docked at Petapolee.

The mestizo had to be roped down into the masoola. Sala Pokkar had fashioned a wooden seat on a rope and used a single pulley to lower the man down into the flat-bottomed boat heaped with cargo to be taken ashore. Idris and Kandavar stood on the deck, watching. 'Are you going down the same way?' Kandavar asked.

'What do you think?' Idris asked, piqued.

Kandavar giggled and said nothing. He hoped Idris wouldn't topple and make an ass of himself.

Idris checked he had his little bag with him. Then, with a fluidity of movement that had everyone else staring in amazement, he slithered down the rope. Kandavar's mouth fell open. Who would have thought this of Aabo? He looked around him with pride. If only the boys at the kalari could see him, he thought.

Before Idris could speak a word, Kandavar slid down the rope and landed on the pile of cargo. 'I am going with you,' he said firmly. 'I will jump into the water and follow you if you make me go back.'

Idris glared at Kandavar, but there was no time to send him back to the ship. He smoothed the folds of his tunic, pretending not to notice the resentment in the mestizo's eyes as he sat atop the cargo – cloth from Paliacatta and cinnamon brought all the way from Ceylon, to be taken to Petapolee and from there on to the distant ports. A breeze blew over the water, but he could see how the open coast drew into the estuary and as they entered the mouth of the river, the mangroves that crowded the banks. They pressed down upon the water, curdling the sweetness of the breeze into a foetid heaviness, so that as the masoola drifted upstream slowly, Idris felt stifled.

As the boat pulled towards the makeshift quay, Andre growled, 'How am I to reach wherever it is I am to be left? Where is that to be, by the way?'

Idris shrugged. 'I am not your keeper, or your brother.'

'What does that mean?'

'It means that my instructions were to accompany you to

where you wished to be left. Not find you a place to stay,' Idris said in an even voice.

The mestizo's face paled. 'But I don't know anyone here.'

'Neither do I.'

Idris saw the man's face crumple. What was he going to do with this creature with a stump for a leg and a sodden cloth for spirit?

'I am going to meet a man. He may be able to help.'

'I have some money,' Andre offered.

Idris didn't speak. When the boat had been brought to the quay, he had noticed two oxen and four men waiting. The men seemed to know their routine well enough. They unloaded the masoola and stacked the bales on the oxen. Without a word spoken, they lifted the mestizo and put him on top of the cargo, then gestured for Idris and Kandavar to follow them.

The oxen and men wound their way along a track of beaten mud and entered the town. It was just another port town, Idris realized, gazing at the bustling throng of people. Merchants, travellers, traders and Gentives, as the people here were called. They stopped near a warehouse. The Dutch agent had gone inland on business, but a petty clerk was available.

The Armenian stared at Idris and Kandavar and then at the man perched on top of the bales. He began to speak in Telugu, then saw Idris's face and switched to Arabic. 'Oh, oh,' he said, frowning. 'Is he part of the cargo?'

'Not really. But he was on the Dutch ship *Hercules* and has to be left behind.'

The Armenian's gaze fell on the stump. He nodded. 'What am I going to do with him?'

Idris didn't speak.

'You see, the Dutch follow a system of book-keeping that isn't really what I am used to. The double entry system. Have you even heard of it? They have one ledger split into three. Zornal, that is a journal to you and me; kaps, which is a goods ledger, and groot boock, which is a personal ledger. Now where can I place this one-legged man?'

'Hey, what are you two jabbering about?' the mestizo growled from atop the bales.

'He is not cargo,' Idris said.

The Armenian's mouth twisted. 'Can't see a joke, can you?'

Idris looked away. Great, a joker for a book-keeper. He drew himself to his full height and glowered down at the smirking Armenian.

'I was told that you would have the supplies for the ship and they have to be fetched from here in the morning. Meanwhile, could you tell me where to find Karnam Krishnappa?'

'I'll send someone with you,' the book-keeper mumbled. 'But the mestizo… I can't keep him here. Not until the Dutch agent returns and says we can.'

'Unload the cargo. I will find him a place, but I need two men to make a pallet and carry him on it,' Idris snapped.

The Armenian clapped his hands and a group of men arrived, running. He spoke to them in Telugu. Idris tried to make sense of the words, but couldn't. How many languages did they speak here in Petapolee, he wondered. In Malacca, he had heard they spoke eighty-four languages at least in the port.

'Karnam Krishnappa is a Chetty, so he lives in the artisan section of the Hindu town,' the book-keeper said as the men helped the mestizo down and offered him a stout stick to use as a crutch.

'What's the difference?' Idris asked curiously.

'The Hindus cluster together based on caste. All the middle castes stick together. On one side of the town are the parayans – the untouchables – who are not allowed anywhere near, and on the other side, the brahmins, who won't allow anyone near them either.' The book-keeper laughed. 'Silly fools. They look alike, sound almost alike, and certainly smell alike, but they behave as if each lot of them are distinct from the other.'

Idris nodded. He was as puzzled about the caste system as the book-keeper. But he couldn't stand here discussing social structure all day, so he interrupted the voluble man with a brusque, 'Could you hurry this up? I need to find him and my son and me a place to stay for the night.'

'Oh, are you staying the night? Go to Ismail Al Saabah's home on Moor Street. He will offer you a bed for the night. But about the mestizo... I don't know.' The Armenian's head bobbed.

He was irrepressible, Idris decided. There was no point trying to shut him up or even squash him. He would talk till Idris reached the end of the street and holler some more thereafter.

Eventually, it was time to go. A man led Idris, Kandavar and the mestizo, who sat on a pallet hefted by two porters, through the streets of Petapolee. The port wasn't big enough for it to be divided into a white town and a black town, but the Europeans tended to congregate in one area and the natives in another, and in between were the Mohammedans and the Persians. Small houses lined the narrow streets, and pigs and dogs roamed the streets of the native sections. Idris felt a wave of disgust. His eyes had got used to the large green tracts of Malabar. The hot, smelly streets of Petapolee repulsed him. How much further, he wondered, as they walked down one street after the other, till the man pointed to a big house with a tiled roof. Apparently, the roofing rules here were different from those in Malabar.

'You look thoughtful,' the mestizo said.

'The man I am to meet lives here. You had better stay on the pallet till I have spoken to him,' Idris said, looking at the walled gate.

'What? Out here in the sun?' The mestizo's voice rose.

'Is there an option?' Idris snapped. He was tired of playing nursemaid.

He knocked on the door that was set into the wall. A man let him in, then beckoned for him to follow. Kandavar went with them.

Idris sized up the man seated under a mango tree in the courtyard, wearing a white dhoti, his upper body covered with a fine muslin cloth. He wore several rings on his fingers, including one with a solitaire that flashed blue lights with every movement of his hand. But what struck Idris was Karnam Krishnappa's hair, which was kept short like a European's. Most Indian men he had seen wore their hair in a tuft.

A manservant brought two chairs and placed one alongside the Karnam and one facing him. The man gestured to Idris to sit. A little later, another man entered through the gate. Idris was surprised to see it was a Mohammedan dressed as he was. Kandavar went to sit beneath the tree. It was good to see the boy had learnt so quickly, Idris thought. Listen but don't make yourself conspicuous. That was the first rule of trading.

'Salaam walaikum,' the man said.

'Wa' alaykum salaam,' Idris mouthed, trying to hide his surprise.

Karnam Krishnappa gestured for the man to seat himself.

Idris watched the two men speak in low tones. The Mohammedan nodded and cleared his throat. 'The Karnam is a term used to refer to the village accountant and Krishnappa used to be one. He speaks no language but Telugu. So he has called upon me to interpret. I trust that is fine by you, brother. You can call me Hussain.'

The Arabic the man spoke was competent, but it was obvious that he was only a traveller to Petapolee.

Idris was struck by a strange sense of dislocation. Kozhikode. Ceylon. Thoothukudi. Paliacatta. Petapolee. His head reeled. What on earth was he doing here? In this past year, how had his life changed so much? Idris Maymoon Samataar Al Guleed was being tossed this way and that, like a catamaran at sea. Or, was it a toni or a masoola? he thought wryly.

He wiped his forehead with a cloth, and said in the gravest tones he could muster, 'My name is Idris Maymoon Samataar Al Guleed. And that is my son.'

The Karnam listened carefully as Hussain translated Idris's words. It wasn't a long speech, but Idris had chosen his words carefully. He needed to let them know that the ship's surgeon had provided the introductions, but he was on his own.

'So what would you like to deal in?' the Karnam asked and Hussain translated. 'Take your pick.'

'Such as?' Idris asked cautiously.

'Iron ore that goes to Damascus for the famous Damascus swords. Or cloth with qalamkari art. Or, there is plain Calico. There is tobacco and carpets from Warangal. There is saltpetre that can be procured. Saltpetre is what goes into gunpowder. And if you have that kind of credit standing, we have diamonds and precious stones which come into the port. So much to choose from. And brother, we are exempt from customs duties, unlike the Europeans. So what is it to be?' Hussain smiled, seeing Idris's bedazzled expression.

'And what will you help locate for us? Pepper will fetch you about 125 rupees for 240 ser. Sandalwood from rupees 450 to rupees 520. Cloves rupees 25 to 45 and nutmeg rupees 135 to 170.'

Idris did the sums in his head. About 4 fanams equalled one rupee and 32 fanams equalled one gold pagoda. He still had a credit note procured from a shroff in Surat for 200 gold pagodas and a hundred pagodas worth of gold and silver in Dutch and English coins.

Idris looked at the Karnam and smiled. 'Tell him that I am on the *Hercules* and cannot trade till we return. When I do, I will want to negotiate a deal with him. To both buy and sell. This is merely a preliminary meeting.'

The Karnam nodded. Idris realized that the man probably understood enough Arabic, even if he pretended he didn't. He watched Hussain and the Karnam whisper to each other.

'The Karnam thinks you are wise to wait. He thinks you should consider diamonds if you are headed towards Masulipatnam. Some of the best diamonds are found inland,' Hussain said. 'The Karnam has his contacts there but he thinks that a man like you would prefer to cultivate his own.'

Idris nodded gravely. The Karnam, he realized, had no intention of sharing any more information till they struck a deal. That was how it should be. In the world of trade, a tip or two was the extent of generosity, anything beyond that revealed a paucity of acumen.

'Meanwhile, he wants to know if there is anything he can do for you,' Hussain said.

'Yes,' Idris said. 'I have a mestizo with me. A sailor who has to be left behind. I need to find him a place to stay and something to do. He will never work on a ship again.'

Hussain frowned. 'Is he your friend?'

'No.' Idris shook his head.

'A servant? Or, is it that you owe him something?'

'Neither. The Dutch asked me to leave him ashore. The man's leg was amputated. How can I just abandon him? Isn't that what our Quran teaches us? To help the needy. Whoever joins himself in a good cause shall have a share of it, and whoever joins himself in an evil cause shall have the responsibility of it, and Allah controls all things.'

'You are not just a trader then, you are also a learned man.' Hussain's voice rose in surprise.

'He is quoting the Quran.' Hussain turned to the Karnam to translate.

Idris touched Hussain's sleeve. 'No, no, I am neither a trader nor a scholar. I am a traveller who needs to make a deal or two to survive. Don't make of me what I am not. That will make you expect too much of me. An expectation I may not be able to meet.'

Hussain smiled. 'The Karnam has a solution for the mestizo. He asks if you need something for yourself.'

Idris looked around him. A little away from the house were palm-leaf mats strewn on the ground. Chillies, coriander seeds and turmeric knobs were being dried in the sun. Idris stood up. 'My son and I need a place to stay for the night. And I need some of that,' he said, pointing to the drying condiments. 'And a small portion of butter. Brother, will you dine with us tonight?'

XXXII

Hussain took them to his lodgings. A house that offered a bed and board for Arab travellers. 'It's run by my uncle, Ismail Al Saabah,' Hussain said as they neared the house on a street that seemed more like a souk in Damascus than in India.

Ismail Al Saabah had come to Petapolee almost two decades ago, when the port was still finding its feet. The English and the Dutch had sought to establish their supremacy by seeking royal dispensations, but the port had survived, independent of who the European rulers were. Despite the mud creeks, the pestilence and the fact that trade wasn't easy, ships called in at Petapolee and travellers began to arrive. Ismail Al Saabah came from Dabhol on the west coast and chose to live on in Petapolee. He built a house that was a hostel for Muslim traders and travellers. And it flourished, for Ismail Al Saabah knew what to offer a man away from home. Whitewashed walls and mattresses stuffed with silk cotton. A prayer room and a kitchen where only halal meat was cooked. Men came there not just to rest their weary bodies but to strike a deal or two, for the hostel worked also as a brokerage house. You discovered new markets or new products. No one went away without having profited from his stay. And as its reputation grew, so did the charges it levied from its customers.

'He is my uncle,' Hussain said. 'That means you won't be turned away even if we are full up, and he will offer you a concession. So don't worry. I am his favourite nephew, which is why he insisted I come here from Dabhol some years ago. Dabhol is a beautiful place, with mountains and rivers and greenery everywhere. I almost died of shock when I arrived here. One day, soon, I am going back to Dabhol.'

Idris listened to the ebullient Hussain with amusement. Dabhol. He remembered the port city with fondness. There was nothing left of its grandeur. Even the Shahi mosque built by Adil Shah's begum was shrouded in neglect. And yet Hussain invested it with greater importance than Petapolee, which held his future. 'So how did you become the Karnam's interpreter?' Idris asked, curious about the strange affinity between the men.

'My uncle knows him well – I took over his duties as interpreter when my uncle discovered that I had learnt to speak the local language.'

Idris nodded. Destiny had been kind to him this day.

'What would you like for your evening meal?' Hussain asked. 'You must be tired of the food on the ship!'

Idris smiled. 'I would like to cook tonight!'

'What?' Hussain stopped mid-stride. 'Whoever heard of a guest cooking? Besides, men don't cook.'

'This man does,' Idris said firmly.

'But…' Hussain began. 'Nobody here,' he said, gesturing with his hand to the street and its people, 'would have heard of a man cooking. Let alone admit to it.'

'Is it illegal?' Idris asked with an innocent expression.

'Brother, you are mocking me!'

For years Idris had stopped himself from seeking comfort in memory. With every passing day, the past became yet another place he had shaken the dust from. A phrase, the musk of a woman's armpit, the feel of a saddle, a particular shade of blue – that was all he chose to remember of the past. But now it seemed to haunt him more and more. Was it because of the boy? Had his change of status from nomad to father caused a tectonic shift in how he located himself on this earth? Or was it merely age? Almost all his life he had been his own sultan, with no allegiance or troth to any living being. He bore no one any ill-will and hadn't suffered the brunt of anyone's wrath. He was everyone's friend and no one's partner. And he hadn't ever felt the need to live life any other way.

But now, something hungered in him. The need to rest his head on the same wooden barkin night after night. To hold to him the warm contours of the same woman. To find succour in the known and familiar, in forgotten scents and sounds.

He felt too a piquant desire to taste all the foods that he grew up on. His mouth watered at the thought of the fluffy softness of the canjeero. When was the last time he had broken a piece of lacy pancake and dipped it in a paste of subag and sugar? Fatima Naaya would make the subag herself, by clarifying butter, and even though it was a luxury, she would dip into the jar of sugar candy and take out a few lumps and pound it into a powder. For her prince, her Idris, nothing was good enough unless she had cooked it herself. She would feed him the triangular crustiness of sambusa stuffed with hot green chillies and ground beef. To ease the fire on the tongue, she would then offer him xalwo, sweet halva dripping with subag.

So when Idris saw the spices drying on mats in the Karnam's courtyard, it stirred in him a memory of what had been his favourite food. Suddenly he felt an unbearable yearning to eat again the niter kebbeh, spiced butter.

'Listen to me, Hussain,' Idris said. 'I have never done this before and do not understand why I am justifying myself, but perhaps I will not have the run of your uncle's kitchen if I don't, and so will you listen to what I have to say?

'Sometimes a man needs something to keep him going. I am not talking of lofty ideals or the thought of jannat awaiting him in the hereafter. Sometimes it is only a meal that he needs to propel him into the next day… a meal that to him is representative of home and comfort.'

Idris saw the wry amusement on Hussain's face. He pretended not to see it. 'You may think it is trivial, Hussain, but tell me the truth, don't you ever long for food from your Ammi's kitchen?'

Hussain nodded. His uncle's cook replicated the dishes that they ate at Dabhol, but it didn't taste the same as his Ammi's.

'And when someone travels as much as I do, home becomes almost a memory. I keep it alive by remembering tastes, scents, colours, textures. So, Hussain, will you help me recreate a taste of my home tonight?' Idris touched the younger man's arm gently.

The hostel was full up but Ismail Al Saabah was as taken by the tall African as his nephew had been. The sheer magnificence of his bearing had him open up the room he kept for any nobility or sufis who may seek him out.

Hussain's eyes widened when he saw where Ismail Al Saabah was leading Idris. It was the apartment at the farthest end of the corridor, with a private, enclosed garden that held a frangipani tree and flower beds. A small stone fountain sprayed the air with a pleasing coolness. Hussain could barely remember when the apartment had been last used.

He followed Idris into the room that had a fine Persian carpet on the floor and at one end, a mattress covered with a fine white sheet and laden with plump bolsters and cushions. There was a table and a chair, and a cupboard, all of which his uncle had procured from the Dutch agent. The windows were open to the garden and a breeze lifted the muslin curtains at the window. 'Will you and your son be comfortable here?' Ismail Al Saabah asked anxiously.

Idris was startled. Who did he think they were?

He smiled broadly, thinking of his bed in the last few days. There had been a pallet in the mosque at Kuttichira and on their way to Galle, they had slept on the deck of the Arab ship. His mind flitted to the small space in the ship to Paliacatta and the bare room in the merchant's top floor. This was almost a palace in comparison.

'It is not what we are used to, but we will manage well enough,' he said in an even voice.

XXXIII

Idris was going by memory alone as he assembled the ingredients for his niter kebbeh.

In the days after Idris had lost his eye, he had been crippled by the most horrific pain. Then, when the fever settled and the eye began to heal, the nightmares began, and they wouldn't stop. Even when he was awake, his dead eye saw the horrific images of a camel in flight, its legs kicking, its teeth bared and eyes rolling in fright. The sickening thud as it slammed against the rock wall. Hamid, the cook, impaled on a staff and in flight with streamers of blood trailing. The screaming and shouting and the howling wind. And then the silence, before the wind resumed. But what terrified Idris more was the deadness that had come to live in his Aabo. Idris would cling to his father, but would feel no warmth in response. What is wrong, Aabo, he would ask every few days.

'Nothing. But we are going back,' Aabo said one day. It had taken them almost four months to retrace their steps back home. What had sapped his strength wasn't the loss of his caravan, or the cargo they had been carrying, but the shaitan wind that had taken his men and gouged out his son's eye. He had heard about the wind on his travels but until it grabbed him in its whirling arms, he had never known its terrifying strength. He had survived pirates, barbaric nomads, even a murder attempt, but this wind was something else. It was inhuman and yet struck with a viciousness that was human in its ability to maim and kill. For the first time, Samataar Guleed had felt fear. What else was out there?

Fatima Naaya had taken Idris to her hut. Samataar Guleed needed to heal as much as his son did. The son was easier to deal with, she knew. His fears could be contained, but when a grown man lost his nerve, how was she to help him retrieve it? So Fatima did the only thing she thought could help. She fed him. Fed the child and the man with food that would build their muscle and prop up their flailing spirits.

Idris lay on a pallet in the corner of Fatima Naaya's hut and listened to her as she went about her day. His eyes had been covered with a paste made by the medicine man from the village and bound with a cloth. His other eye was free to gaze at the world but it was too much of an effort. He preferred to lie there with his eyes shut, the darkness enveloping him in a soothing embrace while sounds and scents wafted around him. Then, one miraculous day, the smell of spices and clarified butter swirled his senses so that he opened his eye and rose from the ground, seeking the source of that wondrous fragrance.

Idris found Fatima Naaya stirring something in a pot and his father looking more like the man he knew him to be.

'Aabo,' Idris said.

His father had smiled. 'Are you on your feet then, son?' he asked.

Idris nodded. It was clear his father was. 'Are you leaving?' he asked, feeling torn. He didn't want to leave Fatima Naaya's hut and the security of its confines. But he didn't want to be parted from his father either.

'Not yet.' His father patted his thigh. 'Come here, Idris.'

Idris climbed into his father's lap. Aabo didn't encourage it usually but that afternoon, Idris felt his father gather him in his arms and nuzzle his neck. For as long as Idris lived, he would remember that moment; the white heat of the afternoon sun and in the shade of the wanza tree, a pleasing coolness, the aroma of the niter kebbeh as it simmered on the fire, his father's breath fanning his neck, the hardness of his father's chest as he leaned back against it, the radiance in Fatima Naaya's eyes and the chuckling croo-doo-doo-do of a flock of laughing doves.

'What is the meat in the dish?' the cook asked, watching the tall, black man as he stood motionless in the middle of the kitchen. Was he going to stand here all evening, wondering what he was going to do next? The cook had chopped, crushed and grated various ingredients as per his instructions. Besides, the cook had the evening meal to prepare.

Idris opened his eye and said, 'Tonight, I fancy a chicken. I am tired of the lamb we have been eating on board. A freshly slaughtered chicken.'

A squawking filled the kitchen. Idris frowned. What was going on? He stepped out of the kitchen into the backyard, where the assistant was chasing a plump chicken that was running furiously, this way and that.

Idris watched the man and fowl run around in circles, raising little puffs of dust. The chicken's terror-stricken squawks rent the stillness of the early evening. Idris strode across into the path of the chicken and in one swift motion, grabbed it.

'Here,' he said, giving the chicken to the cook's assistant. 'Or do you want me to do the slaughtering as well?'

Kandavar stood by the doorway watching Idris. He hadn't thought Aabo could move so swiftly. 'Do you know how to?' he asked.

Idris stared at his son.

'I would have slaughtered the chicken before it even realized its throat had been slit.'

Kandavar's gaze dropped.

'Yar inan, there are many things you do not know about me,' Idris said slowly.

'Would you show me how to?' Kandavar asked suddenly.

Idris was startled. 'Why?'

'So I do not fear the sight of blood. As a warrior, I cannot be frightened of blood. I cannot feel my hand tremble or my gaze falter, Aabo. But I would also like to be able to kill without the person knowing I have taken his life.'

Idris nodded. 'Next time, you will slaughter the chicken. There is no mercy in killing, but you can reduce the horror of it.'

Idris returned to the kitchen and to the contemplation of the ingredients. The cook cleared his throat.

Idris opened his seeing eye. 'Where is the butter I brought from the Karnam's household?'

The cook gestured to a lump of butter placed in an earthenware bowl containing water. 'It is here, as you left it. What else do you need?'

Idris thought for a moment. He asked for a heavy-bottomed copper cauldron. Into it he put the butter, the chopped onion, minced garlic, grated ginger and turmeric.

'I need some spices,' he said, turning to the cook.

The man's eyes widened. Spices were kept under lock and

key, but Ismail had said the African was to be given whatever he asked for. 'Like what?' he asked with a sullen expression.

'Cumin seeds, a stick of cinnamon, a clove, a cardamom, and some fenugreek seeds and coarsely ground pepper,' Idris said, stirring the butter as it melted.

The cook pulled out the spices and watched in horror as Idris took a handful of each and placed them on a brass plate. He looked up and told the cook, 'Don't worry. I will account for this and pay your master. Just make sure that your accounts and mine tally. I know precisely, to each peppercorn and clove, what I have taken.'

The cook gulped. He had hoped to set aside some of the spices for himself. The African may be one-eyed, but he was more astute than all of them put together.

'Do you know how long I have worked here?'

'Yes, three years and two months. That doesn't make you infallible. In fact, it makes you complacent. How you cheat Ismail is your business, but I won't let you cheat him using me as an ally.'

The cook wiped his forehead and said nothing.

The cook watched as Idris added the spices to the frothing mixture. Just how much time had the man spent in a kitchen by a hot stove? Not enough, he thought, as Idris continued to gaze as the butter foamed.

'You have to skim the foam when it rises to the top,' the cook said, offering a ladle to him. 'Or it will change the texture of the melted butter.'

Idris nodded and as the foam rose to the top, he skimmed it off till there was none left. He remembered Fatima Naaya doing so.

Night had set in. Idris had been stirring and skimming for a long time. Finally, when the butter was clear on top and the aroma of it had seeped into every surface and into the pores of the men assembled there, Idris took the pan off the fire and poured melted, spiced butter into another vessel through a fine cloth. Again and again, till the butter had clarified to a clear liquid with no residue of milk solids or spice.

Idris held the bowl to his face and inhaled deeply till he felt its aroma pervade his bones and muscles. The knots in his shoulders unravelled, his clenched nerves unfurled, a sense of settling in... Idris smiled. How could a memory revived do so much?

'This is niter kebbeh,' he explained to the cook and Hussain. 'From the land I come from.'

'Which is where?' the cook whispered to Hussain.

'A small place called Dikhil on the east coast of Africa. It means "waterhole" in the Somali language.'

'But where do you belong to?' Hussain asked.

Idris shrugged. 'When I drink in the fragrance of this niter kebbeh,' he gestured to the cooling clarified butter, 'I am Abyssinian. When I speak the Somali tongue, I am Somali. When you ask me where I come from, I tell you Dikhil, which is part of the Lake Abbe region.'

Hussain and the cook exchanged glances. The cook frowned. 'So, if this is the dish you were cooking, what was the chicken for?'

'Doro wat.' Idris smiled enigmatically, washed his hands and wiped them on a cloth.

'Here is what you do,' he said, handing over the bag of chillies to the cook's assistant. Perhaps he would never have sought to venture into this kitchen if the chillies drying in the Karnam's courtyard hadn't set him thinking and hankering for doro wat. 'You will first toast these in a pan and then grind them to a fine paste. I don't need more than a cup. As for the rest, I want you to pound it with some of the spices I have here.'

Idris carefully laid out two lines of spices. Cardamoms. Cinnamon. Cloves. Fenugreek. Peppercorns. Coriander seeds. Turmeric. 'You will need to add some of the shallots, ginger and garlic to the paste. And salt to both paste and powder.'

The cook sniffed loudly. 'Salt! As if we don't know that. What is this complicated dish you are making? It had better be good for all the trouble it seems to be.'

Idris frowned. 'You are going to be begging me for instructions on how to prepare it!'

Kandavar shifted his feet and wondered if he could go back to the room allotted to Aabo and him. Idris looked at Kandavar. He didn't want the boy wandering off on his own.

'Bilal,' he called loudly.

The boy didn't respond. Idris saw the cook and his helper exchange glances.

'Bilal,' he called again.

The boy returned from wherever it was his mind had drifted to. 'Aabo,' he said. 'Did you want something?'

'Come here,' Idris said in Malayalam. 'I called you twice. You didn't hear me the first time.'

'I did. But I forgot that was my name for a while.' The boy grinned.

Idris frowned. 'You can't forget that you have a new name when we travel. It is important.'

The boy hung his head. Aabo didn't ask much of him. He must remember his given name.

'This won't take long,' Idris said as the cook's helper brought the paste and the chicken pieces.

'Here, rub the pieces of meat with salt,' Idris said, offering the bowl of chicken pieces to Kandavar.

The boy's eyes grew round with shock. What was Aabo asking him to do?

'How will you learn to stomach the gore of battle if you can't handle touching flesh?' Idris asked.

The cook looked at the man and the boy as they spoke their strange tongue. The boy seemed to resist the man's instructions at first, but then changed his mind and began rubbing salt on the chicken pieces.

Idris placed a deep cauldron on the fire and began to put some shallots in it when the cook stopped him. 'You need to wait for the cauldron to heat up. Why don't you let me do it? And don't you need to add some oil first?'

'No,' Idris said, hoping he was right.

When the cauldron was hot enough, the cook drizzled some oil over the shallots when Idris wasn't looking and dropped them into the cauldron. He tossed them expertly so they wouldn't burn.

'What else do you want me to do?' Kandavar asked.

'Nothing. Stay here till this is done. I promise you will love it,' Idris said as he poured some of the spiced butter into the vessel. 'Besides, a warrior has to learn to wait. Cooking teaches you that. You cannot hurry a dish or a war tactic.' Idris tried to hide a smile from showing on his face. The innocence of the young, he thought. How easily they let themselves be manoeuvred and manipulated.

Kandavar watched Idris throw in this and that. The paste that Aabo called berbere went into the cauldron. And the chicken. Steam rose, filling the kitchen. Kandavar felt his stomach rumble.

And then finally it was done. Aabo called it a doro wat. Kandavar didn't care what it was called. Back in their apartment, he ate the doro wat with hot rice and a bowl of curd to temper the heat.

Hussain licked his fingers and said, 'I am glad you decided to cook tonight.'

The cook and his helper tasted the doro wat, more sceptical than eager. But with the first mouthful, that changed to an overwhelming desire to eat as much as they could. 'I hope you remember what you just chopped and ground and powdered,' the cook said to the helper, wishing he had paid more attention.

The helper didn't reply. He hadn't.

XXXIV

The masoola was waiting for them at the pier. Idris oversaw the loading from the bullocks to the boat. Kandavar was quiet. Something was troubling the boy, Idris thought, taking in the boy's features and the stillness of his stance. When Kandavar was happy, his eyes sparkled and his face played host to a thousand expressions. He would hop on one foot, poke the ground with a twig, whistle through his teeth. But when something was eating at him, his face turned into a mask and his body seemed as if it had been confined by a kafan.

Sometimes it was best to leave things well alone, Idris reflected, and wait for them to resolve themselves. Besides, he would soon have to deal with Sala Pokkar sulking about being left behind.

The boy sat motionless, trailing his fingers in the water. 'What is it, inan? What is wrong?' Idris asked, unable to help himself. He touched the boy's arm gently.

The boy looked at Idris and said, 'I don't know. I just feel sad.'

'But something must be making you sad. That's what I want you to tell me.'

Kandavar bit down on the soft pad of his thumb. 'I can't stop thinking of home.'

'Do you want to go home?' Idris asked carefully. Perhaps he had done wrong to take the boy away. He was only a child.

'No, I am not asking to go home. But the thought of going back on the ship... I miss land. I miss open spaces. I keep thinking of what Amma must be doing now. If my sister has begun walking yet. If at the kalari, they have forgotten all about me. Something feels tight within my chest then, Aabo.

But it's all right,' Kandavar said quickly, seeing Aabo's face fall. 'I'll feel better once we are back on the ship. I really will.'

Idris nodded. But he couldn't smother the guilt he felt. He had taken the boy away from his home to fill in him a sense of awe about life; to introduce him to the splendours of the world that existed beyond his horizon. For a brief while, at Thoothukudi, Kandavar had learned something new about life. The dive in the deep seas had filled him with a sense of mortality. One night, he had sidled up to Idris and said, 'If Kesettan had realized what death was all about, do you think he would have chosen to become a Chaver?'

Idris had shrugged. 'All I know,' he said, 'is that what god gave us, we shouldn't treat so callously.'

But what had he done to expand his son's mind apart from dragging the boy from one port to another. He would need to rethink this voyage.

'What is this?' Sala Pokkar asked, opening the glass jar. Ismail had proffered it to Idris. 'A humble gift that you must accept,' he had insisted.

Idris looked at the gilded glass jar with dismay. What was he going to do with something so fragile?

'You can use it to carry some of that spiced butter you made,' Hussain said.

'It's glass. It may shatter,' Idris said, holding the jar up.

'It survived the voyage from Kutch. Why won't it survive the voyage with you?' Ismail laughed. 'Look at it this way. When you have something fragile in your possession, you will take fewer risks.'

'Niter kebbeh... it's clarified butter with spices in it. I thought our taste buds needed to be revived,' Idris told Sala Pokkar, unpacking the few things he had brought back, including the berbere powder.

'What's wrong with him?' Sala Pokkar asked, pointing to Kandavar, who sat staring at the shore. Musa was in his lap.

Idris shrugged. 'He is homesick.'

Sala Pokkar didn't say anything. Instead, he picked up another copper jar and stuck his nose, sniffing the berbere mix before Idris could stop him. Sala Pokkar sneezed, a little sneeze that grew into a volley of sneezes each louder than the other. He ran out, eyes streaming, unable to stop sneezing.

He came back red-eyed and sniffing. 'What on earth was that, Ikka? Something to ward off the djinns?'

Idris looked up and said, 'I think we should break the voyage at Masulipatnam. Kandavar is unhappy being confined to a ship, and I think I may be able to try my hand at a new trading prospect. What do you think?'

Sala Pokkar wiped his streaming eyes and shrugged. 'I'll go wherever you want me to. You are the al-kamal as far I am concerned, Ikka. But will they let us? The ship's surgeon behaves as if you belong to him...'

Idris examined his fingernails. 'I have my means,' he said. 'Don't mention anything to Kandavar yet. But we will leave the ship at Masulipatnam.'

'And what will we do there?' Sala Pokkar asked.

'We'll find something to do.' Idris smiled. 'Do you trust me?'

'I trust you with my life, Ikka.' Sala Pokkar's voice trembled with emotion.

'In which case, leave it to me,' Idris said.

But when Sala Pokkar had gone, Idris looked at the boy and cat who both sat still, staring at the horizon. His shoulders sagged and his forehead creased. A butterfly flapped furiously in his heart. He had no idea how he would set about looking for diamonds when they landed at Masulipatnam.

They weren't happy to hear what Idris had to say. The ship's captain had liked the tall African who knew when to merge with the shadows and when to separate from them. On a confined space like a ship, that was a rare virtue. Besides, Idris had known how to read the stars and the captain had enjoyed their night strolls, with Idris pointing out the constellations to him.

The ship's surgeon was worried. He had come to depend upon Idris for assistance in the surgery.

'Will you stay back if I arrange with the captain to pay you a fee for your services?' he offered.

'No,' Idris said as firmly as he could. 'That isn't going to make me change my mind.'

'How am I to manage?' the surgeon asked dourly.

'Call in a couple of sailors to help you.' Idris refused to be provoked. 'I wouldn't do this if my boy wasn't sickening.'

'What about the other thing you were going to take care of for me?'

Idris smiled. 'That I will do at Masulipatnam. In fact, it is probably best done at Masulipatnam. On your return, when you call in at the port, send for me so that I can hand over the returns of your investment.'

The ship's surgeon mopped his forehead. It was ten in the evening and still warm. He swore this would be his last voyage and he would sail home at the end of his contract. Before which, he needed to ensure he had enough money. 'I depend on you to get me the best there is,' he said.

A silence sprang between them.

'There is something you can do for me,' Idris said abruptly.

The ship's surgeon cocked his head curiously in the direction from which Idris's voice came. They were standing on the poop deck. The sky and the sea were the same inky blue and in the dark of the night, all that the surgeon could see were Idris's eyes: the white of the seeing eye, the gold of the dead eye.

The ship's surgeon blinked. The African's eyes were like stars, he thought. 'And what would that be?'

'If you could get me enrolled as someone in the employ of the Dutch East India Company, I could avail of the privileges allowed to such persons.'

The ship's surgeon stared. What privileges? He hadn't heard anything about this.

'Individual traders in the employ of the company are allowed a percentage of their purchases free of duty and freight charges. So if you could organize for me to become a buyer, I could travel freely and fund my expenses with the money I make on the percentage. That means I can go further inland and find you diamonds at almost cost price.'

The ship's surgeon smiled. For the first time, diamonds had been mentioned.

'Buy me the biggest diamond you can find,' he said.

Idris narrowed his eyes in speculation. Greed has a way of rising to the surface like cream. Fat skin of greed that clings to the tongue. 'I'll bring you what your money will fetch. But if I travel beyond Masulipatnam, I probably will find a better deal. For which I need money. For which I need you to do this for me.'

The ship's surgeon nodded. 'I'll have the papers ready in the morning. You do realize that they are not valid in the eyes of the company, though they will stand up to any casual scrutiny.'

'And they will bear your mark.'

The ship's surgeon swallowed. If Idris went down, so would he.

'You will be careful,' he said.

'I am always careful.' Idris smiled.

The ship's mate was more than worried. He was afraid. Sala Pokkar had carried out his duties with such diligence that it had absolved him of a great deal of responsibility. He had got used to thinking that Sala boy would take care of it. He wondered if he could prevail upon the boy; bribe him with a higher wage, perhaps, to stay back even if the African left. But Sala Pokkar refused to be enticed.

When they docked at Masulipatnam, all of them watched from their individual vantage points as the strange entourage left the ship. The tall black African, his chunky Indian mate, the slender black boy clutching a half-grown kitten. Would they look back, the ship's surgeon wondered.

They didn't.

Kandavar stared ahead at the approaching port. Aabo had decided that they were jumping ship here and it seemed Sala Pokkar, Musa and he had jumped without asking why. One day, he would need to instill in his Chaver comrades this degree of faith. If he called out 'attack', they should heed without questions on their tongue or doubts binding their feet.

'So what do you know about this place, Ikka?' Sala Pokkar asked, narrowing his eyes against the glare of the sun.

'What I know, Sala Pokkar, is that it is at a latitude of 16 degrees and 9 minutes North and 81 degrees and 10 minutes East. And it is one of the first ports the whites came to,' Idris said, latching onto geographical coordinates rather than voice the fact that he knew nothing.

'Right.' What else could Sala Pokkar say? He didn't understand latitudes or winds, elevations or stars. But give him a block and a line and he could hoist an elephant or ten elephants. Not that he thought he could be called upon to hoist elephants at the port of Masulipatnam.

'What are we going to do there, Aabo?' Kandavar asked without turning around. His fingers stroked the kitten's fur, but otherwise the boy seemed hewn out stone.

'The truth is I am not certain yet.' Idris chose his words carefully. 'But I will be, once we have spent a few days there.'

The waves rocked the masoola. The boatsmen looked at the skies and each other. Idris didn't understand their words. But both Idris and Sala Pokkar had read the glance. A storm was coming. The sea and the sky were a dull grey and despite the heat, an ominous chill clung to their skins.

'And then?' Kandavar asked.

'And then, we will see.' Idris smiled.

PART 5

September–October AD 1660

(Muharram AH 1071–Safar AH 1071)

XXXV

Idris found them a house to rent. There were rooms he could rent in the town, but after living on a ship for many months, he needed to have a space free of other people and the intricacies of their lives.

Sala Pokkar looked around the rooms, marvelling at every detail. Kandavar remained strangely unmoved. It would have worried any man to see his son so. But not Idris. The boy was more like him than he had realized. Waiting and watching, every thought held in rein before he spoke them aloud.

'Are you all right?' he asked the boy.

'What will we do here?' Kandavar shot back. He sat down on a padded bench gingerly. He still didn't understand the purpose of furniture. They had bedsteads at home. Wooden cradles. His uncle had procured a mesa, as the Portuguese called it. A flat wooden plank supported by four legs and a caderia to sit on. He thought of the day the mesa and caderia arrived at the tharavad, and how everyone had gathered to marvel at these objects of sophistication, the likes of which none of them had ever seen before.

'Do you know what a diamond is?' Idris asked.

Kandavar shook his head. 'No,' he said.

'It's a stone; a precious stone.'

'Like the one my mother wears as a nose pin?' Kandavar frowned.

'No, that is a ruby. This is a clear stone and you can see all the colours of the rainbow in it. Anyway, that's what we are going to do – find some diamonds.'

'And what will you do with them?' Sala Pokkar asked from the doorway.

'Foster human greed.' Idris laughed.

He saw their puzzled glances and explained. 'Diamonds are worth a lot of money. I will trade in it for profit. To me, it is just a commodity.'

Sala Pokkar understood this. Kandavar didn't. But he was game for anything Aabo wanted to do. 'But where do we find the diamonds?' Kandavar asked. He hoped it didn't involve ships.

'Inland. We have to travel deeper into the land. I would like to go into Kollur. There are diamond mines there. And then we'll see,' Idris said, stretching out on his takht of mattress upon mattress made to order with the finest silk cotton grown in the region and covered with sturdy cotton cloth.

Idris knew he was a secret sybarite even though he denied it vehemently. Sybarites had no place on the road. But a traveller of the world took the best and worst in his stride. That was his position. Now that he could, Idris had his silk cotton mattresses covered in ticking and then made with fine, white, cotton sheets. Even on the hottest day, the mattress was an oasis of cool. He may not sleep at night, but there was no need for him to sit up and wait for the dawn to arrive. He could do it lying down.

Many years ago, a sufi and he had spent a night underneath a tree. The sufi had lain down on the ground, but Idris had continued to sit up through the night, until dawn.

When the sufi woke up, he had gazed at Idris for a long while. Then he said, 'I have to tell you a story.'

'A Bedouin and his dog were once walking through the sand dunes. The desert stretched as far as the eye could see and beyond. The Bedouin shielded his eyes to see if there was an oasis at least in the distance. But there was nothing in sight. The Bedouin began to weep. Soon a group of men on their camels came by. They saw the weeping Bedouin and stopped. 'What is the problem?' they asked.

'My dog is very thirsty and he will soon die of thirst and fatigue,' the Bedouin said even as tears continued to roll down his cheeks.

'But you have water on you,' they said, seeing the skin of water slung over his shoulder. 'Why don't you give your dog some?'

'But I would need that for myself,' the Bedouin wept.

Idris had flushed when he understood the meaning of the story. If you wait for something to happen without helping it along, you would have no one to blame but yourself.

Sitting up straight through the night was not the way to woo sleep. You needed to persuade it to come to you. So, when he could, he found for himself the airiest of chambers, the softest of mattresses, and women who would wrap themselves around him.

Idris closed his eyes. His thoughts swirled, but if he could lie on his back for a while, block out the questions and the conversation, forget what was expected by him, his mind would formulate a plan on its own.

'Aabo is sleeping,' Kandavar murmured to Sala Pokkar.

'He doesn't sleep,' Sala Pokkar retorted.

'Look at him... see how his breath has become even. That's how it is when you sleep,' Kandavar argued.

'Oh, so you are the sleep expert now. Ikka can't sleep,' Sala guffawed.

'Will the two of you shut up and leave me alone?' Idris hissed without opening his eyes. 'Go to the next room, outdoors, wherever. I don't want to hear a sound for the next hour.'

Idris heard scuttling sounds and grinned.

Diamonds, he thought. Diamonds. What was it about those stones that turned men into hyenas? Ready to lie and betray; worse, to kill and plunder. He himself preferred pearls. The lustre of it against a woman's skin evoked a loveliness a diamond seldom could.

He saw in his mind's eye the pearl Kuttimalu wore at her throat, against her polished teak skin. He felt himself quicken. He touched himself almost with loathing.

For weeks together, his body went into a state of hibernation. All sensual thoughts curled into a tight millipede-like ball. And then, from nowhere, a strange arousal. A legion of feet driving and working on desire. So all he could think of was satiation.

Kuttimalu may have cursed him never to be able to find absolution in another woman. But she didn't know how the mind stretched to accommodate the curse of memory. He wasn't a boor to whom all women were the same in the dark. But he knew how to imagine a much loved contour or call on some familiar scent. He knew how to make love to a woman, seeing in her the one he wished he were making love to.

It was the heat, he decided. And the uncertainty. On a ship, there was the breeze to cool his thoughts and a map that determined his passage. But here, in this house surrounded by mango and tamarind trees, the cloud of warm, moist air compounded his restlessness.

A few hours later, Idris sat up with a start. How could he just laze around when there were a thousand things to be accomplished?

'Sala,' he called out.

Kandavar walked into the room. 'He isn't here. He has gone to the market.'

'I am here,' Sala called out from the kitchen that formed the rear of the house.

The merchant who had rented it to them had said that it was a house Arab traders liked to rent while procuring goods. 'It has a kitchen, and I have put in a stack of firewood which you can replenish.'

Sala walked in, wiping his hands on a rag. 'You can't go looking for diamonds on an empty stomach,' he said.

'Not you. We.' Idris smiled. 'We are going looking for diamonds.'

'Even Musa?' Kandavar asked.

'Oh well, why not? I have a khalasi and a boy who wants to be a Chaver, a cat called Musa is not going to make things any more difficult.' Idris stood up and stretched.

Sala looked at the tall black man in admiration. When he stretched, his fingers brushed the ceiling. When he walked into a room, everyone fell silent and waited for him to speak. He made everything seem doable. He made it all seem within reach. Even diamonds. Though Sala Pokkar had never seen a diamond in his life, he felt curiously excited at the prospect of looking for one. Or a hundred. But first, he had to tell Ikka what he had found out at the market.

'We really don't need to go looking for diamonds. There is something else here that you can trade in,' he said.

Idris put his hand to his mouth and stifled a yawn. 'What?'

'Cloth. Why not cloth instead of diamonds? There are some very interesting trading options in cloth,' Sala Pokkar said, dredging from memory the conversation he had overheard.

Idris frowned. Sala Pokkar knew that frown. Tell me more, it demanded.

'The silk that comes from the kingdom of Bengal.'

Idris shook his head. 'The really fine silk that sells is white and the only naturally white silk comes from Palestine. And, my dear Sala, it is almost impossible to procure. The Bengal silk is yellow.'

'Hear me out.' Sala Pokkar walked towards Idris. 'I made some enquiries. There is a place called Kasimbazar. Apparently, the people there know how to use the lye from the ashes of the plantain tree to whiten their silk. The Dutch buy this silk. Last year, they took almost seven thousand bales. And it's not easy. For they have to carry the silk by canal, almost fifteen cos, to a mighty river called the Ganga and from there, it's almost the same distance to where their ships are anchored.'

Idris opened his mouth.

'No, let me finish,' Sala said.

'There is more. If you don't want the Bengal silk, there is the Chile cloth.'

Idris smiled and squeezed Sala Pokkar's shoulder. 'You have been busy. I forgot that you know some Arabic now. But I didn't realize you comprehend it so well.'

Sala Pokkar flushed with pride. 'There were two Moors at the mosque I went into for Asr prayers, and I heard them speak. To them I am just the fool native with no Arabic.' Sala Pokkar grinned.

'Do you want to eat or do I tell you what I heard?' he asked suddenly.

'The food can wait. You, I see, can't,' Idris teased.

'This qualamkar cloth is painted cloth. And they make it here. Near Masulipatnam.' Sala Pokkar paused. 'The only problem, I hear, is that even if you get all the workers together, they can produce only about three bales at the most.'

Idris laughed aloud. 'Cloth is not easy to trade in, Sala Pokkar.'

'Yes, I realize that now. But before we eat, I must tell you this. An amazing story about cloth. A Persian called Mohammed Ali

Baig, when he went back to Persia, took a gift for the sultan. A coconut studded with precious stones. When it was opened, they drew out a cloth that was ninety feet long and so fine that you could scarcely feel it in your hand. One can only imagine cloth like that, Ikka. Have you seen anything like it?'

'I am hungry,' Kandavar said, afraid all this discussion about cloth would stretch into midnight.

Sala sighed and went back into the kitchen. He had dithered in the market for so long, eavesdropping, that there had been little time left to do anything more than throw a hasty meal together. Ikka wouldn't be pleased. Then he remembered that Ikka had picked up some porcelain that had come from China. He would serve the food in it. The exquisite tableware, he hoped, would deflect attention from the poverty of the assembled meal.

Idris cocked an eyebrow as he surveyed the meagre supper. 'Next time, I suggest you cook a meal befitting the plates,' he said and tore a piece of chicken from the bone.

'I heard another story in the market,' Sala Pokkar said hastily.

Kandavar giggled. He knew what Sala Pokkar was doing.

'Yes, tell us the story. We are going to need a story to help us through this mess you call a meal,' Idris said, staring in dismay at the potage of vegetables and meat cooked together.

Sala Pokkar gulped. 'Er… it's this cloth I heard about. They were talking about a cloth that cost one thousand mahmudis a piece. How much is a mahmudi, Ikka, to a rupee?' He stopped, defeated by the arithmetic.

'A mahmudi is worth two-fifths of a rupee,' Idris said. 'Four rupees make a fanam and thirty-two fanams make a gold pagoda.'

Sala Pokkar shook his head. 'I don't understand.'

'Go on. I'll explain it to you later.'

'Apparently, two such pieces were sold. One by the Dutch

and the other by the British. And they were just forty-two feet long. I can't even imagine what one thousand mahmudis mean. Can you, Ikka?'

Idris glanced at Sala Pokkar in amusement. 'When we find our diamonds, you will understand money better. Cloth is for merchants with warehouses and ships. With cloth, you have to be careful. The weavers are all right, but there is always a middleman and they encourage the weavers to cheat.'

'Cheat?' Sala Pokkar's eyes grew round. In Malabar, the Zamorin's justice system put cheating on par with murder. 'But how can they?'

'Quite effortlessly,' Idris murmured. 'They have their means and methods,' he added, thinking of what he had heard. Of how a few pieces of inferior quality would be inserted into a bale consisting of two hundred pieces. Of bricks inserted into bales.

'So, even if we were to procure cloth, we would have to make sure that it isn't ruined during our travels. We will be using ships that belong to other merchants and there is no knowing where our cargo will be stored. Cloth doesn't make sense for us. What does is diamonds.'

'But where do we go looking for diamonds?' Kandavar asked.

'First, we'll go to Bezawada. And from there, to the mines,' Idris said.

XXXVI

The optimism of the first days dissipated into a state of frustration. Idris could make no headway at the Mint House. His gold was still being assayed, he was told every day. And unless he had money, he couldn't plan their expedition to Kollur.

The mint master, or the Darogah, as he was called, was a

hard man. 'The problem is, he is too conscientious,' the Amin at the mint house had whispered in his ear. 'He doesn't trust the Sairafi and thinks he takes a bribe. The mint master thinks the Sairafi is in cahoots with the owner of the coins and the assessment will favour him. So he waits and has the Sairafi evaluate the gold and silver again and again to catch him out.'

Idris had rubbed his forehead thoughtfully. He didn't know who he was supposed to bribe to expedite matters. The Darogah, the Sairafi, the Amin? If he bribed all of them, how could he leave out the account keeper, the Mushrif? In the end, Idris decided to do nothing. Once he began bribing people, he knew there would be no end to it.

So Idris had thrown up his hands in a gesture of helplessness. 'Inshallah! I should have sent in a gold ingot in return for the pagodas. Nevertheless, I am sure no matter by whom and how many times it is evaluated, my rose nobles and Albertuses should fetch me their worth in the Masulipatnam pagodas.'

'What other pagoda is there?' the Amin scoffed, seeing his bribe dissipate into nothing.

'There is the Paliacatta pagoda.'

'Oh.' The Amin frowned. 'They are all the same.'

'No, the Masulipatnam pagoda is worth eight per cent more than the Paliacatta pagoda.'

The Amin looked away uncertainly. The Cafre wasn't going to be easy to deal with. He was proving to be as difficult as the Dutch. 'You said you are a traveller, but you sound more like a trader.'

'I wouldn't get very far as a traveller if I didn't understand money, Amin.' Idris smiled. He had made some enquiries and discovered a few juicy morsels about the Amin. The man loved food, he was told. More than loved, he was obsessed with it. Idris decided to host a splendid dinner for the Amin and see if that would make a difference.

'Brother,' Idris said, 'why waste time and words on what

can't be helped? Come share a meal with me at my home tomorrow night. My man will make you food like you have never eaten before.'

Idris came back to an empty house after a pointless day of trying to make some contacts with diamond merchants. Sala Pokkar had taken to swimming in a nearby water inlet with dense mangroves on either side. He said he liked to float on his back, feeling the tide push him along, while his mind turned over everything he had seen and heard in the last few months. Besides, it was cooler than being in the house where the air moved reluctantly, with sluggish feet and arms firmly clamped to its side.

'You are courting disease, my boy,' Idris rebuked him, seeing Sala Pokkar come in after his evening swim.

Sala Pokkar grinned back and retorted, 'What has survived the white flame of fire will not wilt in the heat of the sun.'

Idris shrugged and went back to contemplating who to approach next. Then he looked up and said, 'You haven't forgotten, have you? I've invited the Amin from the mint to eat with us tonight.'

'No, I haven't,' Sala Pokkar said. 'I've been cooking all afternoon, including your doro wat. I just have to fry the shambusa when he gets here. Why do you think I needed that swim?' he added.

'Where's Kandavar?' Idris asked.

'I've sent him to pluck some green leaves. We are going to smoke out the mosquitoes before they devour us alive in here. I have never seen mosquitoes as vicious as these,' Sala Pokkar said, swatting at one.

'Sprinkle this on the coal and keep it in a corner of the room,' Idris said, opening his teak chest, a new acquisition from Masulipatnam, and pulling out a pouch of frankincense.

Sala Pokkar peered into the chest. 'What else do you have in there?'

Idris pulled the lid down with a thud. 'This and that to keep a traveller alive.'

'You are as bad as an oyster,' Sala Pokkar murmured as he walked away.

They ate together, sharing the same dishes. Kandavar had hesitated, but Idris had rebuked him with a stern glance.

'In the eyes of god, we are all one and we are all the same. So all that is mine is yours, brother,' Idris had said, inviting the Amin to start the meal.

The Amin couldn't stop marvelling and exclaiming: at the plump cushions he sank into on the carpeted floor; at the exquisite blue and white pottery the pilau was served in; the heat and spice of the doro wat; the succulence of the lamb; the dried apricots stewed and served with the top of milk; and at the blue sapphire ring Idris wore on his little finger.

The Amin's gaze fixed on the blue stone with every gesture Idris made. Until he could bear it no longer and spoke up, 'That is a splendid ring…'

Idris peered at it. Sala Pokkar held his breath. Ikka, he knew, was quite capable of taking it off his finger and offering it to the greedy Amin. 'It's a trifle. Yours to have, if you like it so much,' he would say.

Instead, he brought his palm close to his face and murmured, 'It is a splendid ring. I bought it at Ceylon. They have some of the world's finest sapphires.' He paused. The Amin waited. But Idris pretended not to comprehend the pause the Amin waited for him to fill.

The Amin cleared his throat. 'You came to the mint rather than go to a Shroff. I was surprised at that. You realize that you have to pay the minting cost and seignorage. And the minting charges are almost five to six per cent of the value of the coins minted.'

'I needed the Masulipatnam pagodas.' Idris shrugged. 'And I don't know a changer here well enough. Someone I can trust not to cheat me.'

'They are all honest, but you have to make sure that you don't lose more than two per cent on the silver rupees.' The Amin smiled, popping a plump date into his mouth.

'I've heard a story about the assayers. That they collect the gold remnants on the touchstone. But how?' Idris asked, pushing the bowl of dates closer to the Amin.

'Hmm... it's no big secret. They make a ball that is half black pitch and half wax. After every evaluation, they rub the ball on the touchstone. And after some months or even years, they burn the ball and all the accumulated gold is theirs to take.' The Amin laughed. 'Patience and diligence are the only investments in this transaction.'

'I have been trying to make some contacts among the diamond merchants. But I haven't met anyone who is willing to give me a clear indication on how to go about buying diamonds,' Idris murmured a little later.

The Amin fixed his gaze on the ring. 'Everything can be transacted. You only need to know whom to approach and how to fix the appropriate price.'

And then it was time for the Amin to leave and Idris, glancing at his ring again, said, 'You are right. This is a splendid ring and is a worthy prize indeed! Meanwhile, I have a little something for you.'

Idris went to the inner room where the wooden chest was and brought forth a dozen romals. It had been Hussain's idea. 'The best silken handkerchiefs called romals are made in the region around Petapolee. You should lay in a small stock. Not to sell, but to gift. You can always insert a little something in one and the receiver will understand there is more to come. A promise made with no words spoken.'

The Amin smiled, feeling something hard within the stack of handkerchiefs. He would assure the mint master that the assayer had been diligent and he would let the assayer know that the mint master was waiting to catch him out. The Cafre would have his pagodas, the Amin his ring, and god would be in heaven and all would be well with the world.

'I thought you would give the ring away,' Sala Pokkar said when the Amin had left.

'I am not as gullible as you think, Sala Pokkar,' Idris rumbled. 'Occasionally I am known to make a deal.'

Sala Pokkar flushed. Then he yawned and set about clearing up the remnants of the meal.

'You surpassed yourself,' Idris said.

Sala Pokkar grinned. 'There is plenty to buy in the markets here. I like this town better than Paliacatta.'

'When do we leave for the diamond mine?' Kandavar asked. Idris looked at the boy in surprise.

'The sooner we find your diamonds, the sooner we can go home,' Kandavar said.

'I thought you liked the travel,' Idris said.

'I do, but everything seems so strange everywhere. The language, the food, the people…' Kandavar complained. He had found a group of boys playing on the beach, but it had been hard work playing with them. Suddenly he had felt a great wave of longing for Rairu. What must he be doing now? He wished he had asked Aabo if Rairu could come along too.

'Well, that's the point of travel,' Idris said slowly. 'If the place we travel to is just like home, why bother travelling at all, inan?'

Kandavar didn't respond. Instead, he curled up on his side and closed his eyes.

'In the morning, I will make enquiries with the people the

Amin suggested I talk to. And hopefully, the Amin will do what has to be done,' Idris said, bending to whisper in his son's ear. 'We will soon be on our way, inan.'

XXXVII

Sala Pokkar found he was unable to sleep. He felt hot and cold in turns. When he sat up, his head spun. His limbs ached and he felt a chill start deep within him, causing him to shiver violently. 'Ikka,' he called out feebly. 'Ikka.'

Idris, lying on his pile of mattresses, heard a mewling sound. What was with Musa? The kitten had grown rapidly in the fortnight they had spent in Masulipatnam. The previous evening, he had killed a dove and dragged it back into the house with a bloodied mouth and whiskers. 'He is a big boy,' Sala Pokkar had exclaimed in delight.

The mewling sounded like a call: Ikka.

Idris rose and went into the adjacent room that Sala Pokkar had claimed for himself. 'Sala Pokkar,' he said softly. 'What's wrong?'

'I don't know, Ikka,' Sala Pokkar groaned. 'I am burning one moment and freezing the next. And I feel as if someone has put my bones through a mangle.'

'Ssh...' Idris said, laying his palm on the young man's brow. 'You are burning. Lie down.'

Idris opened his wooden chest and brought out a woollen rug bought from a Persian a few days ago for a trifle. The Persian had fanned himself vigorously and said in dismay, 'What will I do with this rug, brother? It's just taking up space and I will never sell it in a place as hot as this.'

'I'll take it off your hands,' Idris had said, offering him a nominal sum while wondering if he was making a mistake.

'You had this in your chest?' Sala Pokkar whispered as Idris draped it over him.

Idris nodded. 'Now don't talk. I'll make you something to drink.'

A little later, Sala Pokkar felt Idris touch his elbow. He opened his eyes reluctantly. Idris propped him up against his chest and held a copper bowl to his mouth. 'Sip it slowly. It will settle your fever.'

Sala Pokkar took a sip and spluttered at the heat. 'What is in it?' he said through streaming eyes, nose and mouth on fire.

'Ginger, cumin and thippali... the long pepper, brewed together. I added some honey, but it wasn't enough, I realize,' Idris said, peering into the copper bowl. 'Drink it now.'

Kandavar came into the room, rubbing his eyes. 'What's going on?'

'Sala Pokkar is unwell,' Idris said. 'You should go back to sleep and stay away from that stream he likes to swim in.'

Sala Pokkar closed his eyes and rested his head against Ikka's chest. He felt a soothing warmth spread through him and his bones felt less like water.

It would be a week before Sala Pokkar found the use of his legs again. On the morning after he fell sick, Idris had gone to the market square and found two physicians seated under a tree. He looked at the older of the two and decided to bring him home.

The old man examined Sala Pokkar and shook his head. 'It's the mosquito fever. We see a lot of this in the hot months. But at this time of the year...'

'He used to go swimming in the stream by the house,' Idris said.

The man slapped his palm on his forehead. 'Is he mad? The water is brackish and who knows what else he must have caught.'

Idris didn't answer. Instead, he counted out the money for the physician's fee.

'Come with me and I will tell you what to give him to kill the fever and the disease.'

There were large, horrible-tasting pills to swallow, potions to drink, the smoke of the Malabar rattle broom leaves to inhale, before Sala Pokkar recovered enough to offer the rug back to Idris. 'It's too hot,' he said.

Idris smiled and hung the rug out in the sun. Later, Sala Pokkar watched as Idris inserted camphor into the rolled-up rug and shoved it back into his wooden chest. That was when it suddenly occurred to him that something was missing.

'Your ring is gone,' he exclaimed.

'The Amin wears it now. Or, perhaps his wife,' Idris said.

'So you have your money?' Sala Pokkar asked. 'So much seems to have happened while I was laid up.' His voice dwindled to a whisper.

'Nothing has happened. I was waiting for you. Two days from now, we'll go and find ourselves what we need for the long haul to Gani.'

'Gani?' Kandavar asked from the doorway. 'So what about the diamond mine?'

'Gani. Kollur. The mine is called by both names. And from there, we will go perhaps to another mine. We'll see.'

Kandavar and Sala Pokkar exchanged glances. Idris seemed to have worked everything out.

The next morning, the three of them went to meet the headman of a nearby village. The Amin had said he would help them.

'They don't look like weavers or farmers. Did you see the

muscles on the one who stood at the entrance of the village? And he wasn't even the guard!' Sala Pokkar whispered as they passed one burly man after the other.

They found the headman seated under a giant banyan tree. On an adjacent piece of land, several handsome oxen stood grazing. A few herons strutted between the feet of the cattle.

The headman frowned at the motley group. The interpreter the Amin had sent with them stepped forward. 'The Amin sends his greetings.'

The big-bellied headman stood up. Kandavar thought he had never seen a belly as big and rotund. It was bigger than the pot they stored tamarind in at the tharavad. And it wasn't a wobbly belly, like he had seen on many men. This one seemed packed with muscle. If he flung a coconut against it, he was certain it would shatter into pieces. 'That is an impressive belly,' he whispered to Sala Pokkar.

'Ssh…' Sala Pokkar prodded him.

The headman smiled and beckoned to Kandavar. He spoke to the interpreter.

The man hid his smile and translated, 'The headman would like your son to touch his belly as he can see that the boy is most impressed by its magnificence.'

Idris took a deep breath. He hoped for Allah's sake that they hadn't violated some code of protocol here. 'Go, inan,' Idris said. 'Touch that belly as if it were a snake. Cautiously, but with a steady hand.'

Kandavar walked towards the headman and prodded his belly with his index finger. It didn't budge.

The headman threw back his head and laughed. He spoke to the interpreter.

The man cleared his throat. 'The headman says he expected more of the boy. He would like him to punch his belly.'

Idris shook his head. 'No, that may not be advisable. The boy has some training as a fighter. He may injure the headman.'

But the headman wouldn't agree. 'He insists,' the interpreter said in a worried voice.

Idris spoke to Kandavar. 'Inan, he wants you to punch him in his belly. But remember, this is not the kalari. He merely wants to impress us. So let him have his way.'

Kandavar nodded and made a cursory punch. The headman frowned and shook his head. He peered at Kandavar and gestured he punch him again and with force.

Kandavar nibbled on his lip. The belly had a marmam; a vital spot that most fighters aimed to locate, for a punch there could kill. But the headman didn't think a boy such as him could inflict such a blow. Kandavar used the side of his palm and sent a vicious chop into the side of that humongous belly, well away from the nabhi marmam, the navel.

Idris closed his good eye while the golden one continued to watch impassively. The headman buckled at his knees. The attendants stood in their places, transfixed by the sight of their infallible headman groaning, doubled over.

Sala Pokkar and the interpreter held their breath. Only Kandavar seemed unperturbed as he examined the side of his palm. It felt sore but he had been careful, he thought. He hoped Aabo wouldn't be furious with him.

The headman straightened. He glowered at Kandavar as if annoyed at his temerity and then, after a moment, smiled. He hooked a finger into Kandavar's curly hair and tugged at it.

'Come,' he gestured to them to follow him.

When the interpreter had explained what they were there for, the headman pulled at a coarse hair that grew from a mole on his chin. 'That is some distance away, but a route we know well enough. I don't have any horses and the terrain is too rough for carts. Hardly anyone uses carts here anyway. I would suggest an ox for the boy and servant and a palanquin for the master.'

'Do I need a palanquin?' Idris asked in a querulous tone. 'I can ride an ox too.'

The interpreter turned to the headman. The big, burly man cocked an eyebrow and mumbled.

'The headman thinks you would need an elephant, not an ox. The length of your legs would… er… you are too tall,' the interpreter improvised.

'What did he actually say?' Idris asked, curious at the interpreter's discomfiture.

'He wanted to know if you planned to wind your legs around the ox's horns.'

Idris guffawed loudly. 'Well then, I can walk.'

'He says you will slow down the others. Besides, no one will see you as a man of consequence unless you arrive in a palanquin. The banias are very good at reading a man from his trappings. No one will offer you a good stone if you look like you can't afford it,' the interpreter said.

Idris exhaled. It seemed he was to don another guise for this expedition. A man of means. So be it.

'You will need about five oxen, three to carry your belongings. Two for the boy and man to ride on. And you will need six palanquin bearers who can double as guards,' the headman said.

Idris blanched. 'We are a small group, as you can see. Do we need all this pomp and fanfare?'

The headman shrugged. 'The terrain is difficult and you don't want to be attacked by a roving band of robbers. The reputation of my men is well known, so no one would dare come even one cos near you.'

Idris smiled at the headman. It seemed he was going to have a caravan of men and animals with him. 'All right,' he said. 'We need to talk terms now.'

'The terms are always the same. You can hire or buy the oxen. That is up to you. Though I would recommend you buy rather than hire them. A pair of good, trotting oxen will cost you about five hundred rupees but again, as the Amin sent you and you need five of them, we will round off to one thousand rupees. On your return, you can sell the oxen and recover most of your money. And you will need a man to tend to the oxen. The palanquin can be rented out and will cost a silver rupee per day and we can negotiate a price depending on which one you like. The attendants will have to be paid four rupees each, all inclusive, and if the journey takes more than sixty days, you pay five rupees,' the headman explained to the interpreter.

Idris totalled it up in his mind. It was fair enough, he decided. The headman gestured for them to follow. 'Now you must choose the cattle. When they are brought to you with the palanquin, you may pay us. Once you pay, we will not return the money.'

The four of them followed the headman to the pasture where milk-white oxen with curving horns tipped with silver chewed on the grass determinedly. Dust flew as one of the men tussled with a year-old ox and threw it on its back. A hot iron was used to create a slit that was a finger wide through the cartilage of its nose. The headman bent down and through this slit, he pushed a small but sturdy green stick with a forked end.

'This way, it won't slip out,' he said. 'When the nose is still sore, we will train him to accept the harness and a rider. In a week and a half, he will be a perfect mount.'

'You can find many breeds of cattle, but my father decided to bring in Ongo cattle from Prakasam. Look at them... short-horned and white and with great agility, so they make perfect pack animals. They are heavy but tough, and mine have a streak of intelligence that you will rarely find elsewhere. They are fine two-year-olds,' the headman said, patting the rump of the one nearest him.

The ox shook its head and the bells around its neck clanged loudly. Kandavar looked at the giant white oxen with admiration. 'This one is mine,' he said, walking towards one.

'He is not good for riding,' the headman said. 'Look at his horns. They are too long. You need a short-horned animal. The horns should not be more than this long,' he said, indicating the space between his wrist and elbow.

'Or, when the reins chafe his neck, or sometimes when flies hover around his head, he will toss back his head and the horn will pierce your belly,' the interpreter translated.

'Who would have thought of that?' Sala Pokkar said, wondering if he should opt to walk rather than ride one of the oxen.

Idris and the headman chose five heads of cattle. Then the headman stopped in front of a beast that had its horns tipped in gold plate. 'He is the best of the short-horned herd. For this tiger cub,' he said, pulling Kandavar towards him. 'Yours to keep.'

When Idris began to protest, he waved him away. 'Do you like him?' he asked the boy with a grin.

Kandavar's eyes flashed. He was a beauty of a beast, with a chest that was so wide and deep that the space between his ribs and hips appeared small. The belly was tight, but his loins were wide, his flanks rounded and well-proportioned and his legs strong. At two-and-a-half years, he had reached his full size, and his hide gleamed with health and vigour.

This was his diamond, he decided. 'Vajra, I will call him Vajra. Tell the headman this,' he said, tugging at Idris's arm.

There was no need to. The headman had understood the word. 'Vajra,' he said loudly and slapped the ox's rump. A diamond among oxen indeed.

XXXVIII

Idris had been inclined to stay a little longer in Masulipatnam. Sala Pokkar seemed drawn and weak and he worried the boy would take ill on the journey. But Kandavar wouldn't agree. 'No, Aabo, we have to leave. We have to go away from this place by the end of the week,' he said.

They had walked down to the beach where Idris liked to stand gazing at the waves. It calmed him down and made him feel less apprehensive about what lay ahead.

Idris looked at his son and saw the plea in his eyes. 'But why, inan?' he asked slowly.

'You mustn't laugh or think I am being silly. But I had a dream. Or maybe it was a vision. The goddess appeared and, like the last time, she sat at the foot of my bed and woke me up. She said we must leave. Don't wait. Tell your Aabo that you have to leave.'

Idris laughed. 'She knew the word Aabo, huh?'

Kandavar glowered. 'You have to listen, I tell you. The goddess had warned me about the snake in the baby's bed... Aabo...' He tugged at Idris's arm again.

It didn't make any real difference, so Idris relented and thus, a month after they had arrived in Masulipatnam, they set out for the diamond mines and thereafter, maybe even the kingdom of Golkonda, Idris told himself, feeling the familiar stirrings of excitement at the start of yet another journey.

It had been decided that they would leave before the sun had set. It is best to travel in the evening hours when travelling inland, Idris had been told. Besides, once it was twilight, the city gates would be closed and they wouldn't be permitted to leave.

'Here,' Idris said, handing a few dabu to Sala Pokkar. 'This is for anything you may wish to buy for yourself.'

Sala Pokkar looked at the copper coins. 'But what do I need to stock up on?'

Idris shrugged. 'A gewgaw? Or something you want to eat? A coil of rope, a handful of spice, whatever...'

In the afternoon, the oxen and the palanquin with its attendants arrived at their doorstep. Idris instructed the men on how to load the animals. The wooden chest would have to be carried on its own, it was agreed. With an extra oxen as a pack animal, all of it was accomplished without much fuss.

Idris looked at the palanquin nervously. It was about seven feet long and three feet wide, with a small rail all around. They had found him the longest one available. A bamboo cane curved over the middle and from it hung brocade coverings. The two ends of the bamboo arc were attached to the bed on either end. The entire contraption was placed on a frame with two poles at both ends. Would it sustain his weight? Idris wondered.

One of the men gestured for him to seat himself.

'Mount your beasts,' Idris said loudly, wanting to delay his advent into the palanquin as long as he could.

Two men helped Sala Pokkar onto his animal, but it was Kandavar whom the men surrounded as they led him with some ceremony towards Vajra, the diamond among oxen.

The animal had been washed and the gold tips of its horns gleamed. Three tiny bells were attached to each horn and they filled the air with a pleasing tinkle each time Vajra moved his head. The horns had been polished with oil and the animal's hooves shod. A white rope dipped in turmeric was slung around its neck, and from it hung a talisman fashioned out of shell and black beads to ward off the evil eye. The headman had instructed his men to take good care of the tiger cub. 'The rannebebulli is afraid of nothing, so you have to be afraid for him,' he had said.

The two oxen that were to be mounted had a ring inserted into the septum separating one nostril from the other and it was to this ring, the bridle, a thong of hide of sufficient length to reach around the neck was attached. The thong was attached to a leather collar four fingers wide around the oxen's neck. The collar stretched over the hump on the oxen's back, keeping it taut without hurting the animal. It was from the collar that the reins were drawn. A sheep's skin with wool on it was placed on the back of the animal and on it a sturdy cloth. All of it was held in place by a rope that was passed three times around the body of the animal. This was to be the saddle. On either side of the animal, a leather loop had been attached to the rope into which a piece of wood had been inserted to work as a stirrup.

The men made Kandavar sit and gave him the reins attached to the bridle. The ox's back was wide as a bed and Kandavar could even sit cross-legged if he chose to.

One of the attendants stepped to the side of the palanquin and said. 'Their walking pace is about one cos an hour. Unlike horses, they need to stop, to rest and chew their cud. So that is going to determine how much distance we can cover.'

The man's name was Golla. Idris was startled to hear him speak Arabic, even if it was with a strong Telugu accent. He exhaled. For the past hour he had worried about how they were going to make themselves understood. He stepped into the palanquin.

'Don't forget Musa,' Sala called out. The kitten, who had been put into a bamboo cage, was placed near Idris's foot.

And so Idris and his entourage set out.

There was a beautiful garden on the outskirts of the town; the ship's surgeon had described it to him. It was a little less than half a cos away and they were soon at its gates. Golla murmured, 'We may not be allowed in there.'

He gestured for them to halt.

Idris stepped out of the palanquin, relieved to be standing on firm ground again.

Sala Pokkar and Kandavar looked equally shaken by their ride. He watched as the men helped Sala Pokkar and Kandavar get off their oxen. It was dusk and the sky was streaked a deep red turning to grey at the edges. The cawing of crows filled the air. Idris raised his arms above his head and stretched.

Golla, who Idris now knew to be the team leader, came up to him. 'Ayana,' he said softly, using the Telugu word for master, 'we may not be able to enter the garden of the Dutch people, but I know a place nearby with a stream and plenty of trees. Let us rest there tonight and leave early at dawn. We have to cross a river some cos away. I would prefer that we do it by day.'

Idris nodded.

Sala Pokkar sidled up to Idris. 'Ikka, how long is this journey going to be?'

Kandavar had Musa in his lap. He smiled at Sala Pokkar's expression. Sala Pokkar had grumbled all through about the ignominy of being perched on a bullock.

'It was this or a horse,' Kandavar had said.

'A horse? They're too high up and horses are known to bolt,' Sala Pokkar said.

'Apart from which, neither of you knows how to ride a horse. And horses can be tricky creatures if they know the rider is a novice,' Idris had called out from his palanquin.

Idris smiled at Sala Pokkar as he stood with one foot on a tree stump as if to stretch it back to its natural angle. 'The distance to Golkonda, which is where we are headed after the diamond mine, is one hundred and twelve cos. It takes about two nazhikas to cover one cos.'

Sala Pokkar's foot fell off the stump. 'I will be an old man before we get there,' he said in dismay.

'Don't be silly.' Idris frowned. 'Besides, we'll stop at Kollur first to find our diamonds.' Idris had reverted to calling the diamond mine by its local name Kollur. Only the Arabs and Persians seemed to call it Gani.

'And this Kollur is how far away?'

Golla appeared like a djinn, gesturing for Idris to go with him.

'Not very far away,' Idris said, walking away. Sala Pokkar, he could see, was inclined to complain and fret like an old woman if he didn't have much to do. He would tell Golla to give him a few chores.

Golla walked down a path, into a clearing. The oxen were grazing by the stream. Across the stream was a narrow bridge made of bamboo poles and on the other side, a copse of trees with a small stone structure.

Idris nodded. They would rest here tonight. Even though they hadn't travelled very far, he felt a great fatigue.

'Come,' he said, walking back to the road where Sala Pokkar and Kandavar waited with two of the men. 'Golla has found a resting place for the night.'

They bathed in the stream that gushed around them with tremendous force. And then Sala Pokkar and two of the attendants cooked the night meal while two men watered the oxen, and two others sat vigil as the night enveloped them.

In the light of the fire, Idris pulled out his journal and writing paraphernalia. He glanced through the pages. There was nothing in there that would make him ponder or exclaim. Most days had passed with nothing of significance to report. Accounting details, dates of arrival and departure, and a few couplets of his hashish poetry. Idris had begun to ask himself: why do I need to keep a journal of my doings? I am neither a scholar nor a keeper of history, it is not imperative that I track my journeys, my doings, my thoughts. And yet, tonight it felt right that he sit here with his journal and ink and write of this momentous journey in search of diamonds.

'Aabo.' Kandavar crept to his side. 'What does that mean?' He pointed to the calligram. 'Almas.'

'It is the Arabic word for diamond,' Idris said.

Musa nudged his way between the father and son.

'And what do you call a cat?' Kandavar asked.

'Quitta, for a tomcat like Musa. Would you like to learn

to speak my language? Do you remember the Arabic letters I taught you while we were in Paliacatta?' Idris asked, struck by a thought. He would like to have taught his son the Somali language, but perhaps in his life ahead, Arabic may be of more use than the Somali tongue.

Kandavar frowned. Then he smiled at the thought of greeting Rairu with a mouthful of Aabo's language. And Aabo and he could converse without anyone else understanding. 'Yes,' he said. 'I would like that.'

Kandavar sat by Idris as he wrote in his journal, poking the fire once in a while and sending out a spray of sparks. The wood cracked and burst.

'You should go to sleep,' Idris said. 'We'll make an early start.'

Kandavar nodded. He thought they had stopped too soon after they left. But both Sala Pokkar and he were unused to riding, even if it was only a bullock, and to ride too far on the first day would have made them stiff, Aabo said. And it was true, his muscles felt sore.

Golla had rolled out three mats. Sala Pokkar brought three thin pieces of cloth for them to cover themselves with. Kandavar drew his mat closer to Idris and curled up on it, pulling the cloth to his chin. He lay there watching Idris till he fell asleep and his last thought was that when Aabo was with him, everything felt safe, everything felt right.

XXXIX

It was the fifth day of the month of Safar. It wasn't yet dawn. Idris sought the sky for a reading before they set out. Al-Zahra and Al-Mushtarie blazed in the skies, but there was Otareed as well. The smallest planet and closest to the sun. To dream about the Otareed meant a project begun would not be completed. But what if one were to see it for real?

Idris looked at the sky again, tilting his head at an angle so only the Al-Zahra and Al-Mushtarie were visible. What he couldn't see wouldn't hurt him, he decided. He didn't want to cast a blight on their journey even before they had begun.

Kandavar was wide awake. It was pitch-dark and the fire had died out. He could hear the snuffling of the oxen and Sala Pokkar snoring. Then he saw the attendants walk towards them. They had been washing in the stream. The oxen shook their heads and the little bells tinkled. He looked around. Where was Aabo?

'Aabo,' he called out, suddenly frightened. Had he left without saying a word?

'I am here, inan.' Aabo's deep, rumbly voice spoke from the darkness. 'You are awake?'

Kandavar stood up. One of the attendants started the fire. He was warming a cauldron of water.

Sala Pokkar sat up, looking shamefaced. 'I overslept. I didn't realize it was time for us to go...' He beckoned to Kandavar and they walked to the stream. By the time they had washed, the animals were loaded and the fire stamped out. 'Here, drink this,' Golla said, offering Kandavar a small brass glass.

Kandavar took a sip. The drink was fiery and sweet and left a trail of fire in its path. 'What is this?' he asked.

Sala Pokkar took a sip and rolled the fluid within his mouth. 'Ginger and jaggery. And some herb.'

'Tulasi,' Idris said. 'It will remove any phlegm from your chest and strengthen your nerves.'

Kandavar drank the brew and went to check on Vajra.

'We will head towards Nidumolu or Milmol, as the whites call it, which is four cos away. We can break journey there. It is a small village, but they are used to travellers and will provide us with whatever we need,' Golla said as Idris climbed into the palanquin.

Kandavar found himself more at ease on Vajra today, and as they set out, he thought: If only the oxen would hurry.

A strong wind started soon and blew around them. Kandavar grew afraid as he saw the wind toss everything in its way. But Vajra seemed impervious to the strength of the wind and trotted to the rhythm of the palanquin attendants' brisk walk. Idris peered through the brocade curtains at the shambling oxen with their curving horns and felt a sudden sense of apprehension. Where were they going?

The terrain was still flat and there were well-worn tracks to the village of Nidumolu. But the wind blew up dust and disturbed the animals. Fortunately, they were at the village gates an hour before noon.

It began raining. 'Nothing unusual about it,' Golla said. 'Rains at this time of the year are expected. The north-east winds have begun blowing and they bring rain with them.'

Through the rain, they marched into the village, where everyone seemed to have vanished.

'There is a house that I know from my last visit here. They set it aside for travellers. We'll have to pay for its use, though,' Golla said, walking along the palanquin.

He had wound a cloth around his head but otherwise seemed as undeterred by the rain as Vajra and the other oxen. Idris saw water dripping down his back. The small cloth wound around his hips to fall just past his knees was soaking wet. For a moment Idris envied him the freedom of knowing the elements on his skin. The wind and the rain and the sun and its warmth; he felt hot and humid in his clothes.

'Yes, of course,' Idris said. 'Will it hold all of us?'

'You want us to share the house with you?' Golla's eyes widened with incredulity.

'We travel together,' Idris replied. 'So we will eat and sleep together. That is the rule of travel.'

'This is the first I have heard of it,' Golla said, not sure if he liked the idea. As for his men, what would they think? Under the stars, it was all right for them to rest together but beneath a roof, differences would show up. The Cafre was either a saint or a fool if he thought otherwise.

'We will deal with that later. For now, let me find my contact in the village,' Golla said firmly and walked into the village, leaving the others beneath a giant ficus tree.

In a little while he returned, holding a plantain leaf over his head. He smiled sheepishly at Idris. 'They insisted.'

Golla led them to a small thatched house. It had been cleaned out by the villager who owned it and within were four cots made of wooden frames and braided rope. Golla pulled two together lengthwise, grinning. 'Ayana can sleep on this.'

Kandavar looked around the house curiously. There were just two small rooms and an enclosed yard with a mango tree in it. He put the bamboo cage down and let out Musa. The kitten stepped out and stretched. Kandavar watched and mimicked its body movements. He felt his muscles stretch and the soreness vanish.

'Change into this,' Sala Pokkar said, handing a dry cloth to Kandavar.

Kandavar took off the clothes that Aabo had someone stitch for him in Galle. He now had three sets of tunics and trousers and long cotton breeches to wear beneath the trousers. 'Why can't I dress like Sala Pokkar?' Kandavar had demanded, thinking of the more familiar blue and white checked cloth Sala Pokkar wore around his hips. It was held at the waist by a broad leather belt and he wore a sleeveless, open tunic above it.

'Sala Pokkar looks like the khalasi he is. But it is necessary you wear the same clothes as I do, so that no one doubts who you are,' Idris had said.

Kandavar had been wearing the tunic and trousers for almost a year now, but it was a relief to be rid of them. He walked into the open courtyard in his loincloth and felt the rain thunder down on him.

From the doorway, Idris watched.

On a whim, he pulled his clothes off and wearing just a cloth around his hips, he too stepped into the rain.

Kandavar stared in surprise. 'Aabo,' he said in a voice full of wonder and exhilaration. 'You will get wet.'

Idris raised his face to the rain. 'I am not salt; I won't disappear if the rain falls on me, inan.' He reached for a branch of the mango tree and shook it so the spray splashed Kandavar's face. The boy giggled and ran.

Sala Pokkar stood with his hands on his hips and watched the father and son gambol in the rain. He smiled at them and then turned to the kitten. 'We are not rain lovers, are we, Musa?'

Musa licked his paw and curled into a ball. And Sala Pokkar went back in to figure out what to cook.

It rained all through the night and well into the next day. Later that evening, two bania merchants heading to Bezawada arrived at Nidumolu. They looked more shaken than exhausted, Idris thought as he saw them walk into the village.

'Where did you come from?' the senior bania asked Idris. He was a man of some fifty years with little hair, a rotund flabby body and a haughty gaze that seemed to dwell on man and beast, leaf and stone and find everything wanting. His companion was a youth with a thin, long face and a quivering voice, who couldn't seem to stop wringing his hands the moment he came into his uncle's orbit.

Idris frowned at the terseness. 'Why? But, since you asked, Masulipatnam.'

The two merchants looked at each other. 'There was a great storm in the early hours of the day,' the senior bania said.

The younger man wrung his hands in agitation as he spoke in short staccato sentences, describing the scene they had fled from. 'Winds that blew houses away and swept many boats out into the sea. Two ships were swept ashore. They stand seven feet deep in sand. Trees have fallen and buildings collapsed. The water rose till it covered parts of the town. Several people have died in the sea and on land.'

Idris felt Kandavar clasp his elbow. 'Whereabouts did the water rise?' he asked.

'In the southern end of the city, where there are some houses. The water rose from the sea and the river and the people asleep in their homes didn't even realize the storm had struck. We had been living there in a house for the last three days, ever since our ship docked,' the young bania answered.

'We came from Surat, and we thought we would build our strength before starting for Bezawada. We had decided to make an early start and so we missed the storm by a hair's breadth.' The senior bania glowered at his nephew in irritation. The boy wasn't letting him get in a word even edgeways.

'That's where we lived too,' Idris said slowly. 'We left two evenings before, or it could have been us.'

Neither Idris nor Kandavar spoke as they went back to their rented house.

'Aabo, this is the second time the goddess has appeared and told me what to do,' Kandavar said, unable to stop his lips from trembling. He knew he had insisted that they leave Masulipatnam. But he hadn't ever thought about what it meant to ignore the goddess's warning. Would they have died as well?

Idris looked at his son with a knot of fear. Had it been a coincidence or did his child have the sight?

'What is it, inan, that you see? Tell me again?' he asked.

Kandavar described to him the first time the goddess had appeared, and then the second. Idris saw how the boy's face turned into a mask devoid of all emotion as he spoke. It was as if he was describing what he had seen happen to someone else rather than to himself. Idris drew his son close. Such a mighty burden for such a small boy. 'Inan, you must forget all about it. And you mustn't mention these visions to anyone else. It is best we keep it quiet.'

Kandavar nodded. He didn't understand, but he was exhausted.

It continued to rain for the next two days and Golla walked around with a worried expression.

'We have to cross a river about four cos away and if it continues to rain like this, the waters would have risen,' he said.

Idris smiled. 'You worry too much, Golla,' he said. 'We will cross the river when we come to it.'

By evening the rain stopped and after the continuous din of water falling on leaves, a curious stillness descended. 'We will leave for Weeyuir tomorrow,' Idris said.

'But we mustn't leave too early. I want us to cross the river in broad daylight,' Golla said.

The banias decided to accompany them. Idris looked longingly at their horses and wondered if the older merchant would agree to swap. The headman had turned down Idris's plea for a horse, saying that theirs was a small group and the oxen would be unable to keep up with the horse. 'You will end up losing your way and it's treacherous country.'

The ground was wet after the incessant rain and progress was slow. They halted early in the evening. Idris yawned and teased Golla as he went about preparing a feed for the oxen. 'Where is your river, Golla?'

The man didn't speak. Instead, he poured a ser of chickpeas into a cauldron of water. 'When this has soaked for half an hour, I will mash it and feed it to the oxen,' he said, looking up. 'Tomorrow they will need all their strength to cross the river.'

Idris flushed. He had been firmly put in his place. 'Oh,' he said, not knowing how else to respond.

'I hope your son and man can swim; I hope you do as well,' Golla added.

That night, as the fire was lit and everyone gathered around it, one of the men began to sing.

Idris had been staring at the blank pages of his journal, unable to pen the banalities of their walking hours and the number of cos covered. He set aside the sheet of paper and put it back in its chamois leather bag. Then he leaned back against a tree and shut his eye. The plaintive notes of the song and the man's high, clear voice filled him with an ache he couldn't name.

How could he yearn for what he had not known? How could he miss what was not his? This thing called life; what was it all about? This relentless searching, this hunger to know, what in the end would it fetch him?

XL

For a moment, everyone fell silent. They had reached the river.

Sala Pokkar got off his mount. Kandavar continued to sit on Vajra.

Idris and Golla stood by the river bank and gazed at the expanse of water. The river was full and treacherous. 'It is just as I feared.' Golla sighed. 'The rains have flooded the river. This is otherwise a gentle tributary of the Krishna.'

'We can't wait for the water to subside,' Idris said.

Golla nodded. He just hoped that at the end of the journey,

the Cafre would reward them for what they were about to undergo in the next hour or two.

'Isn't there a boatsman here?' Sala Pokkar asked, holding his hand to his forehead to shade his eyes as he stared at the silvery waters glinting in the sunlight.

The banias stood undecided. 'What's wrong?' Idris asked them curiously.

The older merchant smiled sheepishly. 'I can't swim. Nor can he. And then there are the horses.'

Idris put his hand on the bania's horse. 'You don't think we will abandon you to fend for yourselves, do you?'

The bania dropped his gaze. He had thought they would.

'The boatsman wants half a rupee, he says, and in silver,' Golla said with a frown. 'He says he wouldn't usually take the raft out in waters like this.'

'Raft?' The bania's voice shook.

Just then, the boatsman arrived. He put his hand out for the payment. 'Where are the rafts?' the senior bania demanded.

'That is how it is,' Golla said. 'They have to be paid first, before they bring the rafts out.'

Idris watched the boatsman walk away. 'Where is he going?'

Golla shrugged. 'They don't trust anyone. He will put the silver rupee into the fire and check that it is real silver before they bring out the coracles.'

'I thought you said raft,' the bania spoke up.

Golla ignored him.

When the boatsman came back, there were three men with him. They carried four shallow baskets about 12 feet in diameter, made of bamboo and covered from the outside with cow hide.

'We are to cross the river on this?' The junior bania voiced the concern that neither Idris nor Sala Pokkar dared to. 'It looks like it can barely hold a pigeon, let alone a man.'

'Why would a pigeon need a coracle?' Golla asked under his breath.

'And is that animal skin?' the senior bania said in horror.

'Well, this is all there is. Or you can wait for the summer, when the river dries up, and you can wade across... that is up to you,' Golla said, as he began tethering the oxen together with a rope. He was vexed with the banias, their rules and taboos, their fears and complaints.

One man led three of the oxen while another took the reins of the other three, including Vajra. One of the palanquin attendants led the horses. All the animals went into the water without any hesitation and stood waist deep as the rafts were pushed into the river. The goods were loaded onto one raft and when the palanquin had been placed on top of it, Golla climbed into it. Idris took Musa in his cage and waded into the water. Sala Pokkar and Kandavar followed him as he climbed onto the raft. The banias and the other men were on the last coracle. The boatsmen pushed their poles into the water and the men leading the oxen and horses put a hand on the rafts and let themselves float along.

Idris thought this must be one of the strangest scenes he had ever seen in his life. The convoy of men and beasts, floating like an island across the water.

The sun shone and the river sparkled. A steady breeze blew, licking at their faces, and for a while Idris felt as if he were in a dream. He looked at his son's face. What was he thinking? The boy trailed his fingers in the water.

'Aabo, will Vajra be all right?' Kandavar asked. The horses were good swimmers, the oxen, reluctant.

'They are used to this, I am told,' Idris lied. He hoped they were.

The current was swift and the raft that held the banias bounced against a rock. It tilted precariously and the young bania fell into the water.

'He can't swim, he can't swim… save him,' the senior bania screamed, flapping his hands.

One of the men in the water swam towards the boy and dragged him back to the raft. He sat wet and trembling till the rafts reached the shore. It was not a long crossing, so they were soon at the banks. The horses and the oxen clambered up the shore and stood in the heat, drying themselves. The rafts were pulled ashore and the goods unloaded. The banias stepped onto the shore, still trembling.

'We will let the animals rest for a bit before we start,' Golla said.

Idris sat beneath a tree, watching Golla knead wheat flour, melted butter and palm sugar. He moulded them into six balls and then, as if it had just occurred to him, he prised a little off each and made two more.

'Here, feed this to the animals,' he said, handing the balls to one of his men.

'They have used up all their strength crossing the river and we still have three cos to go before reaching Weeyuir,' Golla told Idris.

The senior bania sat across from Idris. The younger man brought him some food on a leaf plate.

'What is it like to be a vegetarian?' Idris asked him curiously.

'We are vegetarians from birth and my family, which we can trace back by several hundred years, has always been vegetarian. So it is the most normal thing for me.' The bania smiled. 'We cannot understand the killing of life for food.'

'It is the law of nature,' Idris said.

'But we are not animals. That should make us different,' the junior bania piped up. The senior man silenced him with a glare.

'In Malabar, the killing of a cow is a capital offence,' Idris said.

'That is how it should be,' the senior bania said, nodding his head in agreement. 'The cow is our mother. To kill a go-mata is to commit matricide and it is a crime that must be met with the most serious of punishments. But we believe all life is sacred. So we do not tolerate the killing of any animal or bird, and not just our go-mata!'

Idris frowned. 'What do you mean?'

'Tell him, uncle,' the younger bania whispered.

'Like I said, all life for us is sacred. We especially do not permit killing for sport. But once in a while, a travelling merchant who has too much time on his hands may decide to go hunting.' The senior bania leaned forward as he recounted his tale. 'Once, while I was on my way to Agra, I had to cross a pass near Gopalpur. On the Agra side, some of our people have shops where they sell flour, rice, butter, vegetables and condiments. So I decided to stay on. Besides, there is a river that I had to cross and it was so full and swift after the rain that I had to wait for it to subside.

'Anyway, another merchant from Persia too was staying there. He was waiting like me for the river to subside. One morning, he killed a peacock that was on the road as he rode past. The fool that he was, he had not bothered to find out anything about our customs. Who knows why he did it? Boredom, or perhaps he wanted to prove he could kill. For whatever reason, he killed a peacock for no real reason except that it was there. In kingdoms where Mohammedans like you rule, it is all right to hunt for sport. But the Raja of the region is a Hindu, like we are.'

'And?' Idris asked.

'We were so enraged that we went to the merchant's lodgings and dragged him to the spot where he had slain the peacock. We tied him to a tree and whipped him soundly and left him there for three days so he would never kill an animal again.'

'What happened to him?' Idris asked quietly.

'He died.' The bania laughed. 'He had a huge fortune on

him. About 300,000 rupees, which we handed over to the Raja's treasury.'

Idris looked at the mild-faced bania, unable to decide how he felt. Sala Pokkar nudged him. 'What was that story about?'

Idris translated.

'But how did the merchant kill the peacock?' Kandavar asked. He too had been listening, darting glances at the elderly bania.

'A gun, perhaps. Though I have seen something very curious on my travels. I have seen hunters approach a peacock holding a cloth screen on which a peacock is painted. Once, I saw a giant peacock come close to the screen, and the hunter's partner shot an arrow through its throat,' Idris said.

Kandavar frowned, but didn't speak. Then he looked at Idris and said, 'If he doesn't believe in killing, ask him how it was that he and the other men were able to beat the life out of the Persian merchant?'

Idris smiled and translated.

The bania's face tightened. 'This is different,' he said, rising to his feet.

It was almost dusk when they entered Weeyuir. They spent the night there in the village, and the next day, they finally reached Bezawada.

The rains began again and Golla looked worried. 'What now?' Idris asked.

'We have to cross the river and the Krishna is not as gentle as her sister we crossed before. We need to stay here till the rain stops,' he said.

'Don't look so worried. There will be plenty to see and do here,' Idris said as he got off the palanquin and stretched. He would be glad to have the use of his legs again.

The elderly bania and his nephew looked relieved to have

reached their destination. 'There is much to see here,' the senior bania said as they bid farewell. 'There is a temple, I am told, that has fifty-two columns, each twenty feet high. There are no walls around it, so you can see it from the outside. There is another one on a hill which is reached by climbing 193 steps, each step a foot high. But as a Muslim, I suppose temples mean nothing to you.'

Golla looked at Idris to see how he would respond.

'I have something to ask you,' Idris said. 'You killed a man who killed a peacock. How does one wrong justify another wrong?'

The elderly bania frowned. 'He should have known better.'

Golla hovered by the horses. The banias were notoriously tight-fisted, but he and his men had served them well.

Idris saw the hopeful expression on Golla's face and felt a wave of anger at the banias, who now pretended not to see him. 'My men have taken good care of you and your belongings. It would mean much to them if you were to make a present of some money as a token of appreciation.'

The elderly bania's face fell. His nephew and he had tagged along so they wouldn't have to pay what it would have cost them to hire guards. 'Oh,' he said.

He opened the money bag at his waist and pulled out the smallest copper coin he could find. 'Here,' he said to Golla.

Golla held up the coin as if it were a golden pagoda and peered at it. Then he handed it back to the elderly bania saying, 'This is too much. I don't want you to empty your coffers for us.'

The nephew looked embarrassed. Idris walked away in disgust. Golla went back to his men, shaking his head in amusement. Once upon a time, human pettiness had angered him; now it merely amused him.

The elderly bania gathered the reins of his horse and moved on to find his cousin's home in Bezawada. The nephew followed.

Early next morning, there was a knock at the door of the house Golla had arranged for them. Sala Pokkar opened the door and found the young bania standing there. He frowned. The man asked for Idris and smiled sheepishly as he entered the room. 'What brings you here?' Idris asked, surprised.

'I must apologize for my uncle. This is my own money and I would like Golla and his men to have it,' the bania said, laying down two silver rupees. 'I wasn't sure if they would accept it from me.'

Idris nodded.

And then the young man leaned forward and whispered, as if he didn't even want the walls to hear, 'And when you find your diamonds, bring them to me. I will appraise them for you so that you know their true value.'

'You are a young boy. What would you know about diamonds?' Idris asked in surprise.

'Like many others of our caste, I was trained from a very young age to identify a good stone and value it. I made my first sale when I was twelve. We made a hundred per cent profit. Why do you think my uncle dragged me with him all the way from Surat?' The boy smiled.

Golla was pleased with the junior bania's gift but he was unhappy with their progress. The rains had started again and they would soon have to cross the river. This time the mighty Krishna herself, and not some little tributary.

'Build your strength and that of the animals. It's a long haul from here, I am told,' Idris offered.

Golla nodded, trying not to show how worried he was. Vajra seemed to be sickening for something. He was a curious young ox, given to chewing on anything and everything he found. Golla thought of the clump of trees where the oxen had been left to graze. But the boy had taken Vajra further in. There had been a vine there. Had Vajra eaten some of that? Ten leaves of it were enough to kill a full-grown bull. Golla groaned. The headman would dismember him and throw his carcass to carrion if he discovered that his gift to the boy had been so callously treated.

'Vajra isn't well. It is best we give him time to recover,' Golla said. He walked to the meadow where the cattle had been left to graze.

Kandavar stood near Vajra, coaxing him to eat. But the ox stood with his head bent low and his eyes listless. 'Did Vajra eat any of this?' Golla asked, showing a bit of the creeper he had brought with him.

'No, but by the river he found a plant with tiny white flowers that he started chewing on before I dragged him away,' Kandavar said, trying to remember all that Vajra had taken a bite of.

'Ummetta,' Golla said. 'That's better than what I feared.'

'Will he get better?' Kandavar asked quietly. His heart felt as if it would explode.

'We will make him better.' Golla smiled and went to make a purge.

Kandavar sat by Vajra, willing him to get better. Aabo often said that if you wished for something hard enough, it would happen. All the laws of nature would conspire to make it happen.

On the fourth day, they set out again and crossed the Krishna by boat. No one spoke on the journey, for the sight of the mighty, swirling river stilled all words. They had eighteen cos to travel before they reached Kollur. And they would need three more days, Golla said. Six cos to Kah Kaly and twelve to Kollur. Vajra was better now, but he wasn't fully fit and they couldn't tax him beyond a point.

Idris nodded. As they drew closer to the town of Kollur, all he felt was a queer fear. What would await them there? And what lay ahead of him thereafter?

'You look thoughtful, Ikka. What's wrong?' Sala Pokkar asked as they made camp at a little village in the evening.

Idris shook his head. 'I was just thinking of what awaits us when we return.'

Sala Pokkar frowned. 'I can't believe you said that. What has happened to you, Ikka?'

'Look at Musa,' Idris said, holding up the kitten. 'He doesn't think of tomorrow or the thereafter. I used to be like that once, Sala Pokkar. But once you have a child, it changes everything. Your tomorrows are invested in that child.'

'But your son will be with you. So why do you sound so forlorn?'

Idris shook his head. 'He will go back to his mother. That is the arrangement.'

'Oh,' Sala Pokkar said, nonplussed.

'You should marry again, Ikka. And settle down in Kuttichira or Ponnani, or one of the places where our people are. Enough of this wandering the earth like a homeless nomad,' Sala Pokkar said, clasping Idris's hand.

Idris smiled wryly. 'It's not good for a grown man to sit around doing nothing. It's all this palanquin's fault. The mind does nothing but wander down unnecessary, unwanted paths. Once we reach Kollur, everything will be fine.'

Sala Pokkar nodded. This was the Ikka he knew and understood.

PART 6

November AD 1660–January AD 1661

(Rabi al-Awwal AH 1071–Jumaada al-Awwal AH 1071)

XLI

It was one of the strangest places any of them had seen. A settlement of migrants by the mighty Krishna, and about a cos and a half away, high mountains that cut each other at right angles to resemble a cross. Between the town and the mountains was a plain where the diamond mines were.

They headed towards the settlement. It wasn't particularly pretty or even well laid out. The mines had birthed a town of makeshift homes, and to feed the nearly hundred thousand people who lived there, shops had sprung up. There were a few fine houses with gardens that the merchants had built for themselves, and it was to one of these that Idris went.

The Amin had given him a letter of introduction. 'This should help,' he had said, fondling the little clock that Idris had presented him with the day before they left.

Idris smiled. He knew suddenly who the Amin reminded him of – the Somali crow, with its fondness for shiny objects. Stealing from the food cache of other crows adroitly and shamelessly. Yet, he could be called on to solve problems with an astonishing quickness of thought.

'He will open his home to you when he knows I sent you,' the Amin added. 'Tabriz thinks of me as his older brother. An older brother whose wishes have to be respected.'

Idris paused at the giant gates of Tabriz Ali's home, and

pulled at the bell strung on a rope. He had left the others a little behind so that the merchant wouldn't be frightened by the size of his coterie.

A manservant came to the door and led Idris to a waiting chamber. From there, Idris could see into a room within which was the receiving chamber. It was here the merchant sat and saw his employees, suppliers and guests. Idris could see him now, a youngish, handsome-looking man who sat frowning at a ledger while an elderly man stood alongside, trying to explain its contents. He looked as if he would rather be elsewhere, riding his horse, hunting for game or playing a board game with his courtesan, Idris thought.

Idris took out the Amin's letter and handed it to the servant. 'Please give this to your master,' he said.

Idris saw the merchant scan the letter, drop the ledger and rush towards him.

'Salaam walaikum,' he cried. 'How could that fool of a servant leave you here? Welcome, welcome, to my humble home, Idris Maymoon Samataar Guleed.'

Idris took a step back. 'Wa' alaykum salaam,' he said, surprised by the warmth of the welcome.

'What can I do for you?' Tabriz Ali asked when they were seated in the reception room and refreshments had been called for. The accountant had been summarily dismissed with a wave of his hand and a few mumbled words.

'We are here to procure some diamonds,' Idris began.

'We? Where is everybody else?' The merchant sat up.

'I have left them a few streets away,' Idris tried to explain. 'There is my son and my assistant.'

'That's fine. We have room for everyone here.' The merchant bobbed up and down in his excitement.

'Actually there are also six attendants, six oxen and a palanquin. And oh, I forgot, a cat.'

The merchant frowned. 'I am not sure about the attendants

and pack animals. We can house them with my employees. But the cat is welcome.'

Idris wondered what it was that the Amin had written in his letter.

A manservant was dispatched to do the needful and the merchant called for rooms to be prepared.

'It will soon be time for prayers,' he said. 'I have a prayer room in my home and we may as well pray before we sit down.'

Idris didn't respond. He was given to praying when he felt like it, rather than when it was expected of him. And yet, it would draw attention if he refrained. It would be prudent, he decided, to find separate living quarters soon.

By the time the evening prayers were finished and Idris and the merchant came back to the receiving chamber, the manservant had returned with Kandavar, Sala Pokkar and Musa. Their belongings had been kept in a warehouse that the merchant owned. Golla and his men had taken the oxen to a pasture and had said they would make their own arrangements, the manservant reported.

Idris didn't wait for long to broach the subject of a house to rent. 'Why go elsewhere? There is plenty of room here,' the merchant said, surprised.

'Tell Aabo I cannot be parted from my Vajra,' Kandavar mumbled to Sala Pokkar, when he told him what was being discussed.

Idris darted a look at the boy and smiled. 'My son has a pet ox. He will not be parted from it. We need a house with an open field where it can be tethered. So, you see, we need to have an abode that is suitable. Please do not think that I am being churlish in refusing your hospitality.'

The merchant pulled at his tuft of a beard. 'Yes, if we do not indulge our children when they are children, they will grow up to be adults with childish whimsies,' he said thoughtfully.

Idris wondered what dream of Tabriz Ali had gone unfulfilled as a child. No doubt, he would soon be told of it among other confidences.

'I have an old house by the river. It is some distance from the finer part of the town, if you can call this a fine part. But it is closer to the mines than from here. The only thing is, several of the mining families live there as well. And most of them are Hindus with dogs and pigs.' The merchant screwed up his nose at the thought of having to share space with the devil's own.

Idris put up a hand to hide his smile. He knew he and his men would be safe enough there.

'Yes, I know, but the boy will not agree to be parted from his ox. And so I must forego the pleasure of your hospitality,' Idris said, waving his hand to indicate the grandeur of his surroundings.

The truth was, he feared he would die of suffocation if he had to live amidst all the grand, ornate possessions that Tabriz Ali seemed to need on a daily basis. A clean, bare room was what he longed for.

When Kandavar and Sala Pokkar had been taken to their rooms, the merchant drew his chair closer to Idris and said, 'There is something I must tell you, brother. You will make no real profit if you merely trade. Unless you take the diamonds to the firangi's land. Would you be travelling to those parts?'

Idris smiled. 'That's highly unlikely.'

'Well then, you ought to prospect for the diamonds yourself. Who knows, with Allah's grace, you may even find a diamond to rival the one Mir Jumla had.'

'Tell me more,' Idris said, curious about the stone.

'They say it weighed almost seven hundred and eighty-eight carats. Mir Jumla offered it to Shah Jehan, and so it is called the Great Mughal Diamond. Shah Jehan sent the rough diamond to a Venetian lapidary, Ortensis Borgis, to have it cut. But the great diamond had several inclusions,' the merchant said.

Idris shook his head. 'Inclusions?'

Tabriz Ali smiled. 'I forgot you don't know enough. Here, let me show you.'

The merchant went to an inner room and came back with a chamois leather pouch. He brought out a tray lined with a burgundy-coloured velvet cloth and emptied the contents of the pouch onto it.

'These are some of the not-so-fine diamonds, but they are all I have here,' Tabriz Ali said, seeing Idris's eye flare at the sight of the sparkling stones. He held out a jeweller's loupe. 'Pick a stone and look through this. You may see some tiny specks, which may be foreign materials or sometimes a colour difference... er a cloudy portion.'

Idris gazed at a diamond only a little bigger than a baby's toenail. He couldn't see a thing within it. Allah be praised, he thought, remembering the young bania's offer to appraise his stones for him.

Idris handed back the eyeglass and stone, smiling ruefully. 'It will be many years before I understand diamonds.'

Tabriz Ali put the stones away as the refreshments were brought in. A plate of dried apricots was brought and rose-flavoured water sweetened with sugar. 'The apricots are from Shiraz and the sugar is from Surat,' the merchant said artlessly.

Idris nibbled at an apricot and said, 'Tell me about the Great Mughal Diamond.'

'Well, the gemstone cutter decided to tackle the inclusion by grinding away at the stone till all the flaws were gone. Except that when he had finished, the stone weighed only about two hundred and eighty-eight carats. He almost lost his head. In the end, the emperor fined him 10,000 rupees for his ineptitude. Apparently, that was all the money the gem cutter had!'

Idris leaned back and stretched. It had been a long day, but

Tabriz Ali was reluctant to let him go. He said it was seldom he met anyone who had travelled as much as Idris had. He himself had spent all his life perambulating between Golkonda and Kollur. 'Seven days of travel. That is the story of my life,' the merchant sighed, as he finally bid Idris goodnight.

'The first thing you ought to know is that the diamond has many names. In fact, what we call almas is known by the miners as iri. So make sure you take someone with you who speaks our language as well as theirs. Someone you can trust,' Tabriz Ali said as they walked towards their bedchambers.

The next morning, they moved to their new home. Golla and his men had been persuaded to find living quarters close by. Vajra and the other oxen were tethered in a pasture adjacent to the house, where they could rebuild their strength for the journey back to Masulipatnam.

Idris could see the river from the house. Nothing disturbed his line of vision or his thoughts as he paced the room, deep in thought. He would ask Golla to stay on as his aide and help him with the diamond prospecting. Golla was already committed to be with them till they returned to Masulipatnam. He wouldn't scoff at the thought of making some extra money on the side.

Idris wrote down the fragments of fact gleaned from his conversation with the merchant. Most of it was contrary to what the ship's surgeon had said. The surgeon had thought that the miners and locals could be bought with tobacco, mirrors and other trifles as if they were halfwits who would be easily dazzled and thus persuaded to part with their diamonds. Tabriz Ali, on the other hand, had said they accepted nothing but gold pagodas. That too, only Golkonda pagodas.

Idris sighed and put his reed pen down. A diamond was an exacting master.

The wooden chest and their other possessions had been laid out in the house. It was a damp, old house with a permanent odour of mustiness, but no one minded the discomfort. The magnificence of the river was compensation enough.

'The sea is beautiful, Aabo, but a river is better,' Kandavar said.

The boy had just come back from a swim and drops of water clung to his hair and eyelashes. His skin gleamed, and he looked like he had sprouted a few inches overnight. Idris put his arm around his son and held him quietly for a moment.

'When do you start looking for diamonds?' Kandavar asked.

'Later this day, I will go to the mines with the agent. The merchant we stayed with on our first night has organized for me to lease a piece of land. We will prospect there,' Idris said.

A heron rose from the grassy verge by the river and flapped its wings. Idris saw its flight across the grey skies and felt an incredible sense of peace, followed by a sense of loss: this time may never be his again.

'Aabo, may I go with you?' Kandavar asked. Idris looked at him unseeingly.

'And I?' Sala Pokkar's query dredged Idris back from the space in his head he had retreated to.

Sala Pokkar appeared at the doorway. 'Ikka, I am yet to see a diamond. How will I know what it is until I have seen one?'

'I haven't either,' Kandavar piped up.

'Tell me, what do you boys think? That the ground will be strewn with diamonds like seeds under a tamarind tree, and all you need to do is poke around till you find your own stash of diamonds?'

Sala Pokkar and Kandavar flushed. The thought had crossed their minds.

XLII

Idris hadn't realized it was going to be such an arduous enterprise. Tabriz Ali had found him an agent who had organized everything. The leasing of land, the hiring of miners, the supervisor and security guards, and the paperwork. Two per cent on all purchases had to be paid to the Sultan of Golkonda, as also a royalty for permission to mine. A further duty of two pagodas would need to be paid every day for hiring fifty men. Idris felt a quiet rage gather in him as the agent explained, 'And then there are their wages, which are negligible. For a whole year's work, they earn about three pagodas.'

The workers probably knew more about diamonds than anyone else, and yet they were the ones who profited the least. Idris decided he would make sure they were rewarded without breaking any established practices.

'But you have to be careful. They are completely without scruples. They will hide a stone in their mouth or,' the agent lowered his voice, 'who knows in what orifice, so they can sell it to some fly-by-night operator. We get a lot of those as well. So don't go wasting your sympathy on them!'

Idris saw the emaciated workers with their ribs sticking out, dressed in only a loincloth as they moved about. He said, unable to keep the irony out of his voice, 'They can't be selling too many stones on the sly, judging by how hungry they look.'

'That's just how they are. Even if they ate three meals with ghee in it, they would look like flea-bitten mongrels,' the agent said.

Idris bit back a retort and left, quietly resolving to have as little to do with the agent as possible.

They left at the crack of light. As they headed towards the mine, the sun rose behind the gigantic mountains, covering the slopes in an arc of golden light. Birds tweeted from the trees and a gentle breeze blew. It was a beautiful, languid morning, but at the mines, a sense of purpose dominated.

Two hundred paces in circumference had been earmarked by the mine master, who the agent had said was one of the best. 'He knows the spots better than anyone else. He is expensive, but you don't have the time for trial and error, so you need to invest in him.'

The spot that had been selected had been fenced in by a low wall of about two feet in height. Idris was surprised to see women and children waiting with the men outside the wall. And within the enclosed area were the mine master and a priest.

'What is this?' Sala Pokkar whispered as the mine master and the priest placed an idol by the wall.

'Hush,' Idris hissed. 'The miners are Hindus and must do as they believe. Or, they will later cite this as the reason why the diamonds were of insignificant value. Besides, everyone is entitled to their beliefs, Sala Pokkar.'

The men, women and children prostrated before the idol three times while the priest chanted a prayer.

Kandavar frowned. 'He is saying it all wrong, Aabo,' he told Idris.

'What would you know?' Sala Pokkar mocked. 'It is some Hindu gobbledygook!'

Kandavar pulled himself to his full height, glared at Sala Pokkar and began, 'I should know. I am…'

Idris clapped his palm on Kandavar's mouth. 'Enough,' he glowered. 'Neither of you will speak a word till this is over.'

Golla raised an eyebrow and smiled. The tall Cafre was hiding something. He knew that for certain, but it wasn't his business, so he wouldn't probe.

The priest took a bowl of vermilion and mixed with it water into a thick paste. With his thumb, he daubed the red paste and with his forefinger grains of raw rice on the forehead of each man, woman and child. Golla joined the line at the end and came back to Idris, bearing the vermilion and rice mark on his forehead. 'One of us from the group needs to be blessed so the miners see us as one of them,' he said by way of explanation.

Idris had already paid for the feast that was to follow. Cooked rice was ladled into a leaf plate and each of them was offered a little copper cup with ghee and sugar in it. 'This we must eat,' Idris said in a tone that would allow no dissent.

When all of them had eaten, it was time to begin. The mine master led the gang of workers to a spot nearby. He took the spade and cut into the earth.

'What is he doing?' Idris asked, surprised. 'Shouldn't they be digging within the wall?'

Golla went up to the mine master and spoke to him. He came back grinning. 'Lesson one, that is the mine. This is just where they sift for the diamonds. Lesson two, we should trust them and let them do their job. Those are the mine master's words. Not mine, by the way.'

Idris flushed. What had he got into? Was it always going to be like this? An impetuous thought leading him into situations he knew nothing about. A wild recklessness that goaded him to invest all he owned, and himself, in the relentless pursuit of an elusive dream. And then the wondering and not knowing, the self-doubts and self-recriminations… But he had always fallen on his feet in the end. And so he would, this time too, a little voice of reason murmured in his head.

He watched as the men began digging and the women and children sent baskets of earth from hand to hand till it was dumped in the area enclosed by the low wall. An air of festivity and beginnings suffused the place. Idris moved to seat himself under a tree. Sala Pokkar and Kandavar hovered near the spot where the men were excavating the earth. If a diamond appeared, they would be there to make sure they saw it first.

Golla and the mine master stood together, sharing a chew of betel leaf into which slivers of areca nut and tobacco had been placed.

'Your master knows nothing about the mining of diamonds; I hope he is better at trading them,' the mine master said thoughtfully.

'He is a good man,' Golla said in defence.

'You know what they say: A good man is a good-for-nothing man,' the mine master said wryly, smiling to take the sting off his words.

'He is a trader. A good trader. What he doesn't know, he will find experts to advise him on.' Golla's voice was cold. Cold and hard like a diamond, the mine master thought.

'You really like him, I can see,' he said.

'So will you, by the time he leaves here. There are some men who are natural leaders. They inspire you with their feats of courage, their bigness, their valour and strength. And there are others who, with their quietness, reveal another way of being. You don't always have to be in the thick of things to change the world. You can do it from the sidelines. You can do it with an innate decency and faith in the goodness of the world. My master is like that,' Golla said quietly.

The mine master nodded. Golla was a servant and if a servant spoke well of his master, there must be some truth in it.

'We will do our best for him,' he said.

Golla smiled and clasped his hand. 'And you will see that he will do his best for you, even without your asking.'

A little later, Golla said to Idris, 'It's almost noon. They will do nothing but excavate for the next two or three days. There is no need for you to wait; I will stay on.'

Idris stood up. A peculiar lassitude curled within him. The sense of expectation that had welled within him at dawn had dwindled into a desultory emptiness. Would his life always be this? One port after another, one adventure after another, till he was old and tired and would be condemned to live out his days in a hut somewhere in Dikhil, alone with his memories. What would any of this mean then? Whether he prospected for diamonds or salt, in the end, all that would be left would be a sense of regret for the untenanted rooms in his life.

It was then he saw her. She stood at the other end of the marked land with a pack of dogs milling around her. The dogs ran around, raising little puffs of dust. When one of them barked, she silenced the animal with a look. She was tall and high-breasted with skin the colour of baked clay. She wore a knee-high cloth draped around her hips, with one end pulled over her shoulder, but even from where he stood, Idris could see that the cotton was superior to what the other women wore. There was a tilt to her chin that suggested hauteur. Her heavy-lidded eyes and high cheekbones were emphasized by her hair, which was pulled back tightly into a knot. In her ears were heavy gold discs. A big irregular stone gleamed against the burnished skin of her throat, and around her ankles were ornate silver chains. Idris thought he had never seen anyone as magnificent as this woman.

He stared at her, unable to fathom the feelings that overwhelmed him. It was as if all the anticipation of the days before had resolved itself into this one moment of recognition. In her he saw an answer to a query that had hovered in his thoughts and, even though he knew nothing of her, a beacon that suggested safe anchorage.

'Who is that?' he asked Golla in a low voice.

Golla peered at her. 'I don't think she's one of the diamond workers. Let me find out.'

Idris nodded. He liked this about Golla. Unlike Sala Pokkar, who needed an explanation for everything, Golla seldom asked why.

As he trudged back to their house in the midday heat, Idris decided he would buy a horse. The searing dry heat made every step feel like twelve. A horse would cover the distance easily and perhaps Kandavar could learn to ride as well. Golla had called for the palanquin, but Idris was loath to use it every day. 'I am not a merchant prince,' he had explained to Golla. 'On an expedition, it makes sense to some extent, but not every day. I would rather walk.'

Golla had said nothing, but he had brought Vajra for the boy to ride on. Sala Pokkar preferred to walk.

'I'll stay behind until evening. Datta will go with you,' Golla had said, gesturing for Datta, his trusted lieutenant, to lead the way.

'You think I can't find the way home?' Idris was amused at Golla's punctiliousness.

'It's not about knowing the way home. It's about getting there intact.' Golla sniffed.

'What is he sniffing the air for? Enemies?' Sala Pokkar jeered.

Golla didn't understand, but he sensed the mockery. He turned and fixed his stare on Sala Pokkar's face. The young man dropped his gaze and grin. Golla looked like one of his oxen just before it ran at you and gored you with its horns, Sala Pokkar thought, moving a step back.

Only Kandavar stepped towards Golla and said, 'Aabo, shall I leave Vajra behind for Golla? He will be tired by evening and it would be easier if he could ride Vajra home.'

Golla caressed the boy's cheek when Idris translated for him. 'No, little master. Vajra is your mount and yours alone. But you are kind.'

Idris had felt a rush of pride for his son. You can teach many a thing to a man, but you cannot teach him compassion, he thought.

The cool interiors of the house came as a relief. Idris sank into the pile of mattresses and closed his eyes. He willed himself to think of nothing, but his mind was restless as it sought one image after the other. The landscape of the mine and the craggy face of the mine master, the baskets of earth that went from hand to hand. How in that soil would they chance upon any diamond unless it was as big as an almond? And then, what he had been wanting to linger upon: the image of the tall woman with her soft curves and proud, patrician face.

Idris turned on his side. Some things, or rather some people, were better left alone.

Golla returned from the mines early in the evening. He wiped the sweat off his brow and squatted on a stone by the door.

'They will continue to excavate the mine for the next two days,' Golla said without any preamble.

Idris nodded. 'And then?'

Golla grinned. 'We will have to see. My guess is as good as yours. And to ask the mine master would be to let him know how little we know about diamonds, or their mining.'

Idris cocked an eyebrow. 'You think he doesn't know?'

Golla looked sheepish. 'He does.' Golla sat up suddenly as if he had just remembered something and looked around him. 'Where are the other two?'

'Swimming.' Idris looked out at the river where Kandavar and Sala Pokkar frolicked.

The merchant who had owned the house before Tabriz Ali had built a stone embankment along the river. Steps led from it to the water. The other bank seemed a long way away. Even by boat, they said it took several hours. But Kandavar had no thought for the other bank or what it held. Instead, he jumped and dived in the water, splashing Sala Pokkar and ducking him. Their bodies glistened in the light of the evening sun and Kandavar's high-pitched screams of merriment rang through the air. Youth was so precious. It allowed you to find joy in the smallest of things and the most inconsequent of times.

'The river isn't safe,' Golla said.

'My son swims every day in the river. He knows how to swim with the current rather than against it,' Idris said.

Golla twisted his mouth into a grimace, but didn't pursue the subject. Instead, he leaned forward. 'I found out about the woman,' he said.

'Which woman?' Idris tossed over his shoulder.

Golla smiled at Idris's back. He knew the trader had looked at the woman with more than mere curiosity. He had seen her with the eyes of a man. But he also knew that masters didn't like their minions to point out the obvious to them.

So Golla proceeded cautiously. 'The woman who stood at the edge of the land marked out as our mine.'

'Oh, her.' Idris turned to face Golla. 'What about her?'

A water bird screeched and another rose from the river with a fish in its beak. Golla stared at it, transfixed. Idris followed his gaze. Was Golla playing with him? he wondered.

'Golla,' he snapped. 'You were saying…'

Golla stood up and went closer to Idris. 'Apparently all of that land was her family's. About a hundred years ago, her great-grandfather was digging the land to plant millet when he found a clod of earth that wouldn't crumble in his fingers. So he dropped the clod into a pail of water and within it was a diamond twenty-five carats big. How big would that be?'

Idris thought for a moment and held his thumb and index finger up to indicate a stone the size of a gooseberry. Golla's eyes widened in amazement. 'Are there diamonds that big?' he asked.

'Tabriz told me of a stone that was more than seven hundred carats when they found it, here in Kollur.' Idris smiled at Golla's expression. 'But go on, tell me.'

'Apparently Venkata Reddy – that was his name – met a

diamond merchant who was honest and the story of the stone spread and everyone in Golkonda descended here to try and find diamonds,' Golla finished.

'But what happened to Venkata Reddy?' Idris asked curiously.

'The usual. Everyone profited from his discovery but him. Fortunately, because of his own perversity, he didn't sell his stone. Nor did he sell his land. But he didn't have the money to increase his land base or to mine for diamonds on what was his land. The Golkonda merchants acquired the lease to the land around his and mined for stones. He continued to grow his millet and died a poor man. They say the stone is still with the family.'

Idris thought of the woman. She had worn an enormous stone at the base of her throat.

'Does she have a name?' he asked.

Golla shrugged. 'Everyone has a name. Hers is Thilothamma.'

XLIII

Thilothamma stared at the reflection in the water. 'O nennu illaga untanna? Is this how I look?' she asked herself, puzzled by her own face. Everyone said she was a hard woman. Harder than the diamonds people came seeking in Kollur, they said. Is it because I don't smile? Or, perhaps I don't smile enough? What must he have thought? Thilothamma touched the surface of the pool. As the ripple dissipated the image, she saw a softness blur her features, and she hoped that was how the tall, black man had seen her.

The stream was up in the mountain. A little tinkling stream that came alive with the rains. It had a little catchment basin of stone before the water splashed down its sides and disappeared into the ground. Her great-grandfather had shown her the stream. 'Chippi, ikkadiki ra,' he beckoned her to his side, using his special name for her. 'I am going to tell you a secret, but you mustn't tell anyone,' he had whispered as she had skipped to his side.

She was four years old. Her great-grandfather, who was waiting for his millet to grow, had taken her with him to the fields. 'The millet doesn't need us today so let's go and do something else,' he had said, hoisting her onto his back. She had wound her arms around his neck and her legs around his waist. He had peered over his shoulder at her with a mock expression of horror. 'Abba, how can you be this heavy? You are not my chippi but a little enuga! A baby elephant that is going to break my back by the time we get there!'

'Get where, Thatha?' She giggled, digging her heels into his belly.

'Chippi, stop kicking me. Wait till we get there,' he said, trudging up the mountain path till they reached the stream. He had pointed out her reflection in the water. 'See how pretty you are!' he had said. 'Do you know you are pretty?'

She had smiled, not understanding. What did pretty mean? She had never heard anyone use the word.

The catchment basin was wide and quite deep. He wouldn't allow her to enter it. 'One day, when you are grown-up, but not now,' he said. But he had let her sit at its edge and dangle her feet in the water. The spray from the stream left tiny little drops on her face. And Thilothamma felt several rainbows criss-cross her tiny heart.

'What is the secret, Thatha?' she asked.

Venkata Reddy pretended to frown. 'What a vaagadu kaya you are! Didn't your mother teach you that girls shouldn't be curious?'

She had stared harder. So many new words: pretty, curious. What did it mean? And why was her grandfather calling her a talking fruit? She didn't have a stone in her middle like a mango. She would ask him at night when she nuzzled into the crook of his arm. 'What is the secret?' she persisted, tugging at his arm.

'It is from here that the river Krishna emerges,' he said. 'Do you remember the river?'

She nodded, thinking of the river she had seen when they had all gone to a little temple on its bank.

'The water goes into the land, deep into the mountain, and then emerges far far away.'

'How far far away?' she asked.

'As far away as the skies,' said Venkata Reddy.

'Have you seen it, Thatha?' she asked, thinking he must have. She looked at his face and felt a great admiration for her great-grandfather who knew everything.

Venkata Reddy swatted at a fly that had settled on his arm. 'Now do you want to hear a story,' he asked abruptly.

She would hear many versions of it from him as she grew up. With each telling the story acquired new facets. But somehow she knew the story he told her when she was four was probably the closest to what had really happened.

The day had dawned auspiciously enough for Venkata Reddy but somehow it seemed nothing would go right thereafter. He had twisted his ankle on his way to the fields and it had made digging that much more difficult. He cursed his ancestor who had acquired the land so close to the mountains. The earth was soft in parts and almost rocky in others. The small of his back hurt as he continued to dig. If he had the money, he would have bought two oxen and used them to plough the soil. But misfortune had dogged him for almost five years now.

First his older boy had died of a fever. Then one of his oxen had been mauled by a pack of jackals. And the other one had to be sold to pay off the debt incurred for his son's funeral. It was like the gods wouldn't allow him respite; they kept piling one misfortune upon the other. And this morning, when he should have been able to dig up at least half the field in preparation for sowing the millet seeds, here he was, hobbling on one foot. And where on earth was his wife? He was hungry and thirsty; his ankle was sore, and what seemed like a giant fist slammed into his ribcage just below his heart. How had he even thought that the day was auspicious?

Venkata Reddy decided to stop after digging one more furrow of land. He would sit under a tree and wait for his wife. She would nag him for stopping work, but he would point to the sun in the sky and that would shut her up. How was a man expected to work when his wife was a slatternly creature who did not bring to him his noon meal on time?

Venkata Reddy struck his spade into the ground. The earth was easy enough here, but it seemed like he had struck a rock. He squatted on his haunches and looked at the clod of earth the spade had turned over. His heart sank. He had hoped to dig a larger segment of land at the foot of the mountains so he could plant a greater area. If the earth was rocky, and without any oxen, this would be almost impossible. Well, not impossible, but certainly back-breaking. He may end up like his grandmother, with a bent back, even though he was only half her age.

Venkata Reddy took the clod of earth and tried to crumble it with his fingers. But the clod seemed to have a rock within. Curious, he pulled away the soil from its hard centre and found it impossible to penetrate. He wanted to fling it as far as it would go. Just then, he saw his wife arrive.

He hobbled back to the tree where he had left his stick and cloth. 'What took you so long?' he grumbled, dropping the clod of earth into the pot of water his wife had brought with her. He hadn't meant to muddy the water but the sight of her standing there nonchalantly, as if nothing was wrong, made him angry.

'What are you doing, you mad man?' she screamed. 'Do you realize I have to go all the way back to bring you more water?'

Venkata Reddy didn't respond. He put his fingers into the mouth of the pot and washed the hard, caked mud off the stone. When he pulled it out, he thought he was holding a star in his fingers. A gleaming star that had fallen out of the sky and buried itself in the earth. It was hard and cold and had a strange light.

'Do you see this?' He turned to his wife, holding out the stone to her.

'What is it?' she asked, as awed by its strange beauty as he was.

'I don't know. I have never seen anything like it.'

After a pause he asked, 'What are we going to do?'

'Nothing,' she said, unpacking his lunch. 'While you eat your lunch, I'll go back and fetch you some water.'

Venkata Reddy didn't speak. He ate the meagre lunch his wife had laid out on a banana leaf. But all he could think about was the stone.

For the next two weeks, Venkata Reddy worked diligently in his field. He dug the land till the soil was completely turned and planted korra. He left alone the new portion of land he had earmarked for further cultivation. It was the home of the stone.

Venkata Reddy had taken to carrying the stone everywhere he went. At night, he lay on his side, looking at the stone cupped in his palm. His wife looked at him and shook her head in annoyance. But Venkata Reddy was hardworking as ever and so she had no reason to remonstrate with him.

One evening, a group of travellers set up camp nearby and Venkata Reddy went to meet them. They had come from Bezawada, they said, and were going to Golkonda.

'What is in Golkonda?' Venkata Reddy squatted by the little fire the travellers had lit and warmed his fingers.

'A street of pearls and precious stones; beautiful women and horses, rocks as big as houses and houses that are palaces.' One of them laughed.

Venkata Reddy blinked. An idea was beginning to take shape in his mind. By night, he had made up his mind. He would go with the travellers to Golkonda and find someone there who would tell him what this celestial stone was and what it meant to own such a beauty.

'Anna, do you think I will be able to meet someone there who can tell me about a stone that I found?' He was older than the man, but he thought it necessary to call him big brother. 'I have never seen anything like it!'

'Where is it? the man asked.

But Venkata Reddy was artful enough to say that it was with his wife. A little later, Venkata Reddy went back home as if in a trance. When his wife and children fell asleep, he dug up the little copper vessel buried in the corner of their house. It contained two silver rupees, the sum total of his worldly wealth. He wrapped the stone and coins in a tiny piece of cloth and tied it on a string around his waist.

When dawn broke, Venkata Reddy was ready and waiting. His wife rubbed sleep from her eyes and looked at him curiously. 'I am stepping out. I will be gone for a while,' he said cryptically and set off to join the travellers from Bezawada.

They journeyed for over a week and finally one evening, they saw the city gates of Golkonda in the distance.

'There are eight gates to the city,' one of the travellers told Venkata Reddy. 'We will take the east gate by the reservoir.'

Venkata Reddy didn't speak. He was too overwhelmed by his journey and all that he had seen and experienced in the past week. 'Whatever you say, anna,' he said.

'Tomorrow I will take you to meet a man I know and you can

tell him of your marvellous discovery. You should have brought the stone with you instead of leaving it at home and expecting an evaluation from mere description,' the traveller said. The truth was the travellers were quite weary of shepherding Venkata Reddy, who seemed frightened of most things and clueless about everything else.

They spent the night in a traveller's inn by the reservoir and by mid-morning, they set out for the fortress. The jeweller Venkata Reddy met looked at him and said, 'You may be holding a fortune in your hands. But unless I see it for myself, how can I tell? This stone you have found, if it is a diamond, which is what I think it is by your description, can change your life.'

Venkata Reddy smiled at his little great-granddaughter and said, 'Chippi, one day when you feel there is nothing left in your life and when you turn to the gods, asking them for a sign, just one sign, to indicate that you should continue to live in hope, you must come back here. And dig beneath this rock that looks like a bull's head. The gods will have left you a sign.'

Her eyes strayed to the bull's head rock further upstream. From the edge of the catchment basin, it could be reached easily by a grown-up.

'Is it there now?' she asked.

Venkata Reddy shook his head. 'No, the gods don't think you need it yet. And if you tell this to anyone, the gods will be angry and leave it elsewhere.'

'Not even my nana and amma?' she asked.

'Not even your nana or amma. Especially not your nana,' he said, his face grim at the thought of her father, his wastrel of a grandson.

He had vested all his hopes in the boy, the only living male among his seven grandchildren. He had wanted the boy to love the land as he did and find happiness in it. But the boy's eyes were dazzled by the merchants from Golkonda. He had seen how the earth had thrown up diamonds big as sparrow's eggs and he knew that their land was worth a fortune. But Venkata Reddy had remained adamant and refused to sell his land or even lease it out.

Instead, he grew millet on the piece of land he had found the first diamond in. 'What we earn from here will endure. How can you trust the land will throw up any diamonds for sure?'

Subba had slapped his forehead with his palm in frustration. 'Are you saying the men from Golkonda are idiots? Do you think they haven't considered all of this? They have found several diamonds already!'

Thilothamma had hidden behind her mother as grandfather and grandson had quarrelled. Her father came home less and less often and when he did, he was either drunk and angry, or sober and surly.

When she was eleven years old, one night, her father had begun his usual tirade against his grandfather. 'You won't sell or lease the land. At least let me have the stone you found. That's all I am asking you for,' he had shouted at the old man.

'When I am dead, you can have the land to do as you please,' Venkata Reddy had said in a measured voice. The old man popped a peanut into his mouth from the bowl of boiled peanuts he demanded every evening. Thilothamma, who stood by the door watching the altercation between the two men, thought it was the nonchalant manner with which he had thrown the peanut into his mouth that drove her father over the edge.

Subba had looked wildly around him and Thilothamma had seen him reach for a knife her mother had left on the floor. He had grabbed it and leapt at his grandfather. 'Go on, eat that last peanut, you bandicoot! You will never eat another one again...'

The knife had gone into the old man's belly with an ease Subba hadn't expected. Blood had gushed out and over his fingers. Subba had stood there for a moment, unable to believe what he had done. He looked at his bloody hands and let out a cry that was part howl and part wail. And then he disappeared into the night.

The knife didn't kill the old man. What did was the infected wound and the soreness in his heart. On his deathbed, he mumbled to the shadows on the wall, 'I wish I had never found the diamond. I wish I had never gone to meet the jeweller in Golkonda. It was that man who told everyone about my stone and started all of this... I didn't want a fortune. I just wanted to be left alone to grow my millet and live in peace.'

Thilothamma and her mother continued to grow the millet, keep their chickens and goats and live off the land for another year. Subba had fled after the stabbing and no one knew what had happened to him.

Two days before Thilothamma turned twelve, a group of three men came by and with the casual ease of a scythe cutting the heads of millet, they burnt down the house. Then they set fire to the fields and took away all the livestock.

Thilothamma's mother, who had gone to the weekly market that had sprung up with the influx of merchants and workers, came home to a field of ashes and a daughter who had hidden herself underneath a basket where a hen sat laying an egg. Terrified by the sounds, the hen had huddled quietly without making a sound and so had Thilothamma.

Thilothamma's mother had begun wailing. 'What did they do to you?' she cried, looking at her dishevelled child.

'Nothing,' Thilothamma said stonily. But the people who had gathered drew their own inferences. Overnight, stories sprang up like weeds: the diamond merchant had only meant to frighten the mother and daughter, but things had got out of hand. The girl was alone... they...

The stories were never completed but Thilothamma's marriage prospects came to an end. It seemed that she and her mother would have to rebuild their life from scratch. The diamond merchant who had sent his hooligans to scare them into selling their land, came calling. He wore a look of concern on his face and mouthed comforting words and did his best to hide how petrified he was. The law of the land was severe. Who would have thought that the little prat would have the presence of mind to sneak under a nesting basket? Who would have thought she would see the men and identify his brother as one of them?

Thilothamma set her face in the expression she had seen on Venkata Reddy's face when her father spoke of selling the land and said, 'We lost our home, our crop and animals. And…'

Her mother turned, horrified. 'Go inside,' she muttered through gritted teeth.

'No, I will not. I will tell everyone what I saw and who the men were,' Thilothamma said, wiping away tears of rage.

The merchant made an offer. Thilothamma asked for five times as much. He tried to bargain. But she wouldn't budge. In the end, he agreed.

Thilothamma's mother called for carpenters and thatchers. New livestock was acquired and two men hired. Seeds were planted. She may have become a woman of means, but no man would marry her daughter and bring her under his protection. Thilothamma brought home a litter of puppies she found in a ditch. They would grow up to be fierce dogs who would guard her and all that was hers.

Thilothamma took to walking with the dogs. No one dared approach her, for the dogs' ferociousness scared everyone. No one dared say anything about her penchant for exploring the countryside, for she had become one of the wealthiest women in the village.

'I am breaking no law, nor am I hurting anyone. So why should it matter where I walk? Did any of them come to my rescue when the men burnt our house down?' she told her mother when she protested.

Her logic was irrefutable and her mother ceased objecting to Thilothamma's strange ways. Once in a while, her mother would sigh, thinking of the plenty their life seemed to be blessed with. 'Who is this for? After you and me, who is going to inherit it all?'

Thilothamma would shrug. 'Maybe I'll adopt a child. Maybe I'll just give it to one of my nephews. Or, maybe I'll give it to anyone who comes to my deathbed. How does it matter?'

Soon Thilothamma established a new practice. A small house was built on the fringes of her property and this was opened out to anyone who needed a roof over their head for the night. Thilothamma would offer them food and hear their stories and in the quietness of her life, she let the world come to her. Balladeers and mule keepers, potters and weavers, merchants and mendicants. The house came to be called Pakshigudu, the nest. The rules were unwritten, but everyone who stayed there was aware of what was allowed and what wasn't. No one sought out Thilothamma; she came to you. No one offered any payment, but if you wished to make her a present of a seed or a cloth, a bird or a carpet, she would accept it. And you never stayed more than a night.

When Thilothamma turned eighteen, a wandering mendicant, who said he had come from Nuchela Veedu, brought her a mango.

It was the tiniest mango she had seen. 'It is called chinna rasalu,' he said. 'It is the most delicious fruit I have ever tasted.'

Thilothamma smiled. Most of her guests liked to have her believe their presents were unique. Thilothamma held the little mango to her nose and sniffed it. The fragrance wasn't unusual. It smelt like a mango should. She was about to bite into it when the man said, 'No, don't bite into it. Puncture a small hole in the skin and then suck out the pulp and juice. Squeeze the fruit gently as you do so.'

A cataclysm burst in Thilothamma's mouth in that first draw of the fruit: The golden heat of yellow, the underside of a rain cloud, forgotten dreams and the gushing of a stream and through it all the pure taste of a mango. Sweet, aromatic, flavourful and with that inordinate sense that nothing would ever go wrong if she could feast on a chinna rasalu every day of the summer.

Thilothamma decided she would plant the seed and perhaps procure more seeds if she could, so she would have an orchard of chinna rasalu.

It took almost five years for the chinna rasalu to flower and fruit. And another five years for Thilothamma to have her orchard in place. Within the orchard, Thilothamma built herself a little home of a room and no more. Soon everyone took to calling it the mango house and it was here Thilothamma spent most of her day once she left home in the morning. In the evenings, she would stop by at the Pakshigudu to meet with any visitors. It would be dusk by the time she and the dogs trudged home.

One summer evening, Thilothamma's mother watched her settle down with a bowl of chinna rasalu in front of her and felt her heart sink. What was to become of her daughter?

Thilothamma saw the expression on her mother's face. It was as if her mother had given up on her. Ever since that day when circumstances changed her life irrevocably, her mother had waited for a miracle to happen. She had hoped that her daughter would eventually be blessed with a home and a husband. And Thilothamma had built her life on the bedrock of her mother's expectations. It was her mother's faith that fuelled her courage to be disdainful of everyone and everything. But now it seemed her mother had given up.

Thilothamma couldn't sleep that night. She tossed and turned. She drank some water. Then she lay in bed wide-eyed, thinking about her life. She was only twenty-eight, but she felt a complete absence of hope. She felt tired and defeated. And then from nowhere, Thilothamma remembered what her great-grandfather had said to her all those years ago.

The next morning, she set out for the mountain, tailed by the four descendants of the six-pup litter she had first adopted. Five others were left behind to guard the house, crops and animals. It was sixteen years since their home had been destroyed, but Thilothamma had not lost her fear of what might happen.

Nothing much had changed up the mountain in the ensuing years. The merchants had discovered that the higher they went, the fewer stones there were. The path was mostly overgrown and hardly anyone seemed to use it. The call of the crow pheasant from the shrubs and the chirp of various birds from the trees filled the air. A gentle breeze took the edge off the summer heat. The dogs panted as they clambered and ran through the grass.

Thilothamma found the stream by the catchment basin. It had reduced to a trickle. Once the rains arrived, it would be full again.

She climbed up the catchment basin and standing on its rim, she looked for the rock shaped like a bull's head. Ferns covered most of the rock, but it was still there, just as her great-grandfather had said. She lifted the rock from the groove it had been wedged into and her fingers touched a small leather pouch. She dug it out and with her heart in her mouth, she opened it.

The stone was as magnificent as her great-grandfather had claimed it was. A diamond with eight faces and as big as a nellikai, she thought. So this was what an uncut diamond looked like.

Thilothamma held the stone in the palm of her hand and felt a cold heat shoot through her. Had Venkata Reddy felt the same? Was that why he had been so reluctant to part with it? He had claimed that he had lost the stone on his way back from Golkonda. His son had believed him, but Subba, her father, hadn't. It seemed he had been right after all.

Thilothamma put the stone back in its pouch and walked home thoughtfully. It seemed as though, with its possession, the wavering in her mind had ceased. She would have the stone set as it was and clasp it around her throat so that she would never doubt herself again. She would accept the marriage proposal that a cousin had made. He was a widower and he wasn't young. His wife had died and there was a daughter who had been married off when she was twelve. But no young man would want her, she knew. The old stories hadn't been forgotten.

For the first couple of years, all was well. He had consented to live in her house, so not much changed. If, at night, his foetid breath and the feel of his dry coarse fingers on her body filled her with disgust, she said nothing. He was her husband and it was her duty to give him her body when he sought it. Then Ranga Reddy began to tire of the life Thilothamma had made for herself. 'You make me feel like a flea on an ox. A parasite living off you and serving no real purpose. I swear I am going to leave if you don't start doing as I ask,' he threatened one evening.

Thilothamma stopped chopping the vegetables she had set aside for dinner. 'What do you want?' she asked.

'First I want you to sound respectful when you speak to me.'

Thilothamma brushed the hair off her eyes with the back of her palm. Ranga Reddy was her father's sister's son. In his veins coursed the same blood as her father's. The same impetuous wild streak; the same need to be top dog everywhere he was; the same desperation of the insecure man.

'I...' she began.

'You forget I married you when no one else would have you, despite your wealth and all this paraphernalia,' he tossed at her. 'Have you ever considered that?'

'You know the truth about me,' she said quietly, and began chopping the greens into small pieces.

'So?'

He stood up and walked towards her. 'Does that stop tongues wagging? They think even less of me for having married you and then choosing to live here off your wealth.'

'What do you want?' she asked again, knowing what was coming.

'Sell this land and we will go away from here,' he said.

She looked up and matched her gaze with his. She wouldn't flinch, she thought. And when his eyes dropped, she said, 'No.'

'What do you mean, no?' His voice rose sharply.

'No. I will not sell this land. This is the land my great-grandfather lost his life for. This is the land my father killed my great-grandfather for. This is the land that robbed me of my youth and my dreams. This is the land that defines me and my past. I will not sell it as long as I breathe. Do you hear me?'

She tried to induce calm into her voice and face and began again, 'It is a matter of pride to me that I continue to live here. Live on this land and flourish. To go away would be to admit that I failed. Please try and understand.'

Ranga Reddy went away. No one knew what happened to him. Some said he became a mendicant. Some others said she had him killed. Some said he was killed by a group of thugs. Yet others said he had been murdered by the man from whom he had taken a large sum of money, promising to sell him his wife's land.

Thilothamma watched the horizon as she had after Subba fled. But after a year, she stopped. Ranga, it seemed, had been swallowed whole by the same darkness as his uncle before him. As long as the body wasn't found, he was considered to be alive.

And as long as Ranga Reddy existed in this mortal world, she didn't have to don the widow's role. Thilothamma could remain a married woman, resplendent in her colours and jewellery. If her face grew harder and her eyes stonier, it would be ascribed to arrogance. She would wear her pride as her veil and as long as she had that, she was safe and inviolable.

Someone mentioned the Cafre to her. They remarked about his gold eye and her interest was piqued. So when her workers told her that the Cafre was at the site marked for mining, she had gone to see him. And he had been just as magnificent to look at as they had said he was. Tall, black, and with a head of tight curls. Even from a distance, she had felt his gaze upon her.

What was it the mendicant who had gifted her the mango said? The universe has all the answers. Once you lay yourself open to the universe, someone will appear on the horizon. Someone who will teach you to think another way…

Was he the man on the horizon? Or, was he yet another chimera, a trick of the mind?

Thilothamma touched the stone at her throat.

XLIV

Idris, Kandavar and Golla stood with the mine master at the edge of the crater and stared into it. The workers had been excavating mud for a day now. Idris sensed a presence near him. The woman called Thilothamma had come to stand by his side.

The mine master hid his surprise well. In all these years,

Thilothamma had never come so close. She would stand at the edge of what was her land and make sure no one was encroaching.

'How far will you go?' she asked.

Idris felt as if he had been felled. Her voice was husky; it hinted at twilights and palm sugar; the richness of a plane teak plank; the smoothness of heated, clarified butter... he had never been so aware of a woman. He glanced at her sideways. She had her profile to him and yet he sensed that she was equally aware of him. He felt almost breathless with expectation.

The mine master crossed his arms and stood with his legs apart. 'If we go a little deeper, the chances of finding good-sized stones are better,' he said.

'Get going,' he called to the workers. 'There is no time to be wasted here. Get on with your work.'

Idris walked back to the edge of the land marked as his and stood under a tree. After a few minutes, Thilothamma went to join him.

Idris thought for a moment and hollered, 'Golla.'

Kandavar stared at Aabo. He had never ever heard that note in Aabo's voice. Almost as if he was calling for help. He started towards his father, as did Golla. 'No.' Golla put out his hand and pushed Kandavar back gently. 'You stay here. I will be back in a few minutes. Don't you want to see what happens next? Besides, one of us has to be here to keep an eye on things,' Golla added quickly, since Kandavar didn't seem inclined to obey.

'You will have to translate for me,' Idris said, when Golla reached his side.

'Ayana, but you already know some Telugu, so why do you need me?' Golla asked in surprise.

'I want to understand everything she says. Not guess at what she is trying to say.'

Golla looked at Thilothamma's face. No one knew much about her except what was hearsay. In fact, while everyone knew she kept an eye on the mining that happened adjacent to her property, no one had ever seen her walk onto land that was not hers.

'Namaskara, akka,' Golla said, using the term for older sister and folding his hands in greeting.

'Ask her about herself,' Idris murmured to Golla. 'What you and I know is this and that. I want to hear it from her.' His eyes were fixed on Thilothamma.

Golla opened his mouth to speak. But Thilothamma held up a hand. 'You called me akka. As your elder sister, I have to answer your questions. But I would prefer to answer your master directly.'

Golla grinned and scratched his head ruefully. 'But the master doesn't speak our language.'

She snorted as she began walking away. 'Tell him he must. What he and I have to say to each other must be just for our ears.'

Golla looked sheepish as he translated her words to Idris even though he knew Ayana must have understood her words. Would the master be furious? She was only a peasant woman after all, and the master was a man of the world.

Idris cocked an eyebrow. 'Is that what she said? I thought so too.'

He wiped his brow. The heat hung in the air like a coarse woollen rug, stifling the breeze and baking the earth. 'I learned languages to become a better trader. For the first time, I have to learn a language to understand a woman. So be it. Golla, you will teach me your language. You will speak only Telugu to me from now. I already speak Malayalam and some Tamizh. And I know a fair number of words in Telugu. How difficult can it be to string sentences together?'

As they went back to the crater from where the mud was being taken out, Idris pointed things out to Golla, asking for their names in Telugu.

'We may as well go home now,' Golla said after a while. 'There is nothing to be done here but wait.'

Kandavar and Idris exchanged glances, but didn't probe any further. Where did the diamonds figure in all this? 'Aabo, did you see the stone at the woman's throat? Is that a diamond?' Kandavar asked, poking the ground with a stick as he walked.

'Yes. An uncut diamond. And don't refer to her as that woman. It's disrespectful.'

Kandavar stared at Idris. He had never heard his Aabo use such a bristly tone. 'So what do I call her?'

'Akka. Would it be appropriate for my son to call her that?' Idris turned to Golla.

'Sala Pokkar can call her that. But the little master must call her pinni. It means mother's younger sister,' he said with a bland expression.

'You may call her pinni. It means aunt in their language,' Idris told Kandavar.

'Do you think they found the diamond here?' the boy asked as they walked back into town.

'Apparently, her great-grandfather was the one who first found these mines. Maybe it was one of the first finds,' Idris replied.

'You are not going to speak much Telugu if you continue to natter in your language,' Golla said, watching the father and son murmuring to each other.

Idris smiled wryly and said, 'I suggest you learn to speak Telugu too.'

Kandavar made a face. 'I already do. Didn't you know? How do you think I speak to Vajra or Golla?'

'I didn't realize.' Idris smiled.

'I just hope I don't forget it once we get back home,' Kandavar began and paused when he saw the expression on his Aabo's face. 'What is it?' he asked. 'We are going back? Aren't we?'

Idris nodded. 'Yes, we will.'

'So then...' Kandavar grinned. Then his face lit up. 'No

one would ever have seen an animal like Vajra at home. He is almost human. He understands everything I say to him.'

'Are you planning to take your bullock home with you?' Golla asked.

The evening was still warm and Idris felt rivulets of sweat run down his back. The thought of the voyage home with a cat and a bullock in tow filled him with a mounting dread. He had kept a close watch on the passage of time and so, it seemed, had Kandavar. And here he was, thinking of a whole new beginning even as the end was in sight.

There was no need for them to go to the mine the following day, Golla said. 'So if there is something you would like to finish, you must.'

Idris nodded. He was going to see a man this evening about a horse. If all went well, he would be riding to the mine soon.

In the morning, he went to look at the horse. His breath snagged in his throat. It was one of the finest horses he had ever seen.

'It is a Turkmen,' he said softly.

The man cocked his head. 'It's actually an Akhal-Teke,' he murmured, pleased that the African had spotted the breed. 'You know what they say. The Persians claim that the Akhal-Teke descended from the Turkmen and the Turkmenistanis claim the Akhal-Teke came before. Does it matter?'

Idris went closer to the horse, which stood sixteen hands tall. She was a grey, and her coat shone with a metallic gleam, causing her to shimmer in the evening light.

The horse's almond-shaped ears twitched as Idris murmured in Arabic, 'You beauty, you glorious beauty, how is it you are here in the middle of nowhere?'

What would she cost? Idris wondered. He had sunk a great

deal of money into the diamond prospecting. And yet, he had never wanted to own something as much as he wanted this horse.

'Tell me about the horse, brother,' Idris said abruptly. The man had a stable full of horses. Fair enough beasts, but none as magnificent as this one. Men led horses in and out; two others were rubbing down a horse and two boys were cleaning the ground of dung and straw that had piled on the ground. The Akhal-Teke didn't belong here. Anyone with some sense of horse flesh could see that.

'She was acquired for Mir Jumla,' the man whispered.

'And?' Idris asked, feeling his heart sink.

They were talking about the most powerful man in the Golkonda Empire. The Vizier who ran the kingdom. Apparently, on the day he first went to see the horse, something happened to him and he demanded that the horse be sold beyond the walls of Golkonda. He didn't want its breath tainting the air, he said.

'You mean the horse threw him off when he tried to ride it?' Idris frowned. 'Is this a problem horse?'

The man shrugged. 'I have never had any problem with her. She runs like a gazelle, sweetly, so you feel you are riding a cloud. Unfortunately, everyone here knows the story and no one wants to take a risk.'

'If she throws me, you will have to keep your cloud,' Idris said, stroking the horse. She didn't fidget or shy away as a horse wary of humans would.

'Shall we talk business?' the man said. He unfurled a cloth tied around his waist and put it over his hand. He indicated that Idris offer him his palm beneath the cloth. Idris understood the gesture for what it was: Make me an offer.

Idris thought for a moment. To hold the whole palm would be to indicate a thousand. Just the five fingers were five hundred. And one finger a hundred. No one here in Kollur traded in anything but gold pagodas. He did his mental arithmetic quickly and made an offer.

The man looked him in the eye and moved his fingers up to the middle joint of a finger. He wanted fifty more. Idris took the tip of the finger. He would offer ten more, he responded.

The man touched the end of Idris's finger two times. He wanted twenty more at least, he was saying.

Idris sighed loudly, for that was part of the theatre of horse-trading, and then nodded. The deal had been made. Idris had been sold a horse for only a little more than what he had bargained for. He was quite sure there was a catch somewhere. But he took the reins of the horse and led it away.

Sala Pokkar walked towards Idris with a grin. 'Why are you walking when you can ride the horse? Don't tell me you don't know how to...'

Idris threw him a look that quelled the young man's mirth. 'Stop prattling and find me a place I can stable this horse in.'

Golla had been busy. He had begun building a stall of sorts the moment he realized Idris was going to buy a horse. He had brought in his men to assist him and the stall now stood on its own, at a little distance from the house. He had added an annexe so that Vajra too could be tethered there. Kandavar had approved wholeheartedly. 'Aabo's horse and my Vajra will be company for each other.'

Sala Pokkar had guffawed. 'You forget they are two different kinds of animals!'

Golla had looked up from what he was doing and murmured, 'It is obvious Sala Pokkar has had nothing to do with animals. Tell him I have seen a monkey become attached to a cat. I have seen a bullock and a goat become inseparable companions. I have seen...'

Sala Pokkar made a face as Kandavar translated. 'Yes, yes, you don't need to say more!'

For some days now, Sala Pokkar had been finding his

position increasingly threatened by Golla. Ikka and Kandavar seemed to need him less and less. Yet, how could he feel any real resentment, for he too could see that without Golla, they wouldn't have managed as well.

'Golla has your horse's shed ready,' Sala Pokkar said, keeping a safe distance from the animal.

'Here,' Idris said, tossing the reins to Sala Pokkar.

Sala Pokkar led the horse as if it were a tiger. Kandavar walked towards him. 'Why are you so petrified?' He giggled. 'Horses don't bite!'

'Actually they do!' Idris said and chuckled at Sala Pokkar's expression.

Golla was waiting by the stable. Vajra was already in his stall. He snorted in pleasure when he saw Kandavar.

Golla whistled. 'She is beautiful! What made you think the horse would throw you if you mounted it?' he asked softly.

Idris smiled at the man, thinking again how shrewd he was. 'Too many things. She is too valuable to have been sold for the price I asked. I was then told a story about the horse and Mir Jumla; apparently, this horse threw Mir Jumla, an expert rider. Then there was the offer of the beautiful saddle for a pittance. He really must think I am stupid.' Idris clicked his tongue in annoyance.

'Oh,' Golla said. Sala Pokkar and Kandavar looked at each other.

'Take the saddle off and examine it carefully,' Idris said, taking the bridle off.

Beneath the saddle, a few prickly pear spines had been wedged in. As long as the saddle was empty, it wouldn't hurt the horse, but the moment a rider sat on it, the nearly translucent but vicious thorns penetrated the skin until the animal, in agony, would try and toss the rider off. The horse trader knew that the animal would be sold back to him for a pittance.

'See that on the horse's back.' Idris pointed to the skin

where a few ridges of scar tissue indicated previous instances of the thorn sinking in and the subsequent infection. 'She has been subject to much pain in the name of greed.'

Golla carefully picked out the thorns. 'Are you going to let him get away with it?' he asked.

Idris smiled. 'His first punishment will be when he sees me ride Fiddah. That is my name for her. Fiddah is silver in Arabic. And because she already knows Aamira as her name, we will have to call her Aamira Fiddah. The silver princess.'

Kandavar went towards Vajra. 'Hear that, Vajra,' he murmured. 'Now you have Fiddah, who will be your companion. Tell her our ways, Vajra, for she along with Musa and you will go home with us.'

Golla glanced at Idris's face to see if he had heard. But, as always, Ayana's face was an impenetrable mask.

Idris rode Aamira Fiddah the next morning to the stables he had bought her from.

The horse trader stared in surprise, but didn't speak after the customary greeting.

Idris leapt off his horse and walked towards the man. He looked at him for a moment, then reached across and slapped him hard. 'Greed has no soul. But you do. Never ever do that to a horse or I will come back and make you crawl on a bed of cactus spines and then I will personally dismember you and stuff your genitals in your mouth.'

Idris mounted Fiddah and rode away, leaving the imprint of his palm on the man's face and his ears ringing.

It would take two to three days of digging, Golla had said. It took three-and-a-half days. When they reached about twelve feet deep, they struck water. The digging came to a halt then.

Idris stood at the edge of the crater and watched as women and children began filling pitchers with the water that gushed from the hole in the ground. They had set up a line and each full pitcher passed from hand to hand before being emptied onto the mud heaped in the enclosed area where the excavated earth had been dumped. Another line passed the empty vessel back to the source of the water. Some of the men stood by the enclosure, spreading the heaped earth out and stirring up the mud so that the water spread over the entire surface evenly.

There was nothing more to be done at the mine site while the soil turned to soup, but Idris on a whim said he would pay the workers for their day of rest.

'You are setting a bad precedent,' the mine master told Golla, who had carried Idris's instruction to him.

Golla shrugged. 'Tell them that the master will extract work from them on another day at another place.'

The mine master rolled his eyes. 'What work, and where?'

But he had told the workers and later that evening, when Idris rode into the mine, he was greeted by the sight of the mine workers staring at the soup of mud.

Idris dismounted and joined them. To his surprise, he saw them walk around the wall, pulling out stones from its base. Soon, slime began to ooze out of the holes.

'In the morning, the sun will dry the soil out again and they will throw more water on it. The clay needs to be washed at least two times before they can move to the next stage,' Thilothamma said. Idris stared at her, not knowing how to respond. Even without Golla translating for him, Idris understood most of what she had said. If only the words would form in his mouth for him to speak them.

Why? What brings you here to my mine when they say you have never ever done this before, habibti? There, I have said the word habibti, my beloved. But how can you be my beloved when we haven't spoken a word to each other?

Carefully, he let his tongue form his first word to her: Enduku?

Golla's eyes widened. What did the master mean by asking why? Did he mean to greet her?

'You have to say namaskara,' he hissed. 'Not enduku!'

Idris looked at Thilothamma and asked again, 'Enduku?'

She looked at him and smiled. 'You know why, don't you?'

He drew in his breath.

She walked towards her land. At its edge, she turned and gestured that he follow her.

'Looks like she wants us to go visiting,' Golla said.

Idris put his hands on Golla's shoulders and turned him around to face the enclosed space. 'Not us. I. I am going visiting. You will stay here so that we know what's going on.'

Golla's mouth turned up in a smirk. But he continued to stand as Idris had positioned him. When Idris was some distance away, he called out, 'How long do I stay here? It will be dusk soon.'

Idris hollered back, 'Till the sun is level with the top of the ficus tree to the west of the wall.'

Golla stared at the grove of ficus trees. Each one was of a different height. Why couldn't the man ever give him a straight answer?

XLV

Where am I going? Idris thought as he walked up the path in the direction she had gone. The evening sun wasn't as intense, but the baked earth exhaled dry heat. Idris thought of the river longingly.

The millet stood almost waist-high and the slow evening breeze ruffled their tops, turning the field into a sea of green waves. Idris felt as if the green millet waves, the puffs of dust that blew at his feet, the wispy clouds high in the blue skies and the call of a dove from somewhere in the trees were all portents of a life change.

She was waiting at the end of the dust road. A pack of four dogs stood around her. At the farther corner of her farmland, a house stood on its own. Idris could see a flurry of activity there. She gestured for him to follow her onto a little pathway that led towards a mango orchard. At the end of the orchard was a small house built almost into the side of the mountain. A platform of beaten mud ran around three sides of the house. Thilothamma sat on the platform and patted the spot next to her. But he didn't join her. Instead, he sat across from her on the other side of the doorway. Then he looked at her straight. 'Naku cheppu,' he said.

Her eyes widened. A little smile danced on her lips.

Thilothamma looked at the man seated across her and wondered what she should say to him. Tell me, he had asked.

Then the words came. All of which she had dammed within; whimsical notions and clawed, fanged thoughts… She saw how he listened as if every little detail would help him map his course to a great cavern of diamonds. Suddenly the words paused and her mouth felt dry. She swallowed and pursed her lips to wet them.

'Have you understood any of what I just said?' she asked. 'You see, don't you, that I am not easy to be with. I am too set in my ways. Women should be like trees. Growing towards the light, shaped by the wind, and sinking her roots deep into the mud, knowing that the earth will hold her well. But when a woman has no one to lean upon, no one to mould her thoughts or to draw sustenance from, she becomes like a wall of rock. Hard, impregnable, and immune to everything. That's me.

Why would you want to waste your breath on a wall of rock?' Her laugh was bitter.

He reached across and took her hand between his.

She thought of that moment when the men had come marauding and she had sheltered under the basket with the hen. It had felt like the safest place to be. And the scariest. That was how she felt when her hand lay in his.

Idris saw the trepidation in her eyes and the slight flutter of her lips. She was afraid. Not of him, but of what they seemed to have embarked on. He cursed his inability to tell her what he felt. She and he seemed to have had an almost similar life-changing experience. He in his cage of bones, she in her basket. Was he reading too much into a coincidence? But what then of this strange affinity he felt for her? Almost as if, in another time, they had known each other and had shared a life together.

There had been other women in his life. But none of them, not even Kuttimalu, had made him feel as if he had come home. That he could curb his restless feet and wandering mind and find in her a resting place he would never leave.

One of the dogs stood up, growling. Its hackles were up. The other dogs growled too. He saw her shield her eyes with her palm and peer into the distance. 'Someone is out there,' she said. 'A stranger my dogs don't recognize.'

He nodded. Golla had told him about Pakshigudu – the lodge for travellers – and that she took in every waif and stray that paused at her threshold.

'We must go now,' she said.

He stood up. He felt her eyes on him. He knew it was time to leave. Golla would be hopping from one foot to the other in impatience.

'Will you come again?' she asked, as if unable to help herself.

He ran his finger along her lips, tracing their lines with a sure hand. 'Habibti,' he murmured in Arabic, the language he loved the most and the language most suited to the making of a promise, the wooing of a lifetime. I will.

He bent low and stepped away from the platform beneath the thatch of the little house. He felt a deep yearning to linger, to watch the night fall with her at his side. He would like to have pointed out the stars to her.

He stretched his hand towards her. She looked at his open palm for a moment and placed hers in his. He wrapped his fingers around that coarse, long-fingered hand. She may look like a queen and have all the hauteur of one, but her hands gave away the story of her life. He felt a surge of tenderness for her. Allah, let me not be the reason to cause her more grief than what she has already endured, he whispered a prayer under his breath.

They walked hand in hand through the mango orchard. The sun had begun to set and their shadows walked ahead of them. But their feet slowed as they drew closer to the edge of the orchard.

A plume of smoke curled into the sky from the main house. The evening meal was being cooked. By the Pakshigudu stood a small group of men and women. How did they find this place? Idris wondered.

Golla stood with the group, talking to their leader. He turned as Idris and Thilothamma approached them. For a moment, they seemed as if they were one. An indivisible unit of man and woman, intrinsically entwined. Then the shadows separated and Idris stopped in his tracks. Golla saw him murmur a few words. Thilothamma smiled and said something over her shoulder to him.

Later, as Idris watched Golla rubbing down Aamira Fiddah, it seemed to Golla that his master wore a secret smile. 'How did you speak to each other?' he asked curiously.

Idris shrugged. 'We didn't.'

'So what were you doing then?' Golla laughed.

'We just sat there and watched the breeze flutter the top of the trees,' Idris murmured.

Golla saw that secret smile again on Ayana's lips. The years seemed to have slipped off his master's face. There was an almost boyish ebullience on what used to be a grave countenance. What had transpired between the two? he wondered.

The clay in the enclosed area was washed two times a day, the next two days, until all that was left was a coarse sand. Meanwhile, Idris continued with his study of the language. In the hour before twilight, he went to sit with Thilothamma on the hard earth platform of the Mango House and watched her face as she spoke to him of this and that. He understood most of what she said but when he tried to respond, the sentences he formed were clumsy or jagged. She would smile and shake her head in dismay. 'When are we ever going to have a proper conversation?'

Thilothamma hadn't come to the mine after that first evening they spent together. Instead, Idris sought her out at the Mango House. He had been hesitant, but she had assuaged his fears. 'I have been the subject of gossip since I was twelve. Don't you think I would be used to it by now?'

He had gazed at her, not knowing what to say or do. Salute her for her courage and gather her in his arms or walk away from her for good. So they sat and watched the evening knock at their feet. On the fourth evening, Idris felt that if he couldn't say what he wanted to, he would explode.

He was silent all evening and brusque, which was quite unlike Ikka, Sala Pokkar thought. When Idris began pacing the embankment, Sala Pokkar watched him walk up and down for a while, then went towards him. 'What's wrong, Ikka?' he asked.

Idris shook his head. 'It's nothing… just something that's bothering me.'

Sala Pokkar drew closer and touched Idris on the elbow. 'Is there something I can do?'

'No, not really, unless you can teach me to speak fluent Telugu by tomorrow morning?'

Sala Pokkar's mouth twisted. 'Well, I thought Golla was giving you lessons.'

Idris nodded. 'He is, but either I am not smart enough, or he isn't a great teacher. I seem to be making little progress. How can I make my wishes known when the words don't form on my lips? And those that do are clumsy.'

Sala Pokkar had never seen Idris so troubled. Why was speaking Telugu so important? There were far more important things to worry about. All of Ikka's money was invested in the diamond prospecting. And the next day, the winnowing of the sand would begin.

Sala Pokkar hated having to say it, but it was necessary. 'Ikka, why don't you ask Golla to teach you what you want to say?'

Idris looked at him uncertainly. 'Isn't there something dishonest about that?'

Sala Pokkar shrugged. 'What's dishonest about it? You tell Golla what is in your mind and he provides you the equivalent words in another language.'

Idris smiled and clasped Sala Pokkar fondly. 'You are right.'

Sala Pokkar was relieved. The sooner everything was in place, the sooner they could leave Kollur. He was a khalasi and he didn't think there was much scope for a pulley in diamond prospecting. Keeping house and being Ikka's odd-job man was all very well when he had a definite role in Ikka's scheme of things. It occurred to Sala Pokkar that Kandavar too was becoming restless.

He had seen the boy practise his moves on the banks of the river. 'Why so secretive?' he had asked in surprise, when Kandavar had pleaded with him to not mention it.

The boy had hung his head and murmured, 'Aabo doesn't like it.'

'But why?' The sand was baking beneath their bare feet and Sala Pokkar hopped from one foot to the other. 'And do we have to stand here under the noon sun? Don't you feel hot?'

The boy shook his head. Sweat flew off his brow. 'I don't know. He said, if I practise on my own, I will not do it right and when I go back to the kalari, the Gurukkal will have to make me unlearn all the moves and it would take twice as long.'

'You actually went to a kalari?' Sala Pokkar frowned. 'A child of Islam in a Hindu kalari?'

'I am not a child…' the boy had retorted and then corrected himself. 'The kalari is run by Baapa Gurukkal. He is of the faith.'

'There is something I must ask you,' Sala Pokkar probed. Kandavar stiffened. 'I never see you pray.'

'Neither does Aabo,' Kandavar retorted.

Sala Pokkar had let the matter drop. But his suspicions grew another finger long. Ikka and the boy were hiding something from him. And yet, what secret could this father and son duo have? That they were bound by blood was obvious to anyone who looked at them. Especially now that the boy was taller than both Golla and him.

Sala Pokkar saw Idris head towards the shed where Golla was sure to be. Ikka, he hoped, would at least eat his dinner tonight.

The day dawned clear and bright. The thunderclouds of the previous evening seemed to have dissipated. The sun shone down, radiant and fierce. The previous day, the clay had been washed for the last time and left to dry.

Idris spoke his heart to her. All the way from the house by the river to the mine, he practised in his mind the words he had shaped with Golla's help. It was all he could think of as he mounted his horse. Fortunately for him, Aamira Fiddah sensed how preoccupied Idris was that morning and when he set out on the path towards the mine, she had known it was where they were headed and followed the path.

He had set out earlier than usual. Golla would come with the other two in a little while, but Idris thought if he didn't speak to Thilothamma early enough, along with the clay, the sun would dry up his words as well.

He rode straight to her house. He saw the workers gathered by the mine. But he didn't stop even though the mine master advanced towards him. The dogs began barking when he steered his horse onto the path alongside her millet field. He found a tree that seemed dense enough to protect Aamira Fiddah from the heat and tethered her there.

Should he go to her home or her little house? He hesitated only for a moment. He would go to the Mango House and if she wasn't there, he would go to her home. He didn't think it would bother her.

The Mango House was empty, but on his way back, she met him on the pathway. 'What is it?' she asked curiously. 'I wasn't expecting you for at least two more hours.'

'Ikkadiki ra,' he said softly.

'Where?' She smiled. What did he mean by come here? She was already there.

Idris grabbed her hand and walked back to the Mango House.

'What is this?' she asked, surprised by the violence of the move.

At the Mango House, he pushed open the door and walked in. There was nothing there but a rolled-up palm-leaf mat. He unfurled it and sat down cross-legged without letting go of her hand. Then, as if she were a child, he pulled her into his lap.

She began to rise, but he held her down and tilted her face towards his. 'Hear me out,' he said. 'Please, tipi.'

She felt as if she had bit into a sugarcane. Her eyes widened. No one had called her sweetness before. She was his tipi. She glowed.

'I don't know why you should believe anything I say, but I hope you will. I have never known anyone like you before. Or if I did, it was perhaps in another lifetime, for from that first…' He paused, fumbling for the word.

'Pagalu,' she supplied with a little laugh.

He frowned. 'Not day but that first moment. Takshana. I felt as if I had come full circle. I have known many women, loved a few, even known passion for one, but with you it is something else.'

He paused and searched her eyes. 'Thilothamma, with you, I am me.'

Golla had laughed when Idris had wanted him to say the words. 'What nonsense is this? Instead of calling her your pet parakeet, or the dove of your heart, you say you are you. How can you not be you?'

'She will understand. If she doesn't, she isn't the woman I think she is,' Idris had retorted.

But it seemed now that there was nothing false or awkward about the words. It sounded the most natural thing for him to say to her. As natural as it was for him to take her face between his hands and kiss her. He felt her stiffen and then melt against him. Her arms came up around his neck. He held her lower lip between his teeth and ran the tip of his tongue along it in a feathery caress. They held each other for several minutes in a feverish embrace, unable to let go of each other.

'Not like this, my Idris,' she said against his mouth.

'Why not like this?'

'I barely know you,' she protested.

His hands caressed her waist; the firm, supple muscles of her back sheathed in silken skin. 'What is there left to know, tipi?' he murmured. 'What is there to wait for? Who knows what our lives will be like tomorrow? Or even tonight?'

'Who knows indeed?'

She stroked his hair. The tight curls beneath her fingers felt like pearls.

She looked up at him and smiled. 'Do you realize that you spoke in Telugu? Your own words, and not that rehearsed speech of a few minutes ago.'

He flushed. 'Tipi,' he said. 'I can't. Please. I can't wait.'

She nodded. She didn't want to either. Everything in her protested at this intimacy between a near stranger and her, and yet, she didn't know how to say no.

From outside the little house, the dogs began barking loudly. Someone was approaching.

'Looks like we may have to,' she said. 'Wait, I mean.'

He kissed her deeply before letting her go.

'When then?' he asked. 'Shall I come back tonight?'

'No, no,' she said. 'I am not a whore for you to seek in stealth.'

'Tipi,' he remonstrated, 'I didn't mean to offend you. I…'

'Come to me like a man who seeks his love, not like a thief taking what is not his. In the early hours of the day, I will wait for you here,' she said softly. 'Come to me then, so we can see the dawn break together.'

The winnowing had begun in earnest. Golla was standing with the mine master and watching the men and women prepare the winnowing baskets, each shaped like a fan.

Three times the earth was tossed into the air, and two times they shook the basket sideways. The fine dust flew into the air like chaff from the grain and all around was a fine haze of dust.

The clods of clay remaining in the basket were placed with great care back on the ground.

Idris drew his head cloth around his nostrils, as did Thilothamma. Their shoulders brushed and they looked at each other for a brief instant. An unspoken promise for later.

All of that day and the next, men and women would separate the dust from the earth. 'It's impossible to go any closer,' the mining master said. 'Come back the day after. Hopefully, it will be an auspicious day for all of us.'

Idris looked at Thilothamma. She nodded briefly and walked away.

XLVI

Idris sat cross-legged on his pile of mattresses. The night was fading into a hazy blur, the inky black skies smeared with a handful of ash. He took a deep breath and stood up. He stepped out of his jellabiyad which he wore at night, wound a cloth around his waist and walked down to the river. He looked, as he always did, for a sign from the heavenly bodies. High in the morning sky, he saw the most astonishing sight of his life. A close conjunction of Al-Mushtarie and Al-Zahra. As though the planets too had sought to draw into each other. He had their blessings.

He washed himself, as though he were getting ready for prayers. He would go to her with a body scrubbed clean of dust and grime, and the shadow of past loves.

There was a rock some distance away. He swam towards it blindly. The force of the water was like a battering ram as it slammed into him. But as he pitted his strength against the tide, he felt a fresh vigour course through him. He felt powerful, invincible even. His fingers touched the rock, then he hoisted himself onto it and in the darkness before dawn, he shut his eyes to everything but the sensation of being there.

He listed it in his head: the slapping of water against the rock as it rushed downstream. The wind rustling through the tall grass that lined the bank closer to him. A cloud moving across the moon. The breeze on his back. The droplets of water that clung to his skin. His beating heart. The quietness of the hour.

A few minutes later, Idris stood on the rock and dived back into the river. A straight black arrow that shot through the darkness into the swirling blue-black waters. He cut through the river and climbed up the steps, then walked swiftly back into his room. With great care, he put on fresh clothes. He opened the little box in which he stored his enamelled eye, opened the eyelid of his dead eye and popped it in place.

After all these years, it still stung a bit. Although he knew it wasn't possible for the dead eye to know any pain, just as it couldn't see. But somewhere, in some corner of his brain, a nerve twitched in protest. A phantom sensation perhaps, for at night, when he took the enamelled shield out and bathed his eye in cold water, he felt a strange relief.

Kandavar had watched him for several nights and asked one evening, 'Why do you wear this eye, Aabo? Doesn't it hurt to take it off and put it back every morning?'

Idris had shrugged. 'Perhaps I don't want anyone referring to me as the one-eyed African. Now they call me the African with the jewelled eye. Or perhaps I feel unprotected when my injured eye is there for the whole world to look at. Perhaps I am just vain. Who knows, inan? Who knows?'

Idris walked to the stable, to his horse. Aamira Fiddah neighed at the sight of her master. Idris ran his hands along the mare's neck. 'Aamira, it's time for us to go. Are you ready?'

The horse nuzzled his neck.

A gentle breeze rode with them as they galloped along the

riverbank and Idris felt suddenly nervous at the thought of what lay ahead.

He rode through the town and towards the mines, his heart racing ahead of Aamira's hooves. In the distance, he could see a little lamp outside the house in the mango orchard. The scent of flowers filled the air. His hands shook as he tethered Aamira to a tree. Golla had kept a feed pouch of horse gram in the saddle bag and given him explicit instructions. 'She is to be fed at first light and not before that.'

Idris hesitated. What if he was late? 'Pray for me, Aamira, that our lives go the way we want it to. The only thing is, if it does, you may need to wait for your breakfast,' Idris whispered in the mare's ear.

Aamira snorted.

Idris turned on his heel and strode towards the light.

Four of the dogs lay in the front yard. They raised their heads and looked at him. One of them wagged his tail. The others just stared, but none of them barked.

He bent low and stepped onto the earth platform. The door was shut but not latched. He hesitated.

Then he rapped gently on the door and pushed it open.

She was sitting on the floor. Her back was straight and, in the golden light of the lamp, her skin shone. Idris felt his breath catch. When she stood up, he saw that she wore a green cloth instead of the ochres, reds and browns she favoured. Her eyes were lined with lampblack and her hair had been combed and pulled into a little bun at the nape of her neck. A small hoop of gold was threaded through one nostril and in her ears were gigantic earrings. At her throat, the uncut diamond glittered. She didn't speak.

He walked the few steps towards her and with the tip of his index finger slowly traced the lines of her face. She shivered.

'Come,' she said, leading him towards the mat on the floor. He watched her undulating hips and felt his mouth go dry. He reached out and took the end of the green cloth tucked into her waist and pulled it gently. As the cloth unfurled into a pool at her feet, he saw the lines of her body and felt overwhelmed. The high breasts, the nipped-in waist, the flaring hips and long, firm thighs. She stood there, letting him have his fill of her body, her eyes downcast.

What did he see? Thilothamma wondered. And did it matter? For he was here, and no matter how she may appear to someone else, to him she was beautiful, she was desirable. The thought filled her with courage. She walked into his arms and let her palms slide along his back and over his chest. He drew in his breath sharply, then turned his back to her, pulling his tunic over his head. She watched as he undid his trousers and stepped out of them. She blinked. She thought of the only man she had seen naked before. Her husband, hollow-chested, with his sagging belly and bony limbs. This man who stood before her, glistening black skin stretched tight over a lean body, was wide at the chest and narrow at the hip, his thighs strong and sculpted. She stood still as he walked up to her. 'Tipi,' he said in his low, rumbly voice.

It was the first word he had spoken to her since he had walked through her door. *Tipi.* She felt as though someone had stroked her soul with a peacock plume.

'Yes,' she murmured.

He touched her lips with the tip of one finger and brought it to his own. Then he bent and took her mouth in his.

On one of his travels, Idris had met a scholar who had told him of an Indian text called the *Kamasutra*. According to it, there were five ways of kissing your beloved. But Idris knew there was a sixth one. That which every man and woman had to discover for themselves. As he took Thilothamma's lips between his and sucked on them hungrily, he felt her nipples harden and he knew this would be theirs. He prodded her mouth open and their tongues curled and fought with each other.

He pulled away then and turned her towards the wall, pushing her against it with her hands over her head. She felt his fingers cup her breasts and squeeze ever so gently even as his mouth dropped little kisses at the back of her neck. Thilothamma's back arched in pleasure.

He smiled in delight and trailed his tongue down the curve of her spine, lingering at the well of her buttocks, going down on his knees to lick the back of her knees. Then he rose and turned her towards him, taking her hands and placing them on his chest. 'Touch me,' he whispered.

She did as he asked, letting her palms slide along his back and over his chest, caressing him gently. He groaned in pleasure and she felt a strange power fill her as her hands roamed his body of their own volition, kneading and pulling, cupping and squeezing.

He pushed her head towards his nipple and she took the stiff nub in her mouth and tugged at it with her teeth. She felt him harden and strain against her belly.

He pushed her down on her back on to the mat and kissed her on the neck, where a pulse beat frantically, then moved his lips to each one of her pulse points, his tongue alternately arousing and soothing until she was whimpering in need. Slowly, he slipped down further until his cheeks grazed her thighs, and then his tongue was inside her, probing and licking and driving her into a frenzy. Her fingers clutched his hair as she bucked under him, the pleasure ripping through her body again and again, and making her moan aloud. Idris lifted his head to look at her, then rested his head on her stomach and held her until she quietened. 'Now it's my turn, Tipi,' he murmured, rolling over and pulling her on top of him.

Thilothamma looked down at the man below her and smiled. She had never known that her body had such reservoirs of pleasure locked within. Now she wanted him to know it too. 'Not like this,' she whispered. Guided by instinct, she slithered down the length of his body, her breasts soft against his skin, and bent to kiss his toes, carefully, gently, one after the other, taking each one in her mouth and nibbling and sucking until he was moving restlessly, his hands reaching for her, trying to pull her up towards him. Then, mimicking his earlier moves, she kissed him gently, lips parted, on his ankles, on the back of his knees and the inside of his thighs. She felt his breath catch and then he was pulling her up and kissing her on the lips, his mouth urgent and needy on hers. She lowered herself on him, then tightened her grip and rode him till a moan escaped his lips.

Idris felt a multitude of waves crash against his skull. For some strange reason, his mind returned to the scholar from Benaras. 'A woman who seeks to pleasure you rather than herself will choose the upari suthanam,' he had said, 'for you will feel all of her everywhere and you will know every moment of the path to that point beyond the horizon.'

But it was their first time and because he couldn't wait any longer, he rolled her over and, parting her legs, entered her roughly, his gaze locked into hers as he rode her until it was she who closed her eyes and surrendered to his passion. 'Look at me, Tipi,' he whispered. 'Don't close your eyes. Look at me...'

Later, as they lay side by side, she thought of the fire the priest had lit at the mine by rubbing two arani sticks against each other. May this body of mine be fit for this supreme sacrifice, she whispered. Each time you enter me and offer me your purnahuti, we will know divinity, the fullness of our vital force. You are mine as I am the camasa, the vessel to hold your sap. I welcome you with all of my being. My body is the sacrificial place, the skull of my head is the fire pit, my hair the kusha grass, my mouth the altar, my skin the soma press and my vulva the fire in the middle.

'I am yours,' she said aloud.

He pulled her closer, then struck her playfully. And she him. Gently at first. And then again, so it hurt a little. Pleasure has its dimensions. Who is to decide what the boundaries are, he thought, as he saw her pupils dilate. Did she even know what that stinging slap on his thighs woke in him?

All he had done before, Idris did now. With a sure touch and in the knowledge that she needed it as much as he did. He took in his hands her hair that had opened from its knot and twisted it so that it pulled at her scalp. Skin against skin, kindling an unquenchable fire.

She wrapped her thighs around him and held him tight within her, unwilling to let go, unwilling to forsake the rapture that had been the blessing of their union.

He laid his face against her neck and allowed the tears to seep from his eyes: the living eye and the enamelled one.

XLVII

A distant pounding. The ground hummed beneath them. He stirred and opened his eyes. She lay there looking at him. 'I was watching you sleep,' she said quietly.

He took a deep breath and said, 'I don't know when I slept last. I had forgotten what it is to sleep.'

He sat up abruptly as if the mere admission of sleep was a declaration of weakness. She rose languorously and raised her hands to knot her hair into its customary bun. His breath snarled in his throat. He wanted to reach out and pull her back into his arms again. But that would be admitting to a need. And Idris could have no needs. That was what allowed him to take every day and its outcome in his stride.

She went outside and brought a cauldron of warm water. Then she took a cloth, dipped it into the water, wrung it dry and sponged him with it.

Idris took the cloth from her and washed her body carefully.

Then they dried each other.

She handed his clothes to him. He didn't speak, but put them on and watched her drape a cloth around herself. Unconsciously, his mind spanned the length – twelve handspans long and two handspans wide of the finest cotton. Thilothamma, it seemed, picked only the best her money could buy. She was her own mistress and it showed, even in the smooth economy of her movements as she covered herself. She inserted one end of the cloth into a string girdle slung around her hip. Then, she took the other end and wound it around her, bringing it over her breasts and left shoulder and tucked the end into the waist. She was Thilothamma again, the queenly woman of the millet fields.

He wondered what she would do. Wait for him to leave or go with him? How would she play this?

At the door she said, 'It will be a long day. I suggest you come back here to rest when the sun is overhead.'

Then she was gone.

Idris waited for a while. How could he feel so bereft, he wondered. How could he long for someone so intensely? Someone he barely knew. He looked at the limewashed mud walls of the house. The earth tones had seeped through and the walls were populated with faces he knew and recognized. There was one that resembled Ali, his father's camel master. Ali, who had given him the black pebble from Kaabah. Ali, who had sat vigil at his bedside along with his father. There was another that looked like Fatima Naaya. An elderly Fatima he had seen a few months before she died. With a sunken mouth and a pointy chin. Why was the past crowding his mind with such haste today?

Something had shifted in him. All that had held his equilibrium had moved. Subterranean forces were displacing all that he knew and considered himself to be. Idris pulled his knees to his chin and stared at the faces of Ali and Fatima, the widow from Damascus, the Yemeni, and his father. He would never see them again. He closed his eyes and willed himself to calm down.

The pounding filled his ears. Idris rose and walked towards the diamond mines. Kismet had decided that this was the day his life would be redefined.

Idris walked past Aamira, who neighed loudly. He went across to the mare and rubbed her nose. The feed bag was empty. Golla must have fed her, he thought ruefully.

'What's going on?' he asked Golla as if it was the most natural thing for him to saunter towards the mine from the mango orchard early in the day.

One end of the mine was being raked. The men were pounding the winnowed clods of earth with a long pestle that ended in a base block half a foot wide. Scores of men pounded the earth two, three times as they moved slowly forward, taking a short step at time. No bit of earth was left untouched. The ground shook with the slow, steady pounding and suddenly Idris felt helpless. The wheels of kismet were turning and there was nothing he could do to change what came next.

He had always been a trader. Someone who knew how to use a bargaining chip to steer a deal in his favour. But for the first time, he was a prospector. Of love and diamonds. And there were no opportunities for him to sniff out a weakness or roll a dice. He would have to accept whatever it was kismet decided to throw his way.

All morning, the men pounded the earth. When it was noon, they paused and Golla came up to Idris, who had shifted to his habitual post under the tree. 'I have arranged with Akka for you to be served your food at the Mango House.

You should eat and rest there. In a couple of hours, they will resume work.'

Idris nodded and walked towards the millet fields. There was nothing he could do but chew on each minute as if it were the jaad leaf Ali had chewed on all day.

As in the early hours of the day, the door was shut but not latched. Idris walked in. A little grass mat was laid out and there were a few covered dishes, but the house was unoccupied. He felt a quick sense of relief.

A pitcher of water had been left out for him. He washed the dust from his face and sluiced his arms and legs. Then he sat cross-legged and ate his meal of rice, lentils and spiced meat. When he was replete, he kept the dishes outside and stretched out on the floor. He needed this time to collect his thoughts.

Idris knew that all his life, this need he had to isolate himself had caused suspicion, even hurt. For the people who loved him, it was an act of rejection, his almost desperate need to get away and be on his own. He had wondered if Thilothamma would seek him out. For that too was part of a relationship. The need to examine, analyse and relive again and again in countless ways all that had transpired. Idris had never understood this failing in people. To want to own not just the body and heart of the beloved, but their every thought and breath. The silken ties that bound one in an affair of the heart may not chaff the skin at first, but eventually it did. Bruising and stifling, just as coarse rope did.

Thilothamma, he realized, was perhaps the only other person he knew who was as solitary a creature as he was and yet, she lived in the moment as he did. She knew how to gauge the edge of their hunger for each other. Not just for the gratification of the flesh, but for something else, more intimate – to walk the labyrinth of each other's soul and not be appalled or afraid by what they would discover there.

When the heat of the midday had subsided, Idris returned to the mine. The pounding was complete. The women filled the fan-shaped trays from the earth that was heaped into a pile at one end and passed them to the men who stood outside the wall of the enclosed area, winnowing the soil again briskly and with great vigour. The dust flew redder and thicker, for the clay had been pounded well. And when all the dust had separated from the earth, the men flung it back into the enclosed area and the women spread it carefully with their hands as if it were rice and the loss of even one grain would be a serious depletion of wealth. As dusk fell, the workers finished the final winnowing. Early next morning, they would go over the earth methodically and search for any diamonds that lay hidden there.

'You have had a long day,' Golla said. 'You should go home. The boy and your man must wonder where you are. I'll stay back here with two of my men. We'll stand vigil so that no one enters the mine at night. We'll begin work in the second hour after sunrise. There will be a feast before that. The mine master and I have made all the arrangements.'

Idris looked at him. 'Why, Golla?' he asked softly. 'What makes you so...' He groped for the right word. 'Walaa... loyal.'

The man blinked. It was as though he had been asked if he would like to fly to the moon.

'I have eaten your salt and you have paid for my time. It's my duty to do my best for your welfare.' Golla spoke brusquely. 'Do not question loyalty, Ayana. It is insulting to the one who offers it and to the man who deserves it.'

Idris nodded, chastened by Golla's dignity. In his own way, Golla had taught him so much in such little time. 'I will return early and I'll bring Kandavar and Sala with me,' he said, seeking to lighten the air. 'They will not forgive me if they are not here to spot the diamonds. They haven't seen a diamond ever.'

'And neither have I,' Golla said simply.

Idris mounted Aamira and turned down the path, homeward

bound. Aamira was frisky on the ride back. Idris had to keep a tight rein to hold her in check. Where was Thilothamma, he wondered. If, at first, he was relieved by the space she had given him, it now irked him.

He had expected her to come to the diamond field in the evening and he had looked towards the millet fields every few minutes. But she had stayed away. What was she trying to tell him?

Figure it out Idris, figure it out, he said to himself as Aamira galloped into the night.

Kandavar insisted on riding Vajra to the mining field. 'I named him Vajra for the diamonds and he should be there when the first diamond is found.'

Idris looked at Sala Pokkar's face. 'What about you? Aamira is strong enough to carry you as well. Or you can ride one of the bullocks.'

Sala Pokkar thought of the distance from Aamira's back to the ground. 'Why don't I just walk?'

Idris paused eating and said sternly, 'No, you will hold us up. You only have two options. Aamira or the bullock.'

'The bullock then,' Sala Pokkar mumbled, reaching for a piece of meat in the round bowl they all ate from.

Musa sat in the corner, washing himself. When Kandavar tossed a morsel of meat to him, Idris frowned. 'Don't feed the cat while we are eating.'

The boy didn't speak, but Idris saw the displeasure in the way he twisted his mouth. 'Why, Aabo?' Kandavar asked suddenly. 'What is wrong if I feed Musa while eating?'

The boy was no longer the nine-year-old Idris had first encountered. Kandavar was eleven years old. He wouldn't be the biddable child anymore. Instead, in his truculence, he would demand an explanation for every rebuke or instruction.

'One day Musa will think it's perfectly all right to eat from our bowl even as we are eating. He has been taught that he can't. But if you feed him, you will confuse him with cross instructions. Does that make sense to you?' Idris said patiently.

Sala Pokkar sniffed loudly. He thought Ikka was too indulgent with the boy. If it were him, he would just box the boy's ears and ask him to do as he said.

'Oh,' the boy said. 'What time do we leave tomorrow?' he asked.

'At sunrise. So I would suggest you go to bed early,' Idris said, rising.

That night, they lay in their pallets, unable to sleep. Was the journey they had begun a year ago finally drawing to an end?

XLVIII

They left home at sunrise. Aamira was inclined to gallop, but Idris held her in, matching her canter to the bullock's gait. The dawn was filled with the sound of hooves and the jingling of the little bells attached to Vajra's horns.

The workers were all assembled at the mine. The priest waited, as he had on that first morning.

Idris stood there, unable to make sense of why Golla was bustling around. He sensed her presence at his side. He turned and there she stood, gazing at him silently. 'Why did you avoid me all day yesterday?' he asked abruptly.

'So you could make up your mind,' she said in a low voice.

He took a deep breath. 'And have you made up your mind?'

'When I decided to wait for you in my house yesterday morning, I already had, Idris.'

'Tipi,' he began.

'Ssh...'

'Don't ssh me... I am not like the men you have known,' he said. 'I want you to remember that.'

'That you are not.' Her voice was wry.

Idris frowned. 'So don't look at me as if I am just any man. You and I, what we have...'

But before he could finish, Golla was standing before him. 'You have to offer a ladle of food to each of the workers. And Akka,' he said, turning to Thilothamma, 'would you offer the second ladle? The little master should offer the last ladle.'

Idris stared at Golla uncomprehendingly.

'They will look for the diamonds today. With this meal that is salty rather than sweet, you are telling them to do their best for you and your family.'

Thilothamma looked at Idris. Would he protest? She had been deemed as his family. This man who had escaped commitment for as long as he could, what would he make of it? Perhaps he had no option. What was it her great-grandfather liked to say? Padda peedepurugu uattu. A dung worm stuck in a dung pit with no option of getting away.

But Idris took her hand in his as if it were the most natural thing to do, and led her to the priest. He hollered for Kandavar, who was standing some distance away. When the boy came running, they arranged themselves by the three cauldrons of food and scooped out a ladle each. They first filled the leaf plate the mine master came bearing and then each one of the leaf plates the twenty-five men held out. And then the twenty-five women too, who were not to work that day, but would still be fed, for that too was part of the ritual: My family and I have fed you and your family. Let this thought guide your eyes and fingers as you seek my diamonds. And finally, each one of the watchmen: Golla and his men.

Thilothamma filled two leaf plates for Sala Pokkar and

Kandavar. Idris smiled at Thilothamma. 'Come,' he said to her. He ladled out a portion of food and served it to her. She offered him one in turn. Golla watched them. So did Kandavar. And the two of them had the same thought. It was as if they were making a vow of some sort to each other.

They ate their food carefully. Then the men took off the half-cloth around their hips and clad only in their loincloth, they went to the enclosed area and, squatting on their haunches, set about sifting through the soil with their fingers. Dust rose in the air and drew a veil around them. The watchmen moved closer as they trickled the earth through their fingers.

They may have eaten the master's salt but the temptation to steal had to be curbed. It was hard for a man not to be tempted. For working tirelessly a whole year, at the most he would make three pagodas. And if his wife and children worked as well, perhaps four pagodas; just enough to keep body and soul together. A diamond would certainly make a difference. The workers were made to strip down to their loincloth so that they couldn't hide one on their person. But Golla had heard the story of a man who popped a stone under his eyelid. And of another who had inserted a stone beneath the sheath of his foreskin. It was best not to take chances.

'The first man to find a stone will be rewarded with five silver rupees. So make sure not a grain of earth goes unsifted,' Golla called out half an hour later, when nothing had emerged.

The dust cloud grew dense as hands worked the soil with greater fervour at the thought of the glinting silver coins. It would be enough to set up as capital for a trade, to retrieve a piece of land from the moneylender, or buy a buffalo calf. It was not a reward that could be easily dismissed.

A shout rent the air. One of the men leapt up, his teeth gleaming, his eyes sparkling with excitement in his dust-covered face. He jumped up and down, shouting, 'I found it! I found it!'

Holding the stone close to his chest, the young man ran towards the mine master while the others stared at him with barely concealed envy.

The mine master took the stone to Idris. He washed it in a bowl of water and held it up for Idris to see. Beneath the leafy tree, in the green shadow, the stone threw a blue light. Kandavar and Sala, who had hastened forward, stood transfixed by the sight of their first diamond.

The mine master murmured to Golla, who began to translate, but Idris didn't need Golla's assistance to decipher what was being said. 'This is a fair enough stone. About one mangelin, which is about two carats as the firangis call it. It's valuable enough, but in the night I can tell you how blue the celestial light is. More importantly, there will be more stones for us to compare it with by then.'

Idris looked at Golla's face. He too seemed dazzled by the sight of the stone. Only he felt a strange deadness. What had he expected? A stone that was as big as the Great Mughal diamond? Or was it something else? A certain sense of inevitability about what would follow once the first stone was found.

He held the stone in the palm of his hand. Kandavar and Sala Pokkar came closer to get a better look. Golla was the one who voiced the thought. 'It doesn't sparkle as I expected it to, but the mine master said it would be like a star once it's been cut. But why is it so valuable? It's just a stone after all.'

Idris smiled. Beneath the green canopy, despite it not having been cut and polished, the stone still had a certain magnificence. But it was only a stone, as Golla said. 'It has to do with human greed,' he explained, almost as if he were speaking to himself. 'We covet what isn't easily available. A river pebble worn smooth by the water is just as beautiful, but you don't find diamonds like you do river pebbles. So we stake everything in our pursuit of it.'

'Does it make the river pebble less valuable?' a voice asked from behind.

Idris stiffened. Thilothamma too had heard of the stone, he realized. He took a deep breath. 'I didn't say that!'

'Let me see the stone,' she said, coming into the periphery of his good eye.

He held it out to her. She looked at it carefully and offered it back. 'I'll see you tonight,' she murmured.

He nodded. Perhaps, when he held her, he would feel less apprehensive of what lay ahead.

Kandavar followed Thilothamma to her house. She had asked Golla to bring him to her after she had spotted him with Idris the first time. Kandavar had taken a great liking for her and she for him. Now Kandavar had a hundred queries for her. What did they do with the millet? Had the black hen stopped brooding? Had the brown cow calved?

Idris watched the two of them retreat further and further into the distance. Sala Pokkar remained at his side.

By dusk, when they stopped work, a dozen more stones had been found. The biggest was six mangelin. 'It's a decent enough crop for the first day. Tomorrow will be better,' the mine master said, handing over the pouch of stones to Idris for safe keeping.

Idris was staying at the cottage that night. Till the crop had been harvested, he would spend every night there, he told Kandavar and Sala Pokkar. They were to return to the mine the next day and every day thereafter, he added, seeing the look of dismay on their faces. 'I need you to make sure everything is ready at home for us to leave. Once the entire crop has been brought in, we will have to return.'

Kandavar and Sala Pokkar looked relieved. The thought of home didn't seem so far away, now that Idris had mentioned it.

Idris laid out the stones on the floor of the little house. Thilothamma looked at the line of diamonds.

'Are you pleased?' she asked, trying to read the expression on his face. The sun had set and Thilothamma had lit a small lamp in a corner of the room. Idris sat amidst the shadows, a giant shadow that gave nothing away.

'I don't know,' he said.

She frowned. 'What is wrong?' she asked.

But he wouldn't speak. Instead, he took her in his arms and lay there with her curled into him. Then he made quiet love to her as if he needed to imprint everything about her into his very being, devouring with greed every crevice and orifice, his fingers moving on her with a manic urgency. When he entered her, he did so with a feeling close to grief: The pleasure dome would erupt and the night would stretch ahead of him, empty, desolate, and fanning the fears that had crept into him when the first diamond had been found.

The next day dawned with thunderclouds streaking the face of the sun. The air was heavy and listless. The mountains peered at the fields with a brooding denseness. Idris watched Thilothamma stir. Once again, he had slept through the night. The first time, he had put it down to a combination of reasons: nervous excitement and fatigue, the physical exertion of their vigorous love-making, the early morning air… but a whole night? What magical potion had she fed him? What sleeping draught lay concealed in her?

'You slept.' She smiled.

'Tipi… I did.' He smiled back and pulled her into his arms.

They lay there quietly, watching the sun climb. A little later, she said, 'We have to rise. My millet fields will be harvested today and your workers will soon start as well.'

XLIX

A little after they began, one of the workers, the oldest man in the group, found a stone that was decidedly bigger than any of the stones found the day before. He wiped the stone against his arm to loosen the mud clinging to it, and walked with great dignity befitting the find, to the mine master.

It was a ten-mangelin diamond, a princeling of a stone. As was customary, the worker had to be rewarded. So Idris offered the man a talapaav. Golla had explained to him that this too was expected. A long cotton cloth worth 40 peche, half a pagoda in silver, and a plate of rice and sugar.

'Diamonds have hearts. If you please the man who brought it to you, the diamond takes on a rainbow hue. The lights and colours will shimmer and please. But the diamond is just as quick to absorb a curse as a blessing. Its heart turns black and vengeful and casts a shadow on the one who wears it. Which is why, when we send a diamond out into the world, we must ensure it carries within it only goodness,' the mine master had explained.

Idris looked at the stone and thought that when they were done, he would choose two fine stones and have them set so that Kandavar could wear them in his earlobes when he was home. Twin blessings to guard and protect him from all that life would throw his way. And Thilothamma? What about her? But Idris wouldn't allow the voice in his head to speak. Instead, he turned his attention to the mine master who, now that Idris had stones, had stories to tell of other mines and diamond prospects.

There was another mine to the south-west called Ramulkota, he told Idris. It belonged to the king of Bijapur. Five days' journey from Golkonda and nine days from Bijapur. 'The river

Bhima, a sister of our own Krishna, separates the two kingdoms and the king will not allow a bridge to be built because he is afraid of being invaded,' the mine master said.

Idris nodded. It made sense.

'And there are sub-governors on either side of the river who keep a check on the men and merchandise, and the animals who have crossed from one side to the other,' the mine master said, his voice mellow with nostalgia.

'The stones there are better, but the ones here are bigger,' he added. 'Would the master…?'

The question was left open-ended. Idris shrugged. 'Let me see,' he said, committing to nothing but the prospect of a time together, sometime in the future.

Late in the evening, Idris went back to the little cottage, where Thilothamma waited for him. I could get used to this, he thought as a sense of well-being flooded him.

And so the days passed, and finally it was the evening of the last day of mining. The mine master advised Idris to meet a merchant who, he said, was more honest than the rest put together.

Idris and Thilothamma looked at the cluster of diamonds. There were eighty-six stones in all. From one-fourth a mangelin to a twenty-five mangelin stone.

'You are a rich man, Idris,' she said, holding up a diamond. 'This is a fine stone.'

'It may be a flawed stone,' he said awkwardly.

'Let me show you a trick the jewellers use,' she said. She placed the lamp in a corner of the room, where there was an alcove, and extended its wick so the flame shone bright and true. Then she held the stone up to the light. 'Look,' she said.

He looked at the water of the stone in that light. It shone blue and true, and he understood why it was called the celestial light. His gaze shifted to her smile of knowing, for she had said it was a fine stone and he had claimed otherwise.

Within her was an incandescence, just as brilliant as the celestial light of the diamond. He had seen it once before, in his son, that fateful night at Thirunavaya. He thought of how much he wanted to cherish it. But as keepers of the world everywhere knew, he would have to choose. For how could a man, any man, nurture two lights? Maybe in another place, in another lifetime, he would have the option, but Idris Maymoon Samataar Guleed, previously of Dikhil, lived in the here and now.

He took the diamond from her and put it back in the pouch with the other stones. Two per cent of the value of the stones had to be paid as royalties to the Golkonda Sultan. The stones would fetch a much lower price, almost twenty per cent less than they would in Golkonda, if he sold it elsewhere, but he wouldn't be paying tax on the Golkonda prices. He would make a fine profit even if he set aside a small pouch of stones for the ship's surgeon, who had helped partially fund the diamond prospecting. But the day for departure was drawing closer.

He had promised to take Kandavar back in the Magharam month of the following year, when he left Vattoli tharavad. He was already two weeks late, and it would take at least two months of travel before they would reach Kozhikode. By which time, they would have given up the boy for dead and performed his funeral rites, he thought grimly.

That night, he told her what she mustn't expect from him. For that was easier than telling her what he could offer her, which was virtually nothing.

'I am not stupid,' she said, when she had heard him out. 'I always knew that you would leave someday.' What she wouldn't admit was that like other women before her, she had thought she would be the one who would make the difference. That he would change, put down roots, and opt for a life with her.

'And...' he began, hesitant to even voice the notion.

'And what, Idris? What would you like me to say?'

'Nothing...' he said. 'I...' But he couldn't speak the words. How could he ask anything of her when he couldn't offer her the commitment that he would return to her someday?

Instead, he made love to her and she to him, matching kiss for kiss, caress with caress, and when they shuddered in each other's arms, neither of them knew if it was joy or anguish that they felt.

'In the holy book, there is a prophet called Idris. They say he was considered the epitome of trustworthiness. They called him the interpreter because he could be trusted to interpret the sacred texts. He was among the first men to use a pen, set out weights and measures and read the stars. I only have his name, Tipi. And his ability to read the stars. But I can't even trust myself to say we will see each other again,' he said, clinging to her.

She touched his cheek but didn't reply.

In the morning, she was gone, and Idris knew he wouldn't see her again. He rode Aamira back to the house by the river in a daze. It was over. It really was over. All of him yearned to stay back but he had a zimmah, a responsibility, towards his son. And even when he had entrusted his son back to his mother, he wouldn't be free to walk away. You don't absolve yourself of parental duties till you are dead. That was the truth. You may stop being a husband or a brother. You could even walk away from being a son. But you can't stop being a parent. He would have to stay for as long as his inan needed him. How then could he make a promise to Thilothamma?

She was hurt, he knew. She had asked nothing of him, except that he say to her that he would return when the time was right. But he had been unable to speak even that phrase of faint comfort.

L

It was the day before they were to leave Kollur. Sala Pokkar and Golla had been busy buying supplies for the journey back to Masulipatnam. Idris had work in the town. He had to meet Tabriz Ali and take his leave as well, he told Kandavar.

'Since everyone is busy, I would like to go and see Pinni one more time,' Kandavar said.

'On your own?' Idris asked.

'I am not a child, Aabo.' Kandavar frowned. 'I will be twelve years old this year.'

Idris looked at the boy before him and was startled to see how tall he had become. The childish face showed new angles of maturity, of a boy on the brink of manhood.

'Yes,' Idris said slowly. 'I failed to see you have grown. How did that happen?'

Kandavar shrugged. 'So it's all right if I go visit Pinni on my own,' Kandavar persisted.

Idris nodded. Then, struck by a thought, he said, 'There is something I would like you to do.'

The mine looked forlorn now that there was no one there. The millet fields too had been harvested and the countryside was bare and bleak. The dogs came running to meet Kandavar. Thilothamma smiled at him as if she couldn't stop. He held out a basket to her. 'What is this?' she asked, surprised.

'Musa,' Kandavar said, sliding off the lid of the basket a tiny bit so she could see the cat. 'You've met Vajra and Aamira. I wanted you to meet Musa as well before we left. He is a very clever cat.'

'So has your father decided on the day you will leave?' she asked.

'Yes, we leave tomorrow,' he said.

She served him lunch and watched him eat, piling still more food into his plate. When the household had settled and they sat together by the door, he brought out the parcel Aabo had entrusted him with.

Thilothamma took the little cloth pouch Kandavar handed over to her. Inside it were two stones of a mangelin each. She bit on her lip thoughtfully. She knew that Idris wasn't in a position to spare much. Each dapu would make a difference. And yet, he had sent her a part of his profits.

'When will you return?' she asked.

'I don't know, Pinni. Probably never. When I go back, I'll have to resume training at the kalari.'

'Kalari.' It was a strange word. Thilothamma shook her head in wonder. There was a world out there that she knew nothing about. It was into that world her Idris was returning. 'Take good care of him. Everyone thinks he is strong and can fend for himself. But he is only human. Will you look after him for me?' She touched the boy's elbow.

'Who?' he asked.

'Your father. Idris,' she said.

'Now that we are leaving, Pinni, I can tell you the truth. We just say that. Aabo isn't really my father.' Kandavar grinned. 'I don't think he will mind me telling you this.'

'He is your father. One just needs to see the two of you together – even the village idiot would spot the resemblance. Which is why I said you should look out for him. I know your mother is alive and he doesn't live with her. He has no one but you, do you see that?'

Thilothamma's words resounded in his ears. Everything that had happened since that dawn two years ago played out in Kandavar's mind. His father hadn't known about him till that moment. But once he had, Aabo had taken it upon himself to be there for him. It felt right, he thought, that Aabo was his father.

'I will,' he said, looking down at his palm. He laid his other palm over hers in a solemn promise.

He looked at her face, her downcast eyes, and felt he had to do something to make her feel better. So he took the basket and offered it to her. 'Musa may not survive the journey back. So I would like to leave him with you, Pinni,' he said.

Thilothamma placed the basket on the ground by the cattle shed. She left the lid propped up and waited. Musa emerged with a mew and leapt onto the wall of the shed in one fluid move. He sat there washing himself.

Kandavar looked at Musa. It seemed to him that Musa had already forgotten him. 'He won't ever forget you,' Thilothamma said, reading the desolation in his eyes.

'But…' he began.

'Cats are not dogs. He will miss you in his own way. But don't expect him to behave like the dog you left behind at home.'

Kandavar's eyes lit up at the mention of Maccanto. He couldn't wait to see him. 'You know about Maccanto? Aabo gave me his dog. He is the most handsome dog I have seen,' he said, as they walked together away from the house.

As he walked away, she called out, 'And you must tell your father that if he ever wants a place to rest his head, he has a home here. And that I will be waiting,' she said, finding the words that had eluded her when she was with Idris.

Thilothamma watched Kandavar leave till he became a speck in the distance. She touched the stone at the base of her throat. The thirteen-mangelin stone that had started it all and had brought Idris to her. Only she knew the millet field was a treasure trove of such stones. Like Venkata Reddy, she had guarded it zealously, choosing a crop that didn't need much turning of the land. She made herself a promise: if Idris ever returned, she would let him prospect for diamonds there. All that was hers would be his. Theirs. She touched her still flat belly and felt the stirring of new life.

EPILOGUE

March AD 1661

(Rajab AH 1071)

Idris let his gaze slide across the port. In all his years, he had somehow never been to Ponnani. Ponnani was about sixteen cos away from the north of Kozhikode and it took a man about four hours to walk four cos, and yet he had never been to the port. But now he was here, he would explore it a little before he headed towards home.

Home? Idris's fingers clenched the wooden rail of the vessel. What was he thinking of? How could it be home? Men like him had no home. The world was their home.

'You are deep in thought?' a voice murmured from behind.

Idris arranged his features to nothingness and turned around. Sala Pokkar stood some distance away, smiling.

'I was thinking that I have never been to Ponnani,' he said, deflecting Sala Pokkar's curiosity.

'There is so much to see here, Ikka, and I will show you everything there is to see,' the young man said eagerly. 'We should go to the Juma Masjid there. Ponnani is like the Mecca, they say.'

Idris put his arm around the young man. 'Sala Pokkar, we will. But first I have to take Kandavar home to his mother. She must be waiting anxiously for his return.'

The young man's face fell. Then his eyes lit up and he said, 'Shall I go with you?'

Idris swallowed. He didn't know what he was going to do once he entrusted Kandavar to his tharavad.

In the end, Kandavar made the decision for him. 'It is best that Sala Pokkar goes with us,' he said.

That night the heavenly bodies were all arrayed for battle in the skies. Idris watched the skies, unable to understand who was winning and who was losing. One thing was certain, he realized with a sinking feeling: the day would bring confusion and conflicting emotions. For even as Al-Mushtarie, the father among planets, stood guard through the night, Zohaal with his rings emerged in the last quarter of the night, seeking to cast malignance. And as if to negate the viciousness of the red planet, Al-Mareekh, Al-Zahra appeared in the morning sky.

Next morning, the three of them set out towards Vattoli tharavad. Sala Pokkar and Idris walked, while Kandavar alternated between riding Vajra and walking beside his bullock. For Vajra had travelled back with them, much to everyone's amusement. Golla had offered to look after Aamira and the wooden chest till such time as Idris returned. 'You will return, Ayana,' Golla had said at their leave taking. 'I know it even if you don't.'

Idris had smiled and said, 'Inshallah!'

When they halted at noon, Idris saw Kandavar wander away to sit on a rock. He went towards the boy. Something was troubling the boy, he realized. Kandavar had gone with him to the young bania in Bezawada, who had appraised the stones and helped Idris find a diamond cutter who cut and polished the stones so their value was magnified. Kandavar had seemed strangely relieved to hear that the diamonds were worth much more than Idris had expected them to be. He had been surprised, but had put it down to Kandavar's secret fear that Idris would go seeking yet another prospect if the diamonds weren't valuable enough. But all through the journey back to Masulipatnam, and on the ship from there to Galle and then the ship to Ponnani they had found passage on, he had vacillated between an aloof coldness and a clingy warmth.

'What is wrong, inan?' Idris asked.

Kandavar turned to see where Sala Pokkar was before bursting out, 'I know you are my father, Aabo.' The words tumbled out of his mouth. 'I know. I know.'

Idris felt as if a battering ram had smashed into the small of his back. 'I…' He groped for a word, a phrase to explain, to right the situation.

'And so, there is something I must tell you.'

Idris stood still, unable to speak. The boyish face of his son seemed to have turned into a man's.

'At first I was so happy when I realized you are my father. How could I not be? You mean more to me than anyone else in this world. But, as we left Kollur, I heard Sala Pokkar tell Golla about the caste laws of our land and, Aabo, I am afraid now. You cannot be here with me anymore,' Kandavar said in a flat voice shorn of its childish quiver. 'Everyone who sees us together will know us to be father and son. And you know the laws of our land. My mother and I will lose our caste. They will perform the funeral rites for us even when we are alive. We will be excommunicated. We will be nothing. They will not spare you either. They will kill you.'

Idris's head drooped. He felt a cold fist grab his heart and squeeze it.

'Aabo,' Kandavar continued, 'when we come to the next athani, you must return. I know my way home.'

Idris looked up, aghast at his son's words.

'I will tell everyone that you perished on the voyage home and that you were buried in Ponnani. That a trader from the ship brought me home. It is the only way.'

'Inan,' Idris said, his hand on the boy's shoulder. Kandavar stood still. Then he buried his face in his father's chest. He willed the tears not to emerge. Later, when he was alone, he would weep for thrusting this man out of his life. The man he loved most in the world.

'Aabo, you have to go now,' he said, pulling apart.

Idris nodded. He reached into his pocket and pulled out a pouch. 'I was going to give this to you on the day you returned to the kalari. Wear it, inan. Wear it so you may think of this father of yours even if he is no longer with you.'

He took the diamond pendant, a three-mangelin stone set with tiny rubies around it and slung on a gold chain. He had got it made in Bezawada. He fastened it around the boy's throat and kissed his brow.

'Make me a promise,' he said.

'What do you want, Aabo?'

'That you will never throw away your life for nothing. That you will remember you are the light of my soul. That you will remember all that I have tried to teach you about the wonder of life,' Idris said.

It was early evening. The next athani was only a few minutes away.

'Aabo, what will you do?' the child asked of his father.

'I will find something to do.' Idris smiled. 'Do you remember what I tell everyone?'

'I am Idris Maymoon Samataar Guleed, previously of Dikhil. Now a traveller of the world, seeking the measure of earth and man,' Kandavar said.

'Yes, that is me. So I will seek once again to do that,' Idris said with half a laugh.

'Go to Pinni, Aabo,' Kandavar said. 'She said she would offer you a place to rest your head. She said she would be waiting for you. Go to her, Aabo,' Kandavar said again. 'That way I will know where you are. Who knows, I could even come to you one day.'

Idris looked at his son for a long while, committing every feature of the beloved face to memory. *I have a son. I had a son.*

At the next athani, they paused. Idris stood by the porter's rest stone. 'We will not go any further,' he told Sala Pokkar gently. 'Kandavar will find his own way home.'

It was almost twilight. Maccanto, sitting at the gatehouse door as he usually did, raised his head. His ears cocked and his whiskers prickled. Suddenly, he leapt up with a bark and with his tail wagging furiously, he raced across the fields to the mud track, barking…

Chandu Nair, walking into the gatehouse with a retinue of men, paused. He shielded his eyes with his hands and peered into the distance. He could hear the tinkle of tiny bells.

Who or what was that?

As the figure approached, he realized it was a boy on a bullock.

As they watched the boy draw closer and closer, Chandu Nair sucked in his breath.

A dark-as-the-night boy on a white-as-the-day bullock. And running around in circles, a dog that was half-night and half-day.

Kandavar was home.

Bibliography

The Grandhavari refers to the Mamangams of AD 1647 and 1671. Strangely enough there is no reference to the one that should have been held in AD 1659. Aswathi Thirunaal had ascended the throne as Zamorin in AD 1658. It is hard to believe that he decided to not have a Mamangam in the next year. Most historical fiction is located in the grey area between factual history and conjecture. And so, I too have taken that path of locating my story in the realm of probabilities with reference to the 1659 Mamangam.

For all other details, I drew into the following texts for reference about life and times of the period in southern India:

Books and Periodicals

A. Galletti, *Dutch in Malabar*

A. Sreedhara Menon, *Kerala Charithram* (A Survey of Kerala History)

G.T. Birdwood, *Practical Bazzar Medicines with over Two Hundred Useful Prescriptions*

Joseph Huddart, *The Oriental Navigator, Or, New Directions for Sailing to and from the East*

K. Chidambarayyar, *Thiruvithamcore Charithram*

K. Damodharan, *Kerala Charithram*

K.L. Barnard, *Kerala Charithra Sambhavangal*, 1972

K.M. Panikkar, *Kerala Swathanthrya Samaram*

K.M. Vahabudeen, *Muslims of Kerala*

K.V. Krishna Ayyar, *The Zamorins of Calicut*

Kerala Historical Association, *Ernakulum Kerala History Volume I*

Keralam Monthly, 1105 Kumbham

M.G.S. Narayanan, *Calicut: The City of Truth*

M.R. Raghava Varier and Rajan Gurukkal, *Keralacharithram*

Mathrubhumi Weekly, 1934, October 1933, 26 November3 December 1934

Memoirs of the life and writings of the Rev. Claudius Buchanan, D.D, late vice-provost of the College of Fort William in Bengal

N.M. Nampoothiri, Dr, *Mamankam Rekhakal*

P. Bhaskaranunni, *Kerala in 19th Century*

P.A. Saidu Muhammed, *Kerala Charithra Veekshanam* (Sahithya Pravarthaka Sangham, 1683)

Philip Baldaeus, *A Description of the East India coast of Malabar and Coromandel 1640*

Phillip B. Zarrilli, *When the Body Becomes All Eyes*

Robert Caldwell, Caldwell R. Bishop, *A History of Tinnevelly*

Sanjay Subrahmanyam, *The Political Economy of Commerce: Southern India 1500-1650*

Shaykh Zainuddin Makhdum, *Tuhjat al-Mujahifin*

T.K. Gangadharan, *Kerala: History and Culture*

Tavernier's Travels in India 1640-1676 (Volumes 1 & 2), translated by Valentine Ball

Thomas Roe and John Fryer, *Travels in India in the Seventeenth Century*

Velayudhan Panikkassery, *Sancharikal Kanda Keralam*

William Logan, *Malabar Manual*

Websites

http://www.langantiques.com/university/index.php/Great_Mogul_Diamond

http://www.archive.org/stream/diseasesdisorder00gresrich/diseasesdisorder00gresrich_djvu.txt

http://www.oocities.org/manishashar888/cindex.htm

shodhganga.inflibnet.ac.in/bitstream/.../08_chapter%202.pdf by K.V.N. Raju – 2011 http://shodhganga.inflibnet.ac.in/bitstream/10603/1631/10/10_chapter%204.pdf

S. Babu – Pondicherry University DSpace Portal, *dspace.pondiuni.edu.in/jspui/bitstream/pdy/238/1/T0621.pdf*

http://historicalleys.blogspot.in/2009/07/fanams-of-calicut.html

http://historicalleys.blogspot.in/2009/01/hindus-and-ocean-taboo.html

http://www.heritage-activities.nl/sites/default/files/content/Sri%20Lanka%20Avondster%20article.pdf

http://books.google.co.in/books?id=Fx4OAAAAQAAJ&pg=PA212 &lpg=PA212&dq=Tegenapatnam&source=bl&ots=SmbcO35 Idi&sig=rBzl0M1iCcxZEnxXWMc4FUvST78&hl=en&sa=X&ei=oVEoUMkRjsqsB7q-gYgP&ved=0CEAQ6AEwAzgK#v=onepage&q=Tegenapatnam&f=false;

https://www.piratedocuments.com/Admiralty%20Reports/ship_surgeon_amputates_1703.htm;

http://www.olivetreegenealogy.com/nn/mm_10.shtml

http://www.bataviaphotos.com/batavia_history.html

http://shodhganga.inflibnet.ac.in/bitstream/10603/2580/7/07_chapter%201.pdf

http://itre.cis.upenn.edu/~myl/languagelog/archives/000457.html – posted by Mark Liberman, 15 February 2004

Acknowledgements

I began this book with an image that haunted me. It was as if I had no choice. *Idris* had to be written. But without the extraordinary contributions of the following people at different points of time, *Idris* wouldn't have been complete: M.G.S. Narayanan, C.K. Sivanandan, Karthik, Leela and Kalyanaraman, Hemanth Gopinath, Jayant Kodkani and Mini Kuruvilla.

And as always, this book wouldn't be what it is were it not for V.K. Karthika, who shared my dream and al-kamaled it through.

I owe thanks to Shantanu Ray Chaudhuri, Shuka Jain, Sameer Mahale and Ayushi Srivastava at HarperCollins India, Camilla Ferrier and the team at The Marsh Agency for their sustained support.

Achuthan Kudallur, Gita Krishnankutty, Jayapriya Vasudevan, Patrick Wilson, S. Prasannarajan, Rajini Sunil, Ravi Jose Thanickal, Suma Vijay, Sunil Koliyot and Sunita Shankar – my support group who kept me going with conversation, cheer and the strength of great camaraderie.

And Sunil, Unni, Maitreya and Sugar – for being there for me. Always.